Praise for Jack Cady

"Like John Steinbeck, [Cady] is an accomplished storyteller. His works resonate with the passions and foibles of ordinary people, and he makes his readers care for them."
— Tor.com

" An exceptional writer."
— Joyce Carol Oates

"A writer of great, unmistakable integrity and profound feeling."
— Peter Straub

"[Jack Cady is] a lasting voice in modern American literature."
— *The Atlanta Constitution*

THE CADY COLLECTION

NOVELS

The Hauntings of Hood Canal
Inagehi
The Jonah Watch
McDowell's Ghost
The Man Who Could Make Things Vanish
The Off Season
Singleton
Street

Dark Dreaming [with Carol Orlock, as Pat Franklin]
Embrace of the Wolf [with Carol Orlock, as Pat Franklin]

OTHER WRITINGS

Phantoms
Fathoms
The American Writer

McDowell's Ghost

Jack Cady

FAIRWOOD PRESS
Bonney Lake, WA

MCDOWELL'S GHOST
A Fairwood Press Book
July 2021
Copyright © 2021 by the Estate of Jack Cady

Fairwood Press
21528 104th Street Court East
Bonney Lake, WA 98391
www.fairwoodpress.com

Series Cover Design by Jennifer Tough
Collection Editorial Direction by Mark Teppo

ISBN: 978-1-933846-11-8
First Fairwood Press Edition: July 2021
Printed in the United States of America

The first edition of this novel was published by Arbor House in 1982.

For Carol,
And for the beautiful, singing ladies

McDowell's Ghost

NEVERTHELESS, IF IT can be said that there are many Souths, the fact remains that there is also one South . . . there was the influence of the Southern physical world—itself a sort of cosmic conspiracy against reality in favor of romance. The country is one of extravagant colors, of proliferating foliage and bloom, of flooding yellow sunlight, and, above all, perhaps, of haze. Pale blue fogs hang above the valleys in the morning, the atmosphere smokes faintly at midday, and through the long afternoon cloudstacks tower from the horizon and the earthbeat quivers upward through the iridescent air, blurring every outline and rendering every object vague and problematical.

—W. J. Cash, *The Mind of the South*

Author's Note

The city of Centerville is fictional. It is drawn from my obser-
vations and recollections of Louisville, Kentucky; Knoxville,
Tennessee; and Charlotte, North Carolina.

While this book was still in manuscript it was read by a few
friends. Each of them asked if the characters of Peg, Margaret, and
Becky represented biographical accounts of great singers either
living or dead. Nothing could further from the truth. These three
singers are their own women and their own musicians. The only
similarity in the lives of Peg, Margaret, and Becky to the lives of
any other musicians is the similarity dictated by their art. I have no
doubt that many singers, actors, musicians, and dancers will find
parts of their lives represented here. Their clearest recognition may
well be the influence of "the road" with its dives, its cheap motels,
and its hazards.

Chapter 1

THEY MUST HAVE SANDBLASTED THESE CENTERVILLE COPS. ALL day long the cops had been starched and showy and driving around in clean cars while they hassled people. *They* must of got a government grant, and give a new coat of paint to the whole city council. The sons of bitches kept fixing this town up. The more it got fixed up the uglier it got.

Once, McDowell told himself in a drunken, flashing insight that he knew was dead wrong, this had been a pretty good town for him. He sentimentally remembered great big trees and open streets. The streets had been red brick, real brick, and they ran out to the city limits and became the road. The streets were that kind of brick that said not much was going on, and nothing much was going to come along, either.

Above his head the old neon sign reading Wine—Beer cast a red glow. The sign fizzed with little electrical pops. The red glow mixed with the pale white glow of the modern sign that read Maggie's Hangar Cafe. McDowell liked airplanes as long as he did not have to ride in one. He liked this bar beside the old airport. Both the bar and the airport had been here since he was a kid. A light plane buzzed through the night sky. The buzzing sounded like an amplified version of the fizzing neon sign. Far across town, over toward the river, the overcast sky was lighted by the central city. At his back, where there used to be fields, were rows and rows of houses.

He told himself that he didn't want any part of it. He didn't like it. The sons of bitches sandblasted their cops and painted and built parks. They creamed their jeans about redeveloping the redevelopments. But the town just got worsen-worse. It was the same old town, though. Only now the meanness showed through. The vicious and really snarly part of the town-that part showed up real good.

It was double-tough to be drunk. He had to be total sober in twelve hours. He stumped his toe coming from the bar and told himself it wasn't nothing but a toe. He had nine more of the damn things hanging around down there someplace.

He was outstanding drunk. He was Superior drunk, like the lake. He was Cadillac, Bentley, Lincoln, Rolls Royce, Aston Martin, and antique Packard super-drunk.

He was Kenworth drunk. He was Peterbilt drunk. He could run with a Marmon Harrington.

The summer night was one of those open-mouth, gaspy things that sure didn't clear the head. The heat was like somebody had blown up a thermometer. He wished he could see a big old tree, but all the big old trees had been renewed. Now there was nothing but these scraggledy little things lining the walk and drooping in the heat. The sidewalk was still warm beneath his sock feet, although it had been dark for hours. He dropped one of the Wellington boots he was carrying, walked past it three paces, and then changed his mind. He came back and retrieved the boot.

He had a Cadillac parked around here somewhere. He thought careful about whether he should pass out or try to make it back to the motel when he got back to the Cad.

"Sober is as sober do/get too sober, catch the blues." He hummed, not exactly happy, but humming.

The Cad sat at the curb, looking like a tomb with a convertible top. The Cad had been renewed. Its whale-tail fins were shiny black beneath the street light, and its re-chromed front end was smooth as an undertaker's advertising. McDowell loved it. A good old '57 Cad convertible running on totally rebuilt everything.

The motel wasn't that far off. All you had to do if you *were* somebody, was to sneak it through the side streets, through the alleys. All you had to do was hang your hand around the light switch, ready to blank her out and run or hide when the starched and sandblasted cops showed up.

The engine started smooth and strong. He pulled away from the curb and ran a mile of broad road before he caught a red light. He waited and then hung a left. Halfway down the block a narrow alley disappeared between garages. He was in an older, residential section. McDowell pointed the Cadillac into the alley.

Sometimes, in old alleys, you got to see a big tree. The headlights picked up long rows of garages. There were gaps between the garages. Old cars and garbage cans were parked in the gaps. He came next to a gap and stopped. He turned out the lights. Sometimes there was a big tree in these backyards. He looked through the darkened side window. Maybe there was a tree out there, maybe not. He peered drunkenly into the darkness.

They were throwing a fire someplace, renewing the town. He heard the distant sirens of police cars and fire trucks.

No big tree. At least none he could see. He switched the headlights back on and peered down the alley. There was something like a mist or a cloud down there.

He rolled the Cadillac forward fifty feet. The ghost stood hazy and weak in the glare of the headlights.

"Aw, no," said Dan McDowell. "Not here. Not here in town. Get back out on that road where you belong."

Chapter 2

THE GHOST HAD FIRST STARTED TO APPEAR SOME years before. It came on nights when Dan McDowell, buzzy from drinking and filled with the awful lust that comes with loneliness, left a small town, Indiana bar. McDowell drove an old Mercury toward the farm where he was then working. The ghost came on misty nights, or nights when thunderstorms hit the black, loamy fields. The soil was still hot in the July and August nights. It sometimes seemed to McDowell that the whole dark land was steaming.

The first time the ghost appeared was right before a storm. The weak headlights of the Mercury picked it up as it seemed to rise from an overgrown fencerow. Dan McDowell was drunk enough that he later remembered being interested in what was happening. Then the interest turned to terror. He missed a ninety-degree swap-around and ran off the two-lane road. The battered old blue and white Mercury bounced across a shallow ditch. It bogged down in the soft soil of a cornfield. Corn wiped the summer dust from the car's chipped paint. Once the car stopped, stalks fluttered like cautioning fingers before the windshield. McDowell turned off the headlights, locked the doors, rolled up the windows and passed out. When he woke in a hot, steaming dawn, he was as wet as if he had been wrapped in a rubber sheet.

A week later when the wind was kicking and rain swept the Merc's windshield like a hand, McDowell saw the ghost again. The ghost stood at the roadside like a hitchhiker. It's collapsed, tucked-in lower jaw was stained with spit from chewing tobacco. Its beard and moustache were scraggly and white. The jaw held only five teeth and they were all rotten. Sleeves of the host's ragged military tunic were inches too short. They rode high on narrow, scrawny wrists. The eyes of the ghost were wide and staring, like the eyes of the drowned. Dan McDowell did not understand how he saw all this, but he knew that he saw it.

McDowell was thirty-one during that summer when he first saw the ghost. It was a bad summer. His wife had kicked him out because she thought he was crazy and because she was interested in another man. She had lived with McDowell for seven years.

The rest of Dan McDowell's family—his parents and sister—had sided with his ex-wife. They had insisted that Dan McDowell was crazy for as long as he could remember. They said he was crazy because he would not settle down and help in the family's import-export business. He was crazy because he loved music.

To make the bad summer worse, the night air was filled with smoke and stink. A peat fire burned north of the small town where he did his drinking.

In thirty-one years McDowell had seen a dozen peat fires. Spontaneous combustion caused the fire deep beneath the black-dirt Indiana fields where the peat lay. Invisible fire. Smoke rose vague and spiritlike from the fields. The fires could not be put out. They could only burn themselves out. McDowell knew of one that burned for six years. When McDowell was beery enough, he told himself that the ghost had risen among those tendrils of smoke.

Harvest came and went. McDowell got a job driving local delivery in Muncie. In early November he met a woman named Becky who was singing folk music in a bar. Becky was fragile, loved folk music, was not a very good singer, and believed she needed him. Becky was nearly the opposite of his ex-wife. His ex-wife was short, heavy, and certain in her opinions. Becky was tall and thin and filled with vague notions. McDowell thought that what she did to a guitar was hopeful, but a long shot. He lay beside her, made love to her, rubbed her head when she was having crazy thoughts and feelings. If his ex-wife and his family thought he was crazy, he saw no reason why Becky could not be crazy. He told himself that he was in love, and nearly believed it. He stopped drinking, but he drove more. The ghost did not appear. The night road was boring, straight, unrelieved by fright. The road became sere once the crops were in, and December edged it with crystal frost.

In January Becky was out of work and troubled. She felt she could do better, back home. Back home was North Carolina. McDowell and Becky moved to Durham where McDowell drove a furniture haul out of Hickory. Becky was not as nervous, but she remained as vague. To McDowell it seemed that Becky was always trying to look beyond some invisible horizon. She had fewer crazy thoughts and feelings, but in North Carolina she began to dream. Her dreams were not of fear, but of sadness. In June McDowell and Becky moved again.

Three years later in Knoxville, where McDowell was driving interstate short haul, Becky left. She did not leave for another man. She was still frail but strong enough to believe that she had to live alone.

After the fact, McDowell found out that he really had been in love and knew in the empty, pained spaces of mind and belly that Becky would be a love he would never forget. She was different from his ex-wife. He had already forgotten his ex-wife's face.

It was then that he saw the ghost again. This time it appeared on U.S. 42 along the Ohio River as McDowell kicked a straight International with a twenty-two-foot van on a turn from Louisville to Cincinnati. The road was obscured by fog so thick that McDowell almost believed he had seen a man and not the ghost.

On the river, somewhere in the fog, an oil barge had been on fire. Fog ran on the windshields, and, the wipers streaked the glass because there was so much oil smoke in the fog. McDowell was sober. It was the first time he had seen the ghost without being drunk. This time his terror came from the feeling that something invisible was sitting in the cab beside him. He did not know whether there was one ghost or two. Years later, he would figure the problem out.

By the time he made Cincinnati he had seen the ghost at four different places along the roadside. Each time he had felt the sense of an invisible presence beside him. In Cincinnati, he was in a mood to get smashed. His loneliness seemed as wide and long as the fog-shrouded river. His fear of the invisible presence was like a hot point of light through the fog. The whole time he was with Becky he had not seen the ghost, and now it was back again. Once he reached Cincinnati McDowell passed out beside a decent black woman named Mary who took his cash but left his checkbook and billfold. Later, thinking about it, he wished he had not frightened the woman by claiming he was hexed. She had been afraid of that word "hexed."

Dan McDowell spent his younger years attempting to be the right man for his ex-wife first, and then for Becky. He spent his thirties being overworked, thin, and desperate for a woman. Sometimes he was most desperate for a woman when he was with a woman.

Thinking about it, and he had a lot of time on the road to think about it, he could not figure out why he liked women so much. He liked nearly every one he met. He liked the different ways that women handled sex. He liked women who were clumsy or frigid nearly as much as he liked the ones who were skilled. He liked being with them when they were clothed. He liked talking to women. He especially enjoyed talking to older women, who always seemed to know more about him than he knew about himself.

He felt that women had a hard time making up their minds about him. On that score his record continued to be terrible. When they did make up their minds, it was always a decision to leave.

Dan McDowell, who was not ugly but who thought he was, at first believed that he lost his women because of his looks. He never had time to get a scheduled haircut, and his face was lined. Then he thought he made them nervous because he always seemed to be three moves behind in any game he was playing. McDowell's eyes were blue, and his face seemed all eyes and brows and chin. He walked with a slight limp from the time he managed to get a leg trapped between a concrete post and a forklift. Even if he was skinny, his body worked well because he did a lot of physical work.

When he was thirty-nine, he saw the ghost along the road just outside of Bluefield, West Virginia. It was the same ghost, wearing the same military tunic. It frightened him just as much, and the invisible presence once more rode beside him, but at least the ghost itself was no longer a surprise. The only difference in the ghost was that it seemed covered with coal dust. The smell of sulphuric acid from the open face of a mine hung in the hot, humid night. It was thick as fog. Off toward the base of a mountain was an industrial plant. A column of fire licked at the night sky, rising from a stack.

The fire threw spectral-looking shadows through a strip of woods that lined the road.

McDowell was driving a Corvette that had a few more payments left on it than miles. He was coming south from Detroit fleeing one more breakup. A tiny and hot-tempered woman named Carlotta, a Mexican, had been decent enough to weep when he left. He knew she had stopped weeping before he was fifty yards down the road. He figured he would regain control by the time he got to Roanoke. He knew that she was naturally hot-tempered, and just used being Mexican as an excuse. Carlotta was not going to be a woman he remembered, not with the same empty and sentimental feeling of loss that he felt for Becky.

Plus, he told himself, he was getting less sentimental as he grew older. At the same time, he still had hope.

At age forty-three, after a lot of work and several strokes of pure luck, Dan McDowell found himself making a lot of money as a distributor of quality merchandise. He was not rich, but he had been broke long enough so that he could appreciate the difference.

By the time he was forty-three, the road was changed for the worse. There had always been freeways, but now there were freeways everywhere. Speed limits were down. To McDowell, it seemed like the whole world was afraid to take chances. The broad, slow freeways were like old-age rivers.

McDowell saw the ghost on a steaming, mist-filled night as it stood beside a freeway outside of Asheville, North Carolina. McDowell was pushing a restored '57 Cadillac convertible. He was headed for Centerville, where he did not often go. He had family here. He had promised to see them. He would not have promised if he had not been going to Centerville anyway. There was a singer he knew who was working there. He thought he might be in love with her.

This time when he saw the ghost, there was a real difference. The eyes were as empty and staring as they had always been, but the frame hung limp, as if the ghost was in despair.

McDowell eased off on the gas, drifted past the ghost and continue down the freeway at a dangerously low speed. He kept checking the night road in his mirror so he would not be rear-ended.

He was cold sober. He was lonely, and he was blue. The Cadillac was paid for. He told himself that he had enough of this foolishness. He told himself that he had chewed up enormous quantities of shit in his life. He was in no mood for another plateful.

When the ghost appeared again, rising spectral and old and sad in the realm of the mist-shrouded headlights, Dan McDowell put on the brakes. He pulled to the berm and waited. The ghost stood, fragile as an echo. Its eyes were wide and staring, yet it seemed to be trying to open its eyes. The tucked-in chin sank a little lower. The mouth opened like a showcase for the rotting teeth. The old military tunic was frayed, shiny. Two fingers were missing from the middle of the left hand.

McDowell climbed from the car and slammed the door. As he stepped from the air-conditioned car, the murky heat made him feel like he was swimming. It was wet heat. Forest heat. The fecund plant smell of the forest hung in the smoke-like mist. Somewhere close a farmer had been clearing land and burning stumps. Wood smoke was mixed in with the low mist and heavy heat.

In the subdued glow of headlights the ghost seemed little more than a formation of rising ground mist. McDowell stood and waited. The ghost seemed trying to speak. McDowell watched the ghost, and he was watching his own mind at the same time. He was seeing the ghost, but he was also thinking of the woman he thought he loved. He thought for a moment of music.

The Cadillac's fan and exhaust made liquid, airy sounds. McDowell opened the door, shut off the headlights, closed the door, and stood watching.

In the darkness the ghost was luminous. It seemed to have more substance, but it still did not speak. Dan McDowell took a step forward, then another step. The ghost began to move away, although McDowell could not tell whether it moved in space or through some other dimension. McDowell stepped around the front of the Cadillac and off the berm. The grass and weeds beside the berm were wet with mist. The ghost had disappeared.

McDowell told himself that he knew a dozen-hundred ways of being a fool, but his ears were no fools. The sounds of the rushing air and exhaust from the Cadillac did not seem unnatural. They were like a backdrop, like the motion of a guitar that lay remote behind a slow jazz horn.

In the distance a hound was singing, the long, confident call making strokes through the mist. On a downgrade and through a patch of damp forest, he heard the voices of frogs and crickets. A small body, larger than a mouse but smaller than a rabbit, moved, then stopped. In the hot, humid North Carolina night it seemed to McDowell that a thousand creatures were moving.

He stood, no longer thinking of love, but thinking that he had not actually stepped from a road in years. He had driven through this southern land, but he had never bothered to stop and listen to the land.

He turned back toward his car and hesitated, caught and held by sound. There was a nearly silent brush of wings against air, and then the snap of night wings closing. There was a thump. A small creature shrieked and died.

McDowell returned to his car. He climbed in, fumbled for the gear, then slipped it back out of gear. The feeling of the invisible presence was all around him. For a long time, until another automobile passed and lit the night with headlights and taillights and mechanical rushing, McDowell sat listening, in fear. He finally got the car in gear and moving. The invisible presence rode beside him for the next twenty miles. When he arrived in Centerville he decided to put off meeting anyone for twenty-four hours. He knew he would be busy getting drunk.

Chapter 3

THE WORLD STILL SEEMED A LITTLE BUZZED WHEN HE WOKE IN one of those motel rooms where concrete blocks were shingled with imitation wood and the rooms were divided by imitation walls. Somebody named Madge was giving her old man down-the-road in the next room. Her old man's name was Fowler. McDowell looked at his watch, saw that he had slept seven hours. He sat on the edge of the bed and wiggled his stumped toe to see if everything was working. His stumped *left* toe, he told himself. Nothing ever happened on his right.

"Bibble," said an enthusiastic, childish voice through the wall opposite the wall where good old Madge was giving good old Fowler a basting—which is what poor-stupid-fuckface Fowler got for being married.

"Leggo barfum," said the childish voice.

"Stay outta that bathroom," said a man's voice. "Barfum."

Welcome home, McDowell thought, you alky. You haven't been drunk in a month, and now the minute, the very minute that you hit this town, then drunk is the only thing it makes sense to be.

"If you *really* think so, Fowler," said the woman. "If you really and truly *think* so."

Fowler protested that he really did.

"Stoppit," said the man's voice. There was a smack and a bawling wail. The barfum kid had just taken a butt shot.

And the very best part of it, McDowell told himself, the absolute very best part of it is that you let them get to you, and they don't even know you're in town yet, because if they did, most likely you would be hearing sirens.

The stumped toe wasn't swelled much, but it gave him a twinge when he stood up. Damn fool. Discussing boots with some drunk, and putting your own boots on the bar, and then walking outta there in your sock feet to tiptoe past the police so you wouldn't have to do something stupid like beat on any of them.

Dan McDowell walked to the bathroom, urinated, and felt better. He stood beneath a hot shower for a long time, soaping and rinsing. The voices that came through the walls were blanked by the shower, but he still thought he could hear them. They belonged to people who were with other people; maybe that was good, maybe bad, but it was more than McDowell had. When he returned to the bedroom for fresh clothes, the voices were silent.

He figured old Madge and Fowler had left. McDowell told himself that he had met a thousand people he had never seen, and every blessed son and daughter of them had been on the other side of a motel wall. He had heard them argue and fight and make love and drink. Sometimes he heard them laughing and singing. He felt like he was a secret preacher who hid in motel confessionals and listened to all of that sinful crap. He forgave them all of it, except when they made too much noise. or beat up on each other.

If he was going to meet a woman, especially this woman who he thought he might love, he had to check into a better place. He dressed in light-colored summer clothing, packed his suitcase, then sat on the bed. His mind tried to jump away from something, and that was a bad thing for a mind to try to do.

That ghost had shown up again last night, which made two nights in a row. That was okay by McDowell. It was nothing new. What was new and definitely not okay was that the ghost had the nerve to show up in his, McDowell's, hometown. Always before, it had shown up on the road.

On the road it was almost okay. A lot of weird stuff happened on the road at night—heavy and unmistakable skid marks leading into a calm, surfaced lake—the kind that when you backed up to check them out, they were gone. Night birds and white, giant moths like specters in the headlights. Red light glowing in the sky behind a hill, and when you got over the hill there would be no wreck, no fire, nothing.

Lots of weird stuff. It wasn't just him, either. Guys told about being passed by old, fancy sports cars. Headlights as big as platters rearing up out of the night, and then the car passed and disappeared like it was swallowed by air.

He could just about take the ghost as one more part of the night road, but now the ghost had come to town. For a minute it seemed to McDowell that it should be night outside, right now. The hot sunlight of a late August southern day shone through the pulled drapes. It almost seemed like the sunlight should actually be a house on fire, a wreck, a burning cross, an explosion.

The phone rang. He figured the desk was calling, trying to sell him another day. Or maybe somebody had trashed the Cad, or, prob-ably, very prob-a-blee . . . he paused and told himself that the minute he got to this town he started talking southern. What *prob-ably* meant around here was that you wouldn't admit to a damned thing, especially if you believed it. He let the phone ring three times before he decided to answer, briskly.

Joking about it to himself later, and knowing it was a full-out lie, he told himself that it was worse than any ghost. That voice. Padded with just the thinnest layer of blue velvet, which is how she thought of herself. He could hear that voice coming before it actually said anything.

"You should have called," said his sister, Samantha, when he picked up the phone. "Daniel, at least, you *could* have called."

He could not believe it. She could out-ferret a ferret, but this one he could not, would not, believe. At least, not for a minute or two.

"Hang on," he told her. "Got to get a smoke."

He laid the receiver on the desk, pulled a cigarette from his shirt pocket, and sat on the edge of the bed. He lit the cigarette, then leaned back on the bed.

Let her wait, bitch.

Samantha. Sammy. She hated the name and the nickname. She thought Samantha was a nigger name, and Sammy was yid. How had Sammy-nee-bitch Samantha done it?

That was easy. He told himself he should of gone over to the other side of town instead of hanging around his old stomping ground. That street out there was a main drag. The Cad was parked out front like an advertisement.

It had to be one of them—Sammy or the Wimp or the Citizen had spotted the Cad while they were on their way to the warehouse.

McDowell looked at the ceiling. He thought about the time when he was in a motel that had mirrors on the ceiling. A really shy, Portuguese girl named Marie had been with him. She had hidden beneath the covers the minute she saw the mirrors.

He looked across the room, at the mirror on the dresser. His face was crinkled wrong. The lines that never appeared except under heavy stress were appearing now. They lay over the furrows and deep, regular lines of his face as if somebody had been making sketches of spider webs.

Finally he returned to the phone.

"Sammy," he said, "this is a hick town. A town of the hicks, by the hicks, for the hicks. Hicks everlasting." He could almost see her react to the nickname. He could almost see her standing in the office at the warehouse, holding the phone, a cigarette wired between stiff fingers that she did not even know were tired. He could imagine her tall, thin, frail-looking body, her long brown hair neatly coiled. But Sammy was not frail. More like the frailness of light wire that, when you wound enough of it tightly enough, became cable that could pick up boulders.

"You needn't be abusive," she said. "You were coming to see us anyway. Charles saw your car."

Charles. The Citizen. McDowell's father.

"Charles." He managed to say what he meant with his inflection.

She ignored it. Her voice turned friendly, the way it always did when she was laying a con, pulling the frail act—the world's leading con artist in action.

He listened to her lay her groundwork. This time it sounded like the groundwork for a plot. He knew those intonations. The plot would not be against him because he lived in Chicago. It might be against the Wimp, but McDowell doubted it. That left the Citizen. Her father was the only other person in her world who Sammy would plot against.

While she was talking he looked around the room. Orange bedspread, blue rug, speckled walls of imitation plaster made to remind you of Mexico. He wished he had brought the tape deck in from the car. He wished he could be listening to the full, confident bump of a sax section. Sammy always made him want to find clean air. Outside there, in the street, traffic was humming. Little tin pot cars that went fifty miles on a pint of piss.

" . . . so," she concluded, "it would be best if you just came to the house. Sevenish. Gerald will be home by then."

Gerald. The Wimp. The guy who must have been conceived through fine mesh. Sammy pushed him around, told him what to do, and McDowell had never once seen the Wimp fight back.

"I'll be at a DAR meeting at seven," McDowell told her. "I didn't know it until just now."

She seemed to hesitate between a gasp and a deep breath. A long time ago McDowell had discovered that the only way to deal with Sammy was to keep shoving her off balance.

"I'll come by the office," he said. "Sometime tomorrow."

"That will not be for the best. I promise you." Her voice was promising nothing pleasant. For a moment, Dan McDowell actually thought that his own sister was trying to tell him something for his own good, instead of hers.

"I really do have other business tonight."

"Water finds its own level." She sounded sniffy. "If you must, bring the creature with you." Her voice was so frigid that McDowell thought she ought to hire herself out. Air-condition the whole city. Iceberg Sammy. She was married to the Wimp. Enough to make anybody icy.

He stood holding the phone and trying to imagine Sammy and the Wimp in bed. All he could imagine was a snowplow stuck in a culvert. He laughed, inappropriate.

"I'll call you tomorrow," he said. "It can't be so important that lunch tomorrow won't cover it." He told himself that he would be damned if she railroaded him into an evening at home.

"It's serious, Daniel. Nothing to discuss in a restaurant. The situation . . ." She broke off, murmured for him to hold. He heard her speak to someone, then someone else. The Citizen's voice came loud and strong from the background.

"Sammy," said McDowell, "do you ever see ghosts?" He did not know why he said it, something instinctive probably, and he was cursing himself as he said it. It was his private trouble. He knew he ought never to even hint at private trouble.

"What have you heard?" Her voice was shocked, nearly, almost breathless.

"Heard nothing."

"You've heard something." Her voice was grim, but also frightened. "Charles has just come in from the warehouse. I'll call you back."

"Hang on for a minute." He was suddenly amused. He had her off balance, somehow. Maybe he could get her upset enough so it would spoil her lunch, or make her raise hell with the Wimp.

"You seeing ghosts, Sammy?" he asked kindly.

"What *have* you heard?" She was whispering now. It was obvious that she was sneaking a conversation past the Citizen, who was still hollering in the background. "*Where* did you hear it?"

"Your bank," he told her. "You oughtn't to ever say too much in a bank."

She was frightened, furious, and obviously could not say what she wanted while the Citizen was present.

"I'll call you tomorrow for lunch," he said and hung up, satisfied, even happy. He had won that round. She could sit on her problem for a day and a night. Hatch it, stew it, ferment it. Meanwhile, he had to get moving before she called back.

He was not particularly hung over, but he still felt a little drunk. He would stay that way through a pot of coffee and breakfast. Then, by eleven, the booze would be washed out.

At nine on a Thursday morning in Centerville, the late August sun was already a skull crusher. As he left the air-conditioned room, the sun was on his back and neck like a nightstick. The air felt so full of water that he sucked at it. Sweat began rolling from his armpits as he made his way through the parking lot to the Cad.

When you boozed you sweat . . . ought to remember that. A fortune in it. Build a sweatless booze. Sell it to working alkies. Computer programmers and salesmen and vice-presidents.

Two black children, a boy and a girl, were standing on one side of the Cad. A blonde-haired, nice-looking boy of about twenty was standing on the other side. None of them were touching anything. They were just standing there, admiring the car. McDowell figured that he met an average of twenty kids a week because of that car. He could never bring himself to be tough with any of them, even when they touched it.

He liked them because they were so sincere, even the punks. The older kids, like this white boy, had the road in their eyes. That was as close as they were ever going to get to the road. This kid looked like a natural to end up in some kind of sweatshop where even the customers wore business suits. It was this kind of kid, and that kind of sweatshop, that kept McDowell in business.

The black kids were about eight and thirteen. The girl was older, dressed pretty in a pink dress with a white collar. In this heat. The boy looked sloppity in worn jeans and a ragged-out tee shirt. McDowell looked at them and grinned. Sister and brother, no doubt about it. He thought of Samantha, and of how, years ago, he and his sister must have looked exactly like this. She, pretty. Him, scuffed.

Well, Samantha was no longer pretty, but he was still scuffed.

"Last of a kind," the white kid said about the car. He backed up a step as he spoke, ready to apologize or run. His blonde hair and blue eyes were not appropriate to his face. McDowell looked, saw the story, grinned again. This fucking south.

"One of the last," he told the kid.

In the south, every once. in a while, and in the very best of families, one of these lily-white types would get his pore self born with Negro features. This kid had a bulgy forehead. McDowell had seen it a hundred times. Everyone, the family and friends and the whole social register, pretended nothing was wrong, pretended that great-great-grandpa had not stuck it to great-great-grandma in the slave's quarters.

This immemorial, cracker, hot-nutted south.

"Fresh air funeral car," the girl said and giggled. Sassy thirteen. She was dark, deep dark. She had high cheekbones. Indian blood in there somewhere. Going to be a real beauty.

"It probably is," McDowell drawled. "I think about it sometimes." He grinned a watermelon grin and decided to lay some Georgia bullshit.

"Knew of a pimp, once," the eight-year-old said. "Had hisself a pink Lincoln." The kid was lighter colored than his sister. He had jug ears and a skinny frame.

"You watch that mouth," his sister told him, "or I'll watch it for you."

"That was Daddy," McDowell said. "That was my old pop." McDowell thought of the Citizen. The Citizen had been whipping Lincolns around this town for thirty years. The Citizen probably dreamed of pink Lincolns. Panty pink.

"What'll it do?" The white kid no longer looked ready to apologize or run.

"Now then," McDowell drawled, "these here speedometers was never no good. You can get yourself a twenty percent error on top." He paused, like he was being modest, playing out the game. Good ole Jukes. Good ole Kalikaks. The boys were taking it in. The girl looked like she knew she was being bullshitted. "When you bury the needle," McDowell said, "you catchin' something over a hundred." He pulled the keys from his pocket and unlocked the door. Heat from inside the car seemed to boil into the morning heat and humidity.

"How you afford this thing?" The girl was not going to let him off easy. The girl did not like to be conned. McDowell told himself that there was a child who was looking at a hard road, but she could take care of herself. She deserved straight talk.

"Tax write-off," he told her. "A business where I gotta have this kind of car."

"What business that?"

"Distributor," McDowell said. "Part of it is stuff for good cars. Company is called The Passing Lane."

The white kid's eyes opened wide, like he was in the presence of someone holy. "Shee-it," he said.

"You've heard of it?"

"Who ain't?"

"I ain't," said the girl. "At least not 'til now."

"I got your Jag book," the white kid said, "and the catalog."

McDowell climbed in and started the Cadillac. He left the door open, but got the air conditioner running.

"I haven't been back here in a long time," he said. "Where's a good restaurant?"

"St. Louis," the girl told him. "Nothing between here and St. Louis."

"Three blocks that-a-way," the white kid said, "then hang a right for one block." He looked like he was about to offer his services as a personal escort.

That was the problem with talking to kids. They always wanted a ride with the top down. Or maybe they just wanted a hero. McDowell had met a lot of kids, but he still couldn't figure out what they wanted. He thought that he knew one thing, though. He thought that they didn't want tin pot cars that ran fifty miles on a pint of piss.

He gave a little wave and got the Cadillac moving. He had enough complications in his life. Still, it was nice to waste a little time jiving with kids.

Chapter 4

HIGH CUMULUS WERE WHITE WITH DARK POCKETS OF GRAY AND occasional black. The clouds hung in the blue sky like the background of a painting. Tall buildings were shiny with windows, and they rose into the sky and were framed by cumulus. In the streets the never-ending traffic was like a confused and independent force that seemed determined to shove the city apart. Heat waves shimmered in the streets. The land was a land of heat and mist. During the day the heat was ascendant.

Dan McDowell parked in a restaurant parking lot. He sat for a minute in the air-conditioned car, reluctant to move into the heat. He told himself that those kids had kind of gotten to him. Especially the black girl. He figured that he and that girl both had the same point of view.

He told himself that when you got right down to basics, most of the work he did was because of kids. Kids were young enough to learn, and he thought it was important to teach them about quality. He made good money, sure, but money was only part of the reason he worked.

They would not understand anything but the money part. *They* would not give a damn about the rest of it.

When Dan McDowell talked about *them*, he was talking about anyone who was cheap. He first of all meant his family. His family had been in the import-export business for years. His family did not export much, he told himself, except for sanctimony and bad advice.

His family imported junk. They specialized in high markup, volume sales stuff from Japan and Taiwan and all of the other countries that had learned the junk formula.

Including, he told himself, this frowzy-ass U.S.A.

They included the cheap politicians and the urban renewers who build new slums. *They* included the animal-type cops, the indifferent social workers, the bureaucrats. In fact, he told himself, as he had told himself a hundred times, *they* included just about everybody.

Kids shouldn't have to learn to become that. That girl was only thirteen, probably, and she probably knew already that she shouldn't have to learn that. She had called him on it when he started bullshitting.

That white boy had The Passing Lane Jaguar Book, and he had The Passing Lane catalog. As long as that boy had the catalog and the book there would be some kind of quality in his life. McDowell thought that he was a revolutionary, a man running a company that poured quality into a world which had learned to love cheap shit. He looked across the long, and to him, beautiful hood of the restored Cadillac. He touched the genuine, handworked leather on the seats.

Time to get moving, he thought, get rid of the booze that was left. Time to shove life back in gear. He climbed from the car, walked into the restaurant, and sat in a booth by the windows. Stainless steel in front of the kitchen mirrored his wrinkled face, his medium-length hair and his full sideburns. It seemed to amplify his skinny frame. His toe gave him a twinge where it had been stumped. The custom-made Wellington boots still had a good shine. He liked them because they were the best boots in the world. They were slightly different sizes, so they helped take away a little of the limp caused from that accident with the forklift so many years ago.

A waitress approached. She carried a Silex, and she was looking past him like he was not a member of the universe. She was paying attention to something out there in the street.

He told himself that if there were fifteen waitresses in a restaurant, and fourteen were nice, he would get the ornery one every time. The woman who poured his coffee was short and fat and in her middle thirties. She had bleached hair, a red face, a tough look, and took his order for pancakes like she was not even listening. McDowell slurped at the coffee and grinned at her.

"Like a transfusion," he said about the coffee.

"Sonsovbitches," she said. "Goddamn pork." She stood, fat hands on fat hips, through the window and into the street. She was wearing a purple-flowered blouse beneath the green waitress uniform. He thought the bleached hair looked terrible, but at least she took nice care of it.

McDowell turned look through the window. Two cops had pulled over an old Buick. The car had a bashed front end with jury-rigged headlights. The trunk lid was missing. A white kid with shoulder-length hair climbing out. It looked like a routine hassle, the kind the punk was used to.

"You know 'em?"

"Cops are all same," the waitress said. "The sonsovbitches." She licked her lips like she was getting ready to spit.

"Your regulation cop-mobsters," McDowell said politely. "Just waitin' for a to kill somebody." He did not want to argue, but he had to admit she was mostly right.

"This town used to have good cops." She did not remove her hands from her hips, and she did not call in his order.

"No, it didn't," McDowell told her. "This town is little Chicago. Always has been." He figured she was having her own cop trouble. Either that, or she was one of those who were all the time walking around looking for somebody to hate.

She looked at seeing him for the first time as a man and not a customer. She did the standard double take that people did as she realized that wrinkled face was not the face of a really old man.

"You from around here?" Her voice was almost friendly.

"Chicago," he said "but originally from here."

She looked back toward the hassle. "Now that there," she hissed, "is illegal search. I got a friend that's a lawyer. He told me about illegal search."

One cop stood beside the kid while the kid emptied his pockets and put the contents on the hood of the car. The second cop was writing tickets for the headlights and the trunk lid. The cops' shirts were plastered to their backs with sweat. The kid's sweaty tee shirt was pasted on him like an extra layer of skin. It was not yet ten o'clock and the temperature was above ninety-five.

Welcome to redneck city, McDowell thought. You ought to write a song. Redneck City. Put it on the Detroit jukeboxes so the down-home boys can sit and drink with tears big as horse turds streaming down their cheeks . . . racehorse turds, he amended . . . if it's going to be a song about *this* town.

"About them pancakes," he said.

"Oh, sure," the waitress told him. "Coming right up." She moved toward the order counter but turned back once to look at what was happening in the street.

Welcome home, he thought, you *never* get out of the south. Even in Chicago, it's all around you. The south don't run from east to west and never did. It runs from Asheville-Atlanta to Chicago and Dee-troit. The south is people, and they move around. You never get away.

The restaurant was the usual choreograph of imitation leather seats, stainless steel hardware, plastic-topped tables, vinyl tile, and washable carpet. It was like a sad song, and he had seen and heard it sung from coast to coast. There were places like this all over. The only difference in this place was that it combined the worst of a chintz restaurant with the worst of a lunch counter. A long oval counter sat in the middle of the long, narrow room. Tables lined the walls, and stood along the windows. Because of that oval, there was no place in the restaurant where you could eat without watching somebody's rear end hanging off the back of a stool.

He was lucky. At this time of day the restaurant was nearly deserted. This restaurant did not have fifteen waitresses, it only had three. Besides the fat and ornery one, there was a thin little dark-haired hill girl who looked like she would do better in a country truck stop. She had that furtive, apologizing way of walking that country girls used when they got to the city.

The third waitress was interesting. She had kin back in Georgia. Her lanky frame and her long jaw were cracker all the way, only this girl was a long way from the Georgia pine brakes. She had a real smile. She moved like a dancer, and McDowell figured that she probably was a serious dancer. There was not one dancer in fifty who could make a living at dancing. That was not just true in Centerville, that was true all over.

Not, he thought, because she wasn't any good. Her movements showed how good she was. It was just that there were never no jobs for dancers, unless you wanted to take your shirt off and dance for a bunch of tit freaks in some club.

He slurped his coffee and noticed that the cops were done with the hassle. They climbed in their car and sat waiting. Strictly kid stuff. Cops always tried to intimidate you by just sitting, making you pull away first.

The kid faked them. He climbed back in the red Buick, but instead of entering traffic, he pulled into the restaurant parking lot. The cops pulled away, probably cussing because there was no law against going to a restaurant.

Looking over at the waitresses, McDowell thought of how that Georgia girl reminded him of Becky; of how Becky had looked so many years ago when she lived with him in Muncie, and then later in Knoxville. He never thought of Becky without thinking about being happy, and he never thought of being happy beside Becky without it made him sad.

That Georgia girl, there, wasn't the same as Becky. In a way that Georgia girl had a lot more going for her. McDowell could see that the Georgia girl had heard the sounds, all of them. She had an ear. She could not move that way if she had not heard all the sounds; the shit-kicking music and the laid-back jazz and the sweet-mouth hounds that made their own kind of music.

"Pancakes," the fat waitress said. "Lemme warm that coffee."

He had been daydreaming. It seemed like he did enough night dreaming. Ought to be paying attention.

"Leave the pot," he said, "Put it on the ticket."

"It's two bucks more."

"It's okay," he told her. "I spent last night drinking."

"So did I," she said, "and all by myself." She paused, and when he said nothing, she moved away. She moved slower this time, like all of a sudden the day had gone tired.

Lonesome he thought, lonesome, *lonesome*, I know what you mean. He chewed on the pancakes and felt bad about the fat waitress; he knew why, but did not know what anyone could do about it.

If only he had been a little more crazy, or Becky a little less crazy, then she would not have left. He had thought that a lot of times, and he thought it again.

He had tried all sorts of ways of loving her. One way he tried was to pull an old trumpet from its case. The horn had been sitting around for years, since his high school and college days when he had tried to be a good horn.

And never was one, he told himself. Never was a good lead horn, only a good backup. Never had the bodaciousness to be a good lead horn.

He had played to Becky, fooling around with the trumpet, and she had tried to understand jazz but had no luck with it. She continued to love folk music, and she continued to get occasional work. Her guitar playing improved, but not much. McDowell had laid the horn aside and drove truck. Then Becky left to live by herself. McDowell continued to drive truck. That was the time he saw the ghost outside of Cincinnati.

He did not want to think about that ghost, not now. He would think about it when he saw his sister, Samantha, maybe. Samantha had something going with a ghost, or ghost stories.

"Oinkers," a young voice said. "Pork chops. Sow bellies." The voice was loud and defiant, like a young child asking for a spanking.

McDowell looked up. A kid was sitting halfway down the counter, right at the curve of the oval. The kid was slantwise to McDowell. His face was hidden. Three traffic citations lay spread on the counter like a hand of cards. The kid turned, quick and sassy, looked at McDowell and wheeled back to face the counter. There was something in the kid's motions that McDowell told himself was more than just snotty. He could not quite name it, but that kid was not just a punk.

The kid lowered his voice. He was whispering to the little dark-hair girl. It was the kid from the red Buick. McDowell looked at him and figured he was seventeen, at best.

"Porkers," the kid said. His voice was not as loud and defiant, but it was loud enough for anyone in the restaurant to hear. "Bacon. Side meat."

The little hill girl waitress said something back to him. She seemed to be speaking as furtively as she walked, her voice no more than a whisper.

"They all are," the kid said, loudly. "All of 'em, and I don't just mean the pigs."

Dan McDowell told himself that there was a kid who was looking for more than he maybe wanted, more than he could handle. One day, if the kid kept that sort of thing up, he would run into a

31

man who had no patience. McDowell finished the pancakes, lit a cigarette, and checked his watch. The fat waitress came sweeping by on a routine table check.

"Can I get you something else?" Her voice was brisk, business-like.

McDowell looked at her and grinned. He made the grin just a little lewd, the way you could do when you were going to talk about something else. The waitress was not so much fat as she was stubby—reminded him of his ex-wife.

McDowell pointed to the kid. "Know him?"

"Naw," she said. "He comes in now and then to see Linda." Her voice slowed. It was not nearly as brisk.

"If Linda is the dark-hair girl, she can do better than that," he said. "Anybody could."

"She's his mama," the waitress said. "She's twenty-three and he acts about ten. She's a mother hen."

"But you aren't." He said it like he was pleased.

It was her turn to grin, her turn to be a little lewd. "I had a mother once. The old bitch."

She was okay. McDowell knew it. She was kind of fat and probably pretty ignorant, but she was okay. He wished she was not lonesome, knowing she was the kind who would always be lonesome.

"I'm headed back to Chicago," he lied. "I should've come in sooner."

"Guys come and go," she said. "Mostly they go." She picked right up on the game.

"Next time through."

"If the world don't end, or the creek don't rise. If nobody's doing nothin' else." She began to pick up the dirty dishes. He smiled and she smiled back, and it was clear to both of them that they were doing the best they could for each other.

McDowell finished his coffee, paid up and left. When he walked outside into the head-crushing heat, the red Buick sat like a monument to junk. The tires were bald. The hubcaps were missing. One lug nut was gone from the left front wheel.

He figured he ought to give as good as he had taken. He figured that the kid was sitting at the counter watching him. The kid could use a little lesson about quality.

McDowell walked all around the car. He pretended to himself

that he was a farmer trying to study out the best place to put a pitchfork into a pile of cow shit.

He knew he would have made a good actor. He could actually feel his face change, feel the scorn and disgust twisting in the wrinkles of his face. This, in spite of the fact that he did not give a damn one way or another about the kid and his car. The kid wouldn't know that, though.

When he had taken his walk around the car, he lifted his shoulders in a helpless, scornful way. Then he climbed into his own car. He had a date with a woman who he hoped he could love.

Chapter 5

I'M GLAD YOU LIKE ME. I LIKE YOU."

"I like you a lot." More than that, he thought, but I better not say it.

"Enough, at least, that you drove down from Chicago."

"I came up Florida coast," he said. "A couple of my dealers down there were pushing cheap sidelines. I had to clear that up."

"From Florida, then."

"I think I even love you." He knew he was taking a chance. This woman was realist. What he said was true, but what he was feeling was even more than what he said.

"Try to get figured out." She smiled, but the smile was distant. She did not look exactly displeased, but she was not happy, either. She looked like a teacher who had just received a stupid answer from a student. "That bothers me," she told him. "You're too old be talking youngish."

She was so beautiful. Women were beautiful. She was important or he would be able to talk better. He would not be sounding like some dumb college kid.

Her name was Margot on stage. Her regular name was Margaret. She wore white slacks and a light, green, long-sleeved, buttoned-high blouse that contrasted with her light Negro skin. In spite of this heat she looked comfortable. She sat beside him at the small table.

Sunlight washed the limestone patio. A light breeze that Mc-Dowell told himself must be gladdening the hearts of the cham-

ber of commerce momentarily cooled the sweating customers. The
breeze carried the stink of automobile exhaust. McDowell was not
drinking. He was never interested in drinking when he was with a
woman. When he was with a woman he was not bored. Thinking
*you are used to being alone because you have been so much but you
don't do good at it.* A man who had so much practice at something
ought to be good at it. He knew he had tried to rush her, tried to
press her too fast. It made him feel guilty and childish.

"We're not exactly strangers." Even to him, his voice sounded
sullen. Like a little kid who gave all the wrong answers.

"We had six nights together a month ago," she said. "We slept
together the last three of them."

"That means we aren't strangers."

"It is a very good start on not being." She sipped at a glass of
lemonade. He knew she was the kind of singer who was almost
superstitious about singers who boozed.

Well, he thought, the booze caught a lot of them—some of the
best. Smoking could really fuck up a voice, too, if you did it too
much. She didn't.

In the busy street that lay beyond the restaurant patio, the traffic was a colored wave, like an abstract painting without the sensi-
bleness of an abstract. McDowell watched Margaret, her fine face,
her long fingers, her graceful movements. He wished he could say
something that did not sound stupid.

He wondered why a singer who could command a stage the
way she did, who could walk away with both the audience and the
band, would have a hard time making love unless the room was
almost dark. At least she had been shy in Chicago last month. He
did not know what was going to happen today, plus the weekend.

After Sunday's matinee she would be finished here. On Monday she would be leaving, and he'd have to head out for Indianapolis. He asked her about the next gig.

"I have two weeks in Atlanta. Don't like it. Don't want it. If I
owned hell and Atlanta, I'd live in hell and rent out Atlanta."

"No worse than any place else."

"I was born and raised there."

She was taller than most women he had known, although she
had the smallest breasts he had ever touched. She was not thin, but
she was narrow. Her legs and ankles were narrow. So was her face,

although her mouth was full.

"It's better than it was," she said. "Atlanta. These days the white gentlemen are courteous. They say 'ma'am' when they ask to fuck you." She was joking, sort of. Some of it was not joking, though.

Her face gained dimension because her hair surrounded it like a cloud, lightly brown and almost blonde. Her hair curled and seemed to be in a constant soft explosion. Her eyes were almost hazel, her skin not light enough to be cream colored. It was not quite dark enough to be brown, either.

"We're sitting in my hometown," said McDowell. "Pretty, ain't it?" He said it joking, not mean. He did not want her to think he was mean.

Her hazel-colored eyes were light enough to look transparent, but they were not. They were bright like sun on water. He thought for a moment that it would be one of the worst things in the world if he ever saw them dull. He told himself to quit being so sentimental.

She could be bold-talking, but shy. That was part of the reason she was so important. Sex mattered, and that was part of the reason, too. But sex was everywhere, and most of it was cheap. She definitely was not cheap. You couldn't be honest and cheap both, but obviously you could be honest and shy, both.

"Are you booked after Atlanta?" he asked, hoping she was coming back to Chicago.

Her grin was pretty crude when she wanted it that way. "Nope, I gotta swap spit with a Pittsburgh radio station. I do a couple under-the-table commercials and a guest spot. They make me some tapes."

He always figured that singers and theater people were shy in private because they had to be so bold when they walked through the world. But when they walked out there in the world like she did, then you had to pay attention.

She paid attention with her singing. She could bend a phrase, right to the cracking point and not crack it. He was dumb about most things, but he was not dumb about music, and he was not dumb about her. She had learned mostly from O'Day. Maybe even the way she acted she had learned from O'Day; but she had learned from a lot of others, too. Lee and Fitzgerald, plus Tilton for that occasional phrasing, and from Holiday and Keely for that remoteness, that sadness, in the music. She must've worked herself silly, listening, working, listening to the old records, and working.

And she turned it into her own sadness, he thought. She could learn from the best, but she took the music and turned it into her own. Not that anybody, except maybe him and a few other crazy people, needed a jazz singer these days. Not that anybody, except maybe him in the whole goddamn world, would listen to a scat singer like her and know what he was hearing.

"Suppose you mess up," she said. "Suppose you really do love me. I wouldn't know what to do with it. Do you understand that?"

"No."

She was looking at him with those hazel eyes, as honest as anybody could get. She was lots more open with her eyes than she was with her legs. The three nights they went to bed, she had never really relaxed her legs. She loved to make love in that intense, quiet way some women had—and one man, too, he thought, if you count yourself. Still, it was always like she reserved something for herself. If she ever really trusted a man, he figured that quietness would still be there, but pressing forward, unreserved.

He had heard of her, of course, a long time before he met her last month in Chicago. Her reputation was solid in Chicago and Pittsburg. She was like a lot of musicians. Strong local, but no national reputation. There were all kinds of reasons. Poor agents. Unwillingness to tour. Booze. Bad luck. He guessed this one, Margaret, Margot Haydn, had told too many of the wrong people to go to hell.

And he had heard her on the road, of course. On the car radio. Jazz and the nighttime road.

He first caught her act on a lonesome night when, womanless, he walked into a club where the booths were upholstered like Oldsmobile seat covers. The crowd was dressed about the same way. She was in front of a good guitar, a good bass, and a pickup drummer who had played rock for so long that he could not quite get in back of the music.

"Working stiff," she told him later. "My career isn't downhill, or much uphill. I get work. I pay the rent."

He had her records. All three of them. She had not mentioned them, but he found them. The old one, back when she was a kid, had cost thirty dollars and was not a good copy. He could not decide whether to tell her that he had it or not.

Like Braff, he thought. You got the oldest Braff record, back when he was a working stiff. You got a lot of Spanier. You got the rare ones, and maybe you are the only one who deserves to have them. Maybe only you in the whole wide world are able to hear. But you can't tell her.

Spanier used to drive straight ahead, no fruit salad, just play it without crap. Braff the same, except Braff was educated, in control, laid back.

"Anyway," she said, "if you do love me, and supposing I lost my mind and loved you, you're not built for this life. We'd have Monday and Tuesday nights, maybe Wednesdays. Once every two months."

"You booked that close?"

"Not always, but sometimes."

"I could come to where you're playing."

"We want to go to bed this afternoon," she said. "I won't be worth a thing later on. I get tired or blue after work."

"I wouldn't care."

"I'm glad you wouldn't, but if we lived together or were in love, you would. Later on. I'm not worth anything in the morning, either."

Most women were not. He had learned that one the hard way.

"If you love somebody . . ."

"Dan," she said, "don't be a kid. If you love somebody, you've got to have bodies together. You got to touch. You have to *be* with them, at least half of the time."

He knew it wasn't true, but it was partly true. *All that you have ever tried to do is find out what is right between two people but you never have.*

He figured maybe she knew. He had only known one other woman who was this honest, or at least this blunt. That had been the shy Portuguese girl, Marie. Maybe he should have been paying attention to the shy ones all along.

She was saying something else, and he had been thinking and not listening.

". . . lots of singers do," she said. "Marry nice guys, respectable guys. It makes them feel safe. It's practically an occupational hazard."

"So I'm respectable." It was about the worst thing anyone had ever said about him, but she had said it. At least she seemed to be saying that.

"Not the only reason, " she said. "You've got an ear. You're very loving. The most honest fake I know."

Out there in the street, in the brightly colored wave of traffic, some dumb sonovabitch was leaning on his horn. In a second everybody would. McDowell listened, and the horns began to join in. Probably, very probably, some old lady had got run over. The corpse was holding up traffic.

Margaret saw his anger. She should. She had tried to make him mad.

"Dan," she said, "get it figured out. You hell around in that car. You sneer and talk tough. But, Dan, I been to bed with you. You can be sweet, not tough."

You had to be tough. She was tough. Didn't she know that? She was in the world's toughest business.

"Make up your mind, which," she said. "I love you gentle."

"Love for me to be gentle?"

"A man roughed me up once, when I was a girl. I love for men to be gentle, but that isn't what I said." She was looking right at him, right at his lined face, and her eyes were as open and honest as they had been all along. Her eyes were like her voice.

There was a thunderstorm late that night. It was one of those sky-breakers, part of the weather system that rolled through the Ohio River Valley. The wind got up fast, bringing in a sheeting front of hot rain that steamed on the still warm pavement. The sky lighted as stroke after stroke of brilliant electrical charges rocked Centerville with bright explosions. The lightning walked across the sky like some old god of war. The thunder did not boom like bombs. It had the sharp crack of artillery.

McDowell lay beside Margaret, watching the raging sky as tall buildings came alight with the white-blue green-blue from the bolts. The windows were washed with rain.

She had worked hard that night, maybe because she knew he was in the audience. The performance had taken all of her vitality.

She moved slightly in her sleep, sighed, murmured a name that he did not catch, but the name was not his. She turned on her back, and the sheet, which was more than was needed in the air-conditioned room, slipped almost to her waist. Her small breasts were silhouetted as she was profiled by the lightning that woke the room, shocked the darkness.

McDowell watched her, like he was seeing the subject of a camera that flashed monstrously. Her not quite brown skin was white in the flashes. Her hair looked white. Her nose was not large, but large enough that there was the least suggestion of a bend, a hook, the genes of some long-forgotten, self-appointed southern aristocrat. An extra heavy hit of thunder cracked the sky, rattling the windows. She murmured again and rolled back on her side, facing away from him.

How many nights, he thought, have you lain like this lying beside a woman—curled up beside her sometimes, and sometimes awake and watching—nights in apartments you rented, thinking this is Becky, it's where we live and we'll get something better in a little while—or lying beside some of the others who are so hard to forget.

How many nights when you lay thinking this is the one, you are safe now, and the warmness of lying there.

I love you, he thought, in spite of what you say. In spite of I don't even know anymore what that means.

How many times in too many rooms beside too many women where you knew there wasn't a chance.

And now, this night, lying beside Margaret, with the lightning and sound and the shadows coming and going, he recognized that everything had gone on too long. Life had gone on too long, all of it. When you tried too long it seemed like your heart got tired. You began hiding inside yourself. He thought that this might be the night when he had to think about taking the last chance that there would maybe ever be, and he decided that he was going to do it, he was going to take that chance, because he had to.

Chapter 6

THE NEXT MORNING THE SKY LOOKED LIKE IT HAD BEEN AIR-brushed with blue, then shellacked and polished. The polish gave no shine. It was not the light blue of a clear day in a declining August. There was a cast of darkness to the sky, like the threat of another storm. The tall buildings were shaded by the threatening blue. Windows that should have been throwing glare from the sunlight were dull. The light lay across them the way it illuminated flat paint.

McDowell was headed over to the import-export company. He was going to see his sister, Samantha. Traffic was stalled, inching forward in short bursts of stop and accelerate and screech. McDowell leaned on the Cadillac's steering wheel while his mind idled with less purpose than the Cadillac's idling engine. He thought of Margaret and of music. He watched the people in the cars around him. A dark-haired, attractive woman of about thirty sat in the passenger seat of a small sports car that was hemmed in beside the Cadillac. The driver wore a business suit, and he had his hand resting on the woman's knee. She looked bored, and so did he.

Marriage, McDowell thought. He had never been bored when he was married. He had been sometimes crazy and broke and angry but never bored.

They were holding another fire, renewing the town. Somewhere out there in the distance black smoke curled away from the river, rising high in the air and then blown sideways by a high wind. The smoke made a layer in the sky. It looked like an oil tank was burning.

The attractive, dark-haired woman in the sports car looked at him. He smiled. She turned away and faced straight ahead. Bored.

They were having one hell of a conflagration. The black layer of smoke made the dark sky look purple. It was better to think of Margaret.

The best tunes were the ones with range, and if a singer had good range, the way Margaret did, then there was a chance that you might hear a wizardly-type job done with a tune. Last night Margaret had gotten off, singing "Sonny." The song would not let go of her, and she would not let go of the song. She wrapped herself around the music like she was making love to it.

Any tune with range was good, especially for a horn. With a horn you did not have to worry about sentimental or schlocky words. You could take something old and corny, even something as bad as "Silver Threads." And that, right there, he told himself, was the true heart of traditional jazz. The horn was one-on-one with the tune. You could make love to the music the way Margaret did with "Sonny" last night.

They were tearing out a well-planted divider strip so that *they* could make a new traffic lane. He could see what was happening, although he was still fifty yards away and boxed in by traffic. The little sports car was beside him; some Oriental tin can was in front of him, and a beat-up GMC running local delivery was behind him. He looked forward, toward the construction. The old, old trees that used to be on this divider strip were gone, but the stumps were still there, yellowy and sap-bleeding from the rupture caused by the chain saws. A yellow backhoe was knocking out the old curbings. A bulldozer sat idling, and the idle was high. The injectors were fouled and the thing smoked. Men in orange hardhats were rigging cable from a stump to the bulldozer, and that was gonna be funny. All that cat was going to do was dig in, or snap the cable.

He wished he were not going to see his sister. He wished he were with Margaret.

Margaret was working up something new. She worked a lot with tapes, and she did not like anyone to be around when she worked, except, of course, other musicians at rehearsal.

Last night Margaret had tore up that number. The audience had become quiet and sad and hopeful; and he had felt the power of it running through the audience. When Margaret finally let it go, the audience tried to tell her they loved her, standing and hollering and applauding. There had not even been a recording hookup.

He liked performers for that. He liked the way they just blew the act off into the air with the sounds heading out toward Mars, or at least the moon. He liked the silver-blue-gray of a muted trumpet weaving color behind some outfit that was not worth a damn, except for the trumpet.

He liked it when performers got free, the ones who ever did get free. He liked Bigard and big-ears Trummy Young, because they had been nigger at the wrong time and learned how to make it mean something. Bigard and Young had got more free than he, Dan McDowell, had ever been.

Traffic surged forward and he was even with the construction. He wished he had not promised to see his sister. Or his father. Or his brother-in-law. Of the bunch of them, his sister was probably the worst.

She thought she was sanctified, despite the fact that she once had an affair with a Spaniard wimp, and another time with a wop wimp. Each time her real Wimp had stood around and wrung his hands. McDowell's sister was a madonna, self-proclaimed, and McDowell told himself that he did not give a good goddamn what her real problem was. There was nothing sacred or secret in McDowell's family, except that it was sacred not to talk about what was secret. He wished he did not think that way about Samantha, but she would not allow him any other way to think. He remembered her, though, back when she was wonderful.

He had loved her when she was wonderful. He had thought she was some kind of goddess, or smart spirit, or at least a genius. Sometimes, even now, in these old days—days that seemed as old as those old, old stumps of trees—he dreamed about when they were kids.

He, Dan McDowell, had always been dumb-headed and smartass. Samantha had always been sharp, but always ready to take his part against anyone but herself. She caused him a lot of trouble when they were kids. If anything bad happened, she always blamed it on him.

But, when the shit came down, he thought, old Sammy had always been there protecting him. Once, when they were little kids, she smacked a big redhead kid named Sikes with a ball bat. It was a good thing, too, because old Sikes had been getting ready to totally demolish McDowell's pore ass.

That line across the sky from the oil fire was getting darker and bigger. It looked like the fire had spread to another tank.

The truth was that he hated Sammy now, but he loved her before. He had never had an older brother, but he sure had an older sister. You could love an older sister the same way you could look up to lady teachers who you liked a lot, but who didn't give a damn what you thought of them.

Maybe Sammy had her reasons. She still did not give a damn about what Dan McDowell thought. She did not like what Dan McDowell did either, he told himself. Nope, Sammy didn't like that part at all.

The temp was running a little hot on the Cad, despite the oversized radiator. McDowell flipped off the air conditioner to reduce the load. In a couple more minutes he would be past the construction and free to get into the next traffic mess.

That sky seemed loaded. It looked like a hurricane sky, a twister sky. The smoke from the oil fire was starting to tail upward from the straight line, like curving movements of wind were cyclonic, turning, wrapping themselves into a ball of storm.

A cop who was no more than a kid was directing traffic. He almost seemed like he was having fun. This kid was Africa black, deep black, and his arm and hand motions were exaggerated and loose and happy, like a man dancing. Parked right in the middle of the old median, down by the intersection, a lady cop sat in a cruiser like she was either supervising or standing by to give first aid when the kid got run over.

McDowell inched forward in his lane of traffic. Suddenly he jammed the accelerator, then got to the brakes. He almost lost it. He slammed them on, his foot just catching the edge of the brake pedal. His foot dangled and skidded, but it got the Cad stopped. He thought he was going to scream.

Standing about three yards from the cruiser and maybe fifteen yards from the kid cop was the ghost. It was wispy-looking, pale, but you did not have to squint to see it.

He had jammed the brakes so hard he killed the engine. He reached for the key, and when he found it his hand was shaking so hard that he could not take hold of it.

The ghost just stood there with those wide and vacant eyes. This time the eyes seemed deeper back in the ghost's face, and they had no pupils. Just white and wide and staring. This time the ghost was smiling with its chops clamped together, the lips rolled in against the gums. The smile walked along the crinkles of its old, old face.

McDowell turned the key and nothing happened. The transmission was still in drive. Then he lost the key again. His goddamn arm began jolting, uncontrollably. He thought he was going crazy until he had the clear-eyed realization that he already was crazy. He shoved on the gear, turned the key, lost it again.

Now his legs were trembling and nearly out of control. He swung sideways on the seat and stiff-legged the accelerator since his leg would not bend and still hold a position. He managed to hold the accelerator down long enough to dump some of the flooding from the carbs.

Horns were going off everywhere. The kid cop was walking toward him, and the ghost just stood there. The smile was not a mean smile or a satisfied smile. It was sort of a sad smile. Either that, or it was just the normal way the face was shaped when all the teeth were gone. Maybe the ghost was not smiling at all.

The cop tapped on the window. McDowell fumbled for the power switch. He looked at the cop, and that was a mistake. The cop could see his face, and his face looked terrible and out of control. Finally the window slid down.

"Little trouble, mister?" The kid's voice was friendly. He was not getting flipped out over the traffic stall. The lady cop was climbing from the cruiser, heading for the intersection to direct traffic. When she climbed out she was facing the ghost, practically bumping into it. She did not react.

It was almost a relief. Now he knew he was crazy. If you were crazy, that was one thing. If you were haunted, that was another. Crazy people could at least get cured.

"Got a 'lil dizzy," McDowell drawled. "Feelin' sorta funny." The drawl was automatic, and when the kid answered, he was drawling back.

"Shove on oveh," the kid said. "I getcha out of this heah mess." He smiled real friendly, and McDowell thought that he, Dan Mc-

Dowell, would never badmouth a cop again. He knew he was lying while he was thinking it, but he managed to slide over to the passenger side of the car. There was a feeling of presence, of quiet horror in the car. The passenger side was loaded with it. McDowell watched the kid. The kid was not feeling a thing. He was looking at the car, and coveting it openly as he got it started.

"Jes' lovely iron," he said. "Mention me in yo' will." Then he remembered that he maybe had a sick man on his hands and knew that he had just made a mistake. "Some years hence, a'course." He grinned at McDowell and pulled the Cad away and through the intersection. They passed right by the ghost, and the kid saw nothing.

The kid drove for a block, turned onto a side street and pulled over. He turned off the ignition, got out of the car, and stood beside the open door. This kid was too trusting to be a cop. He had let himself get isolated, and in this town.

"Now a'course you ain't been drinkin'." The kid leaned into the car. His face was kind of pug-nosed instead of flat, and he wrinkled it like he was worried. The pug nose was incongruous to the dark black skin, but the combination sort of worked.

"Not for forty-eight hours," McDowell said. He was getting back in control, because kid or not, this was a cop. His trembling hands were already snaking his driver's license from the billfold. The kid took the license.

"'Cause you don't look so good," the kid said. "'Course if you was drinkin' I prob-ably smell it."

"What it is," McDowell lied, and put on a show of wrinkling his already wrinkly face, "is that I got to listenin' to the radio. A friend of mine got hisself in a wreck last night. Nobody tol' me." His voice ended on a low wail.

"Bad?"

"He ain't alive no more," McDowell wailed on. McDowell imagined his dead friend. He could see the goddamn crumpled steel, the shattered glass, the still form lying across the steering wheel. He could feel the misery and loss crawling on his face—despite the fact he didn't have a friend anywhere near this goddamn town.

"I jes' come on shift," the cop said commiseratingly. "Last night musta been one of them nights."

The kid's sympathy was so apparent that McDowell almost felt ashamed. In fact, he told himself, he did feel ashamed, but what the hell was he going to do? Tell the truth?

The feeling of presence in the car seemed to be lessening. Maybe the acting helped. It took his mind off the ghost. His fit of being crazy must be over, he thought. He was okay now until the next fit.

"I'm okay now," he told the cop. "It was jes' the shock of it, is all." He held both hands up like he was inspecting them. The tremble was nearly gone from his hands. His voice sounded subdued and sad but steady.

"Drive me around the block," the kid said. "Marge so short she gonna get run over, sure."

That would be the lady cop supervisor. You didn't want a short cop in an intersection. Of course, the kid had other reasons. "I'll come around," McDowell said, playing the game. He got out of the passenger side of the Cad, closed the door, and walked around the front of the car. The kid stood watching him, which of course, is what the kid should be doing.

McDowell climbed in, confident and steady. The kid walked around behind the back of the car. McDowell got the engine started, but he waited until the cop had climbed in the car. He pulled away, driving with the easy, observant grace of a professional driver. The kid watched and was satisfied. When they circled two blocks and came back to the intersection, the kid climbed out.

"Marge gonna raise hell," he grinned. "She is jes' crazy for pro-cee-dure."

"If they is anything I can do," McDowell mumbled, "jes' tell me. I shore do thank you." He was glad to be getting out of this. In a minute he could even drop the accent and start talking like a human being.

"Sorry about your friend," the cop said. "This town is hell for accidents." He slammed the door and walked back into the intersection. The cop looked nearly as relieved as McDowell felt. He had dropped his accent.

This play-acting, lynch-happy, fornicating south.

McDowell pulled through the intersection and began looking for a restaurant. What he wanted was a drink, but he knew better and settled for coffee.

He found a crusty little restaurant with a counter where he sat slugging coffee to steady his nerves. If he was going to see Samantha, even one drink would put him at a disadvantage. He sat thinking, first of the ghost, and then of being crazy. Then he thought about the cop.

There were all kinds of different southern accents, but between men who were strangers there were only two basic kinds of drawls. There was the dog-sniffing drawl, where you circled each other. Then there was the dangerous drawl, which was slower, and which sort of smoldered. He and the cop had only just been sniffing at each other.

It's all a play, he thought, a comedy.

A *clown*, he thought, you're a grown-up clown. Margaret is right—get it figured out, then get out of the circus.

All right, he told himself, it is a circus. But it isn't funny. If it was funny, nobody would take it serious, right?

But they all *do* take it serious.

The cop had been serious. He was just a kid, and he had joked, but one false move on McDowell's part—like if he had mistakenly opened the glove compartment—and the joking would have ended hard and fast. McDowell had not carried a gun in years, but he remembered other years when he could not imagine not carrying a gun. There were more guns out on that road than there were in the whole U.S. Army. And the further south you got, the more guns there were.

It was a dirty, grimy joint. He slurped at the coffee and wondered if the cup was clean. His mind kept trying to dodge the fact that he had just seen the ghost in broad daylight. That had never happened before. Not only had the ghost come to town, but now it wasn't even hiding in alleys. He was cold sober and he soberly had to decide whether the ghost was real, or whether he was insane.

Margaret was not one of the clowns. She worked the way any good musician worked. She worked all the time, and she didn't care for the clown show. He, Dan McDowell, seemed to care for the show. He seemed to want to be part of it, clowning right along with the rest of the jokers who took the least little thing serious and laughed with you right up to the minute they killed you or stuck you in jail. What in the hell, he asked himself, was wrong with him?

He told himself that one thing was sure. Samantha could just sit on her problem for another twenty-four hours. He was not going over there in the shape he was in and try to joust with Samantha.

He checked his watch. It was a little after eleven A.M. Five hours before he met Margaret. You could drive a long way in five hours. What he really wanted to do was give that ghost a road check. He had never seen it on the daytime road. If he was in some kind of fight, he told himself, he ought to find out as much as he could about what he was fighting.

He got a cup of coffee to take with him. It came in a styrofoam cheap-cup that was cheap like the world. Then he headed for the Cadillac.

He thought that he had been crazy before, but never crazy in the way he was now. He just could not figure out what in the hell was wrong with him.

Chapter 7

THE LAND THROUGH WHICH DAN MCDOWELL HAD BEEN DRIVING for most of his life is bounded on the east by rolling mountains in which lie the Smokies, the Blue Ridge, and the Cumberlands. It is bounded on the west by the Mississippi River, and in the north by the Great Lakes. The land is fecund and hot six months of each year, and it has a history of violence.

Whether flat or mountainous, the land southward is a land of smoke and mist. Mist hangs silver-gray across fields and slow rivers. It hangs blue above and around the mountains. The mist is ghostlike and cold in a land that is hot. It causes shimmers in the air at noon.

In the land southward, haunts have accumulated through centuries. It makes no practical difference whether the haunts are real or not. People on the land believe in the haunts, and they pass them from generation to generation like keepsakes. Spirits, some black and dying and carried to this land in the holds of rotting ships, murmur and wail and sing over haunted fields. Indian spirits legislate the direction in which a new house will face, and their legislation is as lawful as the sun. Old tales are like a failed crop, turned under, the spoils decaying and fertilizing the shotgun corn of next year's planting. The tales have a renewing life of their own, and the land of Dan McDowell, whether it contains ghosts or not, is haunted.

He cruised the Cad for an hour and got free of the outskirts of town. Dan McDowell shoved a tape in the tape deck. As the best band in the world, at least the best for progressive jazz, began to play, McDowell hooked the Cadillac onto a side road and leaned in a slump over the wheel. The best band in the world and he was willing to prove it, was working with Bach. The brass section was shaping a choral, and the band was Kenton's.

He told himself that he had been driving this road since he was sixteen, back in the days when he pushed a piston-slapping, flat-head Ford. The old road wound through the countryside south of town. Out here there were still farms and old trees.

Out here you could imagine that nothing had changed. There were occasional remains of the old slave fences, the flat limestone that had been laid and layered by slaves and sweated over—although, he told himself, probably, very probably, those things were built in the winters when ol-fucking-massa had nothing else for his children to do. The fences, which were really walls, had mostly crumbled away. Even if the walls were gone, there were still lines along the road or across fields marking where they had been. Around the old houses and the cheap new houses, lilac grew like trees because of the lime.

A good thing too, the broken fences. Only you hated to see that much of anybody's work go down the drain.

To be fair, he told himself, in this neck of the woods old massa was probably one of those small landowners who only had two or three slaves. In that case he would have been out here busting his ass even harder than the black boys were busting theirs.

This was a narrow, good old two-lane road that was in decay because of the freeway. It ran through fields and over small rises, with some pretty tough curves in places. Sometimes a tree overhung the road, shading it and making a dark splash on the sunny, oily-looking surface. The trees looked scraggledy at this time of year. The bugs had been chawing on them for months.

His best recollection of this road was once when he went off against a really beautiful older woman who was pushing a '47 Hudson coupe. He had been kicking a '54 Lincoln. The woman had dusted him off. She drove hot but not crazy, and she had him climbing all over his steering wheel. He came out of it with his gearshift lever tucked in his tailpipe.

McDowell leaned back in the seat, stretched, and steered one-handed and easily at low speed. The sky, which had seemed purple, was now a normal-looking blue. Then, without knowing why he knew it, he understood that the blue sky was ominous. It should not be, but it was. That ghost was somewhere up ahead. He debated turning back as he nervously fiddled with the volume on the tape deck. He got both hands on the wheel, made a decision he did not like, and increased his speed. The music on the tape deck seemed to help lower his fear. Kenton was doing that original of "Peanut Vendor." The trumpets were climbing right on up the range and squalling that flatted fifth, telling the whole world and Dwight Eisenhower to go fuck themselves.

Jazz was revolutionary and always had been. Back in the '50s when the clowns were dressing in gray flannel and getting their systems together, Kenton had made a mockery of their systems. The organization men could not bear the terrible beauty of perfect musicianship and perfect organization.

Good times and bad, he told himself, trying to avoid his fear. He sure did remember that woman in that '47 Hudson, despite only having seen her once.

After she dusted him good, he followed along behind her. Twenty miles out this road was a crossroads gas station where the woman pulled in for gas. McDowell pulled in behind her, grinned, and respectfully, most respectfully, asked what she was running in that heap.

She was running a stock Hudson eight in a six-cylinder coupe, and she could cut rubber in second gear. He remembered the whole thing like it had just happened.

That, he told himself, was back when he was almost still a kid. He figured that the woman had been about the same age then as he was now. She was short and light built and sort of heavy breasted; and she had black hair with lots of gray. She had an open and friendly smile that she used all the time, instead of just grinning.

Very probably, he told himself, he remembered her because she was too self-confident and intelligent to be a white woman and still live in this place where all white women were born with their legs crossed.

He wondered if that old filling station still existed, or if it had been torn down like everything else. He straightened in the seat, lowered the volume on the tape deck, and found that he was feeling pretty confident. Instead of just cruising, he had some place to go.

The road was nearly untraveled. He edged the Cadillac up to a speed where he felt he was romping into the curves. The heavy automobile, with the heavier frame that had been constructed on convertibles, swung into the curves like a lever. The beefed-up suspension that McDowell had ordered when the car was rebuilt lifted the front end in the curves. The rear end was free to break instead of bunching up in an attempt to roll.

Driving was like jazz, he figured. When you were driving like this, kind of happy-driving and going somewhere unimportant, it had the push of a laid-back horn that had just woken up and decided to play games. The laid-back flow expanded, pushed forward, and what was out in front of the horn was not nearly as good as where it was coming from.

Margaret had been the same way yesterday afternoon when they went to bed. Margaret had still been shy but different. She acted like she was going for something that she could live without but didn't want to. Like making it with him was a luxury. He did not know whether he liked that or not, but, he thought, probably not. What he really wanted to feel like was a necessity.

The crossroads station sat at the bottom of a curve and he could see it from a long way off as he crested a hill. The hill twisted the road away from a view of the intersection, then twisted it back. By the time McDowell saw the station the second time it was no more than five hundred yards away. He began to take off speed after he broke free of the curve. He could see that it was closed. He rolled toward it and felt mournful.

Two dogs were sitting along a fencerow among knocked-down weeds. Weeds covered the crossroad station's lot which had once been graveled.

One dog was a kind of whey-faced mongrel with liver-color spots. It carried that slob, tail-wag look of a dog that would maybe knock you down and lick you to death because it loved you so much.

The other dog was a black and tan. Its hound face carried the hound reserve that would not give over to the very nicest sonovabitch in the world until it had checked him out.

McDowell sat in the stopped car and looked the place over. There had once been macadam in the area beside the pumps. Now the macadam was crumbling and the pumps were gone. Weeds grew right up to the old pump island, and they grew through the remains of gravel so that the whole station lot was covered. When McDowell stepped from the car the whey-faced dog came wagging toward him. McDowell absentmindedly made friends with the dog while he looked at the station.

The building stood like a crippled Bowery drunk leaning on a crutch and trying to fool a cop. The windows were long gone; even the shatters of glass that remained had dirt covering the sharp surfaces. It was a small building on a small lot. He remembered it as being a lot bigger.

Beside the building a gutted blue '63 Chev lay on its side where some grease monkey had turned it over to get at the transmission. The bell housing looked like a rusted cave, and the drive shaft leaned into the wreck as a prop to keep it from falling over. Weeds grew around the Chev and up close to the building. Beyond the lot lay a field, and behind the building was a small creek. Old trees stood along the creek and rose behind the building like a windbreak. In front of what had been the small garage, tar and oil were not yet fully leached from the soil. The weeds were thin and sparse in that area. The sliding door to the garage had been ripped away; maybe by the same punk who had spare-parted the Chev. The station was deserted, vandalized, broken and useless. It sat between the field and the road like a page torn from a history book.

The whey-faced dog whined in a happy, hungry way that was asking for an ear rub. Purple thistles and fluffy, seeding thistles stood in back of the station. Alongside the building volunteer hollyhocks looked like sticks, despite some of them threw a splash of red beside the faded, board-weathered side of the building. The red hollyhocks made black shadows on the building. A tea rose edged over beneath the tumble of weeds. He could see a couple of pink flowers.

It was a damned depressing sight. McDowell picked nettles from his pants legs, turned back and entered the small building through the garage. The whey-faced dog followed. The black and tan one sat at the entry.

It had once been a garage, attached to a small grocery. An old guy ran it, and his wife had made home-grown donuts. You could get good coffee. You could even get gas, but you had to pump it yourself when the old man's joints were aching.

Now it was a good place for spiders. Webs were resilient and gluey against his hand as he shoved them aside. Overhead, the sun threw a beam like a spotlight past a peeled-back piece of galvanized roofing. Where a gas space heater had once hung, rusted brackets dangled. The brackets had been wrenched sideways when some impatient, thieving asshole had been in too much of a hurry to go to his truck for the right tool.

In a dark corner was a large pile of cast-off parts and junk. McDowell walked to it, gave it a kick, and dust whirled through the shadows and into the spotlight of sun.

Broken steering wheel from a Kaiser-Frazier, speedometer from a '47 Plymouth, busted gears from a half dozen different wrecks; but he recognized the syncro from one of those papier-mache transmissions that Chev built in the '50s. Cracked headlight ring from a bathtub Nash, a Hudson clutch with the corks worn off because somebody forgot to check the fluid.

He thought of the beautiful older woman who had trounced him with her Hudson. Maybe this junk clutch had come off of her car. It wouldn't of been her who made that kind of mistake. Maybe she had a punk kid, a son, hot-shitting it up and down that road out there and paying no attention to maintaining the best clutch ever made.

He felt like he was at a goddamned funeral. The whey-faced dog whined. McDowell kicked the pile. Broken taillight lens for a '58 Merc, a couple of those old plasticy, imitation bone handles from a Packard, '47 or '48.

A torn and dented fender from a '59 International pickup leaned against the wall. It stood on another pile of junk. McDowell gave it a kick, watched it tumble away as the dust rose through the shadows and headed toward the spotlight of sun. He stirred the pile with his foot, hesitated, leaned over to peer into the dark corner. Then he leaned further, reaching down like a man discovering and picking up a lost and sacred chalice. He hauled the thing from the junk pile.

It was an enameled medallion between chrome braces and it had once ridden between the headlights and across the radiator of a Cadillac. He ran through his memory, and then through his knowledge. It had to be from a car built between '29 and '32. That was back in the days when Cadillac was second-rate, compared to the custom Duesenbergs and Chryslers, the Pierce Arrows and Rolls.

The whey-faced dog whined. The black and tan stood up, suddenly alert, like it was trying to figure out a strange sound.

McDowell rubbed the medallion, watched the dirt come off the surface and stain his hand. He watched the unbroken, glazed-slick surface come clean. This thing that came from a second-rate car was cloisonné. It was not some junk piece of enameled iron or pottery. The thing did not even have a chip. The chrome braces had been so heavily chromed that there was no rust, only dirt.

The whey-faced dog rubbed against his leg. It whined.

McDowell felt haunted. The feeling came all at once, and it was not like being at a funeral. It was a feeling of being haunted like no feeling he had ever had before. It was not a feeling like those he had when he was seeing the ghost. This was a feeling of sadness, and a feeling that all of the past, including his own, was about to disappear.

He felt haunted by women and music and engines, but especially by engines. He seemed to hear the high roar of old cylinders across this hot and humid land. He seemed to hear the cracking sounds of exhausts through a land where there were haunts everywhere; the dead raftmen in the rivers, the dead Confederates, the voodoo that scared everybody, the Indian spirits that could sometimes rend and tear. All of that was in this land. Everyone knew it, only everyone tried to forget it or pretend it was not there.

Now it seemed like there were even more haunts, and those haunts wore wide-eyed, saucer-like headlights, and they wailed with the voices of engines.

The whey-faced dog whimpered. McDowell looked up to see the black and tan walking away, rapidly, into the weed-covered lot. The whey-faced dog gave a shuddery whine, and ran, tail down, as fast as it could go.

Something seemed to be working in the spotlight of sun. It was like the dust was trying to take shape, like the dust had its own mind and was trying to build some form in the center of the light. At first the form was skinny, and it looked like an impressionist drawing of those dry and dying hollyhocks outside. Then the dust shaped some more. A hand appeared, reaching toward McDowell, palm upward as if in supplication. The hand faded, the dust churned, and it seemed that the dust was trying to form into a face. McDowell tried to tell himself that it was interesting, the way accidental things happened. Then he knew he was not watching an accident. At his elbow, a presence hovered. He recognized the presence, but this time it did not frighten him. This time it was different.

It seemed sad, but it also seemed companionable. It was not threatening, and McDowell felt that it was not aiming to do him any harm for the moment. Instead of running, which he told himself he should be doing, he stood and watched the spotlight of sun. The face of the ghost seemed to be abstractly showing in the swirl of dust. The presence at his side seemed to be going from sadness to despair. Then he felt a real change in the presence, and the change was more awful than any threat could ever be. You could handle a threat, because you could at least fight back.

What came to him from the presence was a feeling of helplessness. Here, where old trees stood along the creek bank, here among dust and weeds and junk, it was like the presence was trying to weep, except that the eyes would not and could not issue tears. It seemed trying to grasp at something, but whatever the hand grasped after was invisible, untouchable.

McDowell stood and watched. The medallion with its chromed bars hung from his hand. He waited in awe. The face began to fade. McDowell watched and believed that his hallucination was over, knowing that he would soon try to kid himself into believing that he had hallucinated. The face seemed to suddenly be puffed apart, like the fluff on a seeding thistle. A breeze stirred the dust. The forms in the dust changed. Briefly, but beyond any possibility of making a mistake, McDowell saw that he was looking down upon a river, as if he stood on a high vantage point of ground. There were no towns. Only forest surrounded the river. Far off, down the river, a column of smoke rose in the air.

The momentary impression slid away. The feeling of presence became weaker. The form in the spotlight of sun was diffused. McDowell blinked, rubbed his free hand across his eyes, and everything seemed normal again. The sun outside, beyond the doorway, was clear and bright. The spotlight of sun was only that, nothing more. Dust swirled in the spotlight, but it made no shapes.

He could not figure out why he was now unafraid, or at least not weak with shock. The medallion weighed a couple of pounds including its chromed bars. It felt hard and real in his hand. He lifted it, looked at it, pondered the thin strips of metal separating the enameled colors. For a moment the medallion seemed unreal, ghostly. Only its weight convinced him that it was not spectral and neither was he.

Then he figured out why he was not weak with shock and fear. The ghost had shown him a river, and it had given him a message. The ghost had not threatened him. It had given him a message, not a threat. It had to have come from times long past. Had to. There was not a forested stretch of river that deserted in the entire country anymore. Only, he asked himself, what did it mean? It did not seem to have anything to do with him.

He checked his watch. Time to get going pretty quick now. He still had a little job to do here. McDowell turned and went outside to his car. He opened the trunk, took out a towing cable, then backed the Cadillac toward the junk '63 Chev.

He could just imagine some twelve-year-old kid, fiddle-farting around the way kids were gonna do, pulling that drive shaft away from the wreck. The car would come down slam, and it would be exit one kid.

In the south, in this vandalizing, hump-ass, Christ-ridden south, there was a special name for the kind of white trash that would leave a death trap baited like that. That kind of white trash was called "sorry." The sorry sonovabitch who had left that heap sitting in the air and ready to slam, well, that sonovabitch ought to be de-nutted.

McDowell ran the cable around the frame of the wreck, then hooked it to the frame of the Cad. He got back in his car, watched his mirror, and eased forward. The Chev seemed to be doing a slow pirouette on the pole of the drive shaft. Then it slammed down. Dust flew up from the car, and the tall weeds were momentarily whipped sideways.

As he unhooked the cable he told himself that he was glad the Chev had been left propped up like that. It gave him something to do, some action he could take to close the lonesomeness and the lostness of this place from his memory. When he got the cable unhooked and stored, he walked to the Chev. It was completely gutted. Seats, dash, engine, wheel, all of it. The floorboards were partly rusted out, and bent weeds showed pale green through the holes.

He looked around for the dogs. They were gone, off on some dog business and not worried about what they were doing, or why.

He checked his watch. Time to get moving. He was supposed to meet Margaret at four.

Chapter 8

" . . . A FRIEND WHO'S A COUNTRY SINGER," MARGARET SAID. "I want you to catch her act while you're in town." Margaret lay beside him with a towel tucked between her legs in order to beat having to sleep on a wet spot.

"Country?" He wondered sleepily what'n the hell she was doing messing with country music. The lamp on the bedside table was turned low. It made her nearly brown skin look darker than it really was. In a hotel this good, the air conditioner did not whizz or buzz. It whispered.

"Peg's not really country," Margaret said. "She takes that folk and country stuff and kind of changes it around."

"And probably wears a cowboy shirt. And spurs."

"She's a missionary to the rednecks." Margaret giggled. She sounded like a little kid telling jokes. "Carries this crazy speckle-painted guitar that she can make go for about three chords, but she's got one hell of a guitarist behind her."

". . . and sometimes on top."

"I presume so." Margaret grinned in a way that would have been raunchy if it were not for the shyness. "I expect they switch around." She was warm and funny and naked and beautiful.

"Next time you can be on top." He was wiped out and soft and sleepy.

"Before you forget that promise," she said, "why don't you roll over this-a-way?"

"Already it's three AM." He watched the light and shadow

along her small ribs, and he placed his hand on her belly. They had not had time during the afternoon for anything but talk and an early dinner.

"Take advantage," she told him. "Usually I'm not this way. Usually I'm wiped out after work."

"Wake me up," he said. "Back up your brag." He wanted to see if this was when she got past the shyness and started stuff on her own.

"But when you do catch Peg's act, you come on back here. I want you to *hear* the lady." She flipped the towel to one side. "And if you got anything more to dis-tri-bute . . ." She drawled in a fake, funny way.

"N'mind," he said, "I'll wake myself up."

Fucking was like jazz. It was a way to tell *them* that you did not believe in *them*. McDowell loved all of the disgusting, perverted practices that Baptists only dreamed about.

He loved it this way, with his face between her legs, his tongue inside her and the sweat taste, salt taste, come taste of the earlier romp in his mouth.

Love was a disciple. Always had been. Love was always learning. Fucking was a method.

He loved it this way, with Margaret above him, tall even as she knelt, and the shadows and dim light moving as she moved, the light across her narrow naked shoulders, touching her small breasts.

He believed there was nothing that a consenting man and woman could do in bed that he had not done, and he loved every bit of it. Except one thing. The only time he had ever been scared in a bed was once when a woman wanted him to hurt her.

He figured, and he figured that Margaret figured, that if you got some place past the point of a superlative fuck you were actually making love.

He loved it this way, lying beside Margaret as she had one leg raised, and the way light crossing her face seemed to illuminate that quiet, forward-thrusting intensity that, if she ever really trusted him, would probably be as much or more than he could handle. Her hair was like a cloud in the light, and he did not know which part of her was the most beautiful.

"I don't know whether I got a case of love, or a case of like," she said later, "but I sure am glad we're here."

He was finally, totally, wiped out and sleepy. He was happy and warm and figured that she would figure out whether she liked him or loved him. It seemed to him like it was pretty damn late in the day to be thinking about stuff like that.

"You're a wonderful conversationalist," she whispered. "I could sit and listen to you snore for hours. And probably will."

He rolled on his side. "Snug up," he said. "Catch my act tomorrow. Tomorrow I'll be brilliant." He drifted toward sleep, telling himself to try not to snore. A man ought to have enough control that he wouldn't snore. Or maybe that was one of those senseless, sleepy thoughts. Dan McDowell had little respect for most men because he had made love to so many women, and women talked.

What with one thing and another, he knew that he was not going to get around to seeing Samantha until Sunday night or Monday. If it turned out to be Monday, then he would have to revise his schedule for going to Indianapolis. Sammy was going to be mad. He told himself that she could get mad, and stay mad, or she could get over it.

When he woke on Saturday morning around noon, Margaret as already awake and dressed. She was sitting at the desk, marking on manuscript paper, and making little hums to herself. The printed staffs on the paper were filled with repetitions of the same group of notes, and each group was marked in her own kind of musical shorthand.

McDowell headed for the shower. When he was showered and dressed and ready for breakfast—lunch to the rest of the world— Margaret had packed the staff paper away. She had a yellow pencil tucked behind her ear, placed there and then absentmindedly forgotten. She was wearing a pale blue skirt and a long-sleeved white blouse, in spite of the heat outside. She was happy, really happy, and he could tell because her almost hazel eyes seemed nearly filled with light.

He hugged her, gentle and lovinglike, and swiped the pencil.

"If I worked that hard, it would kill me," he told her.

"Don't go courting death," she said. "If breakfast isn't pretty quick, I'll kill ya with my own two little hands."

He knew that both he and Margaret had the slightly tousled

look of lovers, although he could not actually say that Margaret had so much as a single hair out of place. She was beautifully, perfectly, groomed, but she still looked well laid. He looked as scruffy as ever, although he was wearing well-cared-for clothing like always. His slight limp was not bad this morning. Some mornings it was real noticeable.

McDowell could feel the crap coming down well before it actually came down. He felt it when they entered the dining room, but he did not know at first what kind of crap, or where it would be coming from.

A polished little priss of a guy with a moustache that looked like the streak on a used asswipe, and who was wearing a three hundred dollar administrator suit, had somehow got his pore self stuck with the hostess's job. McDowell could tell that the guy did not like to be seating people, that his mama had raised him to do more important things. McDowell figured that the regular hostess had gotten fed up and walked off the job. This guy looked like an assistant manager. The suit was actually pinstriped, for God's sake, and the haircut was regulation-Rotarian.

The guy took one look at Margaret, a second look at her legs, a third look at her smile. Then he walked ahead of her waving a couple of menus like he was a traffic cop causing wrecks. He did not exactly mince; it was more like he was walking with the traditional cob up his ass. McDowell followed, not thinking much about it, until the man walked too far. He was going to seat McDowell and Margaret all the way at the back of the room, over by the kitchen.

All that McDowell could think of as he followed the man was that here was a guy who couldn't play anything—couldn't even play with himself and not feel guilty—and he had the nerve to be insulting to Margaret.

This guy was a northern or eastern sonovabitch. Either that, or he was plain stupid.

The guy reached the table, snapped the menus onto it like they were wormy, and turned with an official little jerk of his shoulders. It was surprising that he did not click his heels together.

"N-aow," McDowell drawled, "you pick them things back up, and we'll all walk to the front of the room." McDowell was keeping his face neutral, unsmiling, ungrinning.

"Sir?" The priss took a deep, exaggerated breath like he was asking heaven to witness the misery that life was putting him through.

Sure as hell this guy was new in town. He was not picking up on the signals.

"You gonna pass some shit about ever-thang else bein' reserved?" McDowell reached out, grabbed one corner of the table, and picked it up just high enough that the table's setup looked ready to slide onto the floor. McDowell grinned mean, daring the guy, practically begging him to try something. McDowell was drawling slow and happy and hot, but he knew it was no contest. He had it nailed and clenched with this sonovabitch. Margaret stood to one side, looking half angry and half amused.

The man might be northern, but he finally picked up on the signals. He scooped up the menus and quickly led McDowell and Margaret to a table near the front. It was a good table, but not the best.

"Leave it be," Margaret whispered.

"Sure." If you loved somebody, then you ought not make a scene. He pulled a chair out for Margaret and seated her before he sat down. He watched the pinstriped priss take off across the room like he had a pinstriped pocket on fire.

"I'm not your woman," Margaret said. "I belong to me, and I can handle stuff." She was speaking slow and a little sad, but she was also speaking shy. The degrading sonovabitch had got to her.

He did not know how to answer since he did not see that there was anything else he could have done. It would have been worse to just sit and take it.

A high-assed, long-legged black girl came slopping along, pretending to be a waitress. McDowell was furious, but he kept his mouth shut. Then he quickly became almost grateful to the kid. The girl had that sure and ignorant look of a nineteen-year-old who knows nothing, except that she thought she knew it all.

The girl looked at McDowell, looked at Margaret, and then rolled her upper lip in a sneer. She was telling Margaret that maybe a honky could get to Margaret, but no white bastard would ever get near her high-assed muff.

"What's a girl like you doing in a nice place like this?" Margaret's voice was syrupy sweet. "Send us a different waitress."

McDowell figured that Margaret was pissed off at him just

enough that she was ready to start a real fight with the whole hotel.

The black girl left like she was grateful. She signaled to another waitress. At least she did not give them the finger.

"Us southern folks have our little ways," McDowell drawled at Margaret. "When our lovers make us mad, we turn around and smack a stranger."

She looked at him, checking him out to see if he was being critical. When she saw that he was not, she started laughing, and it was genuine laughter. When he realized the true nothingness of the situation, he laughed as well, and then she laughed harder.

"Maybe it was just because we looked happy," she said. "You mean man, intimidating that little nothing guy."

"An' starting fights between colored womens," he said. "It's not as bad as it used to be."

"No," Margaret said. "You're wrong. It's every bit as bad as it used to be, and there's more of it around now than there used to be." Even with air conditioning the room was not really cool, yet Margaret shivered.

"I've never played it 'come fuck me'," she said, but sometimes I've played it 'little girl'. That can be just as bad."

He was not following her. "I was talking race," he explained. "The only people who don't think about it are musicians."

"I was talking mean men." She touched his hand, and she looked apologetic. "Don't want to make a big deal of this, it's not a preoccupation. I had a man force me once." She giggled, kind of inappropriately. "When I called you mean man, it meant a joke."

"I hope somebody killed him." McDowell felt anger rise as automatically as heat would hit when they stepped from air conditioning onto the street. He felt violent, felt his hands clenching.

"A long time ago," she said, "but really mean men still get to me." She paused. "Of course nobody killed him. Nobody even arrested him."

She would not know it, because he was not going to do anything until she left town, but before he checked out of this hotel he was going to remonstrate with that pinstripe. Meanwhile, she had been happy only a few minutes ago. He wanted her to be happy again. Change the subject. Talk about something real. Talk about music. She was doing something special with her musical attack on a note.

"You're inflecting silence on some of your attacks," he said. "I've been listening, and I can't quite figure out how you do it." She *was* inflecting silence, but it was not just some damned dramatic pause. It was like the silence bunched in front of the attack, and then instead of the attack jumping up and over the bunching up, the attack just eased out soft and clear like it had never been impeded. *That's* what she was doing.

"Slide off of the word that comes before," she said, "then dampen it way down to sweet, then bump the second letter of the next word . . . you got to just bump it, not hit it, or it gets corny."

A waitress who was older and easier-minded interrupted and took their orders. She looked like an advertisement for grandmothers, until you looked at her face. A few people had come to terms with the world and liked their terms. She was one of them. The waitress joked with Margaret. Beyond the windows stood small, drooping trees. A sparrow sat in one of them. It aired its feathers and panted in the sun.

"Show me what you mean," he said when the waitress left.

"Like, not *t*aste of *h*oney—like, taste 'a hOney, only it works better with consonants . . . but you got to just barely bump it. First you got to get a little bit of rise on the bump, then you have to decline behind the bump." She looked nearly apologetic. "It sounded corny for an awful long time."

"Decline the end of taste, then slide on 'a,' and then bump the second letter." He felt proud of her.

"Sure, only you got to get some 'little girl' feeling into that slide."

"Then you're really not pausing at all?"

"Nope, but it sure does sound like it, don't it?" She was happy—happy with him.

When you were singing like she did and knew what you were doing, then there was no possible way for the world to love you enough. He loved her, and he did not know how to show it. He could not give her anything. She already had it all.

"Dan," she said, "you hear too much. You couldn't have been that bad a horn."

"Hearing's one thing, doing's another."

"Ever mess with it now?"

"No." Some lies were easy to tell, and they should be told. Besides, for all practical purposes it was nearly the truth. "I'm on the road a lot. There's not enough time."

"We've all heard that one before. " She was not going to let him off easy.

He shrugged, "You can't set any kind of an embouchure in less than a year. It takes a couple hours a day to maintain a lip. You can't play without chops."

"Buy a mute," she said. "Throw that thing in the back seat, and practice muted in hotel rooms. I knew a French horn player did it once."

"Graas?" Graas was the only jazz French horn he knew of, and that was years ago. Graas had shown what a French horn could do.

"My very first lover," she said. "In Minneapolis, way back when. I lost out to the horn." She paused, then pulled a little-girl cute grin. "Of course, he was very, very good on the horn."

"Them symphony jocks is all alike." He was uncomfortable, a little bit jealous; although that, of course, was stupid.

"No," she said, "they aren't. Some play better than others. She giggled, like she was the world's leading expert on laying members of symphony orchestras.

It just made him more uncomfortable, and the problem was that it made him love her even more. He was feeling pretty possessive. Plus, he was a little angry.

The waitress brought the order. Her face was easy and happy, and he could not see how anybody could be a waitress and be happy.

He turned to check the place out. The black waitress was leaning against a coffee counter, checking them out. McDowell told himself he had to do it—just had to—and gave the black girl a long, slow look-over that ended with him raising one eyebrow and chewing thoughtful-like on his lower lip. He pretended that he was in a whorehouse, and he could feel the look of rejection that was passing all over his face. Then the rejection turned to disappointment as he realized he was going to have to go down the street and find a different whorehouse. The girl stood up like she had just been goosed. She turned away madder than hell, and he did not exactly blame her.

The pinstripe was bent over the table of an older, rich couple. He looked like he could not wait to kiss some wealthy ass.

"What are you doing?" Margaret had not caught his act because his face had been turned from her. She must have seen the black waitress's reaction.

"Checking the action."

"What was he doing?" Margaret asked the waitress.

"I expect he was doing something that should get him jailed for juvenile delinquency." The waitress had caught part of it. "I raised three sons," she said to Margaret, and her voice held a sort of funny, exaggerated tone of apology.

This clown-show, baby-faced, killer south.

In Chicago, he told himself, you could almost forget about it. Come anywhere near this town, and you started acting like *them*.

"Most of them grow up eventually." The waitress's voice was so humorous that she was obviously not trying to give offense. She was actually getting him off the hook by making the whole thing into a joke. She was earning a lot bigger tip than she could ordinarily expect, although she did not know that. McDowell was grateful.

"I'll see if I can get him to eat," Margaret said. "If I need help I'll give a holler." She grinned at the waitress and the waitress grinned back. They looked like two football players who had just sacked the quarterback.

"Dan," Margaret said when the waitress left, "what in the world am I going to do? Can't keep you for a pet, and Dan, I must be losing my mind . . . gonna wake up some morning and find out I really am in love with you."

He slurped at coffee and did not answer because he was a little bit pissed about being ganged up on like that. Of course, he told himself, you brought it on yourself.

"Because, Dan, I'm beginning to trust you." This time she did not speak humorously. This time the shyness was back.

He was instantly, totally, no longer pissed. He was as happy as if he really *was* just a little kid.

"People ought not act like dumb bastards." He was talking about the pinstripe and the black waitress.

"I was raised in Atlanta," Margaret told him. "I know you *got* to do it, but figure a way to do it better."

In the south you had no choice. He told himself that in the south you were either Rhett Butler or you were a goddamn sorry redneck. There was no in-between. He did not exactly understand all he knew about that, but maybe she understood. No matter how much she understood, or didn't, he was grateful to her for knowing enough to say that.

"I was wrong."

"You weren't," she told him. "You just didn't plan. Let's not have any apologies between us."

That was a new twist. No woman had ever said that to him before.

"Because," Margaret said, "we don't have that much time left. I work tonight and leave tomorrow. I want you to catch Peg's act tonight."

"Rather catch yours."

"Catch me next month in Chicago. I'm working on something new. I'll have it done by then."

He was happy, really happy, but he was also possessive and lonesome. The time went too fast. In a little over twenty-four hours she was gone for a month. He would have to go back to that crazy, wacked-out world out there—the road and merchandise and his sister Samantha—the world of engines and ghosts.

Chapter 9

A TAIL-DOWN DOG MOVED SLOWLY ACROSS THE SUNLIT PARK-ing lot. It was a short-haired dog, small, and it looked like it was searching for a comfortable place to die. It panted as it walked.

Dan McDowell wished that the weather would cool enough so he could ride with the top down.

The sign read:

McDowell Import-Export
Clearinghouse For The World

A '79 Lincoln was parked in the parking lot. It was black and shiny with a fresh dent on the left rear fender where the Citizen had drunkenly backed into one post or another. At least, McDowell told himself, the old man had not traded down for a new and reduced piece of imitation Lincoln. Dan McDowell approved of the car and sneered at the dent.

Flanking the Linc was one of those two-bit Mercedes that looked like a taxi, and a turbo Saab that could go around corners, but couldn't do anything else. In any straight-ahead world both of those junkers were early out of gas. McDowell figured that Sammy was pushing the Swede, and the Wimp was flogging the Merc.

The sun made the asphalted parking lot look like a lake of oil. The whitewall rings on his father's Lincoln were scuffed and dirty where the old man had rubbed a bunch of curbs.

The Mercedes was painted shit-muckle-dun, and the Saab was money-color green.

It was eleven AM. Monday. Margaret was in Atlanta by now. He had spent last night alone in his hotel room, which still felt a little special because Margaret had been there with him. Her presence did not seem to disappear right away. On Saturday night he had caught that Peg's act, and it made him not understand Margaret. Margaret thought Peg was good. A'course, Peg was good for somebody whose voice was too light. Peg depended on her backup guitar. The guitar *was* good. That guy could find work anytime.

He told himself that Margaret and Peg were friends. Nobody was ever a good critic when it came to their friends. He was glad he had already heard Margaret and knew how good she was before he met her.

And, he told himself, *it's all over now until next month anyway.* Time to quit thinking about it, time to shove life back in gear. Get rid of this foolishness with Samantha, and then tomorrow get out of town.

Still, he sat. He was unwilling to take leave of this weekend, and even more unwilling to confront his sister. Out there in the street traffic was exhaust-fuming and hot and heavy. A couple of cops cruised by, intimidating the multitudes and slowing traffic. Two teenage boys stood at the curb, waiting to cross the street. When the cops passed, one of the kids pulled a hand from his jeans and flipped the bird. The kid looked ready to run if the police car slowed. The other kid was turned around, looking at the Cadillac.

It got McDowell moving. He did not want to hold any car discussions with kids. Not now.

His family's warehouse was big and old and made of brick, which, he told himself, was the only thing about it that had any class. It fronted a corner lot.

The large parking area was on one side of the building and there were loading docks in back. A huge poplar stood at the corner of the lot. Except for the sharp line of shade drawn by the building, the poplar gave the only shade that amounted to anything. The shade was like a small cavern made of dusk. McDowell momentarily thought of the ghost. He shrugged. There was nothing he could do about it now. Right now he had enough trouble

The trunk of the poplar was scarred at bumper height. For as long as Dan McDowell could remember, that tree had been there getting hit by cars which backed up and banged into it. Three years ago, the last time he was here, the big fight had been over that tree. *They*, his family, fought about the tree because *they* could not think of anything else to fight about. Samantha had wanted it taken down, and the Citizen had threatened to have her jailed if she did.

McDowell walked across the parking lot and to the front of the building. When he entered the immense showroom the Wimp was busy telling lies and giving prices to a consumer. The Wimp looked up with a kind of fawning enthusiasm when he heard the door open. When he saw Dan McDowell he sneered and the back of his neck got red. He looked like somebody had just slipped a dog turd into his pocket. The Wimp lowered his voice and returned to his customer. The customer was a muscular balding Israeli with a country look. Probably, McDowell told himself, the guy was some small-timer from downstate who was buying a truckload of dreck to peddle to the homefolks. McDowell told himself that he did not envy the guy. In the small town south Jews got beat to shit, either literally or through isolation.

The Wimp was a tall, thin man with a big ass that was carpeted in a light tweed suit. He had a narrow, sniffy nose that poked out from between fat cheeks and hung over thick lips. McDowell never looked at the Wimp without thinking of owls and pork chops. McDowell truly detested the Wimp, but the Wimp absolutely and truly hated Dan McDowell.

He told himself that there was no sense in starting the ruction. Let *them* start it.

He walked through the showroom and toward the office, telling himself that he was surrounded by schlock: rattan recliners that weighed about three ounces and would last for less than three minutes of use. Genuine-imitation-maple furniture made of decaled fiberboard, low-fired pottery ashtrays that would break if tapped by a cigarette, lamps resembling busted gourds and beyond the furniture, a section of tools that held crescent wrenches with jaws that would not hold; and electric drills and saws all made to sell but never to use, because if you used them they would kill you. One whole corner of the showroom was given over to several tons of plastic artifacts from a dozen civilizations, and there was a section of sporting goods guaranteed to endanger any all-American. Dreck. Goods.

Remnants, mill ends, rubber-backed imitation Oriental rugs, crapola at a discount.

It was colorful, he had to admit that. The surfaces all looked good, but there was nothing beneath the surface. Surface was what was being sold. The whole place was an $89.98 special. The company supplied the small-timers and those mid-range outfits that always advertised nothing down and easy terms. Markup 150 percent.

Somewhere deep in the warehouse, the old freight elevator creaked and groaned. The voices of a couple of warehousemen discussed an invoice. From even deeper in the building came the sound of the Citizen's voice. It echoed and boomed the way it always did, and only "goddamn" could be plainly heard.

The office, enclosed between the showroom and the warehouse, was where Sammy would be trying to make life miserable for the heavyset, aging bookkeeper whose name was Stan. Stan would be ignoring her. There would be one kid secretary, some young girl just out of school who would be getting a heavy dose of "experience." It was so predictable it was boring. The office was bigger than some stores, and it was furnished with nothing but the best. There was nothing in that office that would ever be distributed by his family.

Except, he thought, bullshit.

He had come this far and did not want to go inside. When he went in there, he would be entering a self-contained world, like a small universe that was only important to its few inhabitants. His family had no friends, only business associates. He was willing to bet that Sammy and the Wimp never invited a bunch of people to dinner, never talked about anything but business, and when they went on vacation they were uncomfortable until it was time to head back and go to work.

Get it over with, he told himself. *They* never killed you yet. He reached for the doorknob but could not quite bring himself to grab it. Familiar footsteps sounded behind him. For a moment McDowell felt like a teenage kid who had just been caught jerking off.

"I *will* be dipped in shit," said the Citizen. "If it ain't our man from Chicago."

McDowell turned. The Citizen walked toward him almost eagerly, like he was glad to see Dan McDowell. The Citizen looked older than he had three years ago, and he had looked pretty old then. He was as tall as Dan McDowell and far more muscular. His hair was completely white but still thick, and he was dressed like always. Expensive shirt with tobacco stains, and pants with dust streaks on them caused when he shoved cartons of inventory. Sammy had never been able to get the old bastard to wear a tie, leave alone a suit. The Citizen actually looked happy to see Dan McDowell. That did not make any sense. The Citizen was smiling, and his face was crinkledy, his white brows bushy above blue eyes that had the old bullshit look to them. Only this time the bullshit seemed friendly. The Citizen had a strong chin, a big nose, and his arms were still heavily muscled.

"Pop," McDowell said, "you lookin' good."

"Quit shootin' crap," the old man told him. "I'm seventy-one. Nobody my age is lookin' good." He went to Dan McDowell and then seemed momentarily like he did not know what to do. He made a couple of false motions as if he were about to hug McDowell or hit him. Then he shook McDowell's hand. Dan McDowell appreciated the truly fucked-up try at affection. It was the best the old man could manage.

"Your sister's inside there," said the Citizen. He looked at the closed office door. He jingled keys in his pocket, like he was a man who owned a private zoo, like he was about to offer a tour. "I reckon you've come to see your sister."

"I reckon."

"She's gettin' kind of feeble-minded," the Citizen told Dan McDowell. "Just go along with her. Say yep and nope." The old man looked the way he always did when he was promoting a conspiracy; half sincere and half sly bullshit.

"Shore," said McDowell; "but Pop, you really are looking pretty good."

"Well," said the old man, "that thing still gets hard, but ever' time it does I think I'd ought to have a picture made." He reached for the doorknob and shoved the door open. "We are in one hell of a fix," he announced to everyone inside the office. "The competition just showed up."

Sammy was sitting behind a desk that was longer than a sermon. She straightened up like she had just been goosed. Sammy seemed even thinner than before and she had always been skinny.

Her black hair was now streaked heavily with gray. It was pulled back tight enough that it seemed to stretch her eyelids. She quickly reached for a fifty-dollar automatic pencil to use as a stage prop, the way she always did. She could misdirect your attention with that pencil, hold it up like a magic wand, or pull your gaze away from her face by moving it downward. There was always a suggestion of shyness about Sammy that denied the harsh way she went after things she wanted.

"Daniel," she said, "I was sure that by now you had left town." She said it in such a way that Dan McDowell could not tell whether she was pissed off or not. She stood up, like she was being introduced to an ambassador or a new customer.

This neurotic, ass-kiss, play-acting south.

"I had business," he said apologetically. "I really got tied up."

"Of course." She said it in that sniffy way she used when a small-time customer came in to cover a cold check.

"Son," said the Citizen, "were you with a woman?"

Dan McDowell started to lie, and then realized it would be the wrong thing to do. Then he started to tell the truth and decided against that. Meanwhile, he felt his face getting hot.

"Get off his ass," said the Citizen. "The boy was doin' honest work." The Citizen walked across the office and took a chair behind a desk that, if you fitted it out with engines, could haul cargo. Sammy's desktop was neat, but the Citizen's was even neater. There was nothing on it but his feet.

Across the carpeted room, in the far corner, there were now two secretaries instead of one. A horse-face, lanky Georgia woman of about thirty watched Dan McDowell. Her face showed a kind of humorous reserve but real interest. Her brown hair was long and well cared for. She had styled it in a way that made her attractive in spite of the horse-face. She obviously had the most sense of anyone in the office. A little fat-girl secretary, wearing a flowery blouse and green slacks, managed to look frail, although it did not seem possible that a fat girl could possibly look that way. Stan looked up from the boxed-in, glassed-in cubicle where he worked. He gave Dan McDowell a wave and a shit-eating grin. McDowell stood on plush blue carpet in the center of the office and felt like he was pinned in a crossfire. He shoved away a chair from in front of Sammy's desk. When he sat down, it reduced his profile and he felt a little better, though not much.

"I saw your catalog," the Citizen said. "You got any inventory to back it up?"

"I sell out of the trunk-a the car," McDowell told him. He swore to himself that he was not going to get trapped into the old family argument about fluid capital as opposed to inventory. The Citizen liked to keep a sizable cash float, but he also believed in overloading the basic bread and butter part of inventory. That part always appreciated, and it was easy to find ways to hide the appreciation from the tax boys.

"I got a massive inventory," Dan McDowell said, "and none of it made in Japan." He thought that he had a strong inventory but not massive. Also, he carried a few fine items that actually were made in Japan.

"Don't knock them Japs," the old man said charitably. "Them Japs have made me a heap of money." He grinned and then he wrinkled his nose like he was about to say something wise. "A'course," he said comfortably, "that don't necessarily mean that I *like* the little slant-eye sonsovbitches."

Samantha nearly dropped her pencil. She turned toward the Citizen, and McDowell caught her profile. Samantha had a long, schoolteacherly-looking nose that poked way out because her hair was pulled way back. She was dressed in a dark gray skirt, and a frilly white blouse that looked a little foolish in a business office. She tapped the pencil like she was calling a class to attention. Samantha was about to lower the boom on the Citizen.

"You will say that once too often," she said. "Two of our best customers are Japanese."

"Pete and Sam," the Citizen told McDowell. "They're different. There's good ones and bad ones. Them boys are good ones and they know what I mean."

"I expect they do," McDowell said, and he said it most politely.

"'Cause they ain't like niggers," the old man explained. "I think of them as short yids."

When Samantha got really angry she did not get red, she got white. Right now she was so white that she seemed to be turning blue. "*Five* of our *best* customers are colored gentlemen."

"Same thing, Sammy." The Citizen seemed happy and nearly expansive. "Those boys know the difference." The Citizen was having one hell of a good time annoying Sammy. McDowell had known the old man all his life, and he still did not know how much of that bullshit the Citizen actually believed.

"You hittin' the loud pedal a little hard," McDowell said, "even for you, Pop."

"Now mackerel-snappers," the old man said' kindly, "ain't near as bad despite they're mostly spick and wop."

He was really going after Sammy, and it was not that Sammy necessarily disagreed. When you came right down to it Sammy was more hateful than the old man could ever be. She just thought this talk was bad for business. McDowell decided to break it up before things got hot. In the corner of the office the little fat-girl secretary was whispering to the lanky horse-face secretary. The horse-face lady tried to get a straight face and hold it, then she giggled. The door to the office opened and the Wimp walked in with an order for one of the secretaries to invoice. The Wimp made an exaggerated point of ignoring Dan McDowell.

"All business, ain't he?" McDowell put the statement out there somewhere in the air between the Citizen and Samantha. He swore at himself as he did. He had promised himself not to start anything.

The Wimp was leaning over her desk. He stood up quick, like he had been shot. He turned, and his owl nose was quivering. "Don't be crude," he said. "There is no reason to be ugly. You are insensitive, actually."

There *was* a reason. McDowell *was* ugly. Nobody, and especially the Wimp, could talk him out of that. And especially not here, not in this office.

Plus, he *was* insensitive. It was the only way he had ever found that helped him hold onto what sensitivity he had left.

"Me and Pontius Pilate," McDowell said, "you sonovabitch."

"That is not exactly humorous." The Wimp was not going to actually, physically, fight, but he was trying to give the impression that he would.

"I rather expect it ain't," McDowell said with imitation politeness.

"You can both stop it right now," said Samantha.

"Let 'em go on," said the Citizen. "Let's see what happens." He still had his feet on the desk, and he was plainly and clearly happy. He looked like he was smoking a five-dollar cigar while being surrounded by a half dozen naked women.

Sammy bailed out from behind her desk like a lady cop on her way to busting a couple of perverts. "My brother," she said, "has come to take me to lunch, and not to fight with my husband." She came around the end of the desk like she was riding a broomstick. The Wimp took one look and got the hell out of the office. The Citizen got his feet off the desk, fast.

"You just wait a minute, Sammy." The Citizen was disturbed about something. "I want to talk to the boy."

"Talk to him later."

"Now," the Citizen said. "The dumb shit may not be here later."

McDowell reached in his pocket for his car keys. He handed them to Samantha, whispering, but not so soft that he could not be heard. "Get the air conditioner going. I'll be there in just a minute."

She was outflanked and outmaneuvered, and even to McDowell, who appreciated her genius, it seemed that there was nothing else she could do. Samantha apparently agreed. She took the keys and looked at them like McDowell was handing her a well-used handkerchief. The horse-face secretary giggled and stuck her long nose down deep toward her typewriter. The frail, fat girl watched the horse-face lady like she was seeing visions or was engaged in an unwanted revolution.

Samantha stood looking at the keys. Then she remembered what they fitted. McDowell thought that he could almost see her thought process. If she climbed in that Cad, she would become a spectacle. Everyone would look at the Cad and they would see her. She passed the keys back to him. "I'll meet you," she said and named a restaurant. She gave him no time to argue, just grabbed her purse from a coat hook and walked from the office. McDowell figured that the Wimp was hiding somewhere out of her line of march. If he wasn't, McDowell felt almost sorry for the poor bastard. Sammy was fixing to do something to somebody.

The Citizen was leering at the horse-face Georgia lady, and that lady was laughing with the open, don't-give-a-damn flair of someone who is either laying the boss or doesn't need the job. The little fat girl looked like she wanted to jump into a wastebasket and hide.

"You're stupid," the old man said to Dan McDowell . His voice as kindly, like he was giving 24-karat advice to a seven-year-old. "I seen your catalog. You ain't never going to make a cent handling that shit."

"I seem to be doing okay." McDowell felt his old defensiveness and indignation and anger begin to accumulate.

"You're stupid," the old man said, "but you aren't dumb. You had enough sense to get out of this place."

That was a switch. That was the last thing Dan McDowell had expected to hear. It contradicted everything he had ever heard before. "I thought you wanted me around here," he said, "helping you."

"What the fuck do I need with another incompetent?" the Citizen said. "I'm talking about business."

"You talking about anything else?"

"I want to," the Citizen said seriously. "Let's head back to the warehouse. This is a kind of special deal." He stood up from behind the desk like he was a man thirty years younger. The Citizen sort of collected Dan McDowell as he left the office, taking McDowell's elbow and steering him. As they left, the Georgia lady giggled.

"Name of Sandra," the old man said about the Georgia lady after he closed the door. "She scares the lights out of Sammy. Sammy's got it in her head that Sandra's got it in her head to marry me." The old man grinned. "And so she does."

Aw, *no*, McDowell thought, aw, *shit*. Now he knew why Sammy wanted to talk. The Citizen was getting old, and Sandra was trying to inherit a piece of the action.

The Citizen grinned. "It don't mean a damn thing," he said, "except it sure does plague Sammy." He headed toward the rear of the building, through swinging doors. To Dan McDowell the figure of his father walking between the high-stacked case of goods was both familiar and threatening, but somehow reassuring.

"Pop," he said, "I don't care if you get married. It's none of my business." He said it almost apologetically, and he could not figure why his voice should sound that way.

The Citizen stopped, turned around. His face was momentarily not bullshitty. He looked like he was trying to figure out how to say something complicated in simple words. "You're right. It's none of your business, but that's not the point. The point is Sammy's crazy. Let's get the hell outta here." He turned back and continued walking until he reached the rear of the building. Beside the loading dock was a smaller door that led to the parking lot. "C'mon," the Citizen said, "a pup can't take a leak in this building without someone listening." He shoved the door open and stepped outside into the sunlight. McDowell followed. The heat outside the building was worse than the dry and dusty heat of the warehouse. McDowell blinked his eyes in the strong sunlight. He waited for his eyes to adjust.

"The point is," the Citizen said, "If I did get married, it wouldn't be to some kid like Sandra, and if I did get married, I'd split up the business first. Sammy ought to know that." The Citizen seemed to be waving his hand or wiping his brow. McDowell blinked.

Dan McDowell understood that Samantha really should know that. Dividing the business would be the old man's way. *Only*, he thought, he did not know why he understood it himself. He blinked again. His eyes were adjusting. The world was no longer only dark shadows and bright lights. For no reason at all, nothing he could identify, he suddenly felt both hesitant and fearful. He felt sweat in his eyebrows, and his eyelids seemed as moist as if he had been weeping. He shuddered, wondering if he was getting sick with a summer flu.

A feeling of presence grew beside him. Dan McDowell stood, stunned.

The ghost was old and vague and hideous in the patch of dusky shade cast by the poplar tree. The feeling of presence grew. The presence hovered close to Dan McDowell. This time the ghost was changed. It still had no teeth, but it stood more erect. The blank and staring eyes were not as saucer-like. The presence beside him was getting stronger. The ghost seemed more confident.

Naw, McDowell thought. *Not now*. Not with the Citizen here.

In the distance a siren rose and fell in the air, and from the street beyond the warehouse, traffic was snarled, a buzz, a hum over the sticky and hot asphalt.

The old man was facing Dan McDowell, away from the ghost. He looked at McDowell's face, saw his shock, and then the old man turned. He seemed almost fierce, he was so glad.

"You raggedy-ass sonovabitch," the old man said to the ghost. "You done it to yourself this time." He turned to McDowell. "Now you see that, don't you?"

"See what?" McDowell lied. Out there in the street a siren

broke loud and brutal into the air. A cop was heading for the distant sirens, and his own siren was whipping the air like strokes of violence.

"I got no time for bullshit," the old man hollered above the siren. His voice sounded desperate. "Sammy ain't playing the game. Sammy thinks I'm bananas. She wants to get me certified." The old man was not blank-eyed, but he was wide-eyed. His voice had dropped the gladness, but it was fierce with its own desperation.

The ghost, with its toothless mouth, seemed to be grinning at the departing siren. The presence at Dan McDowell's side was not exactly malevolent, but it was strong. Strong. It glowered with restrained violence, like the uncontrolled violence of fire—except this violence was still in control, at least for now.

"I'm an old man," the Citizen murmured into the silence left by the departing police car. "Sammy could wait a little while. A man ought to be let to die out the same way he's lived." His eyes were dull, lifeless, and his hands trembled.

"She actually wants you committed?"

"She actually does," the old man said. "I wouldn't have believed it, either." The hollowness of his voice was mixed with the sadness of a man who had struggled against a hard fact, and then accepted it.

"She can't do it."

"What the hell does that mean," said the old man. "I know she can't do it. I can hire as many high-price doctors as she can."

"Then it's just more of her high-horse foolishness."

"Naw," said the old man, "think about it. It's the shame of it. It ain't respectful." His face was full of sadness, and his face was honest. There was nothing sly about his looks. "Kin don't do that."

Dan McDowell had never before heard his father sound helpless or pathetic. It was more shocking in its way than was the ghost. The Citizen dangled above his own feet, standing like a whitehaired scarecrow that wore soiled, expensive clothes. His face sagged. He wore his seventy-one years with a despair that to Dan McDowell was horrible. He had never seen his father powerless. He had never seen the Citizen unwilling to fight back.

"Okay, Pop," McDowell said. "I see it. If you're crazy, then so am I—but mind you, I may be crazy."

"Naw," the old man said. "You ain't got much business sense, but you were smart enough to get away from Sammy." His eyes looked better. He was trying to once more take control of the situation. He squared his shoulders and looked at the ghost. The ghost was growing stronger, more defined, and the presence seemed to radiate violence.

The Citizen's eyes filled with fear, but he seemed determined to bull his way through the situation. He was returning to being the kind of man he had always been. He started walking forward. "I'm gonna shoo this sonovabitch away."

Dan McDowell expected the ghost to fade. The ghost had faded on the one time he had approached it, over there in North Carolina.

The ghost changed. The old man stopped walking forward. It seemed to grow upward from the feet as it changed, growing from a human form into a column of smoke. Then fire appeared, vague, shadowy. It burned silent, as the gray, misty smoke rose toward the high branches of the poplar. The Citizen backed away. The form of a man appeared in the fire, clutching, beating the fire on his clothes, rolling into the flames as his hair burned and his face seemed caked with fire. The presence at Dan McDowell's side seemed to be in an absolute fury of joy. Then the scene and presence faded.

"You go see your sister," the old man said in a hollow voice. "Then meet me back here tonight. Come to the back door about nine."

"I dunno," McDowell said. "Maybe we *are* crazy, Pop. Don't know what it means, who it is . . ." He stood in the saturating heat and sunlight. He looked across the parking lot and toward the Cadillac. He wanted to get in the Cad and just drive and drive.

"Shit fire," the old man said, "I know *who* it is. I just don't know what the bastard wants."

Chapter 10

THE LAND OF DAN MCDOWELL IS NOT HAUNTED ONLY BY SPEC-
ters. It is haunted by ethics that are as evident as its ghosts. As mist
and smoke rise from the cuts and hollows, over the hogbacks and
above the high run of hills, the ethical codes are as tenacious as
the spirits. Like the mist, the codes are slow moving and definite.
They press forward as certainly as the voice of romance, which was
their original voice. The Confederacy is still remembered, and it
still lives in the swirling mist. The voices of cracker and planter
are accompanied by the light tread of war-trained horses and the
bugling of sweet-mouth hounds. The echoes are all across the land,
although in the cities and along the roads they are muted.

One of the codes that lived on in the mist and the hills was
that *no* man, *no* where, ever hit a woman, no matter how much
she was asking for it. No man did that, and if any man did hit a
woman, he stopped being a man and became a sorry redneck who
deserved anything that any other man wanted to do to him. You
did not even hit your sister, even if your sister was Samantha. And,
a'course, Samantha knew that.

"You," Dan McDowell said, "have got to be out of your simple
mind." They were sitting in one more goddamn restaurant, and
this one was upholstered in blue and green. Through a closed-off
section of the dining room came the voices of the Rotary singing
"God Bless America." McDowell told himself that he didn't believe
it was happening, even if he was hearing it. Besides, it probably
was not the Rotary. The Rotary met on Wednesday, didn't it? It was

Elks or an old folks' home or something. Some guy who had hammers instead of hands was beating up on the piano. The piano was being hit in the most amateur and illiterate way. The voices of the singers sounded like a sanctimonious church congregation. Some thin voices were mixed in with the thick and certain voices. It almost made McDowell sad. Those thin voices were old, old people. They were survivors. All they could think to do with their survival was to hang around singing crap. Samantha was chawing on a high-priced, used-looking salad. She was looking straight at Dan McDowell. She did not seem to even hear the awful piano.

"You are not with him from day to day," Samantha said. "You don't know how bad he can get." Her thin nose that was not at all like Margaret's was doing a bitch-sniffy number. Sammy looked like she was absolutely revolted by Dan McDowell or the salad or her memories of the Citizen. Her fingers were long and narrow. Her hands ought to be pretty but they were not. Somehow, to McDowell, they seemed like clamps.

"He don't seem any different than he ever was," McDowell said. "You're just pretending he's different so you can feel good about what you're doing."

"I do not, Daniel, feel *good*. Even if it's for his own good." Samantha continued to look straight at McDowell. There was every appearance of sincerity in her voice. She sounded like she actually believed her own line.

"Now I don't like the old bastard," McDowell said. "Me and him have nothing, absolutely nothing, in common except we don't like each other."

She was stiff as dried starch. "I love him," she said. "You went away, but I stayed. I've loved him all my life." She was nasty-hard while she was saying it, and she was melty at the same time. There were tears lying back there in her eyes, but he knew Sammy. Sammy would not have wept at the crucifixion. McDowell figured that if anyone was crazy it was Sammy.

"Then why are you trying to fuck him around?"

She reacted to the word. He knew he should not have said it, not to his self-anointed madonna sister. The Citizen could get by with saying fuck, but Dan McDowell could not.

"I spend most of my life dealing with white trash," she said. "Grow up." The frilly white blouse she wore seemed incongruous.

There was nothing soft or frilly about Sammy.

"I tried to grow up," McDowell drawled. "I most shorely did give it a try. Then I quit." He figured that what she meant by growing up was to be like her. "Pop was okay when Ma was alive," he said. "The old boy is lonesome."

Sammy looked like she was running a calculator. "I could give you a figure if I thought about it. He spent several thousand dollars impressing women last year. Lonesome is one thing he isn't."

McDowell felt slugged by the piano. It seemed like the noise was going to hammer his head apart. Now those people were singing "There's a Long, Long Trail A-Winding."

At the next table a man and woman sat and talked in low and urgent tones. The woman was short and dark-haired, wearing a wedding ring. McDowell watched, saw that she was having an affair, and that something was going wrong. The man was sandy-haired and medium built. He was nervous.

McDowell told himself that he could never explain about loneliness to someone like Samantha. How could you explain that loneliness could not be fucked away or laughed away or even worked away? "It's a credit to the old man," McDowell said. It was the only thing he could think of. Then he thought of something else. "Is he draining the business?"

"No." She hated to say it, but she said it. Sammy was honest in her own way.

"Then it's none of our business."

"It's our estate," she said, "and you are an inheritor. You may want to think about that." Her eyes were lowered like she was being apologetic. He watched her and saw no apology at all.

She was acting. *Everybody* was always acting. He thought of Margaret, of how straightforward she was, and how, if she wanted something, she would just ask. Margaret did not play these games. The goddamn piano would not stop, and he could not tell Sammy—there was no possible way to tell Sammy—just how angry she was making him.

The sandy-haired guy at the next table suddenly stood up. He looked through the front windows of the restaurant and into the parking lot. He whispered something to the woman. Her eyes stopped being urgent as they filled with fear.

"Naow," McDowell drawled, 'let's get a few things straight." He leaned back in his chair, showing Sammy that he was too smart to get too close to her. "It's Pop's estate, not ours. I don't want any part of him. I don't like the bastard and I never have."

"Then you will cause no trouble?" Sammy looked smug, like she had just won something big off a punchboard after spending only a dollar.

"Wrong," he said. "I'll fight you every step of the way. There won't be any quiet way to do it. I'll make noises all the way to your bank." He told himself that he did not know Sammy very well after all these years, but he still knew how to threaten her.

The threat caused her to lower her eyes. Her shoulders tensed. When she looked up, the line of her mouth and the look in her eyes showed that she was in perfect, ridged control. "Daniel, why exactly are you here?"

"You asked me to come, asked me to see you."

"Of course." She spoke like she was tired of listening to constant lies. "I have asked you at other times, and you did not visit then."

"I had business in town this time." It was a mean thing to say and he knew it. Of course, it was also true.

The dark-haired woman at the next table stood. She walked away, nearly running, in the direction of the restroom. The man headed for the telephones. McDowell twisted around in his chair, watching the doorway. He was ready to slam Sammy to the floor and protect her if any trouble came through that doorway.

Sammy once more seemed near tears.

"All my life," she said, "dealing with you nasty country boys." She sat and toyed with the salad. Then she picked up a cup of coffee. Her hand shook and the cup shook. She put it back down quick.

McDowell thought that she looked desperate, like someone who needed something bad and knew he was not going to get it.

He watched her. She was making him feel a way that he did not understand. The piano was hacking away at "My Little Margie." The dark-haired lady was in the restroom. The guy was talking urgently into the phone. McDowell continued to watch the doorway, waiting for some pore madman sonovabitch to come busting through.

The understanding came suddenly, fully bloomed. He understood what was wrong with Sammy. It was almost shocking. It was one of those automatic things that sometimes happened in your brain, like a musical modulation that was not headed toward anything astounding until some horn hopped onto it and began to blow wide and free.

Sammy wanted to be *respectable.*

That was why she stayed with that phony Wimp with his imitation accent and his summer tweeds. That was why she could never get enough money. That was why the Citizen drove her nuts, and why he, Dan McDowell, drove her nuts.

He told himself that it was ironic. All his life he had been trying not to be respectable, while Sammy, going in the opposite direction, had been fighting just as hard. For a moment he felt almost kind, almost brotherly toward her.

"We are country," he said apologetically, "you and me. This town is where we were born. When we were born, this was a country town." He was no longer mad at her. His voice was trying to show her that his anger was gone. "From the standpoint of business, the old man has pulled that country boy act since we were kids. It's worked."

"It doesn't work any longer," she said. "And maybe you can drive around in that awful car like some hick out of Nashville, not me."

For a moment the piano was silent. Probably, very probably, it had been hammered through the floor. The sandy-haired guy was done with the phone and was now headed toward the men's room. McDowell told himself that, of all the stupid things a man could do, getting cornered in a john had to be top-a the list. He continued to watch the door, waiting for the dark-haired lady's cuckolded husband to come crashing through.

"How is the old man different?" McDowell asked, still trying to be kind.

She once more looked like she was running a calculator.

"He no longer knows when to be quiet," she said. "He brags about his women, and his dog—he bought this silly dog. He is insulting to customers. He will interrupt Gerald right on the sales floor in order to tell some wild lie about the past." She paused, like she was a prosecuting attorney about to lay on final and damning evidence. "And he will not stop claiming that the warehouse is haunted. He says he sees ghosts.

"Yeh," said McDowell. "I know." He let it hang for a moment, waiting for her to jump on it. She did.

"How do you know?" Her voice was sniffy again. This time it was suspicious-sniffy.

"Because he told me," McDowell said. "I kidded him along, pretended he was right."

"You knew before, over the telephone. You would not have asked that filthy question if you didn't know—asking if I ever saw ghosts."

"Do you?" He was stalling for time.

"You are impossible." She was disgusted with him, but he could see that she was not going to let him off the hook.

"I heard about it," he said, "at one of my dealerships. I won't say which one."

"I was afraid of that. The talk is starting." She straightened up and pushed the salad away. "At the very best, your father is senile."

His father. When the old bastard did something right, he was her father. Of course, the Citizen did not do something right very often. Not according to Sammy.

"Plus," McDowell said, "you're afraid he'll marry that Sandra lady."

"He told you that as well?"

"He told me it was never gonna happen."

She should have looked relieved but she did not. She sat silently, and then she seemed to dismiss the problem of Sandra from her mind. "Daniel," she said irrelevantly, lightly, with an attempt to smile. "Tell me about your place in Chicago. Do you have a nice place?"

Social talk. He did not want to mess with social talk.

"A sleeper," he said. "I got a whole floor of a big house. Cheap." Then he grinned. "You wouldn't like the neighborhood."

"If not Sandra," she said, "if not that horrible Sandra, then someone else just as horrible."

He was not following her, and *they* must-a hoisted that goddamn piano back up through the rip in the floor because now the hammering started on "I Want a Girl Just Like the Girl."

McDowell watched Sammy and saw that she was once more play-acting. This time when she picked up the coffee cup, her hand was steady. "I'll make a deal," she said. "We can solve this with a deal."

He told himself that it was the way *they* did things. Making deals was the way *they* ran their lives.

"I'll listen," he told her. He leaned back, pretending he was a banker figuring a way to run a railroad through an orphanage without going to the expense of moving the orphans. He could feel the blandness on his face, the sagging wrinkles, and he could feel his cock getting a little bit hard. He listened carefully, admiring the cleverness of her constructed deal. It was such a rotten deal that it could only come from Sammy. She wanted to force the Citizen out, take over the business and the estate, put the Citizen on a cheap salary and pay off Dan McDowell for his help. When she finished, she leaned back in her chair, expecting agreement.

Dan McDowell reached for his hip pocket, got money to pay for the lunch, and casually tossed the money on the table. He yawned and then he scratched, pretending that a nickel had somehow dropped down his shirtfront. Then he stood up like he had to get to an appointment with a customer who was *really* important.

"No deal," he drawled, "but I'll just give you a little ad-vice. If you try that, or anything like that, then be sure to increase your fire insurance." He turned from her and got away quickly before he really did lose his temper. The Elks were singing "Old Folks at Home" as he left.

As McDowell approached the doorway he slowed. Stepping outside, McDowell looked in both directions, like a cautious pedestrian crossing the street. A Fiat buzzed by. It looked like a spraddle-legged bee. McDowell watched, saw the driver. He looked to be in his middle thirties. He was dressed in a cheap summer suit. His hair was black, his face was tense, and his eyes were staring like they were blind. The little Fiat kept cruising the lot. There were parking spaces, but the driver was not looking for a place to park. Instead of walking across the lot, McDowell stepped behind a row of cars and walked around the lot.

A black kid was hovering near the Cadillac. To McDowell it looked like the boy could not decide whether to just admire the car or steal it. At the corner of the lot two long-haired white boys dawdled. They were trying to imitate the manner of experienced drug freaks. They were about sixteen. McDowell thought that they actually looked like nothing more than kids with dirty jeans. One of them had even polished his shoes. The shoes were like two shiny black dots glowing against the black asphalt.

As McDowell approached, the kid beside the Cadillac looked up, looked guilty, and ran. McDowell watched him go. Then McDowell walked all around the Cadillac. Nothing had been touched.

They ran the world by making you want things, and by making you feel guilty because you wanted them. He wondered if Sammy felt guilty. You never could tell about her. If she did not feel a little bit guilty, then she would have just gone ahead and done it, rather than talk to him. Or, maybe, he thought she had counted on him for extra firepower.

The Fiat buzzed past once more as McDowell climbed in the Cadillac. He told himself that he wanted to get away before the shit started. He looked through the side window, preparing to back up, and saw that it was too late.

A police car screeched into the entry of the lot. It was running with lights, but no siren. The blue lights seemed paled in the strong sunlight. At the moment the car began to brake, the whip, whip, whip of a siren began in the streets. A second police car broadslid the corner. Small puffs of smoke rose from beside its rear wheels. Its tires were scorching, squalling, clawing. It did half a donut as it braked into the other entry to seal the parking lot. The whip of the Siren stopped, but the pale blue lights continued flashing. A thin vapor of steam rose from beneath the hood.

Cop bailed out of each car. One was an older guy with nearly silver hair. He bent over and ran like a combat infantryman. He carried a riot gun. The cops were keeping their cars between them and the parking lot.

The two white kids vanished like blown smoke. The Fiat was blocked. It screeched to a halt. The driver slumped forward over the wheel. He seemed to be passed out.

This role-ridden, insecure, grab-ass south.

McDowell figured that the couple having the affair were still huddled and hiding in their separate restrooms. The sandy-hair guy had no nerve. He had hollered "cop." McDowell told himself that the dark-hair lady had better not go home after all of this was over. Any dumb sonovabitch who messed with a married woman could expect what that sandy-hair guy was eventually going to get. McDowell had told Sammy the truth. This was still a country town.

The cops were hollering at the driver of the Fiat. Their words pounded acoss the sunlit parking lot like the thump of shotguns.

The driver of the Fiat slowly came out of his slump. He opened the car door and climbed out. The guy was clumsy and stupid, or maybe he was stupefied by emotion. He was not showing his hands.

He did not know how close he was to death, that little guy. McDowell thought that the cops were actually being pretty good about it, quite professional. One of the cops yelled again. The riot gun was sticking out from in front of a car, pointed directly at the guy's face and chest.

He made confused motions with his hands, until he finally got them in view. McDowell found that he had been holding his breath, waiting for the sound of the gun, and now he could breathe again. The guy finally caught on and got his hands at least as high as his shoulders.

A cop came from behind a car. He walked fast but he did not scare the little guy by charging him. The riot gun was still pointed at the guy's chest. It had a clear field of fire because the cop was coming in from the correct angle. When he was six feet from the little guy, the cop moved hard and quick. He grabbed the guy, spun him, and threw him against the car. The guy's head banged against the car as he stumbled. He raised his head. His mouth was bleeding, the red well of blood almost instantly splattering down across the cheap, ready-made suit. He tried to stand up straight. The cop shoved him again. Then the cop got a fist into the guy's back. Hard. The cop caught him in the center of the back, slugging quickly and efficiently. The little guy finally caught on. He spread against the car. He seemed to be hanging onto the car because he could not stand up. McDowell continued to admire the professional job. A blow in the back was not going to kill the punk, but it sure would slow him down.

The cop pulled a revolver from the guy's jacket pocket. Even from a distance, McDowell could tell that it was a cannon, a horse pistol, totally ridiculous. The guy slumped, listened to what he cop told him. The guy turned around. The cop hit him alongside the head with the heel of his hand. The guy collapsed. He looked happy as he fell, like he was glad it was all over and he had not had to kill anyone after all.

Cheap advice for anyone watching, McDowell thought. One thing you learned early was not to piss against this particular wind. You could safely play nantzy-pantzy-fuck-around in most parts of the country, but in a southern hick town it was still too risky. He sat waiting for the cops to load the guy and unblock the entry. He did not like the little guy, whose dark-hair wife was fucking the sandy-hair guy, but he understood him. The guy was stupid and inept, but he was not a redneck. He was only trying to do what he had been told he had to do ever since he got into long pants.

This tradition-loving, ass-kick, hot-head south.

This woman-worship, vengeance-ridden, shotgun south.

You could not make a woman love you. Either she loved you or she did not. The most you could ask for was that she be honest. McDowell thought back to when he was younger, and even he had played these stupid protect-your-honor games. Only, he told himself, he had not needed no damn horse pistol. When his wife had taken up with another man, McDowell just beat up on the guy a little bit and left town. The guy did not follow, but that was also part of the game. That guy had paid a price. He had probably expected worse. He had probably been relieved.

You could not make a woman love you. If a woman lied, then she was not worth anything in the first place. McDowell told himself that he knew a lot about the pain that came when a woman left. He thought of Becky, who had been honest. Maybe that was the reason why Becky was a woman he would never forget. Becky had been crazy-as-hell sometimes, but she had not lied.

That dark-hair girl should not have lied and sneaked around. It was not the fucking, it was the sneaking.

The whole business made him lonesome for Margaret. Margaret did not lie. He thought of Sammy, which made him even more lonesome for Margaret.

The police cars pulled away. McDowell was free to leave. Instead, he sat.

He reached for the map case that was built beneath the seat. His hand struck a hard object. He remembered it now. He pulled out the Cadillac emblem he had found at the deserted filling station. The cloisonné colors were hard and brilliant. The chrome on the bars was so heavy that it seemed mirrorlike. The luster of the chrome seemed to actually penetrate into the steel bars. It did not seem to be just spread on top of the metal. He laid the thing on the seat, then he reached further into the map case.

Margaret did not know it, but he had her picture. It was one of those publicity eight-by-ten glossies. It was not a personal kind of picture, but it was a good one. He had tipped a kid ten dollars to pick it off from the last place where she had been working.

It seemed to him, looking at the picture, that he could nearly hear her voice. It seemed, in the middle of a hot day when his sister had tried to plot against his father—a day when one more pore cuckolded sonovabitch had tried to commit murder—a day when he, Dan McDowell, ought to be in Indianapolis, anyway, it seemed like Margaret's voice was scatting. It was firm, fast and pronounced. It was syllabic, riding the rhythm, running free and confident and open like only the best scat singers could do. No confusion. No slurs. Margaret was way the hell and gone off to Atlanta right now, but it was almost like she was sending him a message, like she was somehow helping him.

Her skin was darker in this photograph. Her hair seemed lighter. The slight suggestion of the aristocratic bend of her nose was more pronounced. She was pictured almost, but not quite, in profile. Her dress was cut and arranged in a way that suggested moderately sized breasts.

He remembered her lying naked beside him, and her quiet, forward-thrusting intensity. He remembered how easily she smiled. It just made him more lonesome. It made him want a drink.

He replaced the picture and told himself that this was the way a man became an alky. He had to do better then this. He had to attend business, even if only by phone. He would see the Citizen tonight, and then he had to get out of town. His only accomplishment today, so far, was that he had managed to threaten his sister. He tried to take credit for threatening Sammy but he knew the threat meant little. Considering Sammy, and what she had become, his threat would carry about as much weight as one of her Jap-made rattan recliners.

Chapter 11

EVENING BROUGHT NO RELIEF FROM THE HOT WEATHER. THE AIR was muggy, close, and there were no breezes. The sky was orange. The tops of buildings seemed etched against the sky. The orange light outlined the buildings with such clear definition that they seemed reduced and unimportant. They looked as if they were drawn on the sky with a pen. In the streets traffic seemed like a barely controlled force that might explode. As headlights and bar signs began to burn in the hot night, Dan McDowell steered the Cadillac toward his family's warehouse. The city through which he drove seemed both familiar and, at the same time, foreign. The old places he remembered from his youth were mixed in with new and cheap buildings.

This Centerville was transition-city. It was here, and in Hamilton and Louisville, that you saw the best and worst of this land. People came from the south, headed north. Centerville and Louisville and Hamilton were stopover cities, always had been. The population continually seemed to be floating, headed north, headed south, and pausing for a moment to take a breather.

He had been driving through this land all of his life. He could not honestly say whether he liked it or not, but he could honestly say that he thought he understood it.

Lots of kids were out cruising. They peeled out from the parking lots of fast-food joints, tires scorching. A lotta booze out there, he thought, a lotta drugs.

A police car pulled up beside the Cadillac at a traffic light. The cop was not going anywhere, just cruising. The cop checked him out, looked at the Cad, pulled away slow when the light changed green. One-a them tight-mouth bastards with the mean-eyed look of a guy who would like to bust you because you were breathing.

This was cop city. Always had been. He did not know why.

He cruised the Cadillac and thought about it, figuring this was one of those cities where the country boys came to town, and the country boys couldn't handle it. You would naturally need more cops.

But it was like that all over, wasn't it?

No, he told himself, it wasn't. There was something special about this town, and special about Atlanta and Hamilton and Louisville and Detroit. Lots of the down-home boys were okay until they got to town. Then they turned into rednecks.

Samantha had cooked up the most rotten deal he had ever smelled. It wasn't even a deal. It was blackmail. There were money guarantees, of course, and on the surface it looked business-like and humane. What it amounted to was blackmail. It amounted to putting the old man out to pasture. In return for the old man dropping out, Sammy was willing to let him see as many ghosts as he wanted. Sammy was willing to forget about having him certified. In return for his help, Dan McDowell would receive one third of his share of the estate even before there was an estate.

If it was a fight she wanted, then it was a fight she was going to get. He did not want the old man's money. He did not need it. He wanted nothing to do with those people, but he was not going to let Sammy get away with anything.

He wheeled the Cadillac into the parking lot of McDowell Distributing. A single night-light was already glowing at one corner of the lot. Deep back there in the lot the old poplar tree rose silhouetted against the sky. McDowell parked the car beneath the light and sat looking at the poplar. Nothing was moving back there.

Sammy must be pretty desperate. She had always been someone who needed to be in control. She controlled the Wimp. She had controlled him, Dan McDowell, when they were kids. Now she wanted to control the world. He looked at the tree and thought about Sammy. This business was her whole world; so, yes, she wanted to control the world.

It sure was a sick way of living a life.

The Citizen's Lincoln was not parked in the lot. Maybe the old man was getting forgetful. McDowell climbed from the car, locked it, and walked across the lot toward the rear of the building. As he approached the poplar he paused, looking deep into the darkness and gloom beneath the branches. There was no light, no movement.

Sooner or later a man had to face situations. Either he, Dan McDowell, was crazy, or he really was seeing a ghost. Until he discovered that the Citizen was also seeing the ghost, he had nearly consoled himself with the idea that he had a fairly harmless form of madness, a madness that could be cured. Now it seemed that he was not crazy. Either that, or he and his father were both crazy in exactly the same way. McDowell felt that the odds on two people being mad in the same way were so astronomic that he could dismiss that possibility. Especially, he told himself, when the two people were so totally different. He told himself that he had nothing in common with the Citizen.

That left only one possibility. The ghost was real. It was as real as that world of hot pavement and scorching traffic out there. It was as real as that far-distant siren that was whipping away at the night. It was as real as that poplar tree. If that were true, and it must be true, then he, Dan McDowell, had been kidding himself about the world all of his life.

For years he had been driving through this land. For years he had paid almost no attention to the land. He had been a man of the road and cities. He had seen the down-home people, the country boys, the rednecks and the honorable hill people; but he had only seen them in the cities. Once, long ago, it had not been that way.

He remembered his mother and his grandmothers and his grandfathers. They had been country people. A flicker, a sliding sound of memory ran in his mind. It was like the barely touching note of a horn placed perfectly, so that it led into the rising musical attack of a singer.

The ghost was real. He did not know how he knew it, quite, but he knew it beyond logic. He stood in the hot night. The sirens were silent now, but it was only a matter of time before they would once more begin whipping the darkness.

Okay, he thought, it's real. He began walking to the rear door of the warehouse. His father's Lincoln was parked in the shadow behind the building. He wondered if the old man had parked it there to hide it.

When he knocked on the door, it was opened immediately. The Citizen stood white-haired and muscular, outlined against the dull night-lights of the warehouse. He motioned McDowell inside in that sly way that always made Dan McDowell feel vaguely like a conspirator. A form moved at the old man's side. McDowell looked down.

The most beautiful black and tan hound Dan McDowell had ever seen stood beside his father. It was big for a black and tan, and it looked perfect. Just looking at the dog, you could feel its strength and range.

"Get in here," the old man whispered. His voice sounded hurried, nearly desperate. The desperation stopped the moment he closed the door.

That dog had no business here. That dog belonged out there in the hills, calling fox, running twenty or thirty miles a night. The old man ought to know that.

"He's kinda stupid," the old man said proudly about the dog. "I don't bring him here much 'cause Sammy gets mad when he pisses on the merchandise. Four hundred dollar dog and he's too dumb not to piss on the merchandise." He grinned and he was proud. "Name of Shag," he said. "It's short for shag-ass."

"He piss at home?"

"Nope," the old man said. "'Course home's a little different. I mean the sonovabitch *lives* there."

"He's trying to tell you something about your inventory."

The old man looked grieved. "You and me," he said, "are never goin' to get that one settled. You got stupid ideas."

"I got a better inventory."

"You got a bunch of high-price crap. Comes an economic bust and you're going to be flat broke."

"It's a little risky, not much."

"I live as good as any man," said the Citizen, "and I done it by knowing what sells." He paused, like he was looking for further justification. "High price or low price, it's all junk anyway." He turned to walk back into the dimly lit warehouse. He was headed toward the front of the building and the office. The dog stretched in that catlike way of the best and most confident hounds. Then he raised his head, peered after the old man, and began following him. Mc-Dowell followed them both, and he was momentarily envious. He had no space in his life for a dog, but this Shag was perfect.

When they arrived at the office, the Citizen took a seat behind his desk. He had his back to the wall and his desk in front of him. Shag curled up at one side of the desk. The old man looked like he was in charge of a fort, like he was safe behind loaded cannon.

McDowell pulled a chair from beside Sammy's desk. He thought of putting his feet up on it, then decided that would be too pushy.

"I'm passing through," McDowell told his father. "I got to get out of town. Got a business to run."

"Don't bullshit," the old man said. "If you had a business to run, you'd be running it." He leaned back in his chair. He was trying to take the offensive, but he looked defensive.

"I run it different," McDowell explained, "because it is different. I got a good manager."

The old man looked pained. "I heard that one before. At the very best, you're training your future competition. At the worst, you're training him while he's stealing you blind."

"She's not a he, she's a she. Besides, you think I'm so dumb I'm not watching out for that?"

"Yep," the old man said. "Otherwise you'd be in Chicago right now." He attempted to look kindly. It only made him look sly. "You use that business as an excuse to hell around." He grinned. "There's plenty of women in Chicago, but you're out chasing the farmer's daughter. I done it as a kid. I was hell on wheels as a kid."

McDowell told himself not to get sucked into that one. He was forty-three years old and he did not need no damn reminiscences from the Citizen. He leaned forward, about to try to make friends with Shag. The dog looked him over, decided against it, and placed his muzzle on his forepaws.

"And now," said the Citizen, "I got a dog and I got seventy-one years." He leaned back, trying to look expansive, but he momentarily looked feeble instead. He looked sad. "I got a daughter who is tryin' to rob me."

"She's trying," Dan McDowell admitted.

"She made me an offer," the old man said. "I told her to take her offer and a pinch of salt and rub it up her ass."

"Pop," McDowell said, "you could soft-pedal it. You don't have to plague Sammy."

The Citizen looked puzzled. He was fooling around with a button on his shirt, plucking at it, fiddling with it. "Sure I do," he said. "The older a man gets the ornerier he has to be. If you don't stay ornery, you die." His low voice was certain, but it was also as close to being apologetic as the Citizen ever got. "You saw her today," he said. "What did she want?"

McDowell told him about the one-third payoff offer on the estate. The old man took it, sorted it, sat with his feet up, and still managed to look as fixed as a frog on a lily pad.

Then, suddenly, he was crying. The tears seemed independent, coming slowly. They were not loose, the way crying ought to be, but stern and controlled.

"What'd you tell her?"

"I told her to increase her fire insurance if she done it."

The old man's face was set firm as pavement. The tears ran down his set face. His voice should sound choked, but when he spoke it was not. "It's a nice threat," he said, "and I thank you, but no matter what happens, don't do it. If you burn it, I'll kill you. I got too many years tied up in this place."

"It was only a threat," McDowell said. "I wouldn't burn out my sister, but I will sure give her a burn if she keeps pushing. He was uncomfortable because of the old man's tears. He had never seen the Citizen weep. "I think I stopped her, he said helplessly.

"You didn't stop her," the old man said, "but you maybe slowed her down." He did not wipe his eyes. The Shag dog was wide awake and watchful. Shag was picking up on the Citizen's feelings.

"Meanwhile, Pop, maybe we are nuts. Sane people don't see ghosts."

The old man put his feet down. He sat up straight and looked like he was ready to fight. "The hell they don't," he said. "It's insane people who don't see them."

"C'mon, Pop."

"I'm a good old Kentucky and North Carolina boy," the old man said. "Don't pass me no shit." He looked the way Sammy had looked, when Sammy looked like she was running a calculator. "I seen two world wars and a bunch of other ones. I seen a major depression and a bunch of bad downturns. I seen this country when there wasn't a road you could drive on year round. Don't give me no shit."

"I'm trying not to," McDowell said, "but I don't understand what's happening."

"That raggedy-ass bastard that you're seeing is Enoch McDowell," said the old man. "He died when I was a boy, but I seen him plenty. He was a hellion. He killed seven men in one night."

"Who was he?"

"Your great-great-grandfather. He burned down a whole goddamned town." The old man looked happy at the thought. "Of course," he admitted, "it wasn't much of a town. It was a wore-out settlement."

Shag stood up, stretched, looked around suspiciously, sniffing the air. He was beautiful with his head up that way. A hound usually had his nose to the ground.

"You get steady now, Shag. C'mere, Shag." The old man snapped his fingers and the dog walked around the end of the desk and sat beside the old man. "He's hoverin' out back there in the warehouse," the Citizen said. "You can always tell by watchin' the dog."

McDowell had a hopeful thought. The ghost he was seeing did not look like it had enough strength to even kill itself. Maybe he was not seeing the same thing that his father was seeing after all.

"What I'm seeing," McDowell said, "is an old, old man. He looks blind. He's got no teeth."

"That's our man," said the Citizen. "That's the way he was when he died, but in his day he was one ornery sonovabitch." The Citizen seemed pleased with his story. "Enoch cut two men to pieces, shot three, and burned two. One of the burned ones didn't die. So he lynched him."

"And burned the town?"

"It was abandoned, except for a few niggers. He burned it and the niggers run." The old man was totally pleased. "Let the bodies lay. Spent two days hauling cow manure to cover them, but he pissed in their faces first."

McDowell sat in the modern office, his feet against plush carpet. He looked down at his custom-made boots, his tailored pants, and he thought that either he was crazy or the Citizen was.

Except, McDowell told himself, the story was not unreasonable. At least it was a good story if there was a reason for it in the first place.

"Why'd he kill them?"

"They were renegades," the old man said. "Right after the Civil War. Enoch had a place downriver. They come past his farm and raped his wife and a nigger girl. Then they went down the road a piece and camped in this town."

"An' got what they had coming."

"Sure," the old man said. "Enoch came home from a trip upriver. Your great-great-grandma was struck dumb: never spoke another word in her life. The nigger girl went wildcat crazy a week later. Hid in a tool shed. Cut herself. Like to died, but Enoch pulled her through it."

McDowell sat thinking of his grandmothers, of the days when he was a child and of the memory of hearing tales.

"How come I never heard all this before?" he said suspiciously. "A story like that don't get hid, it gets bragged about."

The Citizen looked reluctant, like he was trying to think of a reasonable lie. Then his face got honest.

"Because," said the Citizen, "your great-great-grandmother and the nigger girl were half-sisters. Their mother, who would have been your great-great-great-grandmother, was a coffee-color girl."

Dan McDowell, who for years had prided himself on his scorn for custom, sat momentarily stunned. He chewed over the information, and then he grinned.

"That sure is gonna flatten Sammy's nose," he said. "Sammy is just going to shit a brick when she hears that."

The old man reached over and flopped Shag's ear. The dog looked at him, thumped its tail. "Sammy's dumb," the Citizen said, "and you're gettin' stupid. You ain't to never tell Sammy, never. She shouldn't be doing what she's doing, but we got no right to kill her. That'd kill her."

McDowell sat looking at his polished boots, at the plush carpet, at the oiled and waxed legs of the desks. He was having a hard time absorbing the weight of what he was hearing. He could handle the Citizen's orneriness. He could handle the bullshit, he slyness, the pettiness. What he was now having a hard time with was the Citizen's kindliness. He was shocked to find that the old man had this kind of generosity, this unwillingness to hit back even when he was sorely tried.

"You and Sammy are punks," the old man said. "You been living in this country all your life and you don't know a thing about it."

"Pop," McDowell said, "you raised me. It was years before I got that word 'nigger' out of my system. Pop, you put it there."

"You don't catch on," the old man said. "You lived here all your life, and you don't know what the sorriest, commonest red-neck knows." The old man grinned. "A'course, the sonsovbitches won't admit they know it."

"What?"

"Everybody in the south is two things," the old man said. "Everybody's a nigger, and everybody is English." He sat at his desk with his hound by his side, posing like a squire. He was obviously having a wonderful time.

"Everybody would amount to a lot of people." McDowell felt slugged.

"Everybody—from Henry Clay and Robert Lee right on down the ladder," the old man said. "Everybody. If it ain't in the blood, it's in the bone."

Shag growled. He stood, and his hackles came up. He was braced, big footed, big chested, and ready to attack. He snarled. Shag seemed out of place. He was like an alien in the expensively furnished office, his feet braced in thick carpet.

"Steady-down, Shag," the old man said. "You are one mean sonovabitch, but you ain't that mean."

McDowell looked at his father, and it seemed to him that this man who had raised him was a complete stranger. This harsh old man, sly and vulgar, who McDowell had known all his life, had suddenly gained dimension. He had a history, a memory, a past that was greater than the daily round of sales and inventory juggling and woman chasing.

"He's out back there," the old man said.

"What does it mean? What does he want?"

"I expect," said the Citizen, "that the way to find out is to ask." He stood up behind the desk. He was clearly afraid, and he was clearly ready to fight back. "We got to leave the dog here in the office," he said apologetically. "Shag can't handle it. There ain't nothing for him to sink his teeth into."

He came from behind the desk and walked across the office. Dan McDowell followed his father. He did not know what else to do.

Chapter 12

THE DIM NIGHT-LIGHTS OF THE WAREHOUSE HUNG HIGH ON CEIL-ings which were otherwise invisible in the darkness. It had been a wholesale warehouse since just after World War II. Before that it had been a furniture manufacturing company, and before that it was a Packard dealership. It originally was a drayage company back in the days when teamsters actually used horses. McDowell had always liked the oldness of the building, the brick walls that had never been covered by whitewash or paint. As a child he had sometimes sat on the loading dock and pretended that right around the corner of the building, in the parking lot, horses stamped and waited for dray wagons to be loaded. He had imagined horses standing in the shade of the poplar, knowing it was so old that horses surely must actually have stood beneath it long ago.

Cases of goods were stacked in tall piles under the nightlights. Furniture was stacked three and sometimes four cases high. Cartons of discount paint were stacked ten high. They looked like ridges in the shadows and gloom, like little chains of mountains. Hardware, cheap office equipment, automobile accessories, and freight salvage were arranged for easy accessibility. McDowell knew that above his head, on the second and third floors, were plumbing supplies, kitchen appliances and soft goods.

And all of it crap, he thought. All of it just good enough that it did not break the first time it was used.

The Citizen moved ahead of him like a white-haired spirit, like he himself was a ghost. He seemed to know where he was going.

As he passed a section of carefully sorted freight salvage he paused like he was remembering something. He reached into a carton and pulled out a bamboo cane, the kind that barkers used in carnivals. The old man looked like a carny, himself. He looked like the great-grandfather of all carnies. His face held wrinkles that suddenly seemed to have grown because of years of bullshit, and his eyes were sparkly with bullshit. His big nose wrinkled, like he was sniffing the sweet smell of a dollar bill. He twirled the cane like he had been doing it all his life. He grinned at McDowell, this time with bravado, and then he poked the cane at McDowell. His face looked a little bit sick with fear, but it also looked sly because of his bravado. McDowell thought that the old man was handling this better than he, Dan McDowell, was going to.

"You gonna use that to rap him with?" McDowell pretended to be amused, and his own bravado sounded sick and poorly in his ears.

"You wouldn't know sheep shit from raisins if you found them in the same piece of pie," the old man said. He pulled another carny cane from the carton. "Try it," he said, "an' then quit shootin' your mouth."

Dan McDowell figured he would rather have an umbrella if he was going to be in a clown show. It would be like being in New Orleans, and he would be dancing with an umbrella before the hot mouth of dixieland horns. He would have spats, and he would be fantastically fat and black and big lipped. He would make smooth and subtle movements with his ass. He would soft-shoe and cakewalk for them Creole ladies. For a moment he could actually feel his belly pressing hard against his belt, and his feet felt light, like they were hunting for a rhythm.

He twirled the cane, and then he tapped it on the floor in front of him. Then he remembered where he was and what he was doing. He was shocked with his imagination, and supposed he was enough unbalanced that his mind was trying to hide by using his imagination.

He followed his father and had to admit that the old man was right. There was something solid about a cane, even a cheap one like this. There was something supple about it, like it was full of quick usefulness. You could strike or twirl or lean or point. He had forgotten how good a cane felt in the hands—if, he thought, he had ever known it in the first place. And realistically, he told himself, this thing was solid and real. It helped to be holding onto something that was solid.

"Enoch comes from over that way," the Citizen said. He stood, pointing with the cane. He looked like one of those gentlemanly types who had once been portrayed by the Hudson River painters. He pointed to the far corner, down by the loading dock where the sliding overhead doors were like galvanized curtains sealing the warehouse from the city.

"He come often?"

"He didn't used to. He showed up a couple of times after your ma died, but I never said anything." The old man stopped. He was no longer showing off. He was leaning on the cane, and he slumped. His voice seemed eternally sad. "Your ma would have been seventy-two this coming November." He tapped the cane twice on the floor, like he felt frustrated, or was trying to dismiss the futility of sorrow. "She put up with a lot from me."

"I suppose she did, Pop. Still—"

"I've known a lot of women, and not a one of 'em could hold a candle to your ma."

'That's got to be true."

"Sometimes," the old man said helplessly, "it's a good question why a man keeps goin' on. I guess you do it because you got to." He again started to walk. His voice was now full of anger, and McDowell supposed that memories were hurting him. "You goddamn frowzy sonovabitch," the old man yelled at the corner of the loading dock. "Get with it, potlicker, get this foolishness over." He banged the head of the cane against a case of goods. There was the rattle of breaking glass. "You moley, miserable, sorry . . . you sittin' and quakin' back there like a little dog shittin' peach seeds—get on out here." The old man was waving his cane like he was an old-fashioned planter about to thrash a newspaper editor or a politician.

Dan McDowell cowered. He did not know what he expected to happen next, but it was bound to be bad.

Nothing happened.

The old man stood there among his junk merchandise and cursed, raved, nearly chanted with the cursing. The cursing was metrical, solid, original, and he was not repeating a word. He finally ran down, stood catching his breath and leaning on the cane. "Pop," McDowell said, "I reckon you scared him off. Let's go get a beer."

"Uh-uh," the old man said. "You ain't going to go yellow on me now." He paused, like he was having a happy thought. "I ain't got no beer," he said. "What the hell are you anyway, a sailor? I got good red whiskey if you want some."

"Shore," said Dan McDowell. "I think I want it pretty bad."

"Well," said the old man, "Let's just have us a jolt. That miserable little squeakpippin' two-bit sister-in-law-molestin' blank-eye raggety-tag is takin' his time."

"So he was laying the dark girl, too?"

"I ain't saying so," the old man grinned, "but they's two branches of the McDowell family, and you got some mighty funny-looking shirttail kin." He turned away, walked a few feet, and rummaged in a case of goods until he pulled out a fifth of bourbon. Then he rummaged in another case and pulled out two water glasses.

"This here bottle is a spare," he explained. "Sammy can't keep me from having a bottle in the office desk." He obviously did not want Dan McDowell to think that he had to hide his whiskey. He had the cane hooked in his belt, and he poured into both glasses until they were nearly full.

"That's a lot of liquor, Pop."

The old man did not answer. He sat down on a case of goods and leaned against another case. He put the cane aside and sat drinking the whiskey. "Have a seat," he said charitably. "We'll just wait him out."

"What's going to happen? Let me know what I'm in for."

"Enoch's kind of like a picture show," the old man said. "Except he scares hell out of me and no picture show ever done that." He took another mouthful of whiskey. "I expect I've seen more of the Civil War than that mangy Grant ever saw. Enoch takes an interest in it. He got shot up in '61 at a place called Lucas Bend."

"I know something about that war," McDowell said. "Everybody does, but I never heard of that one."

"Almost nobody has. They had cannon on the bluffs above the river, and they were tryin' to potshot a couple of northern gunboats called the *Lexington* and the *Conestoga*—only the gunboats potshotted them. Phelps had charge of the *Conestoga*, and a guy named Stembel was driving the *Lexington*."

McDowell sipped his whiskey and bet himself that, if pressed, the old man could come up with the size of the guns, the number of them, and the names and genealogy of half of the men who served them. That Civil War was the best documented war in the history of the world, but most of the information was not of the written kind. It existed in stories passed down through families. He supposed that the stories were dying out now, as the old people died. It seemed sad, in a way, and a good thing in another way.

He sipped at the whiskey and told himself that he should not get loaded, although it was an attractive idea. Then he told himself that he was already loaded—was even overloaded, but not with alcohol. It seemed that in the last few days he had been taking on about as big a cargo as any man could be expected to handle. He had decided to really try to love Margaret, to take the chance of once more trying with a woman. *Only*, he thought, *you* didn't have the nerve to tell her yet because *you're* afraid she maybe doesn't want to hear.

He had gotten mixed up with his crazy family, and he did not see any way out of it. You could not just up and leave your family. He did not know why he knew that. He only knew that it was so deep in him that there was no sense asking questions. You could easy leave them if times were good, but you could not leave them when they were in trouble.

Maybe it was Sammy who was in trouble. Maybe Sammy had more trouble than she could ever cause the old man.

He took a jolt of the whiskey, a goodly mouthful, and thought about the rest of it. He had added information to that cargo he was taking on. It could not have been easy for the old man to admit that there was Negro blood in the family.

Or maybe, he thought, maybe it *had* been easy. The old man wore his bigotry like a merit badge. Yet it now seemed almost possible that the old man was not bigoted at all.

Plus, Dan McDowell had never before seen his father weep.

"You gonna wear that glass thin lickin' on it," the old man said. He reached for the bottle, like he was going to top off Dan McDowell's glass.

"This is enough, Pop. More'n enough."

"I may just wet the bottom of this glass," the old man said.

"That's Jewish," he explained, "that expression. When a yid says that, he means fill it right on up there." He poured more whiskey on top of the amount remaining in his glass.

"Pop," McDowell said, "tell me true. Why do you bullshit so much?"

The old man sipped at his whiskey. His white-haired head was in shadow, and his hair seemed luminescent. He had rolled his shirtsleeves up a couple of turns. His heavy, muscular forearms were propped easily over his knees. He sat on the carton with his knees up, almost like a young boy sitting on a riverbank.

"You don't catch on," he said sadly. "Either that, or maybe the times are passing me by. Maybe things really don't work the way they used to." He took another sip of the whiskey. He did not sound loaded, but he was hitting that glass pretty hard.

"I don't understand," McDowell said helplessly. "I don't even know what you're talking about."

"I wish Enoch would show up," said the old man. "The sonovabitch may be dead, but at least he'd understand."

"Try me. Try explaining it to me."

"This family," said the old man, "has produced some outstanding drunks. It has had horse thieves and preachers and murderers, but it never produced no Bilbos. It never produced no rednecks."

"I don't know what that means."

"That's the whole point," the old man said. "That's the main part of the whole thing. You ain't supposed to understand. Enoch would understand." He reached down beside him and picked up the cane. He held it like it was a rifle. He sighted along the cane toward the loading dock. "In these parts," he said, "but not the redneck parts, the trick is to say *exactly* what you mean, but you got to say it in a way that can't be understood." He lowered the cane. You know that," he said sadly, "or if you don't you ain't been payin' attention."

For the second time that night McDowell sat stunned. *That* was the source of the bullshit. That was why *they* made jokes about what hurt them and made serious noises about absolutely nothing. He took another hit of the whiskey. "It shore does make for a damn confusing world."

"You ever see the sonovabitch when it wasn't confusing?" The old man might not be drunk, but he was getting mellow. "It's English, he said, that way of sayin' things. Goddamn, boy, even pimps know that, *especially* pimps."

McDowell chewed on what he was hearing. "You even do it when you're trying to be straight out understood?" He told himself that he must be getting a little bit loaded since he seemed right on the edge of some great realization.

"You got no business bein' in business," the old man said compassionately. "You're too thick in the head." He tapped the cane against a carton. "I worry about you some." His voice was mournful, maybe even a little maudlin.

"You ain't alone," McDowell admitted, "I worry about me some, too." His own voice was not exactly a smashing success. He leaned against a carton.

It was almost like he could hear Margaret's voice, only this time she was doing a ballad. Margaret's voice was sad and lonesome, like waking up in the morning and rolling toward your lover only to remember that you were in a single bed.

Somewhere behind him the air was being ripped apart with sound, a sound that started low. His reactions were a little bit off. He heard the beginning sound, then heard the rising notes before he had really connected with the beginning sound. Shag's voice was making strokes in the distance. The voice was not belling, and it was not singing. It was pure hound, all right, but it was a hound setting sounds of warning into the air.

"I wish I'd left that dog at home," said the old man. "It's so hard on him."

"It's starting?"

"I've never seen a good dog be fooled about something like this."

It seemed to McDowell that the night-lights either brightened, or the darkness and shadow increased. The old man's hand trembled as he raised his glass. McDowell was sure that his father was reacting to the feeling of presence that suddenly engulfed them. The presence was not the focused, singular presence that Dan McDowell had felt on other occasions. This presence spread all over the area around him, and he thought that it might command the entire warehouse.

The presence was not exactly hideous, although it seemed to carry the possibility of horror through the pulsating darkness. It seemed a creature of gloom and sorrow and anger. What made it so terrifying was its certainty. You could not run from it, only deeper into it. It was in overflooding control.

Dim light appeared from the direction of the loading dock and brightened as it moved toward them. The light was like the pale glow of fire that you sometimes thought you saw on the horizon when the night was late and the road long. At first the fire seemed almost pink, cut with streaks of orange. Then it became like the faded ruby glow of distant fire against a sky of dark clouds. The light did not move rapidly. It pressed forward as steady and inexorably as the flow of a slow river. As it became brighter, forms moved like shadows in the fire. They bent in tortured shapes, seemed trying to flee, and if they were making sounds, the sounds were the whispers of shadows. McDowell listened and knew that frantic and violent sound was erupting in ranges just beyond the ability of the ear to hear them. The forms writhed and it was impossible to tell, at first, if the forms were hellish or only human. He continued to listen. Mouths gaped wide with screams but the sound—if it was a sound and not his imagination—was like thin high weeping and choking.

"This is different from other times," the old man whispered. "This one is bigger'n a barn." The bottle rattled against his glass. He passed the bottle to McDowell. McDowell poured, heard and felt the bottle rattle against his own glass. He drank a good deal more than a sip, taking refuge in the clear smell of the whiskey—because now, all around him was the light stench of burned flesh.

The violence started to be laced with feelings of sadness, a sadness that grew. It gained presence until it seemed like sadness was the whole foundation for the world, and violence sprung like an inevitable expression of the sadness. The tormented and twisted shapes in the fire wailed high and thin screams.

Sadness, grief, and frustration entered McDowell's mind until he thought he would weep. He thought he might become insane. He could feel madness crawling in his brain, pressing outward, and his skull seemed like a thin barricade that was barely holding the madness in control. The presence surrounded him. It could do its will with him. He was helpless, cowering, and he thought of running. He began to stagger to his feet, then halted. There was no place to run.

The air became thicker and hotter, although the warehouse had been dry and dusty and warm. Now the heat of a summer day enclosed him. The air was thick with humidity, the way it was in the river basins. It carried the faint smells of a forest, of rotting leaves and the fine smell of carpeting pine needles. The stench of decay was mixed in with the healthy-smelling odor of millions of plants and trees transpiring water into the thick air. The sharp smell of ozone cut the air, the way it did in electrical storms.

The light changed. It grew through a spectrum of color, changing from ruby to red to pink, then it increased and became like daylight on an afternoon of intermittent rain and sun. It preempted the warehouse, like it was an extra dimension that lay everywhere. McDowell was still sitting, but he could not exactly tell what he sat on. The stacks and rows of merchandise could no longer be seen. Instead, the light opened the surroundings as if it illuminated the bare surface of a stage. Dan McDowell saw that he was not watching a stage; he was on one, transported in time. He felt that he had been set down in a vaguely familiar country. The scene changed. He was in the same room with what was happening.

A woman who was dark and a light-skin, nearly white woman sat together in a large cabin. The timbers were raw and new. The cabin looked unfinished. The light-skin woman was cream color, slender and almost pretty. Her face was broad and looked part Indian. Her hair was light, reddish blonde; long and braided. She was talking to the dark-skin woman. Both women were laughing like they were joking.

The dark woman was not Africa-black, but nearly. Her face was more sharp-featured, like she carried the genes of some northern slave trader. Her body was small, her hands small and quick. Both women suddenly stopped with their tasks, as if startled. The dark woman sat, her hand high on the wheel of a spinning wheel. Her left hand was stopped at the bobbin. The light-skin woman was holding a shuttle, about to push it through the warp on a loom.

There were two windows in the room. They held no glass, but animal skins were rolled above them like shades that could be dropped against bad weather. Dull light, like the light of a storming summer day, illuminated the room. Beyond one window was the rich red of tall hollyhocks which grew beside the cabin. The only door to the cabin stood open. Beyond it the lowering daylight seemed to pin a distant landscape in place. Wet trees stood beyond a clearing. Above the trees dark clouds bunched in the way they often did before the barrier of a river and there was the sound of distant thunder.

The doorway was suddenly obscured by the silhouette of a man. The dark form appeared huge as it stood, blocking light from the room. The man was big chested, heavy shouldered, and he nearly filled the doorway. Another man stepped up beside him. A third man's head appeared behind them, and then a fourth. The doorway was blocked by the forms of men. The room was dark but grew darker still as the light-skin woman stood and tried to force a smile like she was pretending she was not afraid. She touched her hair, running her hand backward up her cheek and then down along the braid to her shoulder. Then she pressed both hands outward, straight ahead, as if she were trying to push away an eventual sorrow. She moaned. The dark woman screamed, and the light began to pulse low, churning and changing, returning to the low ruby color of distant fire.

"We didn't see the rest," McDowell whispered with relief.

"Who the fuck wants to," said his father. "Pore old Enoch probably still can't stand to look at it hisself." The old man's voice, which had been filled with awe and fear, was changed. The sadness McDowell heard belonged to his father, not to the presence. The frustration and fury and violence were his father's. Violence had completely taken the old man away from his fear.

In the south, but not in the redneck parts, a man protected the weak. McDowell, feeling his father's fury, felt his own. His lips were drawn back, the wrinkles of his face smoothed out with drawn concentration. He felt something in his hand, looked down, and realized that without knowing it he had gone into his pocket and opened his knife. It lay there in his hand, a little three-inch blade that was good for cleaning your fingernails. He snapped it shut, put it back in his pocket, and sat stunned at his reaction. He touched the cane, like it was a club.

The ruby light lowered, pulsed darkly. A man stood on a dirt street that ran between a series of log cabins and small houses made of roughhewn boards. The man looked like a shadow and moved like one. A brilliant moon illuminated the street. The moonlight came and went as it was darkened by occasional high-sailing clouds. The man moved toward the houses, searching, peering through windows and darkened doorways. He paused, like he saw something that he could not exactly reckon out, and then he moved into the small cabin.

The shadowed forms of two men appeared. They were asleep, wrapped in blankets. The searcher approached them. He was darkly silhouetted against the moonlit doorway. He moved quickly, but as quiet as a trained army scout. He stood above the men and struck twice, quick, slamming a club against each man's head. Then he knelt and pulled away the blankets. He hamstrung the men. The knife cut deep into tendon and muscle and small bones. Blood ran black in the moonlight.

One of the men moaned, stirred, and the attacker reacted automatically and fast. He grabbed the man's hair, pulled his head back and cut his throat. The man rolled, twitched, gasped while blood spurted in thick, dark streams. The attacker knelt beside the man and, two-handed, drove the knife into the groin. There was a muffled snap as the knife cut and broke through bone. The moonlight illuminated another spurt of dark blood, and the attacker wiped his hands and knife on the shirt of the still shuddering corpse. The other hamstrung man, who was a big, heavyset man, lay silent.

Now the ruby light brightened. A large cabin appeared with fire surrounding it. Dry tinder had been placed all around the cabin before it was fired. The fire seemed to hold the cabin like a bright, enclosing hand while columns of smoke rose in the moonlight. Inside the cabin men were waking. A man's form was shadowy as he moved before a window. He coughed, leaned open-mouthed out the window as he attempted to flee. His eyes reflected urgency, but he did not know that the fire was intentionally started. He did not show fear, and he did not have time to know fear. He coughed, his mouth open, as a revolver shot sounded. The man's mouth snapped up the bullet like a frog might snap up a fly and he tumbled backward into the flames. The acrid smell of black powder from the revolver mingled with the clean burning smell of the tinder and the stench of scorched flesh. Inside the cabin men were screaming.

A second form appeared in the doorway as another man attempted to flee the fire. His hair was burning and is mouth was wide, gasping for breath. The revolver sounded again. The man's eyes crossed, rolled, and he looked startled in the same instant that he was dead. The body tumbled backward, into the fire. It bumped against a second man, partly blocked his path, and the revolver sounded. The man grabbed his side. He staggered back into the fire, sat down with a look of amazement, and then sat burning and screaming. Another man ran through the doorway, like a torch with legs. He beat at his clothing, rolled in the dirt, got the fire extinguished and then lay screaming. His face was charred. Sparks smoldered in what was left of his clothing. The attacker leaned over and once more cut hamstrings.

The red light faded into darkness, and Dan McDowell sat shuddering. The fury of the presence surrounded him, and the stench of burned flesh was not an illusion.

"I heard that story all the time when I was a boy," the Citizen said, "but even I never knew that Enoch done that good." His voice was filled with ferocious joy, the same kind of rapacious joy that hovered all around Dan McDowell, celebrating. McDowell, who had sometimes talked murder but never seen it, felt sick and weak.

The light brightened, like the reddening sky of a stormy dawn. Columns of smoke rose from the burning settlement. On the dirt street Enoch stood. Although Enoch did not look like Dan Mc-Dowell, they were built in much the same way. He walked with a bad limp, like a man recovering from wounds. His eyes were slate-like, but not with blindness. They were the hard, cold eyes of directed fury. On the ground before him lay two living men and the remains of five others. Three of the corpses were burned so badly that only their general forms showed that they had once been human. Blackened bone was scraped white in places where it had been cleaned by being dragged along the ground. Skulls showed through the black, peeling flesh that was flayed away from foreheads. The raw red of flesh still oozed slow blood from cracking and splitting wounds.

The insides of the legs of the corpses were charred. Their penises and testicles were reduced like small, cooked meat. It was meat that a man would not even bother with unless he was skinning out something small like a squirrel. Enoch carefully cut the organs away, flipping the bodies back and forth like they were discardable junk. Heads rolled, and the burned remains of arms flopped. The knife probed in blackened, reddened flesh. He took the parts as if they were chicken giblets. He threw them into the street for the health of passing scavengers—rats, mice, skunks. Blood welled slow and thick and black from the crotches of the burned corpses. It was in thick, dark clots on Enoch's hands.

A man who had his throat cut lay with his head twisted sideways so that the flesh of the throat looked like a pleat gathered around the dark, blood-hardened wound. Enoch kicked the head watched it flop sideways, and Enoch seemed lost in thought. He knelt. As methodically as a man dressing out a deer, he severed the head. He felt methodically with the knife, placing it between vertebrae. When the head rolled free, he picked it up by the hair. He seemed to be holding a conversation with the head. Then he spat in the dead face, the spit hitting the cheeks. He spat again into the glazed eyes. Then he tossed the thing aside like a man culling a load of pumpkins to remove those that were rotten.

A living man, covered with burns, struggled feebly. He seemed to be groaning and praying, or pleading. Beside him a man with his wrists bound, and hamstrung, screamed and wept. The bound man was big faced and big bodied. He had heavy eyebrows and thick, dark brown hair. His brown eyes alternately closed, as if he could not bear to see what he watched, then opened a if he could not bear to miss any last sight of earth. His eyes occasionally lighted with some small illusion of hope, then dulled with fear and guilt. He had either struggled for a long time, or had lost a lot of blood because of the hamstring. His struggles were weak, but his mouth kept moving, moving, praying or pleading.

Enoch leaned down and placed a noose around the burned man's neck. Then he dragged the moaning body to a huge poplar tree. The man thrashed about, seemed trying to talk. Enoch threw the free end of the rope over a branch.

Enoch lynched him carefully. Enoch seemed nearly gentle, the way he raised the man. It was clear that he wanted the man to choke, and not just die easy of a broken neck. He cinched off the rope as the flailing body's toes just barely touched the ground. There was just enough contact with the ground to give the victim hope, but still not enough to do him any good. The face began to strangle, then strangle more. The eyes began to bulge. Enoch stood watching, like he waited for the proper moment to perform some final action. The burned tongue began to protrude from between blackened lips. The eyes bulged more. Enoch took his knife, reached up, and punctured the eyes. Compressed fluid streamed across the face and the lynched man flopped, flopped, finally hung limp.

Now the screams began from the big-bodied man who lay bound and helpless. The screams were deep, rising high, running the full range of the notes of terror. Enoch knelt to tear away the man's shirt. The man seemed to be begging, blubbering incoherently beneath the continuing layers of screams. The knife began slow methodical movements, marking out narrow strips of flesh across his chest. Enoch began to flay the man, the point of his knife picking up the corners of the flesh that Enoch then tore away in strips. The screams choked, became sobs, became a low panting. Enoch rocked back on his heels and watched. Then he seemed to come to a rapid decision. He began moving along the breastbone, forcing the knife against the bone. He began to cut out the heart. The bound man struggled, whipped, rolled, and fell silent. The heart was pulled from the chest and Enoch stood, indifferent to the blood that ran fresh on his hands, arms, shirt, and pants. He stood looking at the heart, studying it like he was trying to figure what part such a thing could have in the running of man. Then he threw it in the dirt. Columns of fire from the burning building rose behind him. Enoch stared slate-like at the fires and at the corpses. The light began to fade.

Dan McDowell was sick. "Pop," he whispered, "Pop, I can't hardly stand this. Any more and I'm gonna puke."

"What the hell's the matter," the old man said. "Enoch done good." The Citizen was not whispering. His voice was glad. "I was hell on wheels," he said, "but I couldn't of done no better."

McDowell, who knew that he was not hell on wheels, sat and felt like he was in hell. The presence was all around him in its singing, celebrating fury. McDowell was weak. His glass rattled against his teeth. Whiskey spilled on his chin. He got some of it down. Then came the shock, a shock of realization so bright and hot that it might have been electric. In his mind, from some dark and deep place, a silence was moving. He concentrated on it because it seemed that right now there ought to be a lot of sense in silence. Then he wished he had not concentrated so hard. The silence opened and became form. Dan McDowell knew that his mind understood and *approved* of every action he had seen Enoch make. Something old, ancient, independent of his previous thought and knowledge, agreed with the fury that he felt all around him. It agreed with the fury in his father's voice. It was riding high, like the bugles of hell sounding in his own mind. He still felt weak, but he no longer felt sick.

"They had it coming," he said. His voice sounded strong and capable. He was no longer whispering. "But you got to admit it was goddamn colorful." The light was once more changing, running through the spectrum of ruby to light, orange-colored sunlight.

The light patterned, moved, became like an autumn day. The light-skin women and the dark-skin woman sat on the seat of a wagon that was stacked high with house goods. Enoch stood beside the team of horses. The two-window cabin already looked abandoned. Enoch began to lead the team. The rig moved slowly along a dirt road that cut through the forest. It passed a bend, slowly moving out of sight. A few moments later Enoch reappeared, carrying an old-fashioned rifle. He stood, like a man who is sad, and then he raised his rifle like a man who is filled with hate. He took his time, aimed and moved the muzzle, aimed and moved, deciding on his target. Then he shot the cabin. Splinters flew from the half-open door that stood like a farewell-waving hand. The light faded.

Somewhere behind McDowell a voice was climbing down the range of sorrow. It was running low to high, mournful, like death had just come calling on the one you loved most. Shag's voice was filling the air, calling like the one true voice of all the lament that ever was or ever would be.

Dan McDowell stood, his legs unsteady, and looked around at a warehouse where goods were stacked beneath shadow-making night-lights. He braced himself against a carton. He felt cold sober, although he knew that was not possible. He felt weak, hopeless. He did not know where his feelings of dread were coming from. The presence was gone. The dread had to be coming from himself.

"We got to help that pore dog," the Citizen said. "That sonovabitch is nigh losin' his mind." The old man stood, a little unsteady. He braced on his cane as he walked. He did not stagger or bump into anything.

Dan McDowell followed. He felt disembodied, remote. He listened to Shag's voice. It seemed, almost, that between the calls of the hound, he could hear Margaret's voice. There was no lilt. The words were not articulated the way you really had to do to get contrast and emphasis when you were sick and blue and trying to say how you felt.

"I wish Enoch hadn't had to run away," McDowell muttered. "Them folks never even got their place fixed up."

The old man snorted.

"Enoch didn't have to run," he said. "There wasn't a man in the county who wouldn't have helped him. There wasn't a lawman anywhere who would have said he done wrong." He snorted again. "But that was back then, wasn't it? That was back before this goddamn world got cheap." He waved the cane at Dan McDowell like he was about to thrash him. "They left 'cause they couldn't live there anymore. Enoch's woman couldn't stand it." The old man looked at Dan McDowell and shook his head. He was disgusted. "I worry about you some," he said "but I'm more worried about that dog. That dog may be the last person in the world that understands anything."

Chapter 13

WHEN THEY ENTERED THE OFFICE, SHAG DID NOT MAKE A FOOL OF himself, bouncing or whining or wagging his tail. He greeted the Citizen with quiet but mournful hound dignity. When the old man took a chair behind his desk, Shag lay beside him. Dan McDowell, who knew something about dogs, knew that Shag was dangerous. Not even a ghost had better approach the Citizen. McDowell had first appreciated the dog for its form and beauty and breeding. Now he appreciated it for its character. He told himself that you might look through a hundred of the best dogs and not find one as aware and single-minded as Shag.

He thought again that the dog had no business here. Its place was the hills. This dog could run a fox all night. It was a match for the best fox ever born.

Of course, how could you ever really tell about a dog until you heard it run. Then he told himself that, no, probably, very probably, you could tell. There was an almost invisible sense of authority that the best hounds owned. Shag had as much of that authority as any dog Dan McDowell had ever seen.

"He's trained to fox?" McDowell said it like a question, but it was a statement and a compliment.

"He's born to fox," the old man said. "Them you got to train ain't worth shit." He was fiddling around in his pocket, pulled out keys, and unlocked the desk. In the well-lit office the old man seemed frail, but vital. His white hair and large-nosed face seemed to hover in a weakened manner above his muscular arms and heavy shoulders.

"Even the borned ones can use training."

"Naw," the old man said, "They train themselves. I've seen little spraddle-legged pups that had to be tied, else they'd hunt too soon and a fox would kill them." He reached into the lower drawer of his desk.

The Citizen really did keep whiskey in his desk drawer. He really did not hide it from Sammy.

"Fox is tricky," the old man said. "They're ain't a man born can outfox a fox when it's running. Any sonovabitch shoots a fox and brags on it, well, that man is sorry." He pulled out a couple of glasses. This time he poured slow and measured. His actions seemed more social than sociable. "A'course, sometimes fox get to stealin'. A farmer just has got to shoot, but the sonovabitch ought never to brag about it." The Citizen stood, leaned across the desk and passed a glass to McDowell. Shag raised his head, watchful and ready to move. The old man sat down heavily, rather than easing into the chair.

"I'll tell you what I figger," he said, "but I want you to tell me what you figger first. What in hell was going on back there?"

"Pop," McDowell said, "do you want an explanation, or do you want what I think?"

"Try both. I'll sort 'em out."

"The explanation is that we were hallucinating. Now that ain't a bullshit explanation." McDowell held up his hand, grabbing for quiet. "I'm not telling you what I think. I'm telling you the explanation. That word, hallucination, is the first word those high-price doctors are gonna use. They'll use it whether them doctors are paid by you or Samantha."

"I know what I saw." The old man's face was starting to get red. He looked like he was about to reach for his cane and give McDowell a thumping.

"Pop," said McDowell, "shut your goddamn mouth. You all the time stomping around. You ask questions and then you don't listen." It was the first time in his whole life that he had ever told the old man to shut up. He did not know what to expect. All he knew was that he felt edgy and angry.

The old man looked at McDowell in disbelief and sat silent for a moment. Then he grinned. "The boy's shit stinks a little bit after all," he said. "Tell me."

"Hallucination is when the mind makes its own real things," McDowell explained. "The things aren't real to the rest of the world, but they are real to the guy who is making them." He paused, trying to keep it simple. The best way to get the old man mad was to start throwing psychology at him. "Sane people do it sometimes," he said. "They usually do it when they're going through real hard times."

"That's all thee-o-retical. Don't amount to nothing."

"Cuss it if you want," McDowell told him. "People do it. Sane people do it." He told himself that he was not going to explain a word beyond that. The more he explained the more the old man would say he was lying. He sipped at the whiskey but still felt cold sober.

"Okay, college boy, now what do you think?" The old man's voice was not thick with whiskey; it was thick with scorn.

"We weren't hallucinating," McDowell said helplessly. He was not about to tell the old man that he had seen the ghost off and on for years. "We aren't real drunk, and we're no crazier than we ever were—at least you don't seem to be. I don't know what I think. " He leaned back in his chair, sipped at the whiskey, and wished he could hear Margaret's voice. Better yet, he wished he were with Margaret, not just hearing her voice. If you were going to make a wish, you might as well make a good one.

The Citizen seemed pleased. He stopped acting social and became sociable again. He reached down and touched Shag's head. The dog eased up toward his hand, but it did not lose any of its alertness.

"I got hope for you. You maybe ain't too muddled after all."

"I'm muddled," McDowell admitted. "I don't understand."

"Then you're in the majority."

"What do you think, Pop?"

"Enoch done so good," the old man muttered. He seemed to be talking to himself. He looked at his whiskey glass like he wanted to dive into it. "I'd have done the same had there been occasion."

McDowell wondered if his father was drunk, or just wandering in his mind. The old man's answer was inappropriate. It seemed as if the Citizen had momentarily forgotten that Dan McDowell was present.

"What do you think, Pop?"

The Citizen seemed immersed in some kind of despair or sadness. "I think the times have passed me by when I wasn't even paying attention." He leaned back, pushed the whiskey to one side of the desk, and continued to look sad. "Now, I know you don't want to hear no stories about the old days."

McDowell told himself that if the old man had ever spoken the truth in his life he had surely done so then. McDowell did not want to sit up half the night listening to stories.

"So I won't tell them," the old man said. "But I'll tell you this. Enoch McDowell ain't cursed. He's not doomed to walk for what he done. Get it out of your head."

"I never had it in my head," McDowell protested. Again he felt helpless. "I don't know nothing about this kind of stuff, Pop."

"I do," said the old man. "Only it got less important with the years. Had a family to raise, a business to run. Had a big depression and that shyster Roosevelt." He was suddenly indignant. His face got red and his eyes were nearly bulging. "A'course it got less important," he hollered. "Why the hell shouldn't it?"

"No reason why not," McDowell said politely. He told himself that if talk turned to politics he was going to get away like he was smoke in wind.

"I was raised with haunts," the old man said. "There's three, maybe four dozen kinds. He reached across the desk and dragged the whiskey to him. He sipped at it like he was taking the first judgmental sip. "The main kinds are them who have to walk and them who bring messages. Enoch is tryin' to tell us something."

"Then I wish he'd say it straight out and cut the clowning." Dan McDowell felt his anger rising, and he did not even know why he was angry. He was fed up, plagued, and drinking in spite of his good judgment. He wanted to walk away from this office and his father. He wanted to climb in the Cad and get out of town.

"He can't," the old man explained. "He has to do it with signs. I don't know why, but that's the way it is. It's the way it always was." He looked like he was peering down a long tunnel of the past, recalling tales. "What we got to do is figure out what it signifies."

"What we got to do is stop that crazy Sammy."

"We'll stop her," the old man said. "You'll explain it to her. The most important thing is to figure out what all this here means." For a moment he seemed simpleminded, but McDowell felt that the old man was speaking with the directness of a simplicity that Dan McDowell had never known.

"Sure," McDowell said. "I'll just explain it to Sammy, and she'll just bust both legs rushing to agree."

"You'll help because I can't do it alone." The old man made it sound simple. He stood. "You and me," he said, "we can hell around all night, but this pore dog needs his sleep." He stretched, yawned, gulped off at least an ounce of whiskey that remained in his glass. "C'mon, Shag," he said, "drive the old man home." The dog thumped his tail, then stood up and looked happy over the prospect of leaving. Shag still did not bounce or make a fool of himself.

"Just a minute, Pop." McDowell stood. "We got nothing figured. Whether you believe it or not, I've got a business to run."

"I dunno," said the old man. "Maybe you really do. Maybe even business has passed me by."

"So let's get something settled."

"It is," the Citizen told him. "You're going to figure what this means. I'm going to figure. We'll talk." He laid the cane on the desk, pretending like it was a toy he did not need.

"We'll talk by long distance," McDowell insisted. "I got to get out of town."

"Talk to Sammy before you do." The Citizen was obviously fatigued. The fatigue bent him, and he forced himself to stand straight. He looked almost longingly at the cane. Then he turned his back to it. "Sammy is dumb," he said. "We got all kinds of time to take care of Sammy. I don't know how much time we got with this other." He turned away and Shag followed. McDowell followed the pair of them, knowing that if he wanted to get out of town he should just do it. There was no reasoning with the Citizen when he was in this kind of mood.

As he followed his father through the warehouse McDowell watched Shag. He told himself that you could not trust many people. You could not even trust many dogs, but you could trust this Shag. The night-lights burned high against the ceiling. McDowell saw the stacks of inventory that looked like crap waiting to be picked up by garbage trucks. The old man had complained about the world getting cheap. Who'n the hell had helped to make it cheap?

Shag was neither tail-up or tail-down. He was pushed forward.

His tail looked like it belonged to a setter. As they approached the spot where McDowell and his father had sat on cases of merchandise, Shag's nose went to the ground where a hound's nose should be. He growled. Shag had a scent, and the scent was alive and hot. He growled again. Then he moved fast and straight on the scent. He called as he ran, the hound cry echoing in the warehouse as Shag headed for the loading dock and the closed overhead doors. He got to the doors and was stopped. He braced, confused and growling, then his nose went back down and he began to hunt.

"You better run that dog," McDowell said in a trembling voice. "You already got him chasing mice."

The old man had stopped walking so that he could admire Shag before calling him off. Now he turned. He looked gaspy, shocked, like he had just been hit with a fist. "Don't lie to me. Don't lie to yourself, neither." He was not concealing his anger or his hurt. McDowell thought that the old man was about to start yelling again, but when he spoke, it was in a low and cold voice. "Enoch ain't playing games. There's blood in this somewhere." The old man turned and called Shag off.

McDowell followed his father and told himself that he had it coming. Common, ordinary hounds might go off running a rabbit or digging for a mouse. He had been insulting to Shag and insulting to his father. To this very minute he had tried to pretend that what he had seen might be hallucination.

When they stepped outside, the hot night closed over them like water. Shag moved around, nose down and hunting. He got as far as the loading dock but picked up nothing. He searched back and forth, back and forth, giving little yips and snorts of frustration. He began to widen his circle until the old man called him off.

"You're right about one thing," the Citizen said. "He's got to be let to run. Dog like that shouldn't be in the city." The old man stood in the hot, humid night with Shag beside him. "I shouldn't have bought him. Only bought him . . ." He fumbled for his car keys and turned to the Lincoln. "Me and your ma did good. We did as good as man and woman ever could do, back home." He opened the car door and the dog jumped into the front seat. The Citizen looked frustrated and sad as he stood in the wet, nearly luminous darkness. "I guess I couldn't help buying Shag." He climbed in the car, started the engine, and did not answer when McDowell said good night. He switched on the lights, backed across the parking lot, nearly ramming a fender into the poplar tree, and then drove away.

McDowell felt like weeping, and it was not because of the whiskey. He looked at his watch. Eleven o'clock. The whole thing had taken only a couple of hours, but it seemed like years. He put his hand to his face. His eyes and cheeks were wet.

Times like this, the hard and confusing times, times of age and sadness, of confusion and fear—were when you needed to love her—needed to love her more than you needed her to love you, even. Times like this—

And if he couldn't have her, he thought, if he could not be with Margaret, then he had only one of two choices. He had booze or he had jazz. He stood in the wet darkness, thinking of his father. Then he remembered it was Monday night. No one would be playing. He could not even have jazz.

He drank in a seedy bar a mile from the hotel, and he drank the stuff scrupulously, like it was medicine.

Chapter 14

THE NEXT DAY DAN MCDOWELL BOUGHT THE HORN. HE SUR-
prised himself when he did, because he already had a pretty good
Conn trumpet sitting in his apartment in Chicago. It was a tangled
kind of day, anyway, what with one more woman and one more
situation.

He woke, feeling groggy, and thinking first of his father and
then of Margaret. He sat on the edge of the bed and thought that
Margaret had gone to the heart of the matter, so to speak. She was
in Georgia. McDowell rubbed his forehead, trying to get the grog-
giness to move in one direction or another. He wondered why
Georgia was so different from Virginia and Kentucky and North
Carolina and Tennessee. Maybe the Citizen knew. It sounded like
the sort of thing the Citizen *would* know.

Although he was in the best hotel in town, the muffled sound
of a television could be heard through the wall. McDowell headed
for the bathroom, but he first pulled the drapes and looked down
into the street.

He could feel the heat down there, in spite of the air-conditioned room. He could sense the heat as it rose in nearly visible
waves. Traffic rolled in colored patterns from as far as he could see,
and that was a long way since he was on the tenth floor. The traffic
was causing more heat with its hot engines, overheated radiators,
and tires that swelled on the baking pavement. He could feel the
heat coming from the brick and concrete on the sun side of buildings. For a moment—but it was a strong moment—he wanted to

crawl back into bed, pull the sheet over him, and sleep until dark.

The Citizen had complained about the world becoming cheap. Dan McDowell seriously wondered if there had ever been a time when the world was not cheap.

Time to get moving. Time to shake off these feelings. Time to shove life back into gear. He had been drunk twice in a week. It was past time to get moving.

He showered and remembered that he had to talk to Samantha. Of course, he had not promised, but the old man had made the obligation for him. He left the shower and again sat on the edge of the bed. It seemed for a moment that he could hear Margaret's voice. She was just humming little hums, like she did when she was practicing a phrase. His mind, which sometimes tricked him, seemed to be trying to trick him now.

Maybe it was not time to get moving. Maybe it was time to start thinking. A man could push facts away for a long while but, McDowell told himself, he had enough experience with being crazy to know that you could not keep shoving feelings away. If you did that for too long, it made you crazier.

Last night's experience changed things. That ghost was no longer just something that showed up occasionally and scared you mindless. It was not just a casual, unexplained occult force. After last night, the ghost was personal. It was someone, or had been. It had been a real man with real problems, once, and that man had lived in a real and dangerous world.

Plus, he told himself, he was now having feelings about the Citizen. The Citizen was no longer just one more mean sonovabitch who pushed his way through life like a bulldozer. Last night McDowell had seen his father cry. He had seen the old man refuse to hit back at Samantha, even when Samantha was doing her best to destroy him. Until this very moment, McDowell had believed that he and the Citizen had absolutely nothing in common. Now he had to admit that they had some history between them.

His father had spent his life wheeling and dealing. His father could deal with the best, and with the absolute worst, of the dealers. The Citizen could handle any shyster who came along. The old man was a tough nut, and nobody, nowhere, was ever likely to deny that. Yet, his father had wept.

He, Dan McDowell, was a dealer. Sometimes he was even a

wheeler-dealer, born to it, bred to it. The only difference between him and the worst of the shysters was the quality of his merchandise, but, he told himself, that was not quite true, either. He told himself that although the Citizen handled junk, that did not make him a shyster. Not exactly. Dan McDowell dressed, then packed to leave the hotel. When he pulled on his boots, the stumped toe gave him just the smallest twinge. It was nearly healed.

That ghost was the ghost of Enoch McDowell. Enoch had not been a dealer. Enoch had been a murderer.

But, McDowell thought, Enoch was not just a murderer, either. Dan McDowell stood before the dresser mirror and looked at his crinkledy face. He did not look the least bit like Enoch McDowell.

For some reason that he could not name, he was reluctant to leave the room. He walked back to the window and looked once again into the streets.

Okay, he told himself, maybe Enoch was a murderer, but at least he had lived *real*. Strictly speaking, you could not even say that Enoch was a murderer. He had killed some men, sure, but killing was not always murder, was it? The men had committed a crime, that, in the south, meant death if you were caught. Enoch had acted the only way a man could act, if that man stayed honest. He had not been a murderer. He had been an executioner.

Except, McDowell thought, there was a little bit of a twist in the story. In the south no man dared to rape a white man's woman, at least in Enoch's time. Even in Enoch's time a man would be taking chances if he raped a black man's woman. Neither black nor white did it, not if they expected to live. Those white boys made the mistake of raping a couple of mixed blood ladies without knowing that one of those ladies had a white husband, even if he was only a jump-over-the-broomstick type of husband.

There was even more to it than that, though. The Citizen had said that there was not a man in that county who would not have helped Enoch. There was an answer for Dan McDowell in the story if he could figure it out, at least he thought there was. In the south there were only two kinds of people, no matter their color. There were southerners and there were rednecks.

Of course, McDowell told himself, that *was* back then. Like the Citizen said, that was back before this world got cheap, before the world turned redneck.

A glimmer of understanding came to him. It seemed to tell part of what Enoch was trying to say. Those neighbor men had been southerners, and in the south a man protected the weak. It made no difference whether they were children or women or slaves. That was the tradition, and it did not go redneck until . . . McDowell paused. *That* was the reason why Georgia was different, and Alabama, and Arkansas. They were in the black belt, the big business cotton belt, those states. McDowell felt slugged. The rednecks had been the dealers, and he, Dan McDowell, was a dealer. He felt sick.

He thought of that good Shag dog, and of the single-purpose integrity of Shag. Dogs had breeding, not principles. Few men had either in this redneck world. It was confusing to think about. For a moment it seemed clear that Enoch McDowell and that good Shag dog had more going for them than he, Dan McDowell did.

Down there in the streets, about five blocks away, someone was hurt or dead. Tiny circles of blue light from a police car and the dull red circles from an ambulance were whipping beneath the shadow of a tall building. A crowd was standing around. The little colored dots of people looked like specks of spray paint against the streets. When you stopped to think about it, as he did now, a siren always meant that you were hearing violence. A siren meant heart attacks or wrecks or shootings. It meant fires and robberies and rapes. Sirens were the sounds of violence, and those whipping lights were the colors of violence.

His mind solved something. The solution clicked into place, like the single tick off the rim when a drummer was tipping over from the pause that comes just before music begins to drive.

That was the reason for the cops. That was why they had to have so many police. Dan McDowell finally understood what made a redneck into a redneck. The rednecks were afraid to be execution-ers. They were afraid to have principles, since they might have to back up those principles. They did not have the integrity of Enoch McDowell, or even the integrity of that good Shag dog. Instead, they hired more police.

It was a sad comment on the state of his world, but it surely did make him feel worlds better. Discovering the difference between Enoch and the rednecks was cause for one of the biggest reliefs Dan McDowell had ever felt.

That was why he had not been able to leave the room. Either his own mind, or Enoch's, if Enoch was here, had not allowed him to leave until he figured this important thing out. For the first time in his life Dan McDowell knew absolutely and surely that he was not just a dealer.

Plus, he told himself with a joy that was as fierce as the celebrating joy of the revenging Enoch, he, Dan McDowell, was not no damn redneck, either.

He turned from the window, picked up his suitcase, and left. He could not exactly say that the presence surrounded him. It was more like a memory of the presence was there.

Time for breakfast. Time for the road. He rode the elevator down and remembered that he still had a little chore to do before leaving this place. When he reached the lobby, he looked around, first at the desk, then into the office directly behind the desk. Through the open doorway he could see the pinstripe guy who had insulted Margaret. He was leaning over a secretary who was seated. The girl was obviously trying to talk of some point about work while guarding her shirtfront. The pinstripe stood beside her. He was trying to be commanding while he also attempted to sneak a look at her tits.

McDowell walked beside the long front desk, turned a corner, and opened the little half-door that led to the area behind the desk, into the office. A kid in a blue suit was at the desk. He looked like he had just graduated from a trade school with a degree in motel management. He looked up, startled.

"Sir?" He flapped his hand in a kind of go-away, useless gesture.

McDowell grinned like he was proud of the kid. Then he walked past the kid and into the office.

The pinstripe priss did not see him. At the end of the office, in a rich-looking cubicle, sat a courtly, Henry Clay-type gentleman. Two secretaries were at desks in a corner of the room. One looked up. She was nearly the spittin' image of Samantha: the tight mouth, the starched look, even the frilly blouse and dark skirt. The other secretary was a sort of washed-out looking blonde.

"May I help you?" The Samantha-type said it in a way that showed in which direction she wanted to help him—toward the city jail.

The pinstripe turned, saw McDowell, and looked like a man

with his weenie caught in tweezers. Then he straightened up and put on his number-one managerial look. His mouth tightened with disapproval. The sonovabitch actually began shooting his cuffs.

McDowell walked forward quickly, as happy with the situation as if he had designed it. From the cubicle office the Henry Clay-type gentleman was getting to his feet. McDowell got within two feet of the pinstripe and stuck out his hand. His face was wearing the kind of enthusiasm a man might have for a winning lottery ticket. The priss was startled. He did not know what to do. He did the civilized thing. He took McDowell's hand.

McDowell pumped the priss's hand with complete, boyish enthusiasm, while telling himself that it was like holding six ounces of freeze-dried shit.

"Sonny," McDowell drawled, "I want to con-grat-u-late you. You are one lucky man." He did not release the priss's hand. He just kept pumping away at it. From the corner where the secretaries sat came first the sound of a giggle, and then the sound of a sniff. Mc-Dowell figured the giggle came from the blonde lady, and the sniff came from the Samantha-type. The Henry Clay gentleman arrived.

"Sir? Lucky?" The priss kept trying to retrieve his hand. "What do you want . . ." His voice rose, a little hysteric. He pulled back and McDowell released him. The priss nearly fell on his pin stripe ass.

"Because," McDowell drawled happily, "you ain't been hurted none."

"Shall I ring for security?" The Samantha-type was speaking with the same slow heat as Dan McDowell.

"Please explain what you are doing, sir." The Henry Clay gentleman's voice was soft, commanding, and in complete control. McDowell loved it. The man was not playing Henry Clay and Kentucky at all. He was playing Thomas Jefferson and Virginia. The man's Virginia accent and the pace of his language told McDowell that he had an ally. All McDowell had to do was play the same act.

McDowell stopped drawling but kept his accent. He turned to the gentleman in a way that dismissed everyone else in the office. He imagined that he was on the front porch of a plantation's big house being greeted by old massa. He heard his speech become slow and courtly. He gave a tiny sniff as he turned, and he actually seemed to smell gin and mint.

"Sir," McDowell said, "I've been offered an annoyance by the help. I would not want to put you to any trouble over a matter I can handle."

"I am privileged to offer my service. You are my guest, sir." The Thomas Jefferson gentleman's voice had even more ease and authority.

McDowell pretended to hesitate.

"My staff is like family," the gentleman said. "Please state your complaint." If the gentleman did not believe what he said, he certainly looked like he believed it.

"I came here the other day with a lady," McDowell said. "That lady is a little bit brown. Perhaps that is the point." He paused as if he were judiciously studying the problem. Then he appeared to arrive at a conclusion. "The real point," he said, "is that she *is* a lady, and this person was insulting in both manner and action."

The priss backed up. He was in the middle of something he did not understand. He looked ready to shriek. At the same time, he looked like a man who had been caught shoplifting or embezzling. He looked guilty as hell. The gentleman took note of the priss's look, but he remained courtly. He smiled in a quiet, stirrup cup kind of way.

"The young man is from back east," he said. "You have my word that he and I will discuss the problem."

"Your word, sir," said McDowell, "puts me in your debt."

"Not at all, sir," said the gentleman. "The young man is surely in your debt." The gentleman offered his hand in slow motion. McDowell shook hands in firm, slow motion. As he did he realized that he had to leave with dignity. It was a tough situation. You could not just turn around and walk off. He decided to invite the gentleman for a drink. Then he remembered that it was only about nine-thirty AM.

The gentleman was not an imitation. He pulled a gold watch from his vest, shook his head as if he could not imagine how time had flown. "I customarily take a stretch about this time. May I have your company?"

McDowell could have kissed him. "It would be the greatest pleasure, sir," McDowell said.

"Perhaps," said the gentleman, "I can afford both of us a greater pleasure." He turned to the Samantha-type secretary. "Miss Carolyn," he said, "we would be most honored if you would join us."

The lady smiled, slowly, with a show of the least reluctance at first. Then her face lit with a girlish smile. If McDowell had not known it was coming, he would have been surprised by such a smile on a Samantha-type face. The lady asked for a moment to collect herself. She did not tidy her desk, but she did fluff her hair.

"Miss Carolyn is from Lexington." The gentleman accented the word "Lexington" in that courteous and dignified way which told McDowell that the lady was from the Bluegrass and not the Old Dominion. The gentleman was showing courtesy to the lady by respecting her birthplace, but he was also testing McDowell.

McDowell established his credentials. He mentioned a couple of old family names in Lexington, and a couple of racehorses. Neither horse had won major races, but both had been loved. "Nearly thirty years," McDowell said, "since I saw Red Stuart run. Dark, nearly black."

"I remember the animal," said the gentleman.

When they left the office, Miss Carolyn was no longer sniffy. She had her hand on the gentleman's arm, and Dan McDowell could swear that when she smiled at him she emanated the scent of magnolia. Her efficient-looking pose was gone, and she seemed like a young girl, although she could be no younger than Samantha. If the lady had ever been happy or could be happy, she was happy now. McDowell did not understand how folks could promenade in a hotel lobby, but, he told himself, that was, by God, what the three of them were doing.

This squire-ridden, fox-hound, soft-mouth south.

He promenaded beside them to the restaurant, thinking that this was taking more time than he had planned. At the same time, he told himself, it was more than worth it. That pinstripe would think twice before he was ever insulting to another woman. By the time Thomas Jefferson got done with him, the priss would have learned some brand-new things about the south.

Chapter 15

THE CADILLAC SAT IN THE GLOOM OF THE HOTEL GARAGE, BLACK
and beautiful in the subdued light. Exhaust swirled through the
garage in spite of ventilation fans that were supposed to circu-
late the fumes into the street. The bladelike, angular, whale-tail
fins seemed like small sculptures rising above the streamlined
Porsches, Mercedes, and new, abbreviated Lincolns and Cadillacs.
Dan McDowell stood for a moment, admiring his car.

It was nearly eleven AM., and it was going to be one of those
crazy-days. McDowell had known it the moment he stepped from
the hotel. Crazy-days happened two or three times each summer,
and a lot of places had them. In California there was the Santa
Anna wind that blew and blew until people went mad. In parts of
Alaska it was rain. In Montana it was wind-breathing sky. In these
hot, hot southern cities when the temperature was high and the
humidity just right, people got peculiar. Husbands stopped thinking about killing their wives and killed them. Women shot their
husbands. Mothers slapped their children, and there were always
a lot of wrecks. Cops were meaner on such a day, and everyone
seemed in rebellion. Maybe, McDowell thought, they should not
be called crazy-days at all. They were rebellion-days.

In spite of the heat he was feeling comfortable. He figured that
the Henry Clay gentleman and his lady had been together for a
long time. McDowell was happy for both of them. In a world that
was cheap, they were acting like cheapness did not exist. He supposed that they were the way aristocrats in the south had been

when the south had been right. If, that is, this hot-nutted south ever had been right.

Then he momentarily felt like a damned fool. Just because a hotel owner and his woman had taken an hour of their time to entertain a stranger was no reason to get sentimental.

Then he told himself, no, nope. He was not being a fool. All of his life he had objected to junk, he had fought against cheapness. When you ran into courtesy in any form, you ought not be sarcastic.

He pulled from the hotel garage and began searching for a phone. He could not use the phones in the lobby. You did not walk away from your hosts and trot across seventy yards of plush carpet to a pay phone. Of course, he did not know then that he would be spending at least an hour on the phone.

Traffic was brutal. In the downtown area it seemed that every third car was driven by a cop. The sidewalks were easy to watch because of the slow-moving traffic. They were littered with paper, street grime, an occasional broken wine bottle that gleamed green in the direct sun. Storefronts carried going-out-of-business signs. The signs were tattered and old, washed-out letters that were now pink and gray instead of red and black. The stores made a business of claiming to go out of business. There were hockshops, beer joints, credit clothing stores, walk-up apartments, cheap jewelry stores and places that sold used appliances.

That fine, old hotel he had just left now sat like a tall brick monument in the middle of a commercial wasteland. McDowell remembered when this street had been the main drag through Centerville. There had been fine department stores, restaurants, music stores that sold Steinway grands, and custom tailors. Now it was ragtag, cheap, discount, and dirty. The strong sunlight could not clean the dirt away, and the city sanitation department would not.

He pulled into a parking lot that had replaced a tall, nineteenth-century building that he vaguely remembered. It had been curlicued and ornamented with a facade on street level that had been solid marble. Over the wide, tall doorways the large transoms had held stained glass.

Now, the building bulldozed into oblivion, the place was just another parking lot that mostly held older model foreign cars, and a few big cars that loan company people picked up cheap as repossessions.

There was bound to be a telephone in one of these grimy restaurants or bars. The parking lot attendant was an old man whose white hair showed around the billed cap he wore. The cap was black with a splash of red where the parking lot insignia was sewn on. His face was nearly as dark as his cap and wrinkled more than black faces usually wrinkled. In fact, McDowell told himself, this man's face was nearly as wrinkledy as McDowell's. The man walked toward him. He was tired, arthritic, and moved slow. He looked at the Cad, then at McDowell's tailored clothes.

"I won't be long," McDowell told him. He passed the man a couple of dollars as a tip. "Keep an eye on the car."

"Sure," the old man said, "I'll keep an eye on it. It won't bust just because I lookin' at it." The man was not only tired, he sounded bitter as he tucked the two dollars in his shirt pocket.

"Man," McDowell said, "I never met you before. You got no cause for the hates. Not from me."

"You high rollers is all alike," the old man said. He looked out onto the sunny street, at the traffic that squashed together before a red light. "That there street is put together tight as the county farm," he said, "You goin' to get told that you ain't needed."

"I stopped to use the phone," McDowell told him. "I got nothing to do with local business."

"Sure," the old man said. "That's right." He turned away, slumped, and walked off.

McDowell told himself that he would be damned. He had been taken for a lot of different things before, but never for a pimp. Especially, a pimp trying to muscle in on another pimp's territory. He walked away from the parking lot thinking that a man so old should not have to be out here working, breathing exhaust, and looking at whores and winos and street punks.

Not that he had anything against winos, or the general run of whores. In fact, he had a kind of respect for them. They were not part of the majority. They were not *them*.

He walked along the dirty sidewalk. Feelings at least twenty-five years old, from back when he was a kid, seemed to rise up from the dirt and crud on the sidewalk. The feelings seemed like they were dangling right there in the air, like they came from the fading going-out-of-business signs that were drooping and fly specked. A hustler sat at a table in the window of a restaurant. She smiled at him as he passed. It seemed to Dan McDowell that it was pretty early in the day for her to be working. Her bleached hair above her tan face was brushed. At a table next to her, two white hustlers sat, but they were not working. One had a sad, red-marked wino face. The other had either a bad case of nerves or a medium case of speed.

In the south, this steaming, burning, smoke-ridden south, it seemed to McDowell that the only people worth knowing were the ones on the bottom and the ones at the top. As a kid, he had not been able to understand why that should be, or why hustlers and winos were not treated as good as the racehorse owners. Now, at age forty-three, he could not say that he understood it yet.

Here, in this going-out-of-business place, *they* were only represented by the street punks, and by the moocher style of store owner. The punks here were tinhorn Hell's Angels without motorcycles or nerve, as redneck as your average banker.

McDowell paused before a hockshop. Steel grids over the windows were protecting junk. Cheap guns, cheap musical instruments, jewelry and watches. The paper backing in the window was yellowed and cracked .

A little mutt of a country guy came to the open doorway. He had a Syrian-type, going-out-of-business smile. He was dressed in a striped, hockshop suit that had been out of style for twenty years. His balding head, his heavy eyebrows, and his pale hands with bitten fingernails added to his overall looks. At least he was not faking some "honest John the poor man" routine. He really was broke.

"You look like a man hunting," he drawled. "I got what you need."

The guy could not be a pimp. A pimp could not look that seedy.

"Just looking," McDowell told him. "Just dawdling." He was looking at a bunch of junk instruments, an old Pan American pea-shooter trumpet that was only good to club people with, and one of the early Jap guitars that had the tone of a cigar box. A tired-looking Les Paul electric leaned against a ragged-out amp. Lying loose in the window was a cheater mouthpiece, the cup about as deep as a three-day growth of whiskers. The rim looked as wide as a toilet seat. McDowell had seen a dozen of those things, back in the days when guys with no lip wanted to play like Dizzy Gillespie. With a mouthpiece like that, you could even teach a monkey to get up in the range and start squealing.

"I got better stuff in back," the hockshop guy said. "I used to keep it out, but folks don't want that stuff no more." His voice was commercial, persuasive. At the same time, McDowell thought he was hearing something genuine in that voice.

McDowell had to call his office. He had to get out of town. He told himself that he had no time to be fooling around, thinking about what he had been thinking about. Punks and bankers.

The problem, the absolute main problem, was that you never could tell. He, Dan McDowell, had once known a discount man who operated only a few blocks from here. The guy had done business in the old black slum that had now been replaced by the new black and white and Puerto Rican slum. That guy had been an honest John. He was not a soft touch, but when a family was really down, that guy had been good for a loan with no security. Either that, or he had been good for a job. He had been a local good guy, a kind of hero.

You could never tell. Some of the bankers were not punks, and some of the punks were not punks. At the same time, some of the horse owners were rednecks. Up north you could tell about a man pretty much from the very first time you met him. In the south, even some of the winos were gentlemen.

"I'm in a hurry," McDowell said. "Have to hurry with my dawdling, but I'll take a look." He was not sure why he was agreeing to this but he followed the man down the single aisle of the shotgun type store. The display counters on each side were those large, blocky old things with heavy glass that had been made in the '20s. It was like walking down an alley where the walls were inset with junk. Glass jewelry, wedding rings for one-night stands that, of course, were outmoded now, but McDowell could remember days when it was smart to carry one. A ragtag group of old military insignia that the hockshop guy had picked up from some distress Army-Navy store. Clutter. Trash.

At the back of the room, above and behind a counter, were a bunch of instrument cases. The guy walked to the one he obviously prized the most, pulled it down and opened it. The way he lifted the lid, he might have been opening a case containing diamonds.

It was a tenor sax, a first line Buescher, which meant that it was one fine saxophone. Or had been. The pads were shot, and when McDowell touched some of the keys, the spring action was too soft. The mouthpiece was chewed to hell, chomped on one side. The guy had played out of the side of his mouth, the way you do if your teeth didn't grow in right. The mouthpiece looked like mouthpieces did when a guy lived with a favorite one in his chops for years. McDowell looked at the mouthpiece and felt sad. Almost surely the guy was dead. This was a professional horn, and that was a favorite mouthpiece. Nobody did that much to a mouthpiece and then got rid of the horn. The horn could be fine again, if somebody reconditioned it and loved it.

"I used to play a trumpet," he said to the hockshop guy. "But you're right about this horn. Nobody's gonna come looking for one this good." He flipped the tag on the case. The guy was asking four hundred, which meant he would take three.

"Trumpets I got. I got a bunch of them, an' I got a cornet." Before McDowell could say anything, the guy turned and dragged down a couple more cases. He snapped one open. The cornet was one of those big bore, big-sized German outfits that had come in during the early '60s. It was a concert horn, silver, dull gleaming, and the flowered etching around the bell was as precise as McDowell knew the valve sleeves would be. It was a beautiful, beautiful horn, but it belonged in a philharmonic.

"An' then," the guy said proudly, "I got this."

McDowell recognized the Olds case before he even saw the trumpet. The case was beat up like ten thousand nights on-the-road. He thought he knew what he was going to see before he saw it, and he was right.

It was, strictly speaking, an antique, one of the first professional horns Olds made after the Second World War. It lay in the case, gold and silver, and it carried the offset middle valve built on the theory that you needed it because your second valve finger was longer. It had the kickout slide for the little finger, so dumb bastards like McDowell would not sharp out when they went for low D.

He picked it up with the same reverence he had felt when he pulled that Cadillac emblem from that pile of junk. Some things were beautiful. Some things had every bit as much right in this world as a masterpiece painting. Things that were true never got old; they only got more true. This trumpet, which was a tool, was every bit as true as the first time anybody figured out how to make a wheel.

He fingered the valves. They were a little stiff, but not as stiff as they should be from sitting so long. Either the valves were badly worn, which he doubted, or the sleeves were still true.

"You got oil?" He picked up the mouthpiece. A Bach #4. Sometime or other, this horn had been used by a kid. That was a standard, beginner, utility mouthpiece. Maybe a kid playing his father's old horn, and wishing for something that had more shine. The silver casing over the valves was worn. This horn had seen a lot of nights.

The hockshop guy was rummaging in the showcase while Mc-Dowell turned the horn up. The pads were thin, the corks dry. He pulled on the slides. Stiff, but they moved. Then he blew through the thing, making no sound, testing the slides and valves. Before he opened the valve case he knew that the bore was true. The hock-shop guy passed him the small bottle of oil. He was keeping his big mouth shut, and that was the mark of a good salesman. So many sales were lost when a salesman got nervous and oversold.

"I need a horn," McDowell said, "like I need my head bored for more nostrils."

The guy remained silent.

"I need a horn," McDowell said, "like a preacher needs the clap."

"I hope this weather breaks before Friday night," the guy finally said. "That street out there is heatin' up. Folks are getting nervous. Gettin' crazy."

One thing anybody learned early in the sales business was that there was no sucker like a good salesman when he was in the hands of another good salesman. McDowell grinned as he removed the valves. There was practically no way this guy did not have a sale, but McDowell waited to see if he would fuck it up. The valves were dry but pretty clean. He began oiling them. "It's always that way," McDowell said. "Hot Friday night after a hot week. Folks get to drinkin'."

"They get sweaty and blue," the guy said. "A'course they do it. Why the hell not do it?" He sounded like he was answering Mc-

Dowell, like he was talking about the street, but the inflection in his voice was saying do it, *you'll never get another chance on one like this*.

The guy was so good that McDowell wanted to hire him. "Hold your pore ears," McDowell said, "I ain't played a note in years." It was not the truth, but it was nearly the truth.

The valve action was even better than the action on that good Conn back in Chicago, and, he reminded himself, that Conn was absolutely clean. This horn still needed to be cleaned. McDowell pulled air into his gut, tried to set an embouchure, then ran a chromatic scale. The tone was not bad, not bad at all for a guy with custard lips and a jaw like busted rubber bands. The notes seemed to brighten up the dark tunnel of the store like the sunlight that framed the front doorway. To McDowell the notes were a total contradiction to all of the crap in the showcases. He growled a low F, on down through D, and the D went sharp. He tried it again, kicking the slide. At the same time he lipped it down. The D went flat. He tried it without lipping. The D came in true. There was not a thing more you could say.

He stood holding the old horn that had been made in '46 or '47. If he had been on this thing since the time it was made, then this old horn could talk with the best. It was a damned sad thing to think about.

He flipped the little paper tag tied to the handle of the case. The guy wanted three hundred.

"That's what it cost new," McDowell complained. "That was exactly the new price."

"All in how you look at it," the guy said. "That was a month's wages then, if you had a good job. It's a week's wages now." He picked up the concert cornet, but he did not pick it up like it was merchandise. He stood looking at the horn like there was a mystery in there, like he had important instructions that were written in a foreign language. "This one," he said, "was about eight hundred new. Eight was six week's wages back then. I'll let it go for four. A better deal."

McDowell thought that this guy was a genius. Any good salesman tried to take what you wanted away from you just at the moment he figured you were about to decide. McDowell could not figure what this guy was doing running a two-bit hockshop. He was not only selling the horn, he was selling his price. He was taking away by offering a better deal on something as good.

McDowell told himself, what-the-hell. He knew he could get it for less, but, standing and holding the horn, it seemed insulting to the horn to argue. Nobody in the whole world was going to understand that. Then he told himself, no, nope; Margaret might understand that.

"Of course," McDowell said, "a guy would need a mute." It was only a statement to save face. Mutes were cheap as mud, or nearly.

"And oil," the guy said. "Which those things are naturally on the house." He reached into the showcase and pulled out a new cup mute. Then he seemed to be recalling something. "You hang onto that," he said. "Meanwhile, I got one of them old extension things around here somewhere." He knew right where it was. He pulled down one of those Conn cases that were designed to carry everything including your lunch and a change of clothes. He pulled out a dented, beat-up, wah-wah mute. He placed it on the counter. "I wish," he said, "that someone who liked nice things would buy that sax."

McDowell had to hand it to him. He could close a sale just as well as he could make a sale. There was nothing else to do but pay up and be happy. McDowell paid, and he was happy. He felt eager, like he stood in front of some bright possibility. You could always make money, but you could not often have a bright feeling like that.

"None of my business," McDowell said after the sale was complete, "except you are a good salesman. Why'n hell are you hanging around here?"

"I own the place."

"Why this street? There's better streets."

The guy was a nice guy. He had McDowell's money, so he was entitled not to give a damn. He looked at McDowell, and his eyes, momentarily, were shy in spite of his sales knowledge. "Folks do get blue," he said. "Comes Friday night and they look at the paycheck, and the paycheck ain't hardly ever enough. They got to drink. You know that."

McDowell fished for a business card, knowing that it would probably never be used. "Just in case you ever get fed up. I can always use a salesman."

143

The guy looked at the heavy, textured card and recognized the company. Instead of sticking the card in his shirt pocket, he pulled out his wallet and tucked it away. "I get fed up all the time," he said, "but a'course that's not the point." He looked embarrassed, like he wished McDowell would leave, or like he wished he did not have to say what he had to say. He pointed to the front of his store, to the sunlight that formed a square at the entry. "Nobody has ever died in that doorway," he said. "They pass out. They get beat up, fucked up, drugged up and drunked up, but nobody has ever died in that doorway." He turned away, packing the silver cornet and the saxophone back onto the racks. He did not turn back, and McDowell, knowing it was past time to be gone, walked away from the man's embarrassment. That bright and hopeful feeling ought to be gone, he knew, but somehow it just seemed more bright and hopeful.

Chapter 16

His manager in Chicago was so sharp that McDowell figured he would lose her in another two or three years. He knew he was training his future competition and had told himself a dozen times that he did not give a lordly damn. Nance came to him through his sales department, back when he was just getting started. They made some astounding mistakes together, and some gorgeous successes. If Nance were not married, they would have made even more mistakes and successes. Dan McDowell was not particularly in favor of marriage, but he respected the condition.

He walked the dirty, sunlit street and looked forward to the phone call. The oppressive heat had him sweating all over, armpits, crotch; and his feet felt damp and steamy in the Wellington boots. The trumpet case was light in his hand. It tapped against his leg as he walked. He wanted, among other things, to have Nance send a couple of nice presents from inventory to that gentleman and lady at the hotel. That was the sort of polite thing you could do, when everyone was acting civilized.

Life would change when Nance left. Almost any manager would nudge you a little, and some would steal you blind. Nance was honest. Her scrupulous attention to the business made him money by saving him money. Plus, she put up with him.

He found a joint not far from the hockshop. It was like a dark tunnel after the bright, sunlit street. Two old men sat at the far end of the long bar. One was studying a racing form while the other nursed a glass of wine. Neither talked, but the one with the racing form stood up to walk behind the bar, limping. His bald head was sweaty, and sweaty grime lay in the lines of his face. He looked at McDowell with a resentful look, like McDowell was slumming. Then he saw the horn case and his look changed. It became indifferent, but he obviously no longer thought McDowell was slumming. The old man's eyes were blue and sort of dull. He fanned himself with the racing form.

"Bottle a' beer," McDowell said.

"That hog-head," said the old man. "You gonna be working for him?" He swatted at a fly with the racing form. The fly kind of hopped drunkenly sideways, then settled back on the bar. The second time he smacked, the old man killed it. He turned to the cooler for the beer.

"I'm just passing through."

"'S fucking credit to you," the old man said.

"Which hog-head? He own a joint?"

"Shit, he owns the street. He owns this joint." The man turned away, rang the sale, then turned back. "If you ever do work for him, you'll learn, boy, you'll learn."

"He'd ought to buy an air conditioner," McDowell said.

"He'd ought to in-stall an air conditioner," the old man said. "The sonovabitch prob-ably owns a million of 'em." He once more turned away, limping along the bar, and took his seat beside the other old man.

McDowell walked to the phone that hung on the opposite wall. He stood the trumpet case beside the phone, then called.

Fat Martha, his best secretary, answered. She tossed him a ration of sheer, humorous b.s., and then transferred the call. Nance came on the phone doing her mother-number. McDowell loved her when she did it, because they both absolutely knew it was down-the-road play-acting. Nance was from east of Knoxville.

"You haven't called in a week. You been out sinning?"

"I've been counting my socks," McDowell told her, "in case I'm losing 'em." For a moment he felt homesick for her. She was a tiny, bright, dark-haired lady with brown, kind of oval and Indian-type eyes. She had a mind that could juggle a thousand facts and keep every one of them straight. Her grandfather had been killed in a mine, and her pop had been shot up during the coal wars of the late '50s. Nance had been sharp enough to look around, and then buy a bus ticket.

"You bin to In-dian-ap-o-lis?" She was drawing the admonishing mother-number.

"Can't seem to get out of this town."

"Don't," she told him. "I got a line on some good goods."

She had found a source for handcrafted solid cherry furniture in Centerville. A three-man factory, which meant limited supply, but the design looked good.

"How do we stand with the bank folk?"

"Right now we own the bank," she told him, "but the catalog is burning out. You know it."

When you distributed good stuff, you had to constantly vary the inventory. You could not slop along on standard schlock from one year to the next, which, of course, is what Samantha and the Citizen did.

"And," she said, "what in the ever-lovin' world is a lutist?"

"There's a dictionary on my desk."

"I already know," she told him. "I just wanted to know if you did."

"It's a fancy name for a fiddle maker."

"If you get down around Ashland, you may want to take a look." She told him of a hill town where she had a line on dulcimers, real dulcimers.

"And when you make Indianapolis," she told him, "there's a guy who is doing functional sculpture in solid brass."

"What in the hell is functional sculpture?"

"That," said Nance, "is heaps more than I understand, but check it out."

The horn sat at his feet, more muted by his inability to play it than any mute could ever do. He took the addresses and mentioned the hotel people. Going through the motions, he felt lonesome. He thought of Margaret, of Nance, and, not surprisingly, of Becky. The many, many women, and yet only a few were really memorable and close. He thought again that Nance would be leaving in a few years. Another woman lost, another empty space in the heart.

"Plus," Nance said, "you got a call from your singer-lady. The bitch."

"If you ever shed a husband," he responded automatically.

Meanwhile he was shocked. Margaret would not be calling unless it was important. She was not the kind who would waste her time or his.

"I never will," Nance told him. "I got myself a one-woman man."

You *loved* them, and sometimes it seemed like you loved all of them. But the curious, strange, improbable part was that they loved you back. They said it with jokes, or with bitchiness, or with play-acting. They said it in muted, incredible, silver-voiced ways.

It was not just fucking: it was not. They really loved you, but the shape of life, and the being trapped in a single body, kept them from loving all that they could love. Right then, with the unforeseen fact of Margaret's call, he loved Nance as much as he loved Margaret. He loved Becky as much as he loved Nance, and he had not seen Becky in years.

As he took Margaret's phone number he stood with the phone sweaty in his hand, his sweat caused by the heat of the beer joint, or the closeness of memory. He could almost see Nance, the way she sort of leaned forward over her desk. She did it so she would look commanding, because she was so goddamn little. No woman had ever said of him that he was a one-woman man, but that is what he had always wanted to be, had always tried to be.

"Dan," she said, and her voice still sounded sort of mother-like "are you doing okay?"

"Shore," he lied. "And mostly sober."

"Dan," she said, "drive that goddamned thing careful." Then her voice became all business, and she ended the conversation.

He hung up the phone. She always said that, always. What she did not understand, or maybe she did, was that there were wrecks all around him but not car wrecks. There were life-wrecks, Samantha, and maybe the Citizen, and maybe, just maybe, himself. He touched the horn case with the toe of his boot, took a gulp of the beer, and called Margaret. The good day, the special day, began to change.

"Where you at, Dan?" Her voice was brisk. No greeting, no words about love.

"Where you left me," he told her. "Trying to get out of town."

Margaret sounded more desperate than the situation seemed to call for. Peg had broken up with her man, her guitarist, and Peg was drinking.

That was an automatic wreck, right there. You could sing or you could drink, but sure as hell you could not do both.

"I still have a week and a half here," Margaret said. "And Peg still has a weekend there."

"I'll do what I can."

"I don't want to ask," Margaret said. "I just hate to, Dan, but I'm asking."

For one thing, he told himself, he felt both foolish and awkward. He was talking to the woman he loved, a woman he was willing to try to stay with, in spite of the fact that he was only seeing her once a month. He had been thinking of her constantly, and now, talking to her, he just felt clumsy.

"I got to be in town for a couple more days."

"She can't do it without a backup guitar."

In McDowell's opinion, Peg could not do it without a backup marching band, but he kept his trap shut. He told himself that the country audience was so ignorant that three twangs and a slide on any guitar could probably get past.

"She does this about every three years," Margaret said. "The last time was in St. Louis." Her voice sounded totally sad, and totally pissed. For a moment McDowell almost thought that she was angry with him. He felt guilty, kind of, and did not know why. The horn sat beside his foot, quiet, and somehow without as much of the bright promise as it had before.

It was a lousy conversation. He felt his own anger, or resentment, or disappointment. He could not say what it was. He decided that this call was either going to be real, real good, or it was going to be a catastrophe. He was not going to put up with this. "Now let's just slow down," he drawled. "I got time to mobilize that child, and you can't do anything by worryin'. So let's us just slow this whole thing down."

She picked up on the drawl, on the seriousness of what she was hearing. "Dan," she said, "you're right. Dan, talk to me." Her voice changed entirely. It was no longer pressing forward. It was gentle-like. Loving-like.

If only she were not almost a stranger. He knew her body, and he knew something about her heart because of the music. He knew her shyness, and he knew her professionalism. But he did not know anything about her fears or sorrows. You had to be with somebody for a long time before you understood things like that. And when you were in her business, you walked a narrow, dangerous line. Maybe Peg was making Margaret afraid, because Margaret knew that she was not all that far from stepping over the line, herself. Maybe.

"I wanted to change the subject," he drawled, "because I remember you so much." He could feel the day turning bright again as he said it.

"I wish you were here," she said, "or me there. I've been doing some remembering myself."

The phone conversation became what he hoped it would be. They were still new to each other, still just barely touching some of the personal feelings and memories. By the time they had talked for another twenty minutes he was more in love than ever.

"What," she said finally, "has been keeping you in town?"

"My pop," McDowell told her. "My sister is trying to railroad him." For some reason, probably because he was feeling loved, he did not exactly lie. Besides that, he thought, this whole craziness with Enoch was a part of him. If she loved him, the craziness was a piece of the package. And besides that, he thought, it was a relief to say some of this stuff to someone who loves you.

"He's seeing something," McDowell admitted, "and the old bastard is no more crazy than he ever was."

Margaret giggled. He could not remember her doing that very much, although he remembered the little-girl act that she sometimes pulled. "I see them all the time when I'm working," she said. "This call is costing a million dollars, I bet."

"Tax write-off," McDowell said automatically. "Anything that's on the credit card. Meanwhile, are you kidding?" His voice was way too serious, and he knew it.

"No." Her voice was every bit as serious. "I don't doubt he is seeing something."

"You mean hallucinating?"

"Nope. If you see it, and you're not crazy, then it's real, even if it may not be real to the rest of the world."

"But purty doggone hard to explain." The seriousness just would not leave his voice.

"You don't explain it, at least not with graphs." She took a deep breath. "You've been in front of those lights, Dan. Years ago, maybe, but you've been there. You know what the music does. Dan, some-times I actually see a lady out there in the lights, and that lady is Bessie Smith." She took another deep breath. "Dan, what'n the hell do you think it's all about? Amusement? Only for amusement?"

"Naw. You know better than that."

"Those echoes are what's different with jazz," Margaret said. "And with folk, and revival. Joplin might not be dead right now if she had understood that."

He was not following her, but his feelings understood what she said.

"I'm spending your money with this foolishness. We'll talk later." Then she seemed to think better of it. "Look, sweet babe, we don't belong to the modern world."

"I thought I did."

"Dan, doggonit, there weren't even any factories in these parts until this century. Our people are still going through the fucking industrial revolution."

"It takes some thinking about."

"They're dying out," she said, "these people who come back to tell us things. But those old people who tell things were always real. They might be dying out, but what is left is still real.

"I'll call you as a witness for the defense."

"Let's try to get together soon," she said. "It's important."

"And getting more so."

"Maybe I can find a day between here and Pittsburg."

"Or maybe I could get to Pittsburgh."

"We could talk." Her voice sounded wistful. "We could make love and lay together and talk and talk."

Even after the good conversation, after the love talk, what she said, together with the wistfulness, made him feel slugged with love and lonesomeness. He wanted to lie beside her for the rest of his life, talking.

"I'll be in Pittsburgh," he said. "Count on it." He nudged the trumpet case with his toe. He told himself that he could damn near see the horn shining through the case. He could damn near hear it singing, as sweet mouthed as that good Shag dog. When Marga-ret finally closed the conversation and hung up, McDowell stood for a couple of minutes beside the phone. He did not want to get moving, not just yet. He drained the beer, which had gone flat and awful warm. He had the address of Peg's motel. Plus, he had to call Samantha. He stood, remembering Margaret, and then realized that he had to get moving.

Samantha could damn well wait. The Citizen had been keeping his ass covered for seventy-one years. He could keep it covered for another day or two. Right now, he, Dan McDowell, had to get a heartsick lady sober and keep her that way. It was the least, the very least, that he could do for Margaret. He picked up the horn, gave a backward wave to the two old men who were paying no attention to him, or to each other. At least when you stepped out onto the street, after being in a joint without air conditioning, you were already hot. The heat did not slug you like a fist.

Chapter 17

A LADY COP CHECKED HIM OUT WHILE HE WAS STOPPED AT A RED light. The crazy-making weather was still holding firm. It was still rebellion-day, and McDowell wanted nothing to do with any cop on this kind of day. The patrol car looked like an advertisement for soap and wax. So did she. She was one of those marine-type super cops with a butch haircut. She eyed Dan McDowell like she was taking the pulse on a nest of rattlesnakes. The temp on the Cad was running a little hot because of the air conditioning. McDowell was headed for Peg's motel, and he was practicing on the mouthpiece.

You could not play the horn just anywhere, but you could play the mouthpiece. It would not do a thing to help your manual dexterity, or help relearn the fine balances of fingering. But if you played the mouthpiece, you could build up the lip and the embouchure. If you played it long enough, it was even possible to do something for your musical attack.

The tall buildings were casting practically no shadows with the sun nearly straight up. It burned on the canvas top and liner of the convertible. The sun was like a giant staple that held every thing in place. The traffic light changed and the cop moved away.

McDowell played the mouthpiece and waited for the pickup in front of him to make its left turn. When your lip was soft, you could get almost no sound at all unless you pressed. He practiced at not pressing. He knew that even if he practiced correctly his lip was going to feel like used hamburger for the first couple of weeks.

He cleared the light just as it changed, and just as a siren began wailing. The siren was not far off, and it was approaching fast. It had the heavy, full throat of a fire siren. *They* were holding another fire, renewing the town. McDowell tucked the mouthpiece into his shirt pocket, got both hands on the wheel, and watched his mirrors for an opportunity to change lanes. The fire was somewhere straight ahead. Traffic was already becoming more compressed. He wanted to turn off of the street before he got caught in a jam. He snapped the lane change when a small empty space came along. Behind him, in his mirrors, a horn began blaring as an indignant madman piloting a new tinkle-bell Ford expressed his concern with the way the world was operating.

Margaret believed in ghosts. Apparently, she even knew why they existed.

The whisper of the Cad's air conditioning covered the smooth idling of the engine after traffic had him stopped. The maniac in the Ford was leaning over his wheel, cursing and sobbing. The tin pot Ford looked like a red-painted roller skate, and the madman was just as red. Now he was pounding on the steering wheel with his fists. Ahead of McDowell was a distressed-looking '70 Dodge, and ahead of that a dented, rusty dump truck that blocked the view.

Other sirens began to join in, and they were not far away. Police sirens were whip, whip, whipping at the sunlight. Traffic nudged ahead a few feet. McDowell figured that the lady cop had made it to the intersection and was directing traffic. Another fifty feet ahead an alley cut off to the right. It was one way, going the wrong way. Do Not Enter signs were keeping drivers from doing the sensible thing. Either that, or the alley was blocked because a truck was unloading.

Of course, he told himself, thinking of Margaret, Margaret had been raised black. Her folks and her grandfolks would have been even closer to the old tales and superstitions than were McDowell's.

He blew into the mouthpiece and told himself, no, nope. Margaret was analytical because of her professionalism. If she believed in something, she would know why she believed it.

The madman behind him was getting crazier and crazier. Now he was hunched up over the wheel like he was ready to plow through the back end of the Cad. He began bouncing in his seat, and even in his mirrors McDowell could see the little Ford start bobbing beneath the weight of the bounce.

There were so many, many, unhappy, torn-up, and crazy people. You saw them everywhere, but only in these hot, hot cities did you expect to meet one about every third block. McDowell figured that the guy was riding some frustration, and blaming it on something else. McDowell could remember other days when he had done the same thing. He told himself that probably, very probably, the guy's wife was working him over, and he was also late for an appointment. He would be blaming all of his sorrows on the traffic. Either that, or he would feel guilty and cursed.

The madman took the chance. The guy spun his wheel, eased the red Ford up to the curb, goosed the gas, and climbed onto the sidewalk. The car almost did not make it, and as it buzzed along the sidewalk McDowell could see where the high curb had taken a bite out of the thin steel just in back of the door. The driver was a thin, wild-eyed man with a lantern jaw that was pushed forward like a battering ram, or like he was hoping the world would slug it. His dark hair was crew cut above his white shirt, and McDowell told himself that the guy's hair was the only thing about him that knew where it stood. The little Ford cruised the sidewalk, heading for the alley.

A thin old woman wearing a black shirt and a purple skirt was coming from the doorway of a used furniture store. Her white hair shone, like it had been rinsed with bluing in the wash water. The Ford nearly brushed her as it passed. She stood, bewildered, as the Ford came off the curb at the spot where the alley began. It swung right, accelerated, and a sparkle and sprinkle of glass sprayed from beneath the drive wheel and showered against cars in the street. McDowell told himself that the sonovabitch had cut a tire, for sure, and that the world had finally got some good use out of a wine bottle. The old woman sat down in the doorway, her face gaspy and shocked. She was breathing deep and holding her chest, but her face showed fear and not a heart attack. Behind her the little redhead storeowner appeared, his face white beneath the fluff of red hair. He leaned over the woman, talking, then ran to the entrance of the alley and began cursing and shaking his fist.

This crazy-making, homicidal, heat-struck south.

Now another car turned into the alley, then another. The dump truck seemed to hesitate in the hands of its driver. Then it turned into the alley. The Dodge eased ahead; the driver waited to see if the way was clear, and then turned into the alley. McDowell's turn came and he looked into the alley, saw the departing bed of the dump truck about two hundred yards away, and turned his wheel.

The presence was suddenly beside him. It slipped onto the seat as happily as a hitchhiker who had been waiting all day for a ride. The presence seemed companionable, almost, like it was in a good humor.

Then, like someone had flipped a light switch, the Cadillac was sitting in smoke. Flames rose in the smoke, and McDowell could see nothing. He hit the brake. Behind him he was conscious of a horn that was blaring.

The smoke was dark, heavy, and it fumed and swirled and obscured the view from the side windows. Flames burst directly before McDowell's eyes, a roaring column of flame that seemed to descend from the tops of the buildings that enclosed the alley. The roar of fire was the sound of suction, of air being pulled into the column and feeding the flames. McDowell, in terror, stabbed the gas, then stabbed the brake. He would only be driving deeper into the flames. He struggled for the door handle, fighting to get free of the car, to roll away from the fire, to run. The presence at his side was unthreatening. The presence seemed like it was a tourist reading the Sunday funnies in a hotel room.

McDowell's hysteria swelled, was about to break, to release into a scream: a roar like the roaring flames. Then the feeling from the presence stopped him. He reached up with one hand to feel the convertible top. It was no hotter than it ever was in bright sun and with the air conditioner going. The fire was ghost fire, illusionary fire. It was surrounding the car but not touching it.

"Enoch," McDowell said, "Goddammit."

The presence actually seemed to be laughing. The *seeming*, or maybe it was illusion, was like a man come to town on Saturday night. The laugh was don't-give-a-damn Saturday night.

McDowell still could not see anything but flame and smoke. The laughter existed just beyond the range of McDowell's ear, and it was coming from a nearly recognizable voice, rising above the roar of the fire.

Then the laughter changed and a nebulous shape took form on the seat beside him. The roar of the fire began to subside; the smoke became mistier, thinner, and cut with sunlight. McDowell looked through the unsmoked windshield and began to see the length of the alley stretching in front of him. A horn was blatting from a car that had entered the alley after him. The shape on the seat became less distinct, and then it concentrated. The shape pulled together, like it was using what little existence it owned to cover a small space instead of being spread out. For an instant, before he kicked the accelerator and moved out fast, McDowell saw the face that formed and departed as quick, nearly, as a rifle shot. Beside him, the Citizen had sat, and the Citizen had been looking sly. The Citizen had been laughing his ass off in his own sly way.

Dan McDowell drove down the alley faster than was safe. By the time he reached an intersecting street he was weak, shaken, and his fear that had risen so quickly was gone in the face of a new emotion. He was to-tally, ab-so-lutely pissed.

It was bad enough when the ghost had been scaring him witless. He had dealt with that. But now the ghost was somebody, and was acting just as clown-showy as everyone else. There was no dignity to it. Enoch was dead. When you were dead you ought not to be a clown.

This clown show south. This play-acting, game-running, illusiony south. Even the goddamned dead men joked with you right up to two seconds before they killed you.

McDowell hooked the Cadillac from the alley onto a one-way street, pulled to the curb and parked. He was weak, sweating, angry, and feeling insulted. It was bad enough to be haunted, but to be joked with was too much.

Pulled over ahead of him was the little red Ford. The madman knelt beside the car. He was changing a tire. Tears streamed across his cheeks like a flow from broken drainpipes. His short hair glistened with sweat from pushing his hand to his brow and wiping upward. He was changing a tire. The man was in such a desperate hurry that he had not taken off his white shirt. The shirt was striped with gutter grime, and grease from the tire. The madman knelt beside the car, working too fast. He removed the wheel, shoved it to one side, and reached for the spare beside him.

The car leaned, leaned further, and hesitated like it was trying to make up its mind. Then it fell off the jack. It just barely brushed the man as it came down, but it was enough to knock him backward. He sprawled flat on his back and lay for a moment as if he were completely bewildered.

McDowell began to climb from his car, then stopped. He told himself that the guy was not hurt, and the guy was ready to kill somebody.

The guy sat up. The look on his wet face said that he had just seen the end of the world, and he was glad. Glad. He looked at the dirt on his shirtfront, at the little Ford leaned onto the curb, and at the two toy wheels that must seem to him like they were his nemesis. To McDowell, the guy looked like a man who had been waiting for a long time to crack up, and now the crack-up had arrived. He was damned well happy. The direct sun lit his dirtstained, water-running face. The face took a different tone, the lines of tension forming into the shape of determination.

The guy stood up. He moved slow, like he was as normal as any sane man. He reached down, picked up the dinky jack, and hefted it in his hand. He swung it a couple of times. It looked like a miniature baton, and the guy looked ready to lead a parade.

He twirled the jack, or tried to, and then he raised it over his head. He smacked the rear window of the Ford. As he smacked he yelled.

McDowell hit the button and lowered the window on the driver side of the Cadillac.

The guy backed off and kicked the quarter panel of the Ford. As he did he hollered a name, hollering, "Mil-dred Jean, Mildred." He smacked the window with the jack. Then he kicked the door of the car. The chintzy steel crumpled, and the guy looked happy as he kicked it again; and yelled again, yelling at Mildred Jean. Then, in a madman systematic way, he circled the car, breaking all the glass; and yelling the name. McDowell told himself that Mildred Jean had to be hearing this, even if she was as far away as Ashtabula. The guy was busy whacking the accessories from the car, aerial, mirror, lights. After he had broken everything he could find, he jumped on the hood and began bouncing and hollering at Mildred Jean. The hood dented, drooped, the guy lost his balance and fell into the street still yelling the name.

He stood up, reached in his pocket for his knife, and began scoring the paint.

A crowd was forming. Two winos stood on the far side of the street, squint eyed and openmouthed. Beside them three little black kids whooped and hollered and tried to get up enough nerve to cross the street and help destruct the car. McDowell sat, ready to climb from the Cadillac and warn them if they came. The madman had not worked his way through his sorrows, not yet. He could still be dangerous.

Further down the street, a group of concerned citizens was forming. Men in short-sleeved shirts and business pants stood beside women in washed-out housedresses. A couple of storeowners wore ties, and there were a couple of secretaries. The crowd increased, gesticulating, laughing, and the people were shaking their heads. The madman was paying no attention to them. He was emptying a briefcase, wadding up papers, and getting ready to set the car on fire. He was hollering at Mildred Jean.

McDowell shoved the Cadillac in gear and pulled away fast. In his rearview mirror he saw the blue circling light of an approaching police car. He told himself that it was even odds whether the madman would get that thing burning in time.

As he drove Dan McDowell found himself laughing like a madman. He was laughing with Saturday night don't-give-a-damn. He was sad for the madman, but he was happier for him than he was sad. The guy had finally, at least once in his life, done some thing that could not be hedged. He had committed a real, genuine, definitive act. It was an act that was even more positive than marriage, because the payments on the car contract were spelled out in black and white. McDowell laughed because now, no matter how bad it got, the madman could stop being mad. He could stop pretending.

McDowell felt in his shirt pocket, pulled out the mouthpiece, and began to practice. Traffic was not too bad on this street. You could work up some kind of lip in a couple of weeks.

Chapter 18

A '77 Cadillac sat outside of Peg's motel room. The car was gimmicky with chrome accessories, and McDowell knew that it would be in first-class road condition. The motel was one of those double-decker Republican places where the parking lot would crumble beneath the wheels of anything less than a Buick. McDowell was willing to bet that if he went to the front desk and asked for the President's Suite this motel would have one.

He sat in his car, unwilling to go over to Peg's door and knock. The mouthpiece was a small weight in his shirt pocket. The ghost was a heavy weight on his mind. If the ghost was trying to tell him something, it had to be a message about the Citizen. He leaned back in the leather seat and closed his eyes against the glare that was coming from the polished hood of his car. The motel was removed from traffic at least a hundred yards. A well-planted strip bordered the road, and McDowell figured that by the time those trees and shrubs got high enough to be a buffer, this dump would be ruins.

Margaret did not even own a car. She had traveled to Atlanta on a bus. Margaret was doing a week of work for her money. Peg was doing weekends.

In this shit-kicking south that ran from Georgia to Detroit, it paid to act illiterate. It paid to sing poorly, if you sang the right thing. If you were a radio preacher, or some other type of hate-monger, it paid to act stupid; not dumb, but stupid. Performers in the south, whether they were preachers or singers, had learned that if you were a very sincere-sounding hick it paid.

He sat in his car and was frustrated and angry because Margaret did not even have a car. She worked so hard, and she asked for nothing. Except, of course, she asked him to help Peg.

Almost, he did not want to go in there. Almost, he wanted to say to hell with all of *them*. For a moment, through the orange glow that was all he could see from behind closed eyelids, he felt like another ghost was approaching, and she was singing. He saw Velma Middleton, as he had seen her once, dancing on four-inch spikes and maybe a hundred pounds overweight. The spike shoes had shown too much wear. He could hear Velma's broad opening statement on a note, after her clean attack.

He did not want to open his eyes. He did not want to get moving. From the road came the swish of fast traffic. A motorcycle went by with hot pipes that were not fooling anyone. The bike was down there in the 200 c.c. range.

The mouthpiece felt like a question in his shirt pocket. He told himself that he would have to get a tobacco sack someplace. When you carried a mouthpiece, it could get scored, and it would be a constant mess with lint and dirt from your pocket.

The glare of sun was red beneath his eyelids, like fire that was dying. He nearly opened his eyes because he was shocked by a thought. He told himself that he had better call his father. If Enoch had shown him the Citizen, it might mean something really important to the Citizen. Then, in one of those moves your mind makes that is as unexpected as a reed splitting, he wondered if the Citizen was dead. Maybe the old man had keeled over from the shock of last night and all that whiskey. McDowell opened his eyes.

A tall jerk in a Republican haircut and a white summer suit was standing beside the Cadillac. The guy was looking down at McDowell, trying to figure out if he was drunk or dead. The guy was third generation Arkansas, for sure. His skull looked as hollow as his eyes, and the only difference between him and his great-grandpa was that his face was white, not yellow with jaundice. That, and the guy had the easy look of someone who had the world taped. McDowell, having thought of preachers, figured that this guy was a preacher. McDowell hit the button and lowered the window.

"What the fuck do you want?" If the guy was a preacher, Dowell figured to get the conversation off to the right start.

"I don't know yet." The guy spoke right up, and he was not a preacher. "Depends on if you're smashed, and if you're a registered guest." The man was speaking slow, not quite drawling, not yet. His knobby, farmer, Arkansas hands beneath the white jacket sleeves were still hanging loose. He was being professionally tolerant.

McDowell grinned a play-acting grin. "Naw, I ain't smashed. I just got an appointment I don't want to keep."

The guy looked as relieved as McDowell felt. Now that he did not have to keep his hands unclenched, he clenched them, then let them hang free. Then he grinned back. "This is a shitless job, but it does beat workin'".

"I beg pardon for the smart mouth," McDowell said. "Wasn't three hours ago, some guy took me for a pimp."

Now the guy actually did laugh, but the laugh was companionable. "You mean you're not?" He continued to look at the Cad. "This shore is a nice car," he drawled. "I'm one of the assistant managers." The guy was drawling happy, relieved, and he actually looked friendly.

McDowell, who had occasionally received a pass from one man or another, began to feel suspicious. He had met a lot of homosexuals, never before has he met one from Arkansas. Of course, he could be misreading the signals.

He decided to give the guy a road check. "I ain't registered, but I'm in town for a day or two. I'll be looking for a room." He dropped his glance down. "I could come by the office later."

"You could do that," the guy said, "Only I expect we'll be booked. I can come up with a room at some motel close by." He seemed serious, thoughtful, and smart. If there was going to be a pass, this guy was not going to be the one to make it. He was smart enough not to mix friends and business.

Plus, McDowell thought, if the guy actually was queer, then he had taken enough crap in his life to make him suspicious of any man.

"I got this appointment," McDowell said. "Then I'll check with you."

The guy looked at his watch. "Two hours. I'll be on the desk in two hours."

"Well, then."

"Shore," the guy said. He turned away and headed toward the

office. McDowell sat in his car and watched. The guy looked as straight as anyone else. McDowell told himself that whether the guy was homosexual or not, he had class. In spite of Arkansas.

He climbed from the Cad thinking about how little most people understood sex. When you had been to bed with as many women as he had, and talked to them, not much surprised or offended you. That was something *they* would never understand. It was a price *they* paid for being respectable. McDowell did not feel bad or sad because some people had kinky sex lives. He felt bad because most people did not. He stood before Peg's door and once more thought of the many, many women. He thought of Becky, and how five years ago, in Cincinnati, he had seen a poster. Becky had been playing at a coffee house. Two years ago, he had seen a note in a newspaper entertainment section. She had been in Louisville at a freak-type bar. The sun was hot on the back of his neck. He knocked, waited, and the door opened.

Peg was one of those long-legged, longhaired, large-breasted and white, white girls that the country audiences had to have. At first she seemed more blue than drunk, but she had a glass in her hand. Her eyes were wet, swollen, red. In spite of being miserable, she tried to smile. The smile came out as a silly grin.

"Margaret called. You're Dan?"

"Yep."

"Well, you just get yourself on in here, Dan." She turned away, went back into the room and walked unsteadily to the bed. She sat on the edge of the bed and braced herself with one hand against the headboard. The booze was on the nightstand. The room was full of cigarette smoke. He stepped inside, closed the door, and figured he had better start with a joke.

"I'm from the temperance league," McDowell said. "I do hope you've been dumping some food on top of that." He tried to grin a funny grin. "No offense."

"I ain't takin' no offense," Peg said. "There's a certain amount of b.s. running around this world. It's just your turn to shoot a little." She took a lick of the whiskey. Her face was puffy from crying. She was in her middle thirties, maybe a couple of years younger than Margaret. The nicest thing about her face was that it seemed generous. She had a wide mouth, and blue eyes that went well with her long, brown hair. McDowell saw that when her face was unswollen from tears Peg would be beautiful. She had looked just fine on stage, but almost everybody looked pretty good on stage. Right now she sat dressed in a chintzy orange robe with imitation orange fur around the hem. The robe did nothing for her hair. McDowell thought that it said worlds about her taste. Of course, he told himself, she was singing country music. That was bound to have an effect on anything you thought or did.

The room looked like the aftermath of a typhoon in a department store. An expensive radio with enough bands to pick up Australia was upended on the dresser. A high-priced tape deck and two carrying cases of tapes sat beside the doorway to the john. Western clothes lay all around like mangled bodies sprinkled with gilt. Shirts were balled up on the floor. Some of those shirts would check out at two hundred dollars a copy. A guitar sat precariously on top of the television. The guitar was covered with so much pearl and plastic it was a wonder the thing could make a sound. The whole room looked and smelled like Peg was engaged in slow suicide. McDowell thought of the madman he had just seen; there were so many torn-up, crazy people.

"It must have been one hell of a confrontation," he drawled. He kept grinning and felt silly.

Peg licked at the whiskey. "The sonovabitch got the call," she said. "To Nashville. I pointed him in that direction and gave him a kick." She wiped at her nose with the back of her hand, then wiped the back of her hand on the orange robe. "Missed with the kick because the bastard hit running."

"Nashville, and you didn't go?"

"I'm not going to never get no invite from that bunch of chickenshits." Peg fumbled for a cigarette, lit it, then licked at the whiskey. "It's a club," she said, "Plus, I ain't really got a lead voice. I got a group voice. What that means . . ."

McDowell interrupted her. "I know what it means." Peg's voice was not the problem. It was the jazz figures that kept entering her music. Other country singers did not like that. Plus, Nashville was organized as tight as the Mafia. The professional jealousy and controlled ass-kicking that went on in Nashville was like every private vault, everywhere. Even Hollywood types got pushed around.

"I hope you ain't a guitar player," Peg said. "I got a case of the hates for guitar players."

"Got to get over it by Friday. You got to be standing in front of a guitar come Friday."

"What day is it?"

"Tuesday."

"Tomorrow," Peg said. "I'll get over it tomorrow. That sorry razorback."

"Good musician, though."

"Good musicians are twenty for a buck." Peg started to stand, thought better of it, and remained on the bed. "Look at me," she said. "I got the shit, git, and mother wit. I got the looks. Twenty for a buck."

She was not smashed but she was rapidly getting that way. Mc-Dowell figured that he had better get her moving or get her to pass out. Her hates were going against her. It was nothing new. Making you feel guilty was the way they ran the world. If you felt guilty enough, then you turned on yourself just the way they wanted you to, or else, like the madman, you beat hell out of your car.

"I don't want to sound like your daddy," McDowell said, "but you'd ought to eat something. Let's go somewhere."

She looked helpless for the first time, and the guilt was turning away from hate and becoming pure guilt. She fooled around with the front of her robe, plucking at it, then she looked at him in an honest but guilty way. She was trying to control tears, but her eyes were wet. "I'd puke in the plate. I been at this awhile. You don't need some bawling drunk lady."

"If it helps any, which it don't, I've been crazy a few times." His joking was completely gone. His voice was nearly as gentle as when he made love with Margaret.

"He shouldn't have done it," Peg said. "We'd been through stuff before." Her energy seemed to vanish. She had finally given in to the situation, had released all of her control. McDowell figured that the booze would hit fast now that the control was gone.

"Sometimes you got to be," Peg said. "Got to be crazy." She slumped, looking at the floor like she might vomit. "It pounds in your head, is what it does. Your head gets to hurtin."

A long time ago, years ago, he had lain beside Becky and rubbed her head when she had crazy thoughts and feelings. Becky had even looked a little like Peg, but Becky never had trouble over losing a man. Becky kept losing herself.

"I got myself a woman," McDowell said, and he hoped it was true. "I'm going to sit by you, but I'm just trying to help." His voice was not just gentle; it actually sounded loving and not at all apologetic. He walked slowly, real slow, to where she sat, and sat beside her. "The preachers wrote a rule," he said. "You drink enough and you're gonna puke. Let's go do it." He put his arm around her, steadying her. "Get it up, get a shower, and we'll take care of that pore head."

"This here's embarrassing," she said, trying to stand up.

He held her. Margaret was narrow, but Peg was skinny, real thin waisted, and her hands were musician's hands, strong and direct looking. Right now her hands were helping to brace her as she leaned a little backwards, fighting against being sick.

"You ain't talking to a guitar player," McDowell said, "but you're talking to a member of the club. You didn't invent all this."

"That Margaret knows. You know that, do you?" She leaned against him.

"Let's go." He began to raise her. She seemed momentarily confused, but then began to cooperate. He got her to her feet.

"Knows all about it all, that's what. Knows how to pick a fucking man."

"I sure do hope that's true. Let's get this out of the way."

"'Cause I can't do it. Can't do like her." Peg took an uncertain step, then stopped. She turned, like she thought of making it back to the bed. He supported her and turned her back. "Can't sing," she said, "just show some tit and leg, don't kid me, mister."

"I caught your act," McDowell told her. "You got no cause to say that." He was afraid that the situation was going to get worse, and it was already bad. She was wandering in her mind. He walked her to the bathroom, slowly, and had her get rid of it in the tub. He had to lower her so she could sit on the edge of the tub, and he held her shoulder to steady her while she vomited. He ran hot water, and kept it running, to dilute the smell. She hung onto him and started weeping. A feeling of presence grew, and the presence was easy in its mind. McDowell held Peg and turned to the doorway.

The ghost stood weak and misty. The eyes that had once been blank now seemed to be getting some focus. The form was more nebulous than McDowell had ever seen it—not much more than a light shadow. It was not even as heavy as the steam that rose from the hot water in the tub. At the same time that it was misty and weak, the ghost seemed to be more physically substantial. The teeth were back in the head, or at least McDowell thought they must be there. The ghost was smiling an easy, approving kind of smile and there was no Saturday night go-to-hell about any of it.

He held Peg's thin waist, steadying her, and this time he really looked at Enoch. Enoch was not slumped very much. He stood with his body cocked slightly to one side like he was favoring a bad leg. His face was crinkled with the smile, and there was a peacefulness about him that had never been there before. Either that, McDowell told himself, or Enoch had been such a frightening vision that McDowell had never seen the peacefulness. Enoch even looked hopeful, kind of.

"I got more comin' up," Peg said. "Sweet Jesus, this is bad." She leaned forward. McDowell tightened his hold.

"When you get past this," he told her, "I'll explain about once when I puked on half of Miami." He reached with one hand and got hold of a washcloth. He put it under the hot water, stinging his hand, and gave it to her to wipe her mouth.

"Playing there?"

"Nope," he admitted. "I was running from a lady."

That was the time he had come out of Detroit, after the breakup with that Mexican girl. For a moment he could not remember her name. Then he remembered Carlotta. "I wasn't even checked in," he said. "Just walked into the lobby and tossed every thing." As he talked he watched Enoch. He waited for one of Enoch's fancy tricks, ghost fire or screams. Instead, it seemed to him that there was the cry of hounds. Voices were mixed in with moonlight and a mist-covered forest. The dogs were fresh and on a fresh scent. He could hear the individual voices rising, and the voices were crossing each other like you heard with a good jazz clarinet that sang across the music.

"I wisht I was home," Peg said.

"Where's home?"

"West Virginia." She gagged but nothing came up. "You reckon we got it all?"

"Sit for another minute." The water splashed in the tub, swirled away at the bile and whiskey. Steam rose from the hot water, mist-ing the mirrors. The song of the dogs seemed louder.

"If I was home," Peg said, ". . . had an old fella once, a blue tick hound name of Thunder. He took me to the woods. We used to run in the woods."

"You hearing anything?" McDowell watched Enoch. Enoch seemed more misty, and even more hopeful than before. He looked like a man about to leave on a trip he was wanting to make; a man with his bags packed.

"Let him off the tie-up stake one spring," Peg said. "Early, frosty spring. There shouldn't have been no rattlers."

"You hearing anything?"

"You too? Hound music. Sure."

"Snake bit?"

"Lost him to the rattlers. Lost. Every fucking bit of it lost, Dan."

"What are you hearing?" He steadied her.

"Drunks hear anything, I'm hearing hounds."

"A whole pack. Running?"

"Where you from, boy?" She leaned against him. He rinsed the washcloth and handed it back to her.

"Here. From this very town."

"It's a *pack* when you talk about dogs," she said, "but don't never talk that way about hounds. It's a *mute* of hounds. Any country boy oughtta know that."

"This country boy don't."

"It's English," she said. "You'd ought to know that." Enoch was fading, and he was calm and smiling.

"If I promise not to fall in the tub, will you get me a glass of water?"

He stood, keeping one hand on her shoulder, and managed to unwrap a glass and get it filled. "You feeling better?"

"I'd have to get well to die." She raised one hand backwardly, up to her shoulder, and placed it on his hand. Then she turned away from the tub and looked into the doorway. She seemed to be looking at something a great distance away. Enoch was fading, and then he was gone.

"I didn't smoke that much."

"What do you see?"

"Nothing. Smoke. Wonder what you can get trade-in on a used-up throat?"

"I can cure that throat," McDowell said. "Suck lemon and horehound."

"Make me puke all over again." She looked down at her robe. "Jesus." She grabbed a towel rack to steady herself. "Get me out of this mess."

He helped her remove the robe and he handed her a bath towel to wrap around her. If Margaret was shy, Peg was not. Either that, or she trusted him, or she trusted Margaret's judgment about him. He steadied her, walked her, and got her into bed and between sheets.

"Got the spins?"

"Like a goddamn top."

He sat beside her. "You pass out for awhile. I'm gonna do something here." He began to gently rub her temples, her eyelids, her forehead. "Knew a lady once, had to have the crazies rubbed away."

"That why you left her?"

"She left me."

"Then she really was crazy." Peg curled slightly over to one side, but with her head turned so he could still touch both temples. "Not easy to find a guy with nice hands." She was nearly mumbling, about ready to pass out. He rubbed her head and in ten minutes she was out. It took another ten minutes to clean the bathroom. He moved quietly, although he figured Peg could probably sleep through a train wreck. He picked up in the room, folding clothing, getting the place straight. He told himself that he ought to be a wife. He almost felt that the thought was true, even if it was nonsense. When he had the place straightened up, he sat in a chair and watched Peg. She was so far out of it that she was not even moving, although she was snoring heavy. He checked his watch. It was only two o'clock, and she was good for several hours. He picked up her room key and thought that he should call the Citizen. Then he decided against it, mostly because he wanted to get out of the room. He could call the Citizen from a phone booth while he was getting the lemon and horehound.

Chapter 19

McDowell bought horehound and a sack of Bull Durham at a small, old-fashioned drugstore owned by a white-haired, nearly tiny pharmacist and his even smaller wife. The old couple had the kind of courtesy that showed they were prepared to like you. It was easy to see that they liked each other, and had for years.

He also bought some rock candy. It would not do the job as well, but it would serve in case Peg really could not stand the horehound. Then he fought traffic for nearly three miles before he found a grocery store. The sun was bent toward the horizon but it was still high enough to make the shopping center like a field of heat as the parked cars absorbed and then radiated the sun.

When McDowell came from the grocery, three teenage kids were checking out the Cadillac. They were parked in an old AMX that idled choppily through a broken muffler. McDowell figured the kids could not shut the engine off because the battery was shot. Once the thing stopped they would not be able to get it started again. The kids were openly passing a joint. As he climbed into the Cadillac he saw that they were daring him with the joint.

Two of the kids were brown-haired, the other was blonde. The blonde kid took a toke, held it, then leaned out the window and blew smoke at McDowell. The kid's eyes did not look stoned, he just looked smartass.

McDowell lowered his window.

"For an old man," the kid pointed at the Cadillac, "that is one wild piece of shit."

170

"For a punk," McDowell told him, "that is taking an awful, awful chance."

"You a widow fucker," the kid said. "You rich bastards is all alike."

McDowell put it in reverse, backed out of the parking slot, flipped the bird, and pulled away while checking his mirrors. The punks were arguing. Then the AMX backed from the parking slot like the driver's foot was on fire. The kid who was driving hit the brake, revved the engine as he hit it, and popped the shift into drive. The AMX burned a little of its remaining rubber in a squawk of tires as the kids came after Dan McDowell. McDowell told himself that he might be about to spend a little money on a bumper, but it would practically be worth it.

He cruised the lot slow, nearly idling, and the AMX was following a yard from his bumper. In his mirrors he could see the kid in the center arguing with the driver. The driver was leaning back in the stiff-armed, ten-two position of race drivers. McDowell grinned. Straight fantasy. The kid was thinking he was the Mario Andretti of the shopping center circuit. The blonde kid was leaning out the window, hollering and tossing the finger.

McDowell eased toward the street. As he arrived he pressed his brake only enough to show brake lights. At the same time he sapped the car. The Cadillac jumped forward. The driver of the AMX was caught off guard. McDowell spun the wheel, bringing the Cadillac on a straight line into the street. The AMX had dropped twenty feet back and was beginning to accelerate. McDowell jammed the brakes. The AMX screeched, its front end bobbing down like it was praying. Its bumper barely tapped the bumper of the Cadillac. McDowell drove away happy. In his mirrors he could see the junker sitting stalled in the street and the kids climbing from the car, cussing each other. Traffic was already beginning to back up.

He told himself that kids were okay. Even punks could be okay if they had their asses kicked a few times. He circled the block, entered the shopping center from a different street, and found a phone booth. He called the Citizen. Samantha answered.

"Daniel," said Samantha. "I was certain you had left town." Her voice sounded like it was breathing frost. He could nearly see her holding that phone and fiddling with her high-priced automatic pencil as she fought to keep her anger from showing. Her voice was even more controlled than it had been during their lunch.

"I'm calling for Pop."

"Charles is not here. He left early, around ten o'clock."

"On business? When will he be back?"

"It was not business. We had a discussion this morning."

"Sammy," said McDowell, "don't do it. I'm asking nice. Please don't do it."

"He is irresponsible, Daniel, to the point where he had one of his women here last night. Drinking, among other things."

"I was there last night. There wasn't any woman." He told himself that you could find no dirtier minds, anywhere, than among the true retards who put business before everything else. Samantha was a retard.

"Charles has already admitted that a woman was here," she said. "You need not try to protect him."

So the Citizen had bragged his way into a mess. He had bragged about a woman. McDowell stood, held the phone, looked across the parking lot and told himself that the Citizen was just asking for it. The old man had bullshitted for so many years that he could no longer even figure tactics. From across the lot a blue light was circling in the declining sunlight. A cop had pulled in behind the stalled AMX. At least that part was going according to plan.

"I'm not lying," McDowell said. "Pop was flippin' bull like usual. You know him well enough."

"Far better than yourself, I suspect." She paused like she was trying to decide if there was profit in continuing the conversation. McDowell figured he she had her mental computer running. She took a deep, frosty-sounding breath and made a decision. "All right, if he was lying and you are not, then why were the two of you here?"

"To hear his side," McDowell said promptly. "I did you the courtesy of hearing yours." If she wanted to proceed with phony dignity, he figured he could play her game. He stood on tiptoe, looked out across the parking lot. The cop was making the punks push the AMX back into the parking lot. From the distance the cop looked like one of those overweight bulldog types who went around intimidating grandmothers.

"I would be grateful if you could justify any position he holds,"

Samantha said. "He is my father, after all. This affair is getting somewhat beyond me." Her voice sounded like she was trying to be sad, but, McDowell thought, Sammy was not that good an actress.

"Excuse me," McDowell told her, "my impression is that you are doing this. How can it get beyond you?" He watched a slightly built woman with two small children pass in front of him. The woman was not much more than a kid, herself. She moved as if she were stiff. She wore a long-sleeved blouse and worn jeans, and she carried two bags of groceries. Her face, which should be pretty, was pale and drawn. A girl of about five led a boy who was probably four. The woman walked to a new Volvo station wagon and sat the groceries on the hood. She was wearing large, round sunglasses. As she turned McDowell could see her bruised eye, and sunlight showed that the green and purple bruise ran backward and into her hair that she had brushed forward. He told himself that she did not look like the kind of woman who ran into doors.

"I have nothing to do with this," Samantha said. "Gerald is initiating the action. He is doing it not at my behest, but on behalf of our guarantors."

"Sammy, goddammit." She was like a general covering her perimeters—she had set it all up. The banks would take most of the flak, the Wimp would take a little, and Samantha would take the whole business. All the while it was happening she could sit and mourn for the Citizen because she had built a wall between herself and the dirty work.

The woman with the black eye had her kids loaded in the backseat of the station wagon. She turned, picked up a bag of groceries, and put it on the front seat.

"Gerald is my husband. I have influence with him, of course." Now she was sounding explanatory and seemed defensive. "A woman must in the end accede to the wishes of her husband."

"Especially," McDowell said, "when she tells him what he has to make her do." He did not attempt to hide his bitterness. "Don't hang up. I have something you need to hear."

He stood back up on tiptoe. The cop had the three punks spread against the AMX, running them for drugs. The woman with the black eye turned, fumbled for the second bag of groceries, and the bag tipped and fell. Groceries spilled, oranges and apples rolling in the sunlight. A bottle of catsup shattered. Cooking oil

bounced, broke, and a bag of flour dusted the whole mess. Mc-
Dowell wanted to go to her. He stood helplessly with the phone in
his hand and watched.

"You have to have a hearing," McDowell said. "It has to be
open to all evidence, and I'll be there."

"It will make no difference."

"You can't do it, Sammy. All you can do is shame him. People
don't do that to their fathers."

The woman with the black eye stood above the mess of spilled
groceries. She was tense, the way the madman in the little Ford
had been tense. She touched the side of her face where the bruise
disappeared into her hair. She stood rigid, like she was ready to
scream. Then she got control, looked into the back seat at the kids,
and then leaned over to pick up the mess.

"You are welcome to attend any hearing," Samantha said. "Any
explanation you have will certainly make me feel better."

"If he's crazy, so am I," McDowell told her. "He really is seeing
something, Sammy."

She took a deep, frost-sounding breath. "Daniel," She said, "at
least extend a minimum of courtesy. Stop treating me as if I were
stupid."

"I'm not," he told her, feeling hopeless. "I'm just trying to clear
all this up."

"Because if you could get me to admit even the possibility of
something supernatural, then you and Charles would have the advantage. Correct?"

He was not following her, could not catch her drift.

"And," Sammy said, "it would then be very simple for you to
gain control through your advantage."

For a moment McDowell hated her, really hated her; despite,
he told himself, you ought never to hate your own family. "I'm
your closest kin and I'm not married," he told her. "Maybe you can
get me certified and take my business."

The woman with the black eye tossed a couple of oranges onto
the front seat of the Volvo. She leaned over again then stood back
up. She walked around the car, tilted the mirror on the driving
side, and leaned over to look at herself. She removed her sunglasses. Her eye was as badly bruised as if she had been in a barroom
brawl and on the bottom of the pile. The bruise would be a month

in healing. McDowell wished he could have ten minutes with the sorry sonovabitch who was her husband. Two minutes to wreck him, and eight to rub salt into the remains.

"Don't joke," Sammy said, and there was warning in her voice. "Your testimony might indict you of just that." She took a shallow, frosty breath. "I can have my attorney begin to research the statutes of Illinois."

In the south, in this woman-worship, hot-nutted, retard south, women just got beat to shit. He did not need the lady with the black eye to show him that. He had known that forever. In the south a woman could either knuckle under—and most of them did—or she could fight back. If she was limited in imagination but overstuffed with ambition, like Sammy, then she fought back the way Sammy was fighting.

Now the woman with the black eye had opened her purse. She pulled out a billfold and counted her money.

McDowell told himself that he understood Samantha, and he was helpless. There was not one single thing he could say. Too much history was pressing on him and on his once loved sister. He wanted to swear, weep, make some kind of hopeful promise.

"I'm against you," he told Samantha. "Do what you have to do. Use the Wimp for your butcher knife. Sooner or later, you have to come my way and I'll be waiting." He hung up the phone, turned to help the woman with the black eye, and saw that she no longer needed help.

McDowell told himself that he would be blessed. This was the second one in one day. First the little guy with the Ford, and now this woman.

McDowell, who had fought back so many times, fighting against duty and illusion, watched one more person begin to make her fight. He wondered momentarily what fights Margaret had once made, or, for that matter, Peg.

The woman was holding the bag of groceries that had been sitting on the seat. She was scrupulously going through the bag, pulling out all of the glass and setting the items on the ground.

Then she started flinging things. A box of cereal went in one direction, a loaf of bread in another. She was not volcanic about it. She was methodically tossing anything not breakable as far as she could throw it. She spoke to her kids, then flipped a package of frozen vegetables over her shoulder. It arced through the air and bounced from the hood of the Cad. McDowell stood watching, fascinated. The woman was making an irrevocable move. She was beaten up, but she was not beat. She looked happy, almost. The four-year-old was laughing. The five-year-old sat looking puzzled.

A second whirling light appeared from where the AMX was parked. The cop had busted the kids and called for the wagon. McDowell grinned, walked toward the Cadillac, and was nearly hit by a pound of margarine. He climbed behind the wheel and watched. For a moment he loved that beat-up, black-eyed lady as much as he had ever loved anybody in his life.

The woman wadded up the grocery bag, threw it away, and climbed into the car. She searched in the glove compartment. She began to unfold a road map.

McDowell pulled away, and he was laughing. That woman was winning.

Margaret was not beaten. Margaret had imagination. If she had ambition, it was for music, and music was for everybody. Music was not selfish.

Samantha was beat. She just did not know it yet. Samantha would not know just how beat she was until after she had won.

A tow truck was arriving for the AMX as McDowell cleared the parking lot and headed back toward Peg's motel. He was laughing like Saturday night. He nearly felt guilty for having trapped the punks, then told himself that they had trapped themselves.

The north was nothing. The north was a bunch of cold crotches and liberal slogans that—when you listened careful—amounted to no more than killing everybody who was not somehow linked to Maine and Massachusetts. Only in the north were things organized in a way that it was possible to run pogroms.

In this hot-ass, stupid, role-ridden south you might kick ass. In fact, you did kick ass, but you expected to get kicked back if you went too far. What it came down to, was that an asshole in the north only got sued, while an asshole in the south had to be constantly alert, or he would wind up payin' a hell of a lot more than just sittin' in some lawyer's office. McDowell figured he had just done those punks a favor by teaching them that lesson.

Chapter 20

THE ARKANSAS GUY WAS ON THE DESK WHEN MCDOWELL ARrived at Peg's motel an hour later. Commuter traffic had been brutal, and the only relief was the mouthpiece. McDowell played it as he sat in stalled traffic. By the time he pulled into the motel lot his lip felt like raw meat. His jaws were sore with that stretchy feeling that would not leave for at least a week. He pulled the Cadillac up in front of the motel office and climbed out. When he entered the office the Arkansas guy seemed pleased to see McDowell, but he did not pretend to be surprised. He did not act coy. McDowell told himself that he still could not figure out whether the guy was a fag or not.

"Must have been some appointment." The man's lank Arkansas face seemed incongruous above his white suit. McDowell figured he must really know his business—no motel this good would put up with a gaunt, cracker-looking kind of guy unless he was an absolute expert.

"Sitting up with a sick friend," McDowell said. Peg's problems were none of the guy's business, but McDowell sketched enough in general terms so the man would understand. "I still got a night's work. Dinner, and sit up late enough to get rid of the sorrows."

The guy was not faggy or bullshit. McDowell found himself as attracted to the man as he ever could be to any man; which, he told himself, had never been all that much. The guy grinned. "No call to explain," he said, "but I appreciate that you did."

It was impossible not to like him. He appeared to be one of the few guys who had been around enough to know that bullshit was only a hobby, not something a man just had to do.

The guy shoved a registration blank toward McDowell. "We naturally had a room open up."

"Shore." So the guy was a fag, at least it now seemed pretty certain that he was. McDowell registered, paid, but did not feel ready to leave. The guy might be queer, but he was not bullshit. He was just smart enough to be careful. You did not often meet people who had been around enough that they did not play games. Margaret was that way. Becky had been that way, sort of. Becky had only played games on herself.

"None of my business," McDowell said, "but you're from Arkansas?"

"Southeast corner, black belt and swamp." The guy grinned. "The seat of the Almighty," he said, "and the Almighty's got his big fat ass a-straddle it like a pot." He stuck his little finger in his ear like country folk did, wiggled it around three or four times for the sensation, and started a low and easy laugh. "It's no place for a man like you."

McDowell grinned a purely happy grin. "I wish we had time for a drink."

The guy looked at McDowell, testing Dan McDowell's sincerity. "Maybe we will, later on."

"Because," McDowell told him, "for the last few days I've been thinking down-home thoughts. You forget about that stuff in Chicago."

"You got home trouble?"

"I got this town trouble. I was raised here."

"You're blessed," the guy said. "At least I expect you are." He seemed momentarily reluctant. Then he seemed like he was arguing with himself.

"You ever notice," he said, "how our kind of folks can't get down-home out of their heads?" Now he had his other little finger in his other ear, and he was serious. "I get sick to puking sometimes, hearing southern people talk about the south. I get sick of talking southern, even. And yet, by God, I keep doin' it."

"Everybody does."

"Most everybody. But all they do is talk. They never think about it. Just bawl around like kids with crap in their diapers."

"Or punch a cop."

"They do that, all right. I've thought about this. You might say I had to."

Peg could wait. The Citizen could wait. McDowell felt that he could learn something from this guy, the same way he learned about music from Margaret. And right now, McDowell told himself grimly, he needed to learn anything at all which might help him understand Enoch.

"If you got a minute," McDowell said, "I would appreciate hearing what you thought."

"I've got a minute." The man turned to look at the wall clock. "I've got four more hours." He turned back to McDowell. "We'll probably get interrupted," he said sadly. "Some imitation colonel and his high-priced lady."

"Anyway, until we do."

"I like thinking," the guy said. "I don't like motels, but this job does give you time to think."

"Feel the same way, sometimes, about the work I do."

"So I take time off. Go back home to Arkansas. And I'm always glad when the trip is over." The guy looked at McDowell, not timidly, but looking like he wondered if McDowell was smart enough to understand. "Back home," he said, "I hear too many voices."

"People talking? They talk about you?"

"Sometimes they do, but that's not what I mean. I mean old-timey voices. What college jocks call inferential." The man flipped through a stack of blank registration cards like he was a gambler. "This is one hell of an old-time land."

"You mean like the land is talking?"

"You said it, I didn't."

"You kind of did."

"I guess. History talks, it always has. It's not a new thing." He laid down the cards. "You go to New Orleans, lots of people know about it. Get into the country and people know. Those big cities get folk confused."

"I really want to understand this—what you're saying." McDowell spoke in all seriousness.

"Musicians know it, and alkies. Gardeners and farmers and barbers, even, sometimes they know it."

"Why alkies?"

"An alky is always something else besides a lush. Maybe they start off as barbers." The man's seriousness was friendly. He was not acting like a teacher, and he was not acting like someone riding a pet idea, either. "It's the people on the fringe. Not the big farmers, but the dirt farmers. Not the guys who run electronics stores, but the bozos who are praying for one lousy recording session. It's people who make shapes that disappear."

"If that's lucky, I'll kiss a bug's ass." McDowell leaned against the counter, telling himself that he nearly understood what the man was trying to say. "If you hear things that ain't there."

"Maybe they are there," the guy said. "I would not testify against them. The south is more jealous than God." The guy looked through the window, into the drive. "Look at that thing. Long as a whore's dream and driven by a guy who has got to be a bum fuck."

McDowell turned. A Cadillac limousine had pulled up before the office. A bald-headed guy sat behind the wheel, discussing something with a blonde lady next to him.

"I'm not your daddy," the motel guy said hurriedly. "But I'm going to sound like him for a minute. If south ain't lucky, think of the alternatives." Although he was speaking fast, he seemed momentarily sad. "If a person is maybe different, maybe some kind of malcontent, and if that person is a man, then think of the problems."

McDowell watched the argument going on in the limousine. The blonde lady had her head lowered in a stubborn way that showed she was losing. "There's problems," McDowell admitted, "but I never been able to put my finger on what the hell they are."

"It's a role," the man said. "I got a degree from a big college, lets me talk this way." He grinned almost apologetically. "In this country there are only about four myths a guy can be, because there's only that many myths. In the south you're Rhett Butler."

"Shore."

"In the north you're Horatio Alger. In the west you're the strong silent cowboy. In the far, far west you're Paul Bunyan." The guy grinned, and this time the grin was funny. "There's a lot of vacancies, but only four kinds of rooms."

"Women?"

"Just as bad for the ladies. More different kinds of rooms but none of them amount to a damn." The guy did not point, but he motioned slightly with his jaw. "That blonde out there is in one of the worst of them."

McDowell looked. The argument was over. The bald-headed guy was climbing out and heading for the office. His pants looked full, like he already had at least half a hard-on.

"Sure is a pretty world."

"This is a shitass job."

"I appreciate the talk." McDowell meant it.

"Me too," the guy said. "You don't hardly ever get to talk serious these days." He turned to the door and put on his professional smile. McDowell picked up his key and left. As he passed the bald-headed man he sneered. The guy did not even see him.

He had to walk around the limousine to get to his own car. That put him right next to the blonde lady. He smiled, but she did not look at him. She sat staring straight ahead, her lips just barely moving; talking to herself, or cursing, or saying prayers. Up close McDowell could see that she was hardly a woman at all, but a girl who had made herself up to look sophisticated. He could not tell whether her face was set against fear or disgust. McDowell started his Cadillac and got away fast. He pulled up in front of Peg's room and parked beside her Cadillac. He hoped she was still asleep, and, considering her state when he left, it seemed likely.

The sun was red behind tall buildings. The buildings looked like dark blocks stacked toward the sky. He sat in the car, watching the declining daylight, then reached into the back seat for the horn. He pulled it out, inserted the straight mute and the mouthpiece. When he tried to play without pressing, he got no sound. His upper lip felt raw. He pressed, managed a middle C, managed eight beats of blues. Even with hamburger lips the horn had a tone that spoke clear and truthful through the mute. He laid the horn back and pulled out the sack of Bull Durham. He emptied the tobacco into the ashtray, turned the sack inside out and brushed the crumbs. He put the mouthpiece in the sack, then stuffed it in his shirt pocket. The horn lay in the open case beside him.

It seemed to him that when he went in to see Peg he would be changed by the situation. He would start play-acting, maybe, or he would feel like someone else. The thought was stupid and teenage but he thought it anyway.

He reached beneath the seat for Margaret's picture. His hand hit the hard surface of the antique emblem from the old Cadillac. He pulled it out and laid it beside the horn. It fit in the top of the horn case like it was made to go there. McDowell dug into the map case and pulled out Margaret's picture.

The many, many women, and now this woman. He had never kept track of how many women there had been. It would be disrespectful. It seemed like he could hear Margaret's voice. She was asking questions with the tune, the way good musicians did sometimes. It changed the emphasis, so that emphasis rose on the strong consonants and syllables in the middle and on the end of words. This tune was improvisational, something rising from her own talent and professionalism. He had never heard the tune before, but the questions were clear and strongly asked.

Without even knowing he was doing it, he reached to touch the horn. Then he realized what he was doing and felt sad. In the hands of a real musician that horn would come alive. It would answer questions and ask other ones. A horn like this could talk to a voice like Margaret's, assuming a guy could play it right.

The feeling of presence slipped into the car. It was not sitting beside him, and it had no focus. The presence was weak but calm. For a moment he heard the sound of a horn being played by an expert musician, blowing slow and low, then rising, then running back easily through the range. The horn was a little flat on top, a little sharp on the bottom. McDowell knew what he was hearing. This was the horn of a black man, somewhere in the early part of the '30s or maybe the '20s when the black bands had to work for almost nothing and guys could not afford good horns. This was a fine musician who was chained to a piece of junk.

He touched the antique trumpet, one of the best horns in the world. The feeling of presence died away, and so did the voice of that black guy's horn.

Time to get moving. Time to shove life back in gear.

Still, he sat. He laid Margaret's picture on top of the horn and reached for the Cadillac emblem. The cloisonne colors were hard and bright. The heavy chrome gleamed in the declining sunlight.

Quality. For most of his life he had objected to cheap shit. Now it occurred to him that he had never asked about purpose.

He told himself that he had better ask himself about that right now.

For a moment it seemed that the ornament was more important and true than the second-rate car on which it had once ridden. Of course, he told himself, it was only an ornament, the mark of a manufacturing house. It was not art, or maybe not; and when you came right down to it, the best car in the world was still only a car.

Then he told himself no, nope; the absolute very best cars in the world were not just engineering, but art. Bugatti had built some. He looked at the ornament and knew that it was better to own the ornament than the car on which it had ridden. That car would be worth a couple thousand dollars today, assuming it was a roadster. It would still be second-rate. This ornament was worth ten bucks or maybe two hundred. It was first-rate, but he could not exactly say why. He laid it back down beside the horn.

His mind slid into the realization as easily as the presence had slipped into the seat beside him at other times. The realization was like the easy pickup of a theme by a trombone, where you almost heard the attack, and then the voice of the horn rose above the lowering volume of a softly kicking sax section. McDowell realized that he did not give a damn for his car anymore. This machine in which he sat, and which he had loved, was worthless. As the world went, he could probably sell it right now for twenty thousand, and he did not give a damn for it. Or for any car. Except, maybe a Bugatti, because you could not use one for a car these days anyway.

The realization had come so easily that he did not understand right away how badly shocked he was, or how much trouble this change might cause. He picked up Margaret's picture. Her voice seemed all around him, and this time it was just kind of romping along, all little-girl and happy, like a voice that had suddenly got free of its owner and was exploring some pretty place.

McDowell sat in his Cadillac and wondered if he was crazy. The ghost of Enoch McDowell had made him wonder the same thing, but not with this same kind of sincerity. Enoch was real, and Enoch was actually, probably, a very good guy. Dan McDowell told himself that he was having lots less trouble with Enoch than he was with these new realizations. Then he told himself he really did have to get moving, crazy or not. He put Margaret's picture away, tucked the ornament beneath the seat, closed the horn case and patted his shirt pocket to be sure that the mouthpiece was there. He had promised to get Peg straight. Crazy or not, that was something he could do. He told himself almost grimly that no man in the world was better for the job. He picked up the bag of lemons and the horehound and climbed from his car.

Chapter 21

PEG WAS STILL SLEEPING WHEN HE ENTERED THE ROOM. THE first thing he looked for was her color, which was good. Peg had thrashed around a good bit, if the tangled sheet and blanket could be believed. Now she lay on her side, the sheet falling away so that one breast was exposed. Her long hair was kind of tucked beneath one of the pillows, like she had pulled the pillow over her head to hide. McDowell debated on whether to pull the sheet up and decided against it. If she woke and found him that close, it might make her afraid.

Asleep like that, with her troubles maybe getting sorted out in her dreams, Peg was just beautiful. Dan McDowell, who not only loved women, but loved the idea of women, stood watching her. He felt like he was in a private museum, viewing a masterpiece. Then Peg took a deep breath, blinked her eyes a couple of times, and tried to snug back into sleep. McDowell watched her, saw that she was awake but refusing to open her eyes.

"Dan?"

"Only me," he said, "I'm sorry."

"It was too much to hope he would come back," she said softly.

"He'll do his drinking later on." McDowell walked to the bed and sat down beside her. She pulled the sheet to her chin.

"How's your poor head?"

"Achin', but not hurtin'." She tried to smile but it faded before it even got a good start.

"Gut?"

"Got to pee."

"Okay otherwise?"

"Think so. Toss me a shirt." She sat up, the sheet clutched to her, and then she swung her legs over the edge of the bed and dropped the sheet. She raised both hands to her head. "Oh, Lord, I sure done it."

McDowell grinned and went to the closet. "I figure the Lord done it himself a few times. It just never got put to record." He pulled out an everyday wash shirt and a pair of slacks, thinking that he had known only a few women like Peg. About the only women who were not self-conscious about nakedness were dancers. He tossed the clothes to her, and she slipped them on and then headed for the bathroom.

"That radio's tuned to Pittsburgh." Her voice sounded a little hollow, coming from the bathroom, but it did not sound bad. McDowell silently congratulated Margaret, and then himself, on having stopped Peg's drunk before it got serious. The sound of the john flushing was followed almost immediately by the noise of the shower.

He walked to where the radio sat on the dresser, almost amused at himself because of his quick case of the hots for Peg. It was natural. Just because it was funny did not mean it was not a case of the hots. His balls ached, but he figured he would get over it. It was not exactly a brand new experience.

Think of Margaret. He did, and the hots got no better, they just got more generalized. He switched on the radio, expecting shit-kicking music, and heard the broad voice of a baritone sax. Jazz station, broadcasting as much to Canada as it was to the United States. Canada was good about jazz, better than most of the states.

He had to call the Citizen. He had to get Peg fed and straight and matched up with a guitarist tomorrow. If her sorrows were under control, he had to get out of town. Then he remembered that he had to check a supplier, the furniture factory Nance had told him about.

The shower was still running. The sax dropped the lead and the full voice of the band picked it up. McDowell listened, trying to spot the outfit. He figured it was an old cut by Ted Heath. Heath was a guy who had used the entire band as a solo voice.

Peg's pearl-plated guitar still sat precariously on the television.

He picked it up to place it in the case. The ornamental crap made it seem heavier than it actually was. He chorded G, plucked the thing, but his plucking was clumsy. The guitar seemed to struggle from beneath the pearl and plastic. The tone had some *boing* in it, but it was not too terrible. He put the thing in its case.

The DJ on the radio started talking about flutes. McDowell walked across the room to the phone and began leafing through the phone book. A jazz flute began to play. McDowell found his father's home phone number. He picked up the receiver, ready to dial, then laid it back down. The jazz flute was moving right out, and that was a credit to the guy. In the '60s, when the flutes came in big, most of them had tried to ruin progressive jazz. They wandered around like birds over an ocean.

He was reluctant to dial that phone because of Peg. It was one thing to talk abstractly about ghosts to Margaret. It was another thing entirely to mix the Citizen's situation with Peg's.

Still, the Citizen ought to be told that he, Dan McDowell, had seen the Citizen in the middle of smoke and flame.

He dialed, halfway hoping there would be no answer. The Citizen answered on the second ring.

"Pop."

"Goddammit," said the old man. "Where are you? Chicago?"

"In town. Right here."

"You are up to your ass in it, like a broody hen on duck eggs." The Citizen sounded both urgent and worried. "If you're in town, it follows you got to be some place. What place?"

"I got this evening tied up."

"You only thought you did," the old man said. "Son, where in the hell are you?"

McDowell admitted to the name of the motel and the room number.

"Glue your tail to that roost. I'll be there in fifteen, twenty minutes." The old man hung up.

McDowell told himself that he would be switched. With the best intention in the world he had managed to get himself put in charge of two cripples instead of one. The shower stopped running. The flute stopped playing. The radio was giving traffic advice to everyone in Pittsburgh. In the radio's opinion, the best thing to do was park.

McDowell dialed room service and ordered a big pot of coffee, plus milk and soda crackers. He told himself to take the Citizen and Peg to a restaurant. At least in public the whole thing would not get out of control. Meanwhile, that Peg girl needed some lining in her stomach.

When Peg came from the bathroom five minutes later, McDowell had been standing before the window looking into the darkening parking lot. He was thinking that he was glad the Citizen was still alive. Enoch McDowell might be a pretty good guy, but he was dead and still powerful. The way Enoch looked at things might be a lot funnier to Enoch than to McDowell and his father.

He had wondered about death and spirits and afterlife. The whole thing made no logical sense, and it did not even make illogical sense. He paused. It occurred to him that Enoch made no sense because this modern world ran on explanations, although the explanations were not always scientific. If Enoch had shown up during the fifteenth century, he would have needed no explanation. Those old times were days of faith. These present times were days of explanations. When you looked at it close, Enoch was not illogical; he was just in the wrong time.

And, just before Peg came from the bathroom, Dan McDowell connected the last piece. He remembered what Margaret had said, that the south was not fully in the twentieth century. In lots of places through the south there were not only no factories, there were hill farms so steep you could not use a tractor if you had one. You had to use mules. To be absolutely honest, there were plenty of places left where the people were lots closer to the fifteenth century than they were to the twentieth.

"I'm the one who's supposed to be brooding." Peg was trying to sound cheerful, and almost making a job of it. She was dressed western but conservative, in a brown unornamented pearl-button shirt and a tan skirt that hit just below the knee. Her hair was brushed out straight and spread fanlike nearly to the small of her back. McDowell saw that she was as beautiful as he thought she might be, and knew she would be even more beautiful when she was easy in her mind.

"I got some bad news," he told her. "A crazy man is coming to visit. " He began to explain about his father.

"For God's sake, help me make the bed." She turned quickly, and regretted it. "Oh, my poor head."

As they worked he thought that he should be amused, but was not. He must have helped in this chore a thousand times, but always before it had been a small and loving ritual between people. As they tore the tangled sheets off, then put everything back together smooth, he explained about the Citizen, and about the Citizen seeing ghosts. Peg was saying nothing. She was too busy trying to get straight, and it was taking all her concentration. The coffee arrived. He tipped the kid waiter and told himself that at least Republican motels had room service. Peg drank milk, chewed crackers, and began to look more comfortable.

"Now how's your head?"

"Better than I deserve, probably." Her try at being cheerful was a failure. Her guilts were still going inward. "Not crazy, anyway." She was honest enough not to try to hide her sadness. Her face was set against the idea of tears, but she was accepting her heartsickness. "What the hell else was there to do? Stand on the sidewalk and cheer?"

"Nothing," McDowell said honestly. He had never been able to keep a woman, and never able to figure out why. He knew a lot about losing someone you loved. "You can't kill him, and you can't kill yourself, so there was nothing else to do."

"I'm too chicken," Peg said. "Don't like where I'm at, but don't want to leave." Then her voice got soft. "Wouldn't want to hurt him."

"You did just right."

"I expect that's your daddy, right there."

McDowell turned to look through the window. It was nearly dark, and the headlights of the car that pulled in beside his Cad were just cutting off. The Citizen's Lincoln bulked as wide as Peg's Cadillac, which sat on the other side of McDowell's car. His Cad looked high and narrow, and strangely out of place. Once he was proud of his car, and now he felt nothing. He looked at all of that high-priced rolling stock and it seemed like so much iron. It was a terrible way to feel, especially after you had loved something so much. The Citizen's white hair shone in the gathering darkness as he climbed from his car. McDowell opened the door.

"Take this," the old man said, "and shut up." He handed Mc-

Dowell a paper bag before he even entered the room. Then he shouldered his way past McDowell, saw Peg, and stopped.

"Pop, this here's a goddamn pistol." McDowell stood looking into the mouth of the sack and told himself that he must look like an idiot staring down a well.

"Charles," the old man said to Peg. "Charles McDowell at your service." He did not sound in the least bit bullshitty or billy goat. He was genuinely polite.

"My friend Peg . . ." McDowell fumbled, then remembered Peg's last name. "Martin . . . like the guitar. Pop, this is a goddamn pistol."

"It is an honor and my good fortune." The old man actually made a small bow, and there was nothing silly about it. The Citizen stood tall and somehow stately even in a soiled shirt with rolled-up sleeves. He managed both courtliness and dignity with all of the ease that he managed a smart mouth. "Mistrust this man," he said kindly about Dan McDowell. "He's simple."

"Pop."

"Because," said the Citizen reasonably, "he's standing there explaining what I already know."

"Dammit, Pop."

"Belonged to my pa, your grandpa Ezra," the Citizen said. "He carried it through World War I. Ezra was the second grandson of Enoch."

"Pop, it's a fuckin' forty-five."

"One more cuss in front of a lady and you and me are gonna tangle." The old man turned to Peg. "He's kind of thickheaded. Should have been a schoolteacher."

"Don't say I didn't tell you," McDowell said to Peg. Then he told himself, no, aw-naw, nope. Peg was picking right up on it.

"On the contrary, sir," she said, "your son is a gentleman and a credit to you. I am in his debt."

McDowell told himself that Peg might be from West Virginia, but she had the Virginia act taped. He worked the slide on the pistol. A bullet popped out, tumbling down and across the floor like a fat, bronze bug. "Jesus suffering Christ."

The radio was still playing, although Peg had lowered the volume. A singer with a good voice was trying to scat and was messing it up. The scat was like corn popping. There was just a hint of accent, and McDowell figured her for a German lady who should be singing Wagner. The Germans could not get loose enough for jazz, but they kept trying. McDowell reached down, picked up the bullet, and thumbed the magazine from the forty-five. He reloaded it and laid the magazine and pistol on the dresser. Peg was pouring coffee for the Citizen, and she was lacing it with a shot from her bottle of bourbon. She had gotten the Citizen into a chair and was at his side, leaning in a slight, ladylike way at his shoulder as she poured. Her face was temporarily eased from her sorrow. She was actually smiling and looking like someone about to have a good time. Beyond the window, an automobile pulled up beside the Citizen's Lincoln. The headlights went out, but it was too dark to tell what kind of car it was. The driver did not get out. McDowell guessed it was some guy coming in from an early drunk or dreading a fight with his wife.

"Supper," McDowell announced. "Let's all of us just go out and get a bite."

"Put the loads back in that thing," the Citizen said. "It's not a squirt gun."

The car that had pulled in now backed up. The lights came on as it pulled away.

Peg and the Citizen were talking in low, formal voices. McDowell shoved the magazine back into the pistol. Then he laid the thing on the dresser.

"My treat," he said. "We'll all go to supper."

"Not many women do," the Citizen said to Peg as he continued their conversation and ignored McDowell. "But almost all of the finest ladies appreciate them."

"I'd love to see him. I'd take pleasure." Peg's voice was sincere. It was not bullshitty or phony, but it was not West Virginia, either.

"In that case," said the Citizen, "I'd be more than happy." He stood up. "He's in the car."

"Pop, you'll get us bounced. You can't bring no damn dog into a motel like this." McDowell heard his own voice. He tried to stop whining. "Listen, we got to eat."

"Room service," Peg said happily. "We could have a party, kind of. She went to the dresser to pick up a menu. She shoved the pistol out of the way like it was a trinket. The Citizen was already through the doorway, headed out to get Shag.

"Gimme a drink of that," McDowell said. He sloshed whiskey on top of his cooling coffee.

"Dan," Peg said, "I ain't fakin."

"He's crazy. You don't know him like I do."

"It's helping, Dan. It ain't all an act."

"Sure it is."

"Then it's a good act. Leave it be."

"He's nuts."

"Not around a lady. He wouldn't insult me or hurt me for the world."

She was right, and McDowell knew it. Even if the old man got falling on his ass drunk, he would remain a gentleman. Even when they got kicked out of the motel, the old man would do nothing more than smack a manager or a cop. It was almost a relief to know something that was totally, absolutely certain. He reminded himself that at least when they got kicked out of this room he had the key to another room. They could sneak back in. He took a heavy slug of the coffee-flavored whiskey, then poured a little more whiskey on top. The door opened and Shag came in, followed by the Citizen.

Peg looked the way people were supposed to look when they went to church. She knelt, but not like she was going to pray. For the first time since McDowell had seen her, Peg's face was open and happy. Her eyes were bright with more than excitement; she looked awed, almost.

"Shag dog," she said, "you come here."

McDowell watched and told himself that even Shag was acting like a fool. Shag, who had not made up to Dan MacDowell before now ignored him completely. He wagged his tail, gave the tiniest whine of pleasure, and went to Peg like he had known her all his life.

The Citizen was purely happy. "Can't fool a good dog. Fool most any man sometimes, but not a good dog." The Citizen was sober and looking like he aimed to stay that way.

McDowell decided, just fuck it. If this was the way the game was running, then he would show them how to play. He walked to the window, picked up the phone and dialed room service. In a voice as casual as a breeze, he ordered three medium rare steaks and one real rare. Then he hung up and began to pull the drapes.

Another car pulled up beside his father's Lincoln, or maybe it was the same one that had pulled up before. The lights went out, but the driver sat like a dark shadow behind the wheel. McDowell pulled the drapes, turned, and the Citizen was laughing about the steaks. The Citizen thought it was funny, while McDowell thought mournfully about all of the starving children in India. He took a sturdy mouthful of the barely coffee-flavored bourbon. Shag was busy licking Peg's face, and Peg was loving it.

"Pop," McDowell whispered, "why the fuck do I need a gun?

"Hang onto it."

"Why?"

"I got a sign from Enoch."

"Enoch's a clown," McDowell whispered. "I don't pay no mind to Enoch."

"You'd better." The old man was not whispering. He was speaking low and seriously. "I told you blood would come of this."

The phone rang. Peg flopped Shag's ears, then went to answer, moving quick and lightly. Her skirt swirled around her legs, and she was as attractive to McDowell as any woman who had ever lived. The Citizen watched Peg. He seemed bemused, or overcome with admiration. "You never get over it," the old man said. "At least I expect you don't." He nodded toward Peg, then drew McDowell further back into the room. "That's the wrong woman," he said. "Who the hell are you trying to kid?"

"I don't know what you mean. She's just a friend. We got nothing going."

"You know a brown-skin girl?"

"How'd you know?"

"Light-brown-skin girl, light hair and all?"

"Just a minute, this is serious."

"Doing fine, girl," Peg said happily into the phone. "It's bad, but it's working out."

"You goddamn right it's serious," the Citizen told Dan McDowell. "Enoch showed you like you were bad hurt. Then a brown-skin girl was crying."

"Pop, are you bullshitting? Are you talking English?"

"Dammit," the old man said mournfully, "do you even know how to use a gun?"

"How hurt?"

"How the hell should I know? The picture came and went fast but hurt, son, and I ain't shittin'. The Citizen looked like he was having a pleased thought. "If it's any comfort, you were still on your feet."

"He shore is," Peg said. "Here, talk to him." She motioned to McDowell. "It's Margaret."

"Because you're stupid," the old man whispered urgently. "If you weren't stupid, you would have took this serious all along."

McDowell walked slowly, almost mechanically to the phone. He almost tripped over Shag. McDowell had been in terror from Enoch; he had been mystified, angry, then almost friendly toward Enoch. Now he was feeling dread, and he had not ever felt that before. Peg covered the phone with her hand. "She's worried," Peg said. "I sounded too darned happy. Tell her true." She handed him the phone.

"Dan," said Margaret, "babe, are you all right?"

"Everybody else is." McDowell felt nearly breathless with the dread, and he did not know whether he was afraid for Margaret or for himself. His voice was more serious than he meant it to be, but the seriousness actually seemed to help as he explained about Peg and the Citizen and Shag. "It looks like a long night," he concluded, "but she's doing okay."

"It takes years," Margaret said seriously, "to really show somebody how you love them. You're showing me you do, though."

"I really do." The dread was all mixed in with longing, and with happiness from what she said.

"We can make it work, Dan. I didn't think so before." She paused. "Could be fooling myself. I miss you a lot right now."

"Every time I hear your voice," he said helplessly.

"I've got a surprise. Just came today." Her voice momentarily sounded little-girl. Then it sounded proud. "I never believe it until I actually see it," she said. "My agent mailed me a promo copy. I've got a new release."

She had never even hinted that a new recording was in the works. He was so happy he was nearly incoherent. "We will totally destroy Pittsburgh," he told her. "Celebrating." Then the dread returned. "You're okay? Safe?"

"They had some trouble at this place last month. Some freak. I start working nights Thursday, and being extra careful."

"It's nights I worry about."

"I been at this a long time, Dan. I'm always careful. Usually I get a ride home with one of the guys."

"I got a room here." He pulled the key from his pocket and gave her the number. "Call me."

"Or Peg," she said, "to leave a message, of course." She sounded like she was laughing.

McDowell turned, seeing the Citizen, who was seated and nursing his spiked coffee. Peg was sitting on the floor with Shag's head in her lap. They looked corny, but not terrible. At least they looked better than anything out of Stephen Foster.

"Get it out of your head," McDowell told Margaret. "It's you I love." He turned to look toward the door, looked away, looked back and was startled. He could swear he had seen the doorknob being turned, like someone was testing it. He looked again. Nothing.

"I'm lots better in bed than she is. You can take my word." Margaret giggled. "Of course, I'm not there and she is." This time she did not even try to hide the laugh.

"You're the best there is," McDowell said fervently, "and you are causin' a miracle here. At least you are causin' growth."

"We got to stop this," Margaret said. "Otherwise I'll be getting on a bus."

This time the knob was definitely turning. McDowell waved to get Peg's attention. The old man had his back to the door, and Peg was not looking his way. McDowell stepped toward the door, stretched, and the phone nearly fell from the table. He shot the deadbolt. The knob stopped moving.

"I'll call before work on Friday," Margaret said. "I'm loving you between now and then." She made something that sounded like a purr, sort of, and hung up.

McDowell replaced the receiver and got away from the closed drapes. He turned off the table lamp beside the window. The room went dark except for light from the bathroom. Shag stood quickly and shook himself. His ears actually flapped, he shook so hard.

"What?" The Citizen was immediately on his feet.

"Someone was testing the door," McDowell said. He stepped to one side of the window, lifted a corner of the drapes and looked out. A car was backing from the parking slot beside the Citizen's Lincoln. The taillights flared as it turned away. It was a small car, but he could not tell what kind. "Gone now."

"I can make a guess," the old man said. The Citizen looked like a man who had come to terms with a private grief. "You could make the same guess if you thought about it."

"I don't understand."

"Of course you don't. You see things right in front of your face, and call 'em something else." The old man turned to Peg. "I have to talk to my boy." His sadness was mixed with dignity. "It isn't private, but it's family. I hate to take your time."

"I'd be grateful if you did take my time," Peg touched the Citizen's arm. She was behaving genteel, but also motherly. "If you mean ghosts, I was raised with them." She seemed to be wondering if that was enough to say. "I always know when I'm singing good. When I'm really good, I feel them all around me."

"It's ghosts," the old man admitted. "There's dead ones and live ones. That was a live one at the door."

"Pop, what'n the hell are you saying?"

"That was Samantha."

"She tailed you? Can't be. Naw."

"I told you Sammy was crazy," the Citizen said, "but I told you in that way where you say exactly what you mean, only you can't be understood." The sadness was all over his face. He slumped, looking as old as McDowell has ever seen him look. "Maybe it was me who caused it," the old man said. "I'm hell to live around. That was my daughter out there, and my daughter is insane."

Chapter 22

McDOWELL DID NOT NEED HIS FATHER'S EXPLANATION, BUT HE listened. The old man remained slumped in his chair, oblivious to the whiskey. If there was any comfort in alcohol, the Citizen would not accept it.

"This is a big town," he said, "but it's still a hick town. By tomorrow the news will be all over."

"She's shaming you, Pop?"

"If she's crazy, she can't be blamed."

"Not unless she loves to be crazy." McDowell thought about what he had heard himself say, and then decided to drop it. He did not want to have to try to explain that. Peg sat on the floor, flopping Shag's ears, looking quiet and respectful.

"It isn't private business. Sammy runs Gerald. This morning she ran him down to a lawyer. The lawyer is moving for a restraining order against the time of the hearing, and he'll get it." The Citizen had rolled his shirtsleeves down. His large, work-hardened hands were clasped in his lap in a nearly feminine way. "The lawyer will get it, because Gerald has a bank guy in his pocket. The bank guy and Gerald have been playing a real estate game on the side."

"Gerald is Sammy's husband," McDowell explained to Peg. "We call him the Wimp."

"*You* call him the Wimp," said the Citizen. "Gerald ain't real bright, but he's a good man."

"Naw."

"He's lived over twenty years with a woman who just gets crazier and crazier. A man don't run away when people are sick. You know that."

"I know it."

"He surely does," Peg said, but it seemed that she spoke to Shag and not to the Citizen.

"It just builds up," said the Citizen. "You pay it no mind, and then one day you look around you, and you've been living in the middle of crazy."

"What does she do, Pop?"

"Acts like things are true. She gets an idea and that idea is only an idea." The old man looked helpless. "But she operates like it's true." He turned to Peg. "I have a lady friend, works for me. She's not the first, and God willin' she's not the last. Sammy has already got us married off, and she's got Sandra in court, and the estate all settled."

"Pop, is that for true?"

"It's real to her," the Citizen said. "It's like the whole thing is already fought out and done." He leaned back in his chair, fatigued. "Honest and true, she carries that with her at the same time she's toting this other. My daughter sees two of me, the man who's already dead, and the man she's got to get committed."

It all slipped into place. McDowell listened and thought about what his father knew. The Citizen could read any contract. He could hit general principles of politics from events reported in the news. When it came to book learning, he had almost none. The Citizen would not know paranoia from pineapple. At the same time, as the old man talked, McDowell starting connecting what he was hearing with what he had heard his sister say. He remembered Samantha's irrelevancies, her question about his apartment in Chicago which had made no sense at the time. He remembered her on the phone, how she set Gerald up and then pretended that she was out of control of the situation. Except, McDowell thought, maybe Samantha was not pretending. He remembered her twisting his intent, implying that he and the Citizen were trying to get control over her by convincing her that there really was a ghost.

Something clearly was awful, awful wrong with Sammy. McDowell thought of symptoms, of fixed personality and rigidity of character. In textbook terms Samantha had slipped into a classic paranoid-schizoid type. McDowell told himself that everyone had those tendencies, and maybe Sammy was not very sick. He sat grieving, and then, finally, indignant.

This crazy-making, woman-worship, woman-hating south.

In the south, all over the south, it was practically a tradition that you had to have at least one crazy lady in your family. It was almost like a family was not valid until it had produced at least one madwoman. And that, McDowell told himself, that right there was definitely, ab-so-lutely, English.

"So what can Gerald do," the Citizen asked reasonably. "He can't commit her, 'cause she's his wife. Besides, by now she's driven him so crazy himself that he don't even know she's crazy."

"Had an aunt," said Peg, "did the same. Married a preacher. Preacher lasted eight years and hung himself." She looked at Dan McDowell. "I can tell a man who don't like country music a mile off, but I forgive you."

McDowell felt like they were ganging up on him, like he was paranoid himself. "I don't know what that has to do with anything."

"Just that you won't understand country music until you understand about my aunt."

"What's to understand?"

"She helped him with the noose . . ." Peg paused, "because she loved him so much."

There was a knock on the door. McDowell stood, stared.

"That's room service," the Citizen said. "Sammy don't ask no more. Sammy wouldn't knock."

McDowell answered the door, then stood in the open doorway as the kid from room service entered and began setting up the table. He was a nice-looking kid with short hair and a kind of babyishness or girlishness about his mouth. The hot night pressed on McDowell as he stood listening to the fast rush of traffic from the street. Over toward the river, as predictable as hound voices in the hills, he heard the distant whip whip whip of sirens. He looked around the darkened lot for a car that looked like Sammy's. He thought that if Sammy had been testing the door, and apparently she had, then it meant that the world of her need or desire or madness had finally become more real for her than the real world. He turned to tip the kid and found that the Citizen had beat him to it. The kid left and McDowell looked for Peg and Shag. The two of them came from the bathroom where Peg had hidden Shag. Peg looked sassy and proud, and Shag looked satisfied.

The Citizen seated Peg, and then himself. He was being court-ly. "What it comes to," he said to McDowell, "is that this time to-morrow I'll be restrained from entering my own business."

McDowell listened and tried to pretend that he was Samantha. He felt his mind begin to become sharp, cold, and brilliantly emo-tional in a way that seemed logical and not emotional at all. The back of his neck began to tighten, and his peripheral vision faded as his eyes clearly saw the details of each wrinkle on his father 's face. He looked at Peg, saw the nearly invisible wrinkles around her eyes, and those wrinkles looked as deep as gullies across erod-ed land. His mind was becoming even colder, freezing, centering. Then his mind began to laugh at him. He blinked.

Something was wrong. Always before when he wanted to act a part, he could act it. His whole life had been spent play-acting one thing or another. Now he could not even act out a simple case of paranoia. He absentmindedly pulled the Bull Durham sack from his shirt pocket. The radio was playing so low he could hardly hear it. A brass choir was playing a number adapted from Bach, and it should have been good but it was not. He felt the mouth piece through the thin cloth of the sack. Peg misunderstood his intent. She left her dinner, went for her smokes, and handed him a cigarette.

Why was the play-acting not working?

He absentmindedly tucked the cigarette in his shirt pocket. Peg and the Citizen were eating and glancing at him, then looking away.

"It must be something in the air," the Citizen said, "or else in the blood and the bone."

"Where you wandering, Dan?" Peg did not seem so much hung over, as she seemed favoring her stomach. She was really packing it away. Shag lay beside her chair, being polite. He was not trying to con bites of steak. Shag's own steak and baked potato and mixed vegetables and coffee cup and silverware and napkin sat at one end of the table.

When he had done that damn fool thing, ordered a steak to feed to a dog, he had been play-acting. Now that he could not play-act anymore he felt ashamed and embarrassed. He laid the Bull Durham sack beside his plate and began to eat. Peg and the Citizen looked relieved. McDowell chewed and thought that something was missing, or at least needed explaining about the Citizen's story.

"Is Sammy in on that real estate deal?"

"Nope." The Citizen was relieved that McDowell's preoccupation had come up with what seemed like a sensible question.

"What is the deal?"

"Land development. Gerald and the banker pulled a cheap buy on some no-good land with taxes owed on it." The Citizen grinned. "'Course, what they didn't tell the tax people was that a big factory was gonna be built ten miles down the road."

"Samantha's let the Wimp off the leash?"

"Naw," the old man said. "Sammy don't know anything about the real estate stuff."

"If she did?"

"She'd stop it. You know that."

"I think I do," McDowell said. "She really would stop it. That's why I'm asking."

"Shag dog," said Peg, "you just lost your baked potato." She forked it from Shag's plate. Shag thumped his tail and looked up, hopeful. "I'll feed him directly," Peg said. "These are just elegant potatoes."

"You been starving this girl?"

"Sammy would nix the real estate, because the distributing business is her whole world?"

"Yep. More and getting more so." The old man looked like he hated to confide something, then he did confide it. "Got to the point where she patrols the warehouse. T'other day she actually took to shoving some cartons. Driving my warehouse guys crazy."

"Then it isn't her whole world," McDowell concluded. "Her whole world is in her head, and that distributing business is only a sign. It's a sign that makes what's in her head real."

"Beg your pardon, Miss Peg, but have you been to college?" The Citizen looked like he was about to get mad but was holding it in.

"Baptist College," Peg said. "Lasted one term."

"College boys are all alike," the Citizen said. "I never know when to trust 'em." He turned to McDowell. "If you got something to say, then cut the double talk."

"It ain't double talk, but it's complicated." McDowell tried to reduce Sammy's problem to simple terms. He failed, tried again, and failed again. The harder he tried, the more he floundered.

"It's a way of being sick," he said inconclusively. "But each person who gets sick that way does it according to their own minds. It's like a room full of broken chairs, but each chair is broke in a different way. A person comes in and sits down in the chair they like best." It was not a good description, but it was the best he could do.

"How'n hell you gonna sit in a busted chair?" The Citizen was getting red and chawing fiercely on the last of his steak.

"I sort of understand it." Peg was finished with the second potato and was reaching for a couple of rolls beside Shag's plate. "When I was a little girl, I used to have an imaginary friend."

The Citizen understood that. "Kids do that. Almost all kids do that."

"Shore," Peg said, "but kids grow out of it."

The Citizen sat and blinked. He was having a hard time connecting what he was hearing with what Peg was making him feel. "If you don't grow out of it," Peg said, "and if the world won't let you have an imaginary friend, then you either got to have a real friend or make a substitute."

McDowell told himself that he would be damned. Without knowing she was doing it, Peg was proposing a whole new way of looking at one kind of psychotic behavior.

"Maybe," Peg said to the Citizen, "your daughter substituted the business for a friend. Maybe she couldn't find the right friend, and she didn't grow out of it."

The Citizen really understood Peg. He turned to McDowell. "College," he said with disgust.

"Shag dog," said Peg, "it comes on to your turn." She began to cut Shag's steak into big bites. Shag sat up, but he was still being polite. As Peg gave him the steak pieces he licked them right out of her hand.

"When I get a handle on something, I can figure it right out." The old man turned to Peg. "So Sammy needs a friend?"

"I don't know," Peg said honestly. "Maybe stuff like this goes on too long. Maybe there comes a time when you can't."

"Can't what?"

"Can't change over. Maybe your daughter has made your business such a big imaginary friend that she can't make no real friend anymore."

"Sammy needs a shrink," McDowell said, "but how we gonna get her to one?" He hesitated, not wanting to sound too discouraged, but wanting the Citizen to understand just how serious Sammy's problems might be. "It could take years to get it all worked out."

"Bullshit," said the Citizen. Then he turned to Peg. "I do beg your pardon for the cuss, but the boy gets me mad." He looked at McDowell. "Maybe the times have passed me by, but I know one thing. When you got a problem, you solve it. I don't care how modern the times get."

"This kind don't solve easy, Pop."

"You telling me what I already know. It might not solve easy, but it can be solved fast." The Citizen looked almost completely heartbroken. "She's my daughter, and she's in trouble. You got to help your daughter no matter what it costs." His heartbreak was spilling over onto McDowell. The old man looked carefully at him, but he did not seem exactly critical. "You should have been a schoolteacher," he said mournfully. "You're one of them flighty types."

"Pop, quit making me put up with this. I do my job."

"No, you don't. You do *a* job." The Citizen looked sly. "And for Christ's sake get a haircut."

"You talking English?"

"I'm talking haircut."

"Pop," McDowell said in complete misery, "I don't understand you one damn bit, not a' tall."

"I sort of do," Peg said. "He's telling you not to get a haircut."

"That don't mean a thing."

"He's telling you," Peg said, "not to make the same mistake your sister made." She sat Shag's plate on the floor for Shag to lick.

The Citizen was looking at Peg with a kind of love on top of his respect. "No offense, Miss Peg," he said, "but if I were a younger man."

"You are a good man, sir," Peg said. "You surely are one good man." Now Shag was busy licking Peg's fingers.

The Citizen sat and looked proud. Then he looked the way he always did when he was about to make a business decision—cool, nearly detached; like he was going to agree to something, then pile on an additional demand, and quickly agree to the whole works while the other guy was still slightly confused. He stood. "You be at the warehouse Thursday night," he told McDowell. "Nine o'clock."

"I got a business . . ."

"To run. Sure. Yep. But you be at the warehouse nine Thursday night. If Sammy really does get that restraining order, then Thursday night we'll all meet and I'll show you how to make Sammy well." The old man was like he always was after a business decision—nearly indifferent, like he was thinking of other things in the future and had no more time for what was already done. He made a small bow to Peg. "I have to go along," he said. "Your company has been a pleasure."

"I feel lucky to have met you." Peg was patting Shag. She seemed reluctant to allow either Shag or the Citizen to leave.

"Pop," McDowell said, "we still haven't settled this here business about Enoch. Enoch showed me something about you."

"I expect he did," the Citizen said. "I seriously ask you not to tell me." His voice was formal, dignified. "Take care of yourself, boy." He reached to touch McDowell's shoulder, looked like he was about to hug him or hit him. Then he reached further down and touched the back of McDowell's hand. "I can handle Enoch, but son, you take care of yourself." He walked to the door and opened it. "C'mon Shag," he said, "drive the old man home." Shag took a last look at Peg, then followed. Fifteen seconds later the Lincoln's starter kicked the engine alive. Headlights came on, glowing through the pulled curtains, and the Citizen backed away. McDowell sat feeling a terrible feeling. It was not premonition, but goodbye. He could not understand why he felt it, but he felt that he would never see the Citizen again. He felt like weeping. He felt loss, sorrow, and more than anything else he wanted to be held. He wished he could be beside Margaret, her talking soft, or giggling like she did sometimes, or maybe them just lying warm and silent together. He looked at Peg. Her eyes were sorrowful, and not just because of her lost man. She was feeling bad about the Citizen.

"He loves you," she said.

"I know it," McDowell told her simply. "But he couldn't say it if his life depended on it."

"Not his life. If it was yours, he probably could." She stood, walked to McDowell, and put her hands on his shoulders. Her hands were strong, musician's hands. They were touching him personally but not intimately. Then the pressure changed, and it seemed like her hands were loving.

"I don't want to, but I've got to go," McDowell said. "If I stay, I'll end up touching you back."

He could not see Peg because she was standing behind him. Her voice sounded amused, along with the sadness. "That's why Margaret loses them. They get wimpy."

"You're her best friend."

"The best friend you ever saw." Peg moved, pulled a chair and sat beside him. "You think she sent you here to hire a fucking guitar player?" She grinned through her hurt. "I know where the musician's union is. I can get a guitar player any old time."

"She wanted me to get you straight," McDowell said honestly. "When folks are bent, really bent out, it's hard to get straight."

"She's a one-man woman if she ever finds the man, I know her. I think she hopes she just found that man."

"I distinctly remember. She said catch your act, but come back to her. That didn't sound too generous."

Peg was not pretending surprise. She really was surprised. "She said that on the phone?"

"Last week. In bed."

Peg giggled and looked relieved. "Honey, what do you say in bed? Boy, you say anything."

"She keeps meaning more and more to me," McDowell said. He was feeling the earlier case of hots coming back, and they were not slow building.

"Me too. I feel the same, and now we got to quit talking." Peg leaned toward him, put her hand on his face. "I just lost a man, and I got poor feelings about your Pop." She stood, tugged at his hand, and he followed her. He had known all along this was going to happen. Women had left him. He had known all along how lonely Peg must feel. Peg kissed him, friendly-like, and began to undress. McDowell patted his shirt pocket, remembered that the mouthpiece in its tobacco sack was still on the table. He began to unbutton his shirt.

The wheelers and dealers were nothing. Life was the real wheeler-dealer. Peg stood, naked, beautiful, and as comfortable with her nakedness as if she were dressed.

"Dan, you ain't my man, but you're not just any man."

"Your best friend's."

"You're her man, and that's next best to having a man of your own."

He did not understand, although he had a feeling that it might be possible to understand. It might be, if he had talked to Margaret, first.

He decided to try to love Peg, and to be careful and do his very best. He would be slow and gentle, touching her as well as he could—because whether he did right or wrong, Peg was a woman worth loving. Maybe he could not actually love her, but he could try. The worn-out heart, his tired heart, might not be big enough to do for Peg as she deserved, but at least he could be god enough with the lovemaking.

It turned out, as he knew it would, that Margaret was wrong. Peg was every bit as good in bed as Margaret, but different, naturally. Margaret had that quiet, forward-thrusting intensity. Peg was more open, more accepting, and not quiet at all. Of course, he reminded himself, Peg had just lost her man. A part of her response was bound to be desperate. It was not until after the lovemaking, and talk, and more lovemaking, that she really shocked the living daylights out of him.

He was lying beside her, feeling dreamy and glad and guilty, all at the same time. He had one arm across her, kind of cuddling her breasts. She lay silent, not exactly lonesome, but probably thinking more of her lost man than of him.

"If I don't have you," she whispered, "I'm glad Margaret does."

"I'm glad I'm here," he whispered back, "but I don't know what in the world to tell her."

"Just tell her the truth." Peg stirred. "You as sleepy as me?"

"Sleepier than anybody."

"One thing in this business," Peg whispered, "is I can sing us both to sleep." She rolled away from him, crossed the dark room, and picked up the tape deck.

He wanted to say, please, no. He did not need no damned sproingy guitars and nasal country music, but he said nothing. You could not make love to somebody and then tell her you did not want to hear her voice.

Peg carried the tape deck back to the bed, punched the play button, and then turned the volume low. Then she snugged in beside him.

Peg's voice began to make figures in the air, slow, nighttime jazz in front of a gray and silver-voiced trumpet. A jazz guitar was laying low, giving a slow kick to the voice, and the drum was on brush. The drum was a little corny, not much.

Peg's voice was in control, and it worked perfectly for that music. She did not have Margaret's range, and she did not have Margaret's ability for sustained volume, but hers was a first rate jazz voice. McDowell, who had been sleepy, was suddenly wide awake.

"Why?" he whispered.

"Why what?" She was giggling.

"You know. When you can do that, why do the other?"

"Margaret's pop worked for the post office," Peg said. "You know what that means?"

"Nope."

"It means he always had a steady job," Peg whispered. "Margaret was an only child. You know what that means?"

"Nope."

The music dwelt in the darkened room like mountain mist, like the slow heat of humid valleys.

"My pop had forty acres, twenty straight up, and twenty straight down. He had seven kids. Now do you know what that means?"

"Yep," McDowell said unhappily.

"Margaret has been broke, lots of times," Peg whispered, "but she's never been poor. I can't stand to be poor, ever, ever again." Then she lay silent, listening to the figures of music, the confident voice and the confident horn. She took McDowell's hand that was resting on her hip and placed it back to her breast. "Go to sleep, babe. It's okay. Just stay close."

Chapter 23

WHEN HE WOKE BESIDE PEG, HE FELT A SENSE OF RELIEF AND could not spot the cause. Peg's long hair was soft against his chest as she laid facing away from him. The light through the draped windows was subdued. The air conditioner made a low whisper that could be heard in spite of the early morning traffic on the distant street. Dan McDowell lay quiet, not wanting to wake Peg. She would soon enough have to face her work and her sorrow. Her work was easy enough. She had to hire a guitarist and practice like crazy for a couple of days. Her sorrow, he could do little about.

Plus, when she woke, he would be right back into the world of problems, and love, and guilty feelings, and fear, and ghosts, and that crazy damned Samantha. Plus, he did not know how in the world he was going to explain all of this to Margaret.

He could not figure out why he felt relieved.

Then he thought that in the last few days, as he met people, the meetings had been different. He met a lot of people all the time, but he usually did not remember them so much. There was the tired, broke guy at the pawnshop, the black kid cop and the fat waitress.

He looked at Peg's hair in the subdued light. It was not cloud-like, the way Margaret's was, but it was just beautiful. Then, he thought, there was the old bartender, the Arkansas fag, the stoned kids, and the madman who stomped his car.

Peg breathed deep, kind of snorked a little, and snugged back into sleep. There was the lady who threw away groceries, and Peg, plus his manager, Nance. There was the Citizen, the kid in the red Buick, the old parking lot attendant, the pinstripe priss and those hotel folk. There was Margaret. And, for some reason, he had been thinking more than usual about Becky. Last, of course, there was Enoch.

It suddenly seemed to Dan McDowell that every blessed person he had met in the last few days had been trying to tell him something.

He turned his head, looking around the room. Over on the table beside the dishes from last night's meal, the mouthpiece lay in the tobacco sack. On the dresser, like a threat, was the black, cold and deadly forty-five. He tried to pretend he was using the gun. He felt his thumb wrap comfortably about the grip so that the saddle of his hand lovingly depressed the rear safety to fully arm the weapon. He felt the weight of the pistol, pulling up and pushing forward. His mind directed itself along the line of sight, his vision narrowed to the target-and then his mind balked. It did not laugh at him this time. It sneered. His mind was not putting up with his play-acting.

Plus, he remembered with a deep feeling of misery, his car no longer meant a thing to him. Dan McDowell felt momentarily lost; lonesome in a world he could no longer even pretend to understand.

He allowed his mind to drift, and his mind seemed trying to go back to sleep. It did not want to work at figuring all this out. Then, like it was allowing him one small piece of information, his mind told him the reason for his relief.

The weather had broken. Beyond those pulled drapes the subdued light meant a thin cloud cover; but it was more than the light. In spite of the imitation comfort afforded by the air conditioner, there was a different feeling in the room. The humidity was less, the barometer had dropped. McDowell had seen it a thousand times. When he went into the streets, everyone would seem a little bit giddy, kind of silly-happy. It would not be the same town for awhile. Life would be more exciting, a little.

With the giddy feeling, his worn-out heart did not seem so worn out after all. He watched Peg, or rather the back of her head and her flowing hair, the contour of her body beneath the sheet, and thought of her voice.

Then he thought of the mouthpiece, of placing it in the horn and the horn walking quiet and strong behind Peg's voice, Margaret's voice—he thought of Becky. His mind was allowing this. It was not balking or sneering. For a moment he loved all three women, and he did not really love one more than the other. For a moment it was like he could hear all three voices, even though he had not heard Becky's voice in years.

But nearly—he told himself—but nearly. Five years ago when Becky had been working in Cincinnati, he had been dreadfully tempted to catch her act. He finally decided against it, and not because he was afraid of how it would hurt. He had not wanted to take the chance of Becky seeing him. That would have hurt her, maybe. At least Becky was catching work, here and there.

Feeling the love, and glad he could feel it, he touched Peg's hair and snugged toward her a little. She sighed in her sleep, snugged closer to him, and for the minute or two before she woke, Dan McDowell lay wishing that he did not ever have to do anything but this. He wanted to be loving and warm beside a woman.

But that was not strictly true. The understanding came to him like a masterful run high off the neck of a guitar, the notes like a sparkle of sunlit rain. The women he had really loved, loved the most, were not just women. The important women were the ones who were doing something they knew was important, and doing it with skill. They were professionals first, and women second. Even Nance, his manager, was that way. Maybe she was not a musician, but she believed in what she did.

To be loved by a woman like that, that was the best way of being loved in the world.

"Dan." Peg's voice was soft and full awake. She must have been awake for quite a while, remembering where she was and who she was with.

He touched her shoulder.

"Gimme a smoke." Now she sounded bright, happy.

"Shore, but you've got to work."

"One never hurts. Or even ten."

"Maybe ten." He rolled over, got the cigarettes and an ashtray from the nightstand. He lit two smokes, passed one. Peg lay on her back, smiling and happy, and feeling the relief of the changed weather.

"Good day to work," McDowell said.

"Yep, and we got to do it. I got to go down to the union hall."

"I got to check out a factory."

She seemed genuinely happy, looking forward to the work. Then she moved one hand down his side, toward his groin. She giggled. "Sort of loose down here."

"But not remaining that way."

"Actually getting sturdy." She tapped the ash from her cigarette, rolled toward him. "You ain't going to understand this, but put up with me." She rose, knelt over him, and gently eased herself around him. "I ain't worth a doggone at this in the mornings, but it's friendly. Awful friendly some mornings." She was not moving on him at all, just surrounding him and squinching her eyes against the cigarette smoke. McDowell, who believed he had seen most everything, told himself that he had never actually seen sex used for friendliness and not at all for sex itself.

"Any man who would leave you for a goddamn job has got to be nuts."

"It wasn't just the job." Peg's light blue eyes, her long hair, and her full breasts were only a little obscured by the smoke from McDowell's cigarette. She looked both strong and vulnerable at the same time. She butted her smoke, lit another. "He's one of them jealous types. This bust-up has been building."

McDowell felt suddenly possessive and then wondered what in the world was wrong with him. After all, Peg was not his lover, even if he was inside of her right now and holding a casual conversation at the same time. "But you didn't give him any cause?"

"Had lunch with a former lover. Guess that was enough."

"Just lunch?"

"It was only lunch, but one mighty powerful former lover." Peg reached to touch his chest.

"Either that or a powerful lunch."

"You don't stop loving somebody, just 'cause you stop living with them." Peg seemed happy with some memory.

"There's a lot of jealous guys," McDowell said. "Honey, you don't know the half of it."

"Ladies, too."

"Everybody's lonesome, Dan." She took a deep drag on the smoke. "Lonesome, and times are changing. Scares hell out of me sometimes." Now she was stroking his chest, loving and gentle.

"You been with a lot of ladies, you know about being scared."

"How did you know? "

"You got a man's body, but you got a woman's touch."

"I tell you true, I never meant it that way. My ladies leave me."

"Margaret won't, if you don't hold on too hard." Peg grinned and gave a little wiggle, like she was teasing. "Me either, if you were my man, and if you didn't hold on too hard." She butted her smoke, leaned down to him, took his cigarette and butted it. "You go ahead with me if you want, baby. I'm no good mornings, but you go ahead."

"Rather just hold you." He drew her down to him, her full breasts against his chest as he held her thin body. He rubbed her back. Her hair was full across her face. They lay, petting each other for a couple of minutes, and then Peg sat up.

"Going to leave you now. Gotta get to work."

"Friends?"

"You understand it," Peg said, "and almost nobody does. Friends in the morning, lovers at night."

It was one more highly original view of sex, McDowell thought as she rose, gave him a pat on the knee and headed for the bathroom. He was momentarily lonesome for her, and then he lay feeling something else. He had rarely felt so well laid in his life, and technically nothing much had happened.

He rolled out of bed, went to the table, and picked up the mouthpiece. His jaw gave a twinge and his upper lip was sore. The shower began to run, but just before it started, Peg's voice was making little hums. He returned to the bed, leaned naked against the headboard, and practiced. Today would be a sore day, and tomorrow, and then the lip would level out a little. In two weeks he would begin to have something firm to work with.

Across the room the pistol lay like it symbolized the crazy, younger times in his life. There were more pistols out on that road than there were in all of Chicago.

You could not get rid of your grandfather's pistol. It would be just plain sinful. At the same time, it was stupid to carry the thing. The Cad was a rolling advertisement. Cops checked you out, and kids always checked you out. It was one of the prices you paid for having something wonderful.

Only, he thought with misery, it was no longer wonderful; and the very, main, absolute problem was that he did not understand why. He worked with the mouthpiece, and for the first ten minutes or so got some pretty good play. Then the lip pooped and the control dropped away. The shower stopped and Peg was still making little hums, although now they were country hums.

Peg came from the bathroom just as Dan McDowell believed that he understood something she had said. Peg had said that he would never understand country music until he understood why a woman would help a man hang himself because she loved him.

That, McDowell thought, was kid stuff. That was worse than the glandular, liquid preoccupations of kids. This childlike, ignorant, innocence-ridden south; ridden with a romance so unlettered that it could only express emotion through action. Peg was singing for romantic kids, even if some of them were seventy years old.

And that was why jazz was real, he figured, and country was not. Jazz came from those black people who had no reason in the world to be romantic. Jazz came from realists. It seemed to McDowell, as he sat playing the mouthpiece and waiting for his turn in the shower, that the black people of the south had always been sort of female, and the white people had been male.

"So that's your vice." Peg pointed to the mouthpiece. She was dressed in the conservative beige outfit she had worn the night before, but her long hair was tucked up now in a businesslike way.

"Used to be."

She grinned an openmouth country grin and looked him up and down. He was no more embarrassed by nakedness than was she, though he suddenly felt a little self-conscious. "Very cute," she said. "If Margaret don't want you, I reckon I could find house space." She pointed at the mouthpiece. "Can you back somebody up with that?"

"Nope." He was more embarrassed with his answer than he could ever be with nakedness. "I used to, but now I'm just fooling around."

"Well, keep on fooling, Dan." Peg was checking out the speckle-painted, plasticy guitar that lay in its open case. She picked it up, sproinged it a couple of times, and looked moderately pleased. "This country is tough."

"Humidity?"

"Heat and humidity. I've seen cheap ones, and some not so cheap, crack or come unglued." She snapped the case shut on the guitar, picked it up, and walked with it to the bed. She leaned over, gave him a wifely sort of peck which hit approximately on his nose. "Meet you back here for dinner?"

He was doing nothing much until he met his father on Thursday night. After that, no matter what else, he was getting out of town.

"How's your poor head?"

Peg slowed down for only a moment. "Like you'd expect. Sad, partly glad."

"Six o'clock."

"At least," Peg said and looked him up and down like she was pretending to be lewd, "I don't have to feel like a calf being weaned." She carried the guitar across the room, stopped beside the dresser, and shoved the pistol away like it was a toy. She checked her purse for car keys before she was through the doorway and then headed for work.

Chapter 24

MIXED SUNLIGHT CAME AND WENT THROUGH THIN, LOW-SAILING gray clouds, and the thermometer was right on down there around eighty degrees. The tall buildings rose against the gray sky, and from the street, traffic roared, popped, cracked. From one corner of the motel parking lot the blue lights of a police car flipped, flipped, where a traffic cop was giving someone a ticket. Dan McDowell, who felt an obscure sense of duty to his car, lowered the convertible top. The pistol, hidden in the paper sack, was stowed beneath the seat. McDowell secured the tonneau cover and made certain that nothing was adrift in the car. Then he picked up the horn and his suitcase. He climbed to the second deck to stash the horn in the room he had rented. In the room he dialed the desk, reserved another day, and was nearly regretful because the Arkansas guy had not answered. Then he got out of the Republican-style room.

Standing on the second deck, looking out across the parking lot, he could see the traffic running in the street. There were not as many horns honking this morning. The break in the weather made people less likely to take offense.

A money-color green Saab was turning into the lot, cruising past the flicking lights of the police car. McDowell told himself, no, aw, no, nope. Sammy was descending like the wicked witch of the west, and he did not want any part of it. The Saab was coming slow, like Sammy was tired or drunk or heartbroken.

He told himself not to let her trap him in a room—if Sammy wanted to talk, she could do it in the parking lot. He walked the length of the double deck toward a stairway at the end of the building. It would allow him to approach her from behind. When you dealt with Sammy, any little advantage was a help. He paused at the top of the stairs before descending. He felt tired. Too much had happened too fast. For years his family had not pestered him, or him them. For years Enoch had pestered him only once in awhile. Now, when he finally thought he had a woman, life began to come apart. Too much Sammy, too many confusing appearances of a ghost.

With the weather broken, and in the gray light with the reality of traffic rushing past in the street, Enoch no longer seemed real. He was like a dream, almost. McDowell paused, struck with a new thought. Maybe Enoch was a dream. Or, if not, then maybe Enoch was something other than he seemed. Dan McDowell realized that Enoch might be an expression of something, some force, perhaps. Enoch might not simply be a ghost at all.

Of course, he told himself, it was still possible that both he and the Citizen were crazy in some brand-new way that had never been identified.

Maybe everybody was nuts. Except, of course, Margaret, and maybe Peg.

Now Sammy's car was pulled in beside his. He could see her sitting behind the wheel as he descended the stairs. She was making no motion to get out. Her head looked kind of bowed. Then she raised her head, pushed her chin forward, and stared at the closed door of Peg's room. McDowell walked toward her, pretending he was a psychiatrist. His mind almost let him get away with it. His mind seemed to grow wider, more generous, and indifferent to any surprises. His pace slowed, and then his mind balked.

Maybe that was good. He figured it was a poor thing to be too generous or open around Sammy. He walked to her car, tapped on the window. She turned, startled but in control. She seemed nearly mechanical. He attempted to open the door but it was locked.

Sammy rolled the window down on the driver's side, but she stared straight ahead all the while. McDowell walked around the front of the car, stood leaning down toward the window. Sammy was dressed in still another frilly blouse, but this one was light blue. She was wearing a dark skirt that fell across her lap in a way that showed her to be even thinner than she looked. She sat absolutely still, and McDowell could feel her tension.

"Nice morning," McDowell said, "what with the heat coming off." He waited, expecting her to give him a mean look, or to start lecturing, or to do something else Sammyish.

She did not look at him. The Saab's engine was churning along in an ambitious-sounding way, and the pinball lights on the dash were sending obscure signals.

"Of course," McDowell said, "maybe it ain't a good morning." The Saab's air conditioning was blowing a cool stream and he could feel it coming from the open window. "For folks who stay up late." He was pushing her a little too hard and knew it.

"If everyone," Sammy said in a small, cold voice, "did exactly as I asked, then the whole world would be happy."

He stood, looking down at his sister, and told himself that she had to be kidding. Nuts was nuts, but it seemed like there ought to be limits. He made his voice sound kind, and it came out sounding even more kind than he believed was possible. At the corner of the lot the lights on the cop car switched off. "Of course," McDowell said kindly, "you don't always tell folks what you're asking. How are folks to know?" The Saab's engine had that breathless, whirry, hot-dogging sound of engines rigged with turbo. This turbo was badly out of adjustment. It sounded like it was trying to cut in on a fast idle.

Sammy said nothing. She sat staring straight ahead, and while he could not quite see her eyes, he knew there were no tears in them. "Samantha, I really have work to do. If you want to talk, then do it." His voice was still kind.

"He gets in enough trouble," Sammy said, "without you introducing him to cheap women." She finally turned and looked up at Dan McDowell. "Daniel, what exactly are you trying to pull?" Her eyes were nearly brilliant, staring straight at him.

He thought he should turn away, go to his car and leave. Then he regained control. "I don't know any cheap women. Never, not a one."

"That's hardly for you to say." She lowered her head again. "Something was going on here last night. I want to know what."

"That is my lady friend," McDowell lied, "and my father. Folks can get together for a good time without it being a conspiracy."

It was the wrong word to choose, and he knew it as he was saying it.

"You named it," Samantha said, "not me." She turned back and looked at him. "Taking advantage of an old man. Daniel, exactly how much money is involved?"

She really was crazy. He had almost not believed it, or at least he had not believed it was this bad.

"Sammy, what in the hell are you talking about?"

"Lie to him if you must, but spare me these stupid deceptions." Now she raised both hands to the steering wheel. Her thin fingers were wrapped around the wheel. Her knuckles were white, she was gripping it so hard.

"I'm not lying," McDowell said helplessly. "I really don't know what you are talking about."

"He's going into business with you," she said. "That's the only clean motive I can think of, and on your part it's dirty." She looked at him, blinked like she was about to cry, but McDowell knew it was an act. Sammy never cried. "He's my father," she said. "You went away, but I've loved him all my life."

"You got a goddamn funny way of showing it." He told himself to hang onto his temper, but he was not hanging on very well.

"When a man cashes out his securities and closes his personal bank account and deeds personal valuables to a silly museum . . ." Sammy kind of choked, seemed unable to continue, then got control. "He's moving to Chicago, isn't he? To your big apartment in Chicago. Daniel, you stole him."

McDowell told himself, hot dog, oh, boy. The old man was protecting his own ass. Before he could be restrained, the Citizen had gotten hold of some capital. McDowell could not help grinning. "You should of thought of that, Sammy. You just made yourself one whale of a big mistake."

Her knuckles were so white they looked dead. She actually seemed to be shivering, she was in such tight control. "I fear that you have made the mistake, Daniel. The results of that hearing are now a foregone conclusion. The money will be retrieved, or most of it. Your plans will fail." She gave just a little wisp of a cold smile. "And those plans must have been terribly expensive. You lose, Daniel."

She was right about that. He had lost. Lost a sister, and in some way he could not yet explain he had lost his father. He felt sad, hopeless, and the bright-feeling day caused by the good weather now seemed dead and dull. "I can't help what you think," he told Samantha. "Go ahead and think it, but you're wrong."

"Only, I suspect, in a few minor details." She put the Saab in gear. "Now, if you have no further explanations."

"I don't have any explanations. There ain't nothing to explain."

"Perhaps there will be, later." She looked up, her eyes brilliant with their direct, tunnel focus. "You too, Daniel. I've loved you all my life. You're my brother." She backed the car, spun the wheel, pulled forward, and drove slowly from the lot. McDowell stood, watching, wanting to weep.

He had no doubt that on some perverse level of madness his sister really did love him. He also had no doubt that it would be wise to stay away from her. If Sammy loved you, it seemed like a good idea to start wearing armor plate. For an instant, but only that, Dan McDowell nearly felt sorry for the Wimp.

He walked to the Cad, climbed in, and sat for a few moments before he pulled away, thinking about the Citizen. The old man was just protecting himself. He had touched no company funds, but he was probably still in pretty good shape. At least Sammy could not make him dependent, or a pauper, because the old man had been sly for too many years. He could hide a buck right under Sammy's nose and she would never find it.

He pulled away, entered traffic, cruised along looking for a gunsmith who used to be in business out this way. He drove for a mile, doubled back, and found the small store, which did not seem to have changed much. It was nearly a cubbyhole instead of a store, and the miniature building was painted yellow. The windows were as dirty as he remembered, and McDowell loved it. This place had survived while *they* were renewing the town. He pulled the forty-five from beneath the seat, unloaded the magazine, and tossed shells, magazine, and gun back into the paper sack. He started to get out of his car, intent on having the gunsmith mail the gun to him in care of a gun store in Chicago. He stopped.

The presence did not slide into the car; it simply opened up like it had been there all along. McDowell sat, blinking, waiting for something to happen. The presence was sitting right there on the seat beside him, and although it did not seem forceful or demanding, McDowell still felt a hint of warning. He settled back in his seat, waiting, and this time he tried to be calm and objective.

It seemed to him that he was living in the middle of a mystery. All along he had been fooling himself by thinking that his problem was a ghost. He tried to analyze what he knew. The ghost of Enoch McDowell had never done him harm, only frightened him speechless. The presence had exhibited a variety of force. Sometimes it was strong, with the confidence that could only come from complete power. Sometimes it seemed weak. Its power ebbed and flowed and seemed to depend on some circumstance or unknown law that McDowell could not guess.

He picked up the magazine and pressed the fat, chunky bullets one by one onto the stiff spring. He laid the loaded magazine beside him, opened the receiver, looked in. The thing was shiny and new looking. He held it up, looked down the barrel. He could just about swear that the pistol had never been fired. He tried to remember his grandfather and had only a vague memory of a face surrounded by flowing white hair and a white beard, the way religious members of the House of David used to wear their hair. McDowell wondered if the presence sitting beside him was his grandfather.

Then he told himself, nope. This presence might show ghosts, or cooperate with ghosts, but this presence was some *thing* and not some body. He shoved the magazine back into the pistol, then shoved the pistol beneath the seat. Margaret's photograph was down there, and so was the antique Cadillac emblem.

The presence still sat beside him, but the minute he decided to hold onto the pistol instead of having it mailed, the feeling of warning was gone. The presence obviously wanted him to keep the pistol.

McDowell started his car, got moving, and nearly expected the presence to blow away in the wind stream. He headed for a main route that circled the city, figuring he could save time getting to the furniture factory. The factory was in the city limits, but on the other side of town. In fifteen minutes he was on the main road, circling the suburbs. In places, the road even ran through fields.

The land was not yet sere, but it was faded in these last days of summer. Grass was yellow and a few of the trees were already beginning to change. In the distance, the city seemed vaguely obscured through shimmers of haze. The land rolled away toward the eastern mountains. An ancient land, and time in this land could be seen in every curve of the rolling fields.

But, he told himself, that had nothing, absolutely nothing, to do with him. He was a man who traveled over the face of the land, detached from the land. He was a man of the cities and roads.

In denying that it was his land, he made a discovery, and the discovery was as startling in its own way as any ghost.

This *was* his land. He had come from here; born, bred, raised from here. This land was a part of his blood, his bone, and it was a part of his mind. He could no more leave this land than could his grandfather—or Enoch—or his father. Made no difference he told himself, if he, Dan McDowell, moved ten thousand miles away and learned to speak a foreign language. This land was always and forever a part of him.

At some point in his thinking, the presence slipped away, and he found the correct turnoff that took him back into the city. He found the street he wanted and cruised, checking addresses and looking for the factory. Where the proper address should have been there was nothing but a wide dirt lane. McDowell pulled into the lane and stopped.

Sometimes, even now in these modern and overbuilt days, remains of other times survived. Here, surrounded by tract houses and cheap businesses, was an entire wooded city block. The lane disappeared into trees. Some of the trees were immense, and this piece of land sat like an antique, nearly ancient voice that spoke softly trough the hum of traffic and city business. McDowell put his car in gear and cruised slowly up the dirt road.

Where the road dead-ended he approached an old barn that stood beside an even older house. The house had new white paint with gray trim, and it was surrounded by old trees. There was a patch of lawn in front, while fields ran up to a kitchen garden in back. The barn was medium sized, like the barn of an ambitious homesteader. It had been restored, red, of course, with white trim. On one end of the barn an open-faced shed sheltered neatly stacked lengths of rough-cut lumber. McDowell pulled into the driveway.

An old black hound lay in the mixed sunlight beside the house. Tied on two long lines, a pair of young hounds began to ruckus. One was black and tan, the other fawn colored. The old hound looked up, stood, stretched, yawned, then lay back down in the sunshine. The two young dogs continued to bark and growl and tried to sound important.

A man emerged from a small doorway at one end of the barn

moving like a kid. McDowell figured that one of the hired help was coming to check him out. As the man approached, McDowell saw that he was not a kid at all; he just walked with the looseness and confidence of a kid. He was at least as old as McDowell, and he seemed glad for the interruption. As he got closer Dan McDowell saw that the man was at least in his fifties. He was dressed in khaki work clothes, was slight built, and was growing a bald spot. His light brown hair was cut with streaks of gray. He hollered at the young dogs. The dogs gave a couple of woofs to show that they had the last word and then shut up.

"Pair of hot shits," the guy said as he approached McDowell. "Shame to keep them tied, but there's a lot of traffic out on yonder road."

"Weather will break in a couple of months. Then you can take them out and let them run." McDowell offered his hand and gave his name. The man shook hands in an easy, friendly manner.

"My name's the same," he said, "only the first name is Jim. Reckon we're kin?"

"I don't doubt it."

In this inbred and secular south almost everybody was every-body else's cousin. Old folks could trace lineage of everyone in a county. Their tracing almost always proved an intricate, if dim, re-lationship to every old family.

"Sure," the guy said, and nodded toward the dogs. "Come heavy frost and they can run. Then we treat cuts from barbwire and run-to-hell dogs." He grinned. "I never learn. Just never lived without hounds, I guess."

McDowell passed the man a business card. "Hoped you might show me around."

The man looked at the card, then at McDowell. "I can't do you a lick of good, but come on along." He was smiling, friendly, and what he said sounded like the truth and not just a sales ploy. He started walking back to the barn and McDowell followed.

"I heard of this." The guy held the card in his left hand and tapped it with his right index finger. "I'm glad somebody's trying it."

"More people should."

"Tell me true," the guy said conversationally. "Suppose some-body did. Is there room for another quality house outside the east coast?"

McDowell, who sold a lot on both coasts, told himself that he did not honestly know. "I do fine, but damned if I can answer your question." They arrived at the doorway to the barn. It was heavy, like barn doors almost never were, and it was perfectly fitted in its frame.

"It might work," the man said seriously. "Way I figure it, the whole country's trained to trash."

He opened the door that moved solidly on tight hinges. Mc-Dowell stepped inside.

"Only people get sick of trash." The guy stepped inside and closed the door. "I figure there ain't a person in the whole world who wouldn't like to have at least one nice thing, if they could afford it."

"My trade secret," McDowell said. "If folks can't have a nice car, they'll buy the best book about a car—and not no damn picture book, either." He looked around the barn. The long work benches and the machinery seemed too small for the space. A narrow section was partitioned off for an office, and another section was a showroom. Two old men were working at benches. A blonde-haired kid was hanging around, like he was waiting to be told to bring coffee or sweep the floor. There was room in the barn to work at least eight men, ten if you squeezed.

The man led McDowell to the little showroom. Before they entered he turned. "These are all sold. We keep everything we make for three months before shipping. Like to live with it, kinda." He actually ushered McDowell into the room.

Five pieces of furniture stood there. They all showed a companionship of design, and an easy link with history. The furniture was not reproduction, but it incorporated the skilled design of pieces made in the seventeenth century that were later called early American; which, McDowell told himself, were not strictly American at all. The design was frontier, and some of the best of it had come from European-trained cabinetmakers. Those men had changed and become generous and free with their lines, because in a brand-new country there was an inexhaustible supply of wood.

Dan McDowell pulled the drawer on a square but graceful chest. The drawer was heavy. He was willing to bet that two drawers of this piece would weigh as much as the total weight of a quality, manufactured chest. The drawer slid so easily that it seemed to jump at him. He closed it by pushing with his little finger.

"Not a nail or a screw in it," the man said with pride.

The ends of the piece were solid. They were not framed and paneled in the cheapening styles of the middle nineteenth century. McDowell looked deep into the hand-rubbed finish. He could not see the bottom of the finish; it was like staring into an ocean. He could not even feel the bottom. He looked the chest over, walking around it, could not find a joint. The wood flowed into shape, as if a tree had grown to that particular form. Beside the chest was a desk that was large but not massive. It looked like a desk on which you signed treaties. The quiet authority of the piece suggested power. McDowell told himself that he had handled quality, but never anything like this.

"How come you can't help me?" McDowell was looking at a spool bed that he knew did not have a lathe mark on it. The handrubbed finish on the back of the bed and on the rails was as deep and clear as on the surfaces that would normally show. It was a bed to be born in, raised in, make love in, give birth in, and die in. It probably belonged in a museum.

"Got a six-month back order." The guy was happy, but apparently not with the back order. He seemed to be happy just in the presence of his product. "C'mon to the office, and I'll tell you why." He led McDowell to the cubicle office, which was furnished with a good desk, but nothing special. There were chairs, a coffee pot, and a drawing board. The guy poured two cups of coffee, passed one.

"Because," the guy told McDowell, "I'm not set up for you. Around here only two pieces are being made at any one time. Some of those pieces are a month's work for a man and a boy." He grinned like a kid would grin, proud and sort of innocent. "Sometimes more than a month."

"I see some production machinery."

"Used to run a production business." The guy took a seat behind his desk, sipped at the coffee. "Might as well keep the machinery. It gets a little use."

"And might again?" McDowell sipped at the coffee, looked through the outside window and on to the land. He could not see the road.

"My trade secret," the guy said. "No more production. Make the very best and sell it dear. You always sell it."

"You can make a living?"

"That desk you saw in the showroom goes for ten thousand. I'm back-ordered two of them." The man swiveled in his chair, pointed to his shop. "You see those two old men?"

"Yep."

"Look close, 'cause you're looking at two of the last real cabinetmakers alive. One's French, one's German." The guy shook his head, was amused. "Hell of a running battle between them. Fight all the time, and they been friends for years."

"The kid?"

"The German's grandson. Apprentice. If I didn't slip him a few bucks on the side now and then, we'd have lost him." The guy eased back in his chair. "Squareheads are tight, and my men make better than they could anywhere else. Point is, there ain't anywhere else they are let to work the way they want."

McDowell lit a smoke, sipped at his coffee, and decided to push just a little. "There's a lot of good cabinetmakers. You could run more."

The man searched in a desk drawer for a pipe and began loading it. "I'm glad you dropped in. Hardly ever get any visitors." He tamped the tobacco, puffed away at lighting the pipe, and then laid it aside so that it immediately went out. "You're right, there's a lot of good cabinetmakers. Including me. But I'm not talking good, I'm talking master craftsman. There ain't never many masters." He glanced at his drawing board. "I only take responsibility for design, an' even then, sometimes, they'll change it on me." This time when he lit the pipe he kept puffing. "Suppose I did tool up? You'd place a good order, a big one. I'd run my two old boys crazy having a bunch of punks around. Then your line would burn out and you'd drop me."

McDowell did not want to admit it, and he was not about to admit it to the guy, but he would admit it to himself. What the guy said was true.

"Besides," the guy said, "you can't manufacture a masterpiece, you got to create her. Masterpiece is what's going on out there." He tamped the pipe without burning his fingertip. Smoke surrounded the guy's face and he sniffed at it appreciatively. "I got a theory. Came to me just before I stopped production. Theory about people and quality."

"That's my business," McDowell told him. "I sure would like to hear it."

The guy nearly seemed to be hiding behind his pipe. He nearly seemed shy. "This here country claims to be a bunch of individualists. The average guy out there is about as individual as one orange in a crate of 'em. I wanted to stop being an orange in a crate, no offense."

"I'm not taking any," McDowell said, "but that's a hard line to sell."

"And around these parts it's even worse. This whole area all the way to the coast, is just soaking with that individual idea. Always has."

McDowell thought of the Citizen, of Enoch, and he thought of the dog-sniffing drawls between men. He thought of the blue, turning lights, and the whip, whip, whip of sirens, of the Saturday night don't-give-a-damn, and of the madman who had busted his car. What this man said was causing him to understand a few things he almost wished he did not understand.

"Guys think they own themselves, but they don't?" He asked it like he was puzzled, but he thought he understood too well.

"Guys think they're supposed to," the man said, "and maybe they are supposed to. Only guys get trapped." The man looked completely apologetic, hiding there behind his cloud of tobacco smoke. "Ought not to say this, but think about it. You handle the very best of the good stuff, but you ain't set up to handle a masterpiece." The man began to get red in the face, blushing, and momentarily shy. "I talk too goddamn much, 'cause people hardly ever come by. It's a good thing, what you do."

McDowell told himself that he was pissed. Then he told himself, nope. He was shocked, and he was sad. Then he told himself to get the hell out, think this over, because new thoughts seemed to be churning all through his head. He stood, made himself a self-satisfied grin and offered his hand. "One of these days I'll send a personal order."

"Make it soon," the guy said. "Those old boys won't live forever." He shook McDowell's hand, looked shy. "I honest to God mean no offense."

"I take none."

"When those two old boys die, the game is up. The kid might

make it twenty years later, if he has luck and if they live long enough to train him right." The guy once more picked up his pipe, lit it, puffed like he was trying to keep busy.

"What'll you do?"

"I think about it sometimes. I got this place, an' I ain't a spring chicken. I'll probably go ahead, trying to do as good."

"If you ever get to Chicago . . ."

"I'm obliged, but I'll probably never get there." The man looked fatigued, like the talk had worn him out. "It's just an idea," he said almost apologetically, "but I followed it. Trouble is I got a late start."

McDowell left a little faster than was seemly, but he could not do the necessary play-acting. He walked past the showroom, which was like a small museum, went through the doorway and into the sunlight. The Cad was parked about twenty yards away. He walked toward it like he was walking to a mass production tin pot from any of a dozen countries. He understood now why he no longer loved his car. He told himself that no matter what that guy said, he, Dan McDowell, was not no damn orange in a crate but he feared that he was lying to himself.

Chapter 25

LATER, LOOKING BACK ON IT, MCDOWELL DID NOT UNDERSTAND how he got through that particular Wednesday. He figured that if it were not for Peg and Margaret he would have thrown a real drunk. Even Enoch, or at least the presence, seemed to help.

He left the factory and spent the rest of the day driving. The mouthpiece hung with its small weight in his shirt pocket, but he did not touch it. The road ran through a changing pattern of town, city, country. It passed rural volunteer fire stations, junk cars abandoned in fields, and brushy gullies grown about with trees. The gully trees looked like tall, winding fences across the land. The road ran through small towns, past general stores and post offices which were hardly larger than shacks. The small flags in front of the post offices hung limp in the windless, sun-and-shadow day. In a vague way he knew where he was in relation to Centerville, but for a long time it did not seem important to return.

He fed tapes into the tape deck, the music swelling up into the wind that suctioned across the open-air car. He thought of music and quality, or lack of it. He thought of jazz and country, and about the quality that resided in things.

The furniture guy had given him a terrible licking, and probably did not even know it. He, Dan McDowell, was not set up to handle a masterpiece. He, Dan McDowell, had objected to junk for most of his life. He had tried to fight back, to make a living by distributing quality. He thought of his inventory, and how all of it seemed like junk. You could not manufacture a masterpiece.

Except for jazz, he told himself, he could not even tell what a masterpiece was. That made him a wheeler-dealer, no more, no less. At least it seemed that way.

He thought of the Citizen and of Enoch; of Peg, who had been poor, once, and of his manager, Nance, who had been poor, once. He thought of himself and Margaret, often broke but never poor, and of crazy Samantha who surely wanted only to be respectable. Sometimes, he thought, it was like each and every one of them was play-acting.

Even Enoch. The Citizen had said that Enoch was trying to give a message. The trouble was that Enoch was no more plain in his meaning than was anyone else.

At that point, and it was getting late in the day, he paused. Margaret was plain in her meaning. Peg was. He almost believed that. Then he did not believe it at all. Dan McDowell, who had made love to so many women, told himself that he was catching mixed signals from those ladies. For a brief, nearly hysterical moment, it seemed that Margaret was shoving him at Peg so she could get rid of him.

He lost the thought as he ran up too fast on a mean curve. As the road fish-hooked, the heavy car humped its rear end, began to break sideways, and he seesawed it around by entering the oncoming lane. The mistake frightened him.

Time to shove life back into gear. Past time.

He found a side road, turned around, and headed back toward Centerville. The evening rush hour was beginning as he entered the suburbs. The traffic lights were timed against him, so it took nearly an hour to work his way across town and to the motel. Other drivers checked out the Cad when he was stopped by traffic lights. Police checked out the Cad. Now, as people looked at his car, he felt that they were really looking at him. Maybe they were wondering if he was a rich playboy or a pimp.

When he arrived back at the motel, Peg's Cadillac was parked outside her room. He checked his watch and remembered that he was supposed to meet her at six. There was time for a shower, if he moved fast. He hopped from the car, unhitched the tonneau, and raised the top. As the top flopped into place the car became shadowed and seemed safer, less conspicuous. For a moment he nearly took pleasure in the car.

Once back in his room, he showered, changed clothes and put on his last fresh shirt. He debated on whether to call for laundry service, then ruled against it. Tomorrow night he would meet with his father. On Friday he would call Margaret from Indianapolis, and that evening return to Chicago. He told himself that if he absolutely had to have a change of clothes he could always buy one. He shook his head. There was so much junk in the world, so much merchandise. It occurred to him that Enoch had probably owned no more than two shirts and two pairs of pants, linsey-woolsey both. Both made by his women.

Time to get down and see Peg; in fact, he was five minutes late. He hesitated, felt in his shirt pocket, leaned down and pulled the horn from beneath the bed. The old wah-wah mute lay dented and dull in the case. He placed it in the horn, inserted the mouthpiece. His lip felt pretty good, but he knew that the feeling would not last. Dan McDowell blew softly into the horn, but it was not very soft because his lip was not in shape. He ran a scale, dropped off, tried, almost embarrassedly, the opening of "Limehouse Blues." The horn walked right on down there, not sharping out. The notes shaped, formed, were suggesting something he had never heard from himself before. What he heard was not bodacious but it had the lack of fear that a horn needed in order to be bodacious. The tune rose and he followed it. He got halfway through the tune before he cracked a note.

McDowell lowered the horn, blinked, could not believe what he had heard. He told himself that it was a fluke. The horn hung in his hand as close to him, somehow, as if it were a lover or a friend. He did not want to leave it, and he was afraid to try to play it again for fear that it really had been a fluke. He put the horn and mute away, and as he descended the stairs to Peg's room he blew softly into the mouthpiece.

The mixed sunlight had disappeared as the sun moved toward the horizon. The tall buildings looked like black sculptures against a brilliantly orange sky. Traffic was running heavily in the street. A tow truck was pulled over beside a stalled car. The red lights on the truck were turning, turning, and yellow flashes were pale in the orange light. From a side street, over behind the motel, came the sound of scorching tires as some kid or madman laid the heat to his poor, suffering car.

The voice of the horn stayed with McDowell. He could not believe that he had heard such a thing—at least not from a horn played by him.

When Peg opened the door McDowell was still musing and thoughtful. He looked at Peg, smiled a kind of hello, stepped inside and stood looking at her. He felt befuddled. Then he saw that he had better stop being that way. Peg was just beautiful, and trying to look her best.

She was wearing a blue, low-cut summer dress which helped to make her blue eyes sparkle. The dress was full, so that when she turned it whirled around and made her long legs seem even longer. Her hair was brushed out and moved as freely as the dress. He was willing to bet that if she had anything on under that dress it would take a microscope to find it.

"Get on in here," Peg said. She was smiling like a kid. Then he saw that her smile was more than kidlike. Peg was shy, and trying to cover her shyness. "I go to the trouble and expense of a seduction scene. Don't you mess it up." She gave him a peck on the cheek, the way she had kissed him when she left for work that morning.

He was suddenly glad, happy to be with her, and if he felt guilty about Margaret, which he did, he was still not going to deny that he felt happy. "Ain't you done sinnin' yet?"

"Nor ever will." This time when she kissed him it was not a peck. It was not lustful, but it was a kiss that was asking for a promise. He held her, laughed, kissed her again. "You want to get on with this seduction?"

"Strengthen you up first." She turned to where room service had set up coffee and buffet sandwiches. "Figure we have a little something now. Go out later." She waved him to the table, then crossed the room and turned up the volume on the radio. A singer seemed to fall off the scale, hit tip-toe on a note, and then sprawl flat. She was attacking light, then smearing the heavy, breathy accent after the attack. Peg shook her head.

"Little much what she's doing there." McDowell poured coffee.

"I know her," Peg said brightly. "Whores shouldn't never try to sing whorehouse." She moved quickly to the table, sat, grabbed a sandwich. Then she looked serious. "That ain't professional jealousy. I ain't jealous, Dan."

He listened to the voice. "No reason you should be."

"With the hype she's got going? Sure there's a reason. You know who it is?"

"Yep."

"I've had my men," Peg said, "but never, not once, not ever, did I make it with some guy so I could get a job."

"Some do."

"Or Margaret, either." Peg was talking as she chawed on the sandwich. "That girl has told more people to go to hell than they got ticks in Georgia." She took another bite, then a slurp of coffee. Her shyness was not exactly gone, but it was no longer so evident.

"Looks like you had a big day."

"Good one," Peg said. "Got a guitar guy who can walk all over that thing." She grinned, drawled, "Unfortunately, the sonovabitch is married."

He was relieved and did not know why. A small feeling of jealousy came, then left. He believed that if any jealousy had shown on his face he had managed to keep it covered.

"Which means you got an act?"

"Which means I can scoot through, anyway. Work again tomorrow." Peg had knocked off two of the small sandwiches. "Dan, it's gonna be lonesome when you leave. I got to tell you something." Her shyness had returned, but she was not embarrassed. When she picked up her coffee cup, her hand did not tremble. At the same time, the shyness made her seem nearly timid.

He remained quiet. He was afraid she was going to say she loved him and he was afraid she was not going to say it.

"I want to thank you, babe. Deep down. I mean it." Peg set the cup down, looking at him lovingly, if not in love.

He did not understand why he was being thanked. As near as he could tell, all he had done was help her get straight and made love to her on that first, worst night of being alone. When you had been left by your lover, as he had so often, you knew how important it was to be wanted on that first, worst night. He began to dismiss his importance, knew it would be the wrong thing to do, and remained silent. She was waiting for him to say something, and that something was not "you're welcome."

Now he felt shy. "Maybe you can tell me . . ." He fumbled, stopped. "You and Margaret, two of the three best women I've ever known . . ." He fumbled again. The shyness would not go away, and she was watching him with that loving if not in-love look. "Why me?" He heard himself, and he was whispering. "There's lots of guys. Good ones."

She giggled, which seemed to him about as inappropriate as anything she might have done. Still, when she answered, her voice was also whispering. "Two answers," Peg said. "You get one of them. The other answer is for Margaret to tell you." She reached across the table, touched his hand. "There aren't lots of good guys. That's one answer."

There were not all that many good women. At least not for him. It was simply that he had always assumed something was peculiar about him, not about the women he tried to love.

"I want to thank you back," he told her.

With the whispering, and with everything being so personal, the radio seemed even louder. A drummer was doing a tickety-tick number behind a slow-walking sax, but it did not sound corny.

"So if I'm going to be lonesome for awhile," Peg said, "I don't want to be lonesome now. In fact, I'm not." She grinned kind of countrylike, slurped the rest of her coffee, and stood. "Now's the time to get on with the seduction." She seemed happy but not particularly lustful. She turned her back to him. "Had hell's own time with those buttons. Suppose you'd better help."

This time when they made love Peg was not urgent. She was taking time to go slow, time to enjoy her own sensuality as she built nearly to climax, rested, teasing herself, then building again. She moved as gently with him as he did with her. He became as lost as she did in the slowly building, friendly, nearly-in-love movement of their bodies.

He loved it this way, and what he loved most, when it was this way, was the changing shape of her body. He loved the shadows that crossed her shoulders, the endless variety of curving lines as her breasts found their own forms when she moved through different positions. He loved the delicate, nearly fragile feel of her small ribs as he touched them. For a while, as the radio played a ballad, they were in an unspoken agreement of movement with the music. Then the physical compulsions began to take over, and the friendly, almost-in-love feelings moved aside as heat, experience, and the lawlessness of loving climaxed in a sweating tangle of mouths, hands, and voices. Startlingly, moving almost instantly away as their bodies pressed together, her eyes looked into his and he felt that she was trying to imprint his face inside her body.

He loved it this way, afterward, when the world was still timeless, soundless, and he was lying beside her and inside her, holding her face close to his and feeling the aftermath of small contractions in her body. He was, and he knew enough to know that she was, present but still away. It was like the private world of the body, joined with another, was intact, but at the same time it searched for intactness. His mind felt present and close to her, but it also felt that it moved through some far reaches from which it shortly must return. As it began to return, the opening notes of yet another ballad came from a softly playing trumpet.

"Sweet Jesus," Peg said softly, "where did that one come from?" She snuggled closer to him, if that was possible, her leg propped over his.

"Be with you in a minute. I'm coming back." He was breathing heavy, loving it all, the warmth and sweat and sight of it. The trumpet eased toward an intro. Peg shivered, listening.

"Uh-oh," she said, "hold me, Dan. Don't leave. Something more is coming, but not down there." She put her arm over him, tentatively, as if she did not know exactly what was going to happen next.

Margaret's voice filled the room, moving slow, doing what she had known all her life and what she had also learned, maybe, from the old records of Keely. Margaret was happy on top and sad underneath, remote, singing about love and loss and hope all at the same time. It was an old, sad sort of number that was not too slushy. Margaret was singing, "They can't take that away . . ." and McDowell knew it was part of the new release.

He was getting soft, fast. He held Peg, but he was holding her too loosely and knew it. He pressed himself against her, confused, and Peg reached to him, touched his chest gently, as he had touched the breasts of so many women. She rolled toward him, kissed him where she had touched, and he understood. The understanding was one of the best things he had ever known, because it was clean and open and unthreatening. Dan McDowell, who loved women, and who had jokingly even thought to himself that had he been born a woman he would have been a lesbian, held Peg tighter.

"That lover you had lunch with?"

"Doggonit," Peg whispered. "It was for her to tell you, and I done it, didn't I?"

He was getting hard again, but not with passion or lust. He was not even trying to move in Peg. It was like he was trying to caress her with his whole body.

"I'm not jealous," he whispered. "You ain't going to understand that." There was no possible way he could explain it. If he tried to explain, all he could tell her was that he was not a woman, and if he needed a woman, or Margaret did, that was separate, from him. He had made love to so many women that he understood how unthreatening and decent it was.

"You ain't gonna tantrum? You're not going to feel sad?" Peg moved her upper body slightly away, so she could press her leg closer around him.

They would never know this. This came from trying to love. It came from the openness that experience taught, from years of trying to love well. You could be glad for love, even when you were only a part of it. Dan McDowell understood that for all of his life he had tried to be everything to a woman. When his women left, and, most often, confusedly, it was maybe not because of him after all.

"I'm not gonna tantrum," he said, "but I sure would like to hear about it." Margaret's voice was moving hauntedly through the room. Her attack that worked so well on an upbeat number was working in a different way on this slower number. The pause that was really not a pause, but emphasis, caused a quiet thrust to the remoteness. He held Peg, loving her, and was so deeply in love with Margaret that he wanted to weep.

"There isn't much to tell," Peg whispered. "We've been best friends for ten years. Three years ago I lost a man and she lived with me for a month. Last year she lost one and I lived with her." Peg wiggled sideways. "Leg's tired. I'm gonna turn, but stay with me. She turned her back to him. He pressed closer to her. The record ended. Margaret was fussy with the ending, doing careful stepping, clearly enunciated phrasing that was a slow ride-out.

"We got each other," Peg whispered. "No matter what else happens."

At first he believed she was talking about him, then realized she was talking about Margaret. "I don't understand," he whispered. "Why don't you just live together?"

Peg giggled. She reached between her legs, touched his balls. "Three reasons," she said, "and here's two of them. The other reason is when we're together too long, we drive each other nuts." He could understand that. If they did not fight about music, which they would, they would fight because Peg was naturally outrageous and Margaret was not. Margaret was only outrageous in her speech, and only then because she had to compete in the world's toughest business.

"Takes some getting used to."

"Damn right," Peg said. "The first time I thought I was queer."

Now he was giggling. "You couldn't fool me."

"It's friends," Peg whispered seriously. "I never had the itch for no other woman, or hardly ever."

Dan McDowell, who thought he knew what there was to know about men loving women, lay beside Peg and told himself that he was a babe in the woods. At the same time his mind was flipping alternatives, trying to understand this new situation. Then his mind found a question that seemed intelligent. "Margaret liked me because she thought I'd understand this?"

"Yep, but more than that, but that, too. Now if you've got a twin brother . . ."

He nearly moved away from her, told himself to stay, whispered, "That's a hell of a thing to hear."

"No, it ain't," Peg said brightly, and she was not whispering. "Margaret loves you. It's just that she lucked out. That's all I'm trying to say."

In that case, he thought, it was a wonderful thing to hear. "Then it's not just because of what I think?"

"I'm gonna leave you now," Peg said, "'Cause I got to turn toward you." She eased away from him, turned, looked right at his face in much the way she had looked when it seemed that she was trying to imprint his face in her body. She touched his wrinkledy cheek and smiled. "Dear dumbshit," she said, "You don't understand about you." She paused, thinking about it. "Either you're all man, the way a man should be . . . or you're something else." Then she seemed embarrassed. "Don't pay that no mind. There ain't many good men."

A trombone was doing a happy number. It was kicking along, not quite slurping, and because the slurp was almost there the music sounded humorous. The guy was laughing through his horn. McDowell watched Peg, her seriousness, and heard the laughter in the music. He did not understand a thing about himself, but he suddenly understood something about jazz. Jazz was not sex, but gender. Jazz was female, always had been. Jazz came from the south, from black realists who could be happy because they were realists, or blue because they were realists. Jazz was a woman.

Chapter 26

THE SOUTH WAS A WOMAN. THE THOUGHT CAME TO HIM AS HE woke on Thursday morning, and at first it made no sense. It was almost like he could hear the Citizen's voice saying that in the south everybody was nigger and everybody was English. McDowell lay beside Peg, after a night of dreams. He and Peg had not stayed up late. They had gone to dinner, then back to the motel to sleep because she was looking at hard work the next day. Almost, he thought, they were like a couple who had been together for years and learned how to fend for each other. It was a warm, happy thought, and it was his second thought when he woke.

Dan McDowell watched subdued light filtering through the closed drapes. The feeling of easy weather was still in the room but his mind was not easy. In the subdued light Peg looked nearly frail. McDowell resisted the impulse to pull her close to him, as if he could protect her. He lay, still waking and figured that the impulse must surely have come because of his dreams. It had been one of those crazy nights when his mind seemed overloaded.

He had first dreamed of fire and darkness, a dream of heat that kept returning to haunt the other, really nice dream. He remembered the dark, fiery dream while the whip, whip, whip of siren sounded from the streets. A cop was headed somewhere in the early morning when the sound of sirens was rare. In the dream of darkness and fire he had seen the Citizen, Enoch, Samantha, and, strangely, Margaret as well.

Then the dream had changed. The warm, good dream came

with Margaret's voice and Peg's voice all mixed together. Then, even more strangely, like one more layer of music, came Becky's voice. He had not heard Becky's voice in years. It was so far in the past that it could now only be heard in his dreams.

The south was a woman. *This woman-worship, woman-hating, hot and fecund south.* He knew that what he was thinking was simpleminded. At the same time he understood that the feeling was true, even if all of the facts did not fit.

In the dream of darkness and fire he had stood helpless. Awake now, he could not remember why he had been helpless or what the fire consumed, but he remembered the feeling. It was like trying to strike out when you had weights tied to your wrists. Each time the dream got to that point it disappeared and the other, really nice dream had returned.

The room was cool enough so that he and Peg were lying beneath both the sheet and the spread. Peg was turned toward him, and her lips were making almost imperceptible movements that seemed childlike. She looked like a little kid who dreamed of sucking her thumb. Peg's long hair was loose behind her, falling away from her face so most of one of her ears showed to break the smooth, curving line of her cheek and the flat plane of temple. He lay, loving her, and feeling a particular kind of sadness that was as old as he could remember.

You only had one self, or at least you only had one body. Even if you loved more than one woman, you could really only live with one if you were going to do any kind of job. Maybe, he thought, three people could live together.

Then he told himself, no, nope. He could no more have with Peg than could Margaret. He would not be able to stand the shit-kicking country scene she worked with. Becky had been different. Now, wide awake, it seemed to him that he could hear all three of their voices, the way he had heard them in the dream.

Then, just before Peg woke, he remembered his horn, and yesterday, and how the horn had climbed right on down there, confident and strong. He actually shivered, thinking of what he had heard come from that horn. He told himself again that it was a fluke, had to be.

Peg pooched her lips together, like she was imitating a goldfish. Then she kind of snugged into herself, like she was fighting against waking. Then her eyes opened. She blinked a couple of times, yawned wide enough that he could check her back teeth, smiled at him and reached to touch his face. He told himself that he did not give a sweet damn about reality, not at this moment. He loved her right now, and the love was exclusive, right now.

"It's a big morning," he said softly, "waking up and looking at you."

She did not answer. The smile went away, and there was hesitation or trouble or question in her eyes. "Baby, baby," she whispered, "you come here." She scooched toward him, pulling his head toward her. She brought his face to her breasts, cuddling him here like he was a little kid. "Gotta get awake," she said, "give it a minute." With one hand she was petting his back. "Helluva night," she said. "Crazy dreams." She released him turned on her back, raised her hands and held her breasts like she loved them and was surprised by having them at the same time. She looked at the low ceiling. The subdued light made shadows across her face. He lay beside her, waiting. She seemed puzzled, like she was trying to remember something and could not.

Then she sat up, not urgent, but the puzzlement did not leave her face. She clasped her arms around her knees seemed to be staring way off into space, even though she was only looking at the far wall of the room. "I trust this stuff, if only I could remember. Somebody's hurtin."

The feeling of dread he had experienced on Tuesday night when the Citizen gave him the pistol returned. He thought of Samantha and her madness, and wondered if she had somehow finally nailed the Citizen. He wanted to draw Peg to him once more, to protect her. He wanted to deny Enoch, to throw that goddamn pistol into the river, to scoff and scorn at the presence, which, suddenly, seemed to lightly fill the room. The strength of the presence was no more than the diffused smoke from a cigarette, but it was there. He watched Peg.

"You're hurting," Peg said. "But you ain't the only one."

"You?"

"A little, I reckon. Your pop, too." Peg continued to stare off somewhere, concentrating. "Dan, what's happening right now? Is someone in this room?"

"Some *thing* is," he said. "You scared?"

"I'm pissed." She turned from him, got out of bed, as easy with her nakedness as some old, mythical goddess. She walked across the room, opened the guitar case, pulled it out and came back to bed. The presence remained light, quiet, nearly indifferent because it was so confident. Peg leaned against the headboard, arranged the guitar around her to accommodate the awkward position. Her right breast was pressed against the guitar and was pushed sideways. "Got big tits," she said, "and it's one damned mixed blessing." As she began working on the guitar McDowell remembered Margaret, her nearly miniature breasts, and kept his mouth shut. One thing no woman would ever understand, at least not about him, was that it was not a woman's size and shape that counted. It was the woman, herself, who she was and what she did. Peg was doing a light strum, fooling around, and then she began to pick the guitar.

She was shocking him almost as much as when he had heard her singing jazz. She was walking all over that guitar, lightly, delicately. He lay silent, not wanting to break her concentration. He was learning something private about Peg that not even Margaret knew. Peg could play that thing, and was playing it so easily that he almost believed she did not need to concentrate. The only reason Peg ever needed a backup guitar was to give her the extra voice she needed to make her own light voice sound more solid. Her guitar was improvisational, like it was asking questions about what kind of questions it should ask. The figures were not jazz, but they were not country, either.

Peg began a modulation, heading for a tune.

"When I was a kid starting out," she said softly, "I worked everyplace. Everywhere. Worked for a dollar or a dime. Worked the hills."

She moved into the tune, and the music spoke to Dan McDowell's dread, but it was also speaking to a sadness he had not even known he owned. The music was direct. It was calling up the voices of the hills, the coal hills. It talked about both hope and hopelessness, about tooth-rotting pregnancy without calcium pills or doctors; about exhausted, frightened men stooping above failed crops, and about the city myths that haunted the hills, telling of telephones and cars and electric lights.

"Worked a dance," Peg whispered, "down by a place called

241

Stinking Creek. There was a school bus ran in that county, and on the side of that bus was painted Stinking Creek School. Kids rode on that bus." The music hauled on down there with just the suggestion of a blues beat, but the music was Peg's and original. It was not folk, any more than it was country or jazz.

"You want to know why I sing it," Peg asked, but she was not talking to Dan McDowell. She was talking to the room. "I'll just fucking-A tell you why." The music rose, there was another modulation, not of key but beat. The guitar was coming into a country beat.

"I make 'em cry," Peg whispered. "They get to hurtin' in the cities and don't know who to kill. If they can cry, they get rid of it. They don't have to kill each other."

The guitar drove hard into the country beat, twanging, spradle-legged, ringing like don't-give-a-damn Saturday night. Then it eased back, as if Peg was daring the presence to do something. She was holding the guitar like she could spray reality from the neck, pointing it like a rifle. McDowell watched Peg, her musician's hands on the guitar, her left breast rising free as she chorded, and he had never seen anyone more defiant and beautiful.

"You holey, miserable, old-timey, country sonovabitch," Peg said. "Ain't you killed enough? Ain't enough good men dead?" She moved high up on the neck and the guitar started an intricate plaintive, and nearly wailing figure that Peg sustained, laid on, would not let go. "Dan," she said, "get rid of that goddamn gun."

"You seeing Enoch? You seeing an old, old man?" Dan McDowell was seeing nothing, only feeling the presence. The presence seemed stronger and was glowering, dark.

"I know what it is," Peg said. "Get the fuck back to those hollows," she said to the room. "This is my Margaret's man. Get outta here."

"I think he's only predicting something," McDowell whispered. "Pop said he was only predicting." He told himself that he had lived with the ghost for so long that he was almost used to it. Now, here was Peg, and she thought it was important enough to fight against. "It's just a prediction," he whispered.

"Like hell," Peg said. "He's causing it to happen. He's no different than a preacher teaching shame."

"What is he causing to happen?"

"Dan boy, keep it shut a minute. I'm gonna make the old potlicker lonesome." Peg was crossed over with her right hand above her left. The guitar sounded more like a dulcimer than a guitar.

Now the intricate forms became lighter. They began to sing, like water running, like the straight down-falling creeks and streams of the hills. They were calling up new grass, new leaves, pale new laurel, columbine, the summer cool of mist and high forest, fern, dogwood, low-limb pine. Peg stayed up there drawing pictures, and then she came off the crossover. She slowed her beat. The presence seemed to hesitate, and sorrow filled the room like invisible weeping.

Peg stopped. The silence in the room deepened with the weeping. "I'm gonna give you this," Peg whispered, "despite you don't deserve." She sat straighter, moving the guitar, adjusting herself to get air deep down so that she could push it with her belly. She sat with her head back, opening the passages for air and song. The guitar sounded one note, then another. Peg began to sing "Mingo Mountain," the purest of the pure music of the hill. It was simple, true, like Bach was true; and the pureness of Peg's light voice, soft and controlled, made Dan McDowell sickly with lonesomeness for hills he did not even know well.

Peg sang the measured, slow beat of the short song. When it was finished it still seemed to exist in the room, like a voice that wanted to say more but already knew everything had been said. "You go away now," Peg whispered. "Go home. If you can't go home, then just go way."

The weeping increased, until it seemed likely to stop being invisible sound and become real sound. Then, like suction, the presence left. It did not fade or wink out; it fled. Peg went to middle range and began strolling on the strings like she was taking a walk with friends through a sunlit field.

"You gave it a beating." McDowell was whispering, and he was awed.

"I've known of that mangy old fellow all my life. He's got a hundred names, maybe more. Back home they call him Old Man."

"The old man?"

"Just Old Man."

"You run him off."

"I wish I did," Peg said, "but I doubt it. That is one tough copperhead."

"Gone now, though."

"City boy," Peg asked, "what'n hell do you think this is all about? This ain't a joke."

"Not saying it is," McDowell whispered, and he was grim.

"When men kill men, that old boy is always with 'em. You ever see a man with a knife in his throat?"

"Nope."

"I have." Peg stopped playing, laid the guitar down. "My only husband. I was his third wife. The other two died." She touched McDowell's chest gently. "I wouldn't have gotten out if he hadn't been killed. Couldn't stay no more with him gone."

"How old were you?"

"Fifteen. Him forty."

"Pretty big difference."

Peg picked up the guitar, seemed to be studying it. "Shit, Dan, what's wrong with you? He was a good man, a good one."

"Just the age. Kind of young."

"No," Peg said softly and touched the strings. "About average. Pop's farm was what it was. Too many mouths to feed. All the young men moved to town. I've seen fifteens married to sixties."

"What happened?"

"Drinking happened. A guy looked at me wrong. Ended up, one man with a knife in his throat, one with a knife in his gut. Two dead men, and Dan, they was just drunk." Peg popped a chord hard, twice. "I hate women who start shit. I never started no shit in my life." She damped the strings, reached to touch his chest. "You got to believe that."

"Can't tell you how much I do believe it."

"Everything dried up in July," Peg said. "Crop didn't make. Coal was only bringing sixteen dollars a ton at the tipple. They had to drink, you know that."

"I know it now. Yep."

"He had a hard life," Peg said. "First wife died in birth, second a week after birth of infection. He done what he could." Peg began playing the lower ranges. The guitar began walking like it was sad and tired, nearly plodding. "He took the mule seventeen miles to get a doctor, 'cause the coal company doctor wasn't really a doctor. He thought he had his second wife saved."

"Kids?"

"Girl died during her borning. The boy drowned in a creek

during a spring rise when he was three. My man was in the mountain, underground and between rock. Preacher's wife was watching the kid." Peg looked like she was going to cry. "I was ten years old at the time. Could have done a better job. I would have watched after the kid."

The hills. Where there was no anesthetic except drink. Where in many places, still, no one had ever heard of birth control. "I'd be so afraid to have anything to do with a man if I was a woman."

"It's part of who you are," Peg said. "Dan, you ought to understand that."

"Maybe. I hope so."

"Dan, babe, you go to Margaret. I halfway wish you were my man, but there isn't a chance. You and Margaret have your work to do, I've got mine."

"I'm confused as any one man can get."

"Margaret's your woman. I can do one thing. I can be honest."

"Peg."

"I've got me, I got my own life. I like it or not, but I do what I've got to do." The guitar was still walking tired, plodding. "He wanted a kid so bad, and I'm goddamned if I'll ever understand why." The guitar began to move out a little, picking up its feet. "It is music," Peg said, "despite what you city folks say. This land is more than any city can show." She closed her eyes. "Don't talk to me now. I'm going away for a little while." The beat picked up. In middle range some of the high range figures began to return, like high range was spring and mid-range was summer. The guitar started fooling around, like a young girl strolling through the cool of a forest. Peg kept her eyes closed, her strong, musician's hands working with the guitar as she entered some private, remembered world.

McDowell lay beside Peg, wanting to weep and wanting to pray. He found that he could do the first, but not the second. Tears started so easily, that at first he did not even realize it was happening.

No one, nowhere, could ever imagine the kind of courage and work that Peg must have shown to get where she was, from where she had started. If her man had ridden a mule, then she had really been back in the hollows. There would have been no passable road, only a railroad to the mine. And what Peg had done was just nothing compared to what she believed.

The tears were not forcing anything, but they were giving him something. The realization began as light as an echo. Then it began to build with the full authority of an anthem. The realization frightened him, made him glad, and so filled him that his tears stopped. It was no time for tears. It was time for determination. He thought that he must have known this for a long, long time. Maybe forever. At least he had known it for days, and had been avoiding the knowledge.

He had to get on that horn and stay on that horn. Even if he did it bad.

And he *would* do it bad. Every horn out there had him spotted anyway twenty or twenty-five years. Years when he had been fucking and trying to make love and drinking and making a buck. All of those horns could do better, and maybe they always would.

Something in his heart, though, the worn-out heart, told him that it was okay to be broke. It was okay to be afraid. It was okay to fight back. No fight he would make would ever be as big as the one Peg had made.

It was okay if you had memories, the hot and haunted memories of the voices of horns. It was right and good if you could distill them and make something new, strong, a voice as true as the voice of a sweet-mouth hound.

Peg was winding it up. She stopped playing, opened her eyes, and laid the guitar aside. She looked at him, more tenderly, he knew, than he deserved. She reached to touch his wet cheeks and she looked like she might also cry.

"Be right back," she whispered. "I'll bring something for that poor nose." She rolled from the bed and headed for the bathroom. McDowell waited, unashamed of his tears. He remembered thoughts that had occurred to him earlier, thoughts about time. Peg, sitting in this expensive room here in the late twentieth century, had crossed over centuries. Where Peg came from had been closer to the seventeenth century, way closer, than to the twentieth. Where Peg came from life was stark, direct. He understood that Peg was not outrageous at all. She was only direct.

Then he thought that the Citizen was the same way. He was not really outrageous, not when you understood the directness that came from another time; a time with average life expectancy of maybe thirty-five. McDowell, thinking about people, suddenly understood a whole new way of looking at jazz. You could get that directness into music.

He lay waiting, thinking that this was not going to be easy, not at all. He could live for quite a while from what he got for the business, if he lived cheap. He could sell the business to his manager, Nance. He wiped his nose with the back of his hand, sentimentally wondering if for old times' sake Nance would pull one more of her play-acting mother numbers. Would Nance understand? He figured, nope, but she would try.

"I should have brought a couple of towels, looks like." Peg came back to bed, passed him some toilet paper. McDowell swabbed at his nose.

"If you can play that good, how come you don't play it for the audience?"

"Because the audience wants a singer." Peg sat on the edge of the bed, watching him. Her light blue eyes first showed concern then relief. Peg seemed to understand that something big had happened, and that it was not bad. "Besides, you don't ever want to draw too much attention off your backup man."

"Do it solo?"

"You need a man behind you," Peg said, "for more than music. There's so many lonesome guys, and there's always a few nuts. A good backup man keeps a lot of shit from coming down."

"Feel like a target?"

"Naw," Peg said, "but some do. Don't care how you play it, the lights make you more sexy than you are." She shook her head, like she was trying to shake a thought loose so she could examine it. "Dan, I got poor feelings this morning. You done dribblin'?"

"Yep."

Peg lay down, moved toward him. "Let's just hold each other, all naked and warm. If you want more, tell me."

"That's exactly what I want." He held her, wondering how anyone so strong and fine as Peg could still seem nearly frail. He cupped one of Peg's breasts in his hand, moving it a little, but only friendly-like. He wanted to tell her what had happened. She snugged in closer to him. He knew that he could not tell her, not yet. He had not yet done the work that would back up his determination. Someday, not this year, and maybe not next—but someday he would tell her. When the horn had its own voice, he could thank her for what she had given him.

"Part of the dream was nice," Peg said, "just me and Margaret." She touched his hand that still held her breast.

"I ain't jealous," McDowell said. "Most you two can ever do is be with each other once in a while."

"Friends. That's what it mostly is." Then Peg stiffened, held his hand tight against her. "Part of it was bad, and I remember part. Part of it was fire."

Chapter 27

IT WAS TOO EARLY FOR THE FALL RAINS, BUT WHEN McDOWELL left Peg's room, the horizon was dark and the sky looked vague with light mist. The temperature was beginning to climb. The break in the weather was not lasting. He figured there would be at least one more thunderstorm before autumn arrived.

Peg had left for work. McDowell was to meet her at six that evening. At nine that night he would meet with the Citizen. And, he told himself, probably, very probably, Samantha and the Wimp.

He stood outside of Peg's room and listened to the swell of sound coming from the street. The motel lot was full of expensive automobiles. Here and there a sports car was parked, a colored dot beneath the heavy, gray sky. The rest of the cars were big, painted in dark colors. McDowell idly fingered the mouthpiece in his shirt pocket and told himself that the motel must be holding a convention for embalmers. Then he grinned and told himself, naw, nope—he was just looking at the cars in a new and different way. Once, and not very many days ago, he would have been interested in some of those high-priced cars. He would not have noticed that most of them were dark.

The mouthpiece felt friendly beneath his fingers. It had damned well better be friendly. He, Dan McDowell was going to need every bit of help he could get. He was forty-three and starting something new. It was not going to be easy.

Then he told himself that nothing else had ever been easy for him, so why was he worried? Other people had done similar things, and they were no smarter than he was. He thought of the man who owned the furniture factory. That guy had closed down a production business so that he could help build masterpieces. The furniture guy was even older than Dan McDowell, and he had made it.

This evening, when he left the meeting with the Citizen, he planned to spend one last night with Peg. On Friday, he would drive to Chicago and get together with Nance. McDowell did not know where his company stood in terms of net worth, but Nance would know. They could make a deal that would serve them both. Nance would get a distributing business, which is what she wanted and needed. He would get enough money to buy the time it took to work with the horn.

He had to have a lot of time. Whether he could be one of the best horns or not, he was going to try to be one of the best. The whole proposition felt clean. That kind of feeling was not a new experience, but it had not happened so often in his life that it threatened to become a habit.

He told himself that this was no different than starting any new business. Peg had made it, and she had come from a lot further back than anyone else in her business. But, of course, music was more than just business.

He turned away and climbed the stairway to the second deck and the room he had rented. It was almost a relief to know that this would be his last night in this kind of room. His days of the tax write-off were over. He turned before entering the room. Cars were running as regular as current. The dark horizon and the gray sky seemed oppressive. He thought of his dreams, of Peg's dreams, and told himself that he should be worried. Instead, he only found that he was eager to get started.

Once in the room he pulled the horn from beneath the bed. It hung in his hand, as close nearly, as thoughts of Peg and Margaret. He put the mute in the horn, pulled the mouthpiece from his shirt pocket, and went to work. The horn started to cooperate right away, although his lip and fingers did not. He stayed in the middle and low ranges, listening to what he was hearing. What he heard was clumsy, cracked, too loud. At the same time he was hearing some of the authority in the voice of the horn that he had heard earlier. The voice held promise. It was not just a backup horn. The voice was trying, already, to get something done. McDowell fooled with it for a while, then ran scales. In less than an hour his lip felt totally demolished and his jaw ached.

He laid the horn aside and sat on the edge of the bed. While the lip rested, there were other things he could do. He sat planning, getting ready to leave when the phone rang.

They would not leave you alone. *They* could not even imagine that you had a right to be alone. *They* told you about everything that was wrong with you. The phone rang again.

McDowell swore. He promised himself that after tonight he was done. After tonight, he was never coming near this town again, even in his dreams. The phone rang again. He picked up the receiver.

"Sammy," he said, "you're in the wrong business. You ought to be training bloodhounds."

There was a light gasp, a moment of hesitation, and then a click as the receiver on the other end was hung up. McDowell sat back down on the bed, waiting. He wanted to get the conversation over with. At the same time he was glad to have jolted Sammy with what was, after all, not a guess. Still, it must seem like magic to her.

He sat imagining how she looked as she stood in her office, looking down at the telephone that had seemed to trick her. She would have a cigarette going, or would be lighting one. Her hands would be trying to tremble, and she would exercise stiff control so that they did not. Her face would look pointed, nearly, because of her coiled brown hair. She was collecting herself, putting a leash on her temper, and when she called back, she would be running a con. It was so predictable it was dull.

He lit a cigarette and waited. When he was done with Sammy, he had to find a music store. He needed a cheap guitar, a set of sticks, and a practice pad. He had never been a good guitarist, never wanted to be. He had never been a good drummer. Still, a guitar and a practice pad would allow him to work on his manual dexterity. It would strengthen and loosen his wrists.

The phone rang. This time McDowell answered brisk.

"The switchboard cut us off," he said happily, stealing Sammy's lie right out of her mouth. "How's Pop?"

"You probably know better than I, Daniel." Her voice had that thin layer of blue velvet, which is how she thought of herself when she was in perfect control. "However, that is not why I am calling." Her voice sounded as content as Sammy ever could sound. In her own icy way she sounded victorious.

"Hang on a minute." McDowell laid the phone down and walked to the bed to get the horn. He carried it to the phone and sat in a chair with the horn in his lap. If bad news was coming, it was a comfort to have the horn close.

"You buy a judge?" he asked Sammy.

Her victory must have seemed complete to her. Her voice would sound smug if it were not so icy. "I leave it to close relatives to suborn the legal system."

"Yeah, the Wimp."

"Not at all, Daniel. You know who I mean."

"Still," McDowell said reluctantly. "You got to admit that it was fast work." He nearly admired the Wimp. That Wimp must still have connections. He touched the horn and thought that he must take it with him to the music store. He could get he pads and corks renewed. Sammy was talking. He reminded himself to listen.

". . . and when he moves to Chicago, which I fancy has already happened, then this is a prima facie case."

He no longer had the advantage. Sammy was just kicking the hell out of him, and she did not even know it.

"Just a minute," McDowell said. "This is serious."

"I assure you that it is."

"Goddammit, Sammy, when did you last see him?" McDowell had last seen the Citizen on Tuesday night. Now it was Thursday. The old man had used all of Wednesday to do whatever he was doing.

Sammy picked up on the urgency in his voice. She knew she owned the advantage. "Tuesday morning," she said comfortably.

"And you tailed him Tuesday night."

"Nonsense," she said. "I came to see you. I did not even know he was there until I saw his car."

McDowell wanted to pick up the horn and blat it open bell into the telephone. He felt childish. Fortunately, his lip hurt and he did not want to be insulting to the horn. It would degrade the horn if Sammy even knew he owned it. He was momentarily speechless, reminding himself that facts meant nothing to Samantha. If she was as crazy as she seemed, she had already cataloged the facts and arranged them in a way that allowed her to absolutely believe her own version. There was no sense in fighting with her. It was better to be persuasive.

"Sammy," McDowell said gently, "no matter what you believe, this is important. When did you last see Pop?"

"Technically, Tuesday morning," she said. "I did not actually see him when you introduced him to that cheap woman." Her voice sounded like she was lying down a trump card, or like a lawyer presenting unshakable evidence to a jury.

"Sammy, Sammy." There was no reason to argue with her, none. He had to keep reminding himself of that. "What has Pop been doing?"

"Moving, I presume. His house is closed and the furniture sold, although it has not yet been removed." Now Sammy was bitter. "You stole him, Daniel, but all you have is a tired, broken old man." Then her voice caught, like a sob. "You stole my father."

It had been a force-out. McDowell could see it plainly. Rather than go through the shame of the situation, the old man had pulled out. "How do you know about the furniture?" He did not even bother to listen to her answer, if she answered at all. He knew. The Citizen had sold it to one of his customers, some guy who ran a used-furniture business along with his discount trade. Then the customer had told Sammy. Simple.

"And so," Sammy finished, "he is doubtless in Chicago."

The old man was doubtless someplace, but it was not Chicago. The old man was too sly. Somewhere in this town the old man was holed up and ready to make his next smart move. McDowell believed it because he knew the Citizen. The Citizen was too tough to just give up without some kind of fight.

"Sammy," said Dan McDowell, "you got to know that isn't true. A man don't live in a town most of his life, then just pick up and go." He wanted to say more, then told himself that he had already said too much. No sense in giving her any more ideas.

"A man would do it if he were no longer competent. I have the papers here to prove it."

Her papers proved nothing. They only proved that enough fast work among lawyers could get a man temporarily enjoined. They only proved that you could force a man into desperate actions because he had old-fashioned ideas about honor. McDowell held the phone, feeling helpless.

"I'll see you tonight," he muttered.

She paused, like she was running a mental adding machine. Then she made up her mind. "That would be delightful, Daniel. Our house at seven. Gerald will be home by then."

Something was awful, terrible wrong. Apparently the old man had said nothing to Sammy about their meeting at nine o'clock. Maybe he had changed his mind. Maybe being enjoined actually had run him out of town.

"I'll call back directly," McDowell told her. "I have an appointment, but I'm sure it's possible." He had no appointment, except to be with Peg. He was goddamned if he was going to Sammy's house. He was only stalling for time.

He hung the phone up and felt whipped around the head worse than if he had been in a fight. It was a terrible way to feel, especially since he had wanted nothing to do with the situation in the first place.

Now that he was finished with Sammy, or, he told himself, now that she was finished with him, he packed the horn in its case and left the room. Outside the room, leaning against the second floor railing, he stood for a moment looking into the streets. Somewhere out there the Citizen was in trouble and hiding, but then you never could tell about the Citizen. He was direct, like Peg, but not always direct in his meaning. For a moment McDowell wondered if Sammy was not correct. Maybe the Citizen had just given up and left.

Maybe, out there in those traffic-bound streets the old man drove his fender-dented Lincoln, heading for Chicago, or Indianapolis, or St. Louis.

Off toward the horizon a police helicopter was chip chip chipping at the gray sky. Maybe the old man was drunked up from grief and had gotten in a fight or a wreck.

Then McDowell told himself, nope, naw. The Citizen was a tough old nut.

He turned, heading for the office to settle his bill. He walked down the stairs. The horn was a good-feeling weight in his hand. The weather was getting oppressive again. His sister was winning, and he, Dan McDowell, had embarked on a new, scary business. In spite of all that, he felt nearly optimistic, although the rest of the day would be spent in trying to find the Citizen.

The Arkansas guy was on duty when McDowell entered the office. He looked up and gave a slow grin. His lanky, cracker face, his skinny frame, and knobby hands made him look countrified. The expensive, tailored suit only helped to increase the impression. "You been a long time on shift," he said. "How's your friend?"

"Healing nicely." McDowell told himself that there was no possible way not to like this guy. "I got to pay for tonight, then get moving tomorrow."

The guy began making up the invoice. When he spoke, his voice was neutral. "Which way your nose pointed?"

"Chicago."

"If it ever points back this way, we might have that drink." His neutral voice held just a hint of shyness.

"You'll be the first to know." McDowell told himself that he was nearly saying the truth, at least some small part of it was true. For a moment he had a feeling that was not about himself but about Peg and Margaret.

"I been thinking over what we talked about," McDowell said.

"Like what?"

"How you only got so many choices in this country."

"Shore," the guy said easily, "Rhett Butler."

"We all talk about it," McDowell said, and he was unhappy. "But I never saw that movie, not since I was a little kid."

"Don't make much difference if you never saw it. It ain't the movie, it's what caused the movie." The man paused like he was making sure his judgment was correct. "The movie didn't even quite exactly do the job." He was finished with the invoice and passed it to McDowell. "It's English, that way of acting. Even the pimps in these parts want to be squires."

"My pop says the same thing, but I don't know what it means."

"It's an old, old way of behavin'," the guy drawled. "If you were a gentleman, you had to be tender and strong when you were with the ladies. At the same time you had to be ready to kill any man who offended them. You carried a rose and fuckin' sword, so to speak."

"And that's English?"

"That's one big part of it." The man now looked objective and he attempted to keep his voice neutral. McDowell told himself that if he, Dan McDowell, did not have such a good ear, the guy's voice really would sound neutral. Instead it sounded shy.

"The same sort of thing has worked between men sometimes," the guy said. "But that's Greek or Hebrew, not English."

"I never studied none of that," McDowell said. He felt helpless.

Now the man was trying not to blush and was doing a pretty fair job. "With men," he said, "at least with some, it's not the fucking. Anybody can get laid . . ." He paused. His embarrassment was still hidden, almost. "It's talk," he said. "Not many men can really talk to other men."

McDowell told himself to be careful. Then he reminded himself that he was in a new business now and did not have to be careful. In fact, he was not even supposed to be careful. Jazz was not jazz if it asked for insurance. He passed the guy one of his cards. "I'd ought to know your name."

"Jackson. And I hope I ain't no distant kin to that scraggle-dyass Andrew. I probably am, though." The man was now definitely blushing but holding off the worst of it. He tucked McDowell's card in his jacket pocket.

McDowell, knowing it was time to get away from the man's embarrassment and leave him in peace, shook hands and left. His feeling of optimism was coupled with a small feeling of loss. He did not really want to leave that Jackson, not exactly.

The sky was beginning to clear and the heat was getting stronger. It was several degrees hotter than it had been a few minutes before when he left his room. From the street were blats of horns and occasional squalls of brakes. The motel parking lot was nearly empty as he walked to his Cad.

If he wanted to find the Citizen, McDowell supposed that the best place to start would be the old man's house. McDowell drove through the late morning traffic, the cars of businessmen and salesmen, the station wagons of ladies with kids, and the busted-up junkers of teenagers who were fiddling away the last summer days before the start of school.

He passed country-and-western bars, with their scams, glittery signs, and pickup truck ethics. He passed tall, grimy churches covered with the smog and soot of the city. He was headed for an older residential section.

The town began to look even seedier as he got into the old area, but at least there were still some big trees. Most of the houses had been changed into apartments. Since the big houses had originally been built close together, there was now a lot of crowding. Even now, nearly at noon, the streets were parked up pretty tight. McDowell wondered how folks could stand it when they came home from a hard day's work and had to cruise, looking for a place to park. There were plenty of alleys. Maybe they parked in their backyards. When he got to the Citizen's house, only three parking spaces were left on the entire block.

He pulled in behind a nondescript Chev stake body truck that had been turned into a van. The guy had done a rednecky job. Plywood was bolted to the racks and over the top to form the van. The plywood was unsanded, raw painted, and the jerk had a decaled Confederate flag flying just beneath the marker light. There were hundreds of trucks like this, but some not so ratty. Across the street a couple of Oriental tin pots sat. Both looked broken and tired. One had a flat. Cracks along the wall of the flat tire showed that the car had been sitting for a long time. Behind McDowell's Cad sat a new, abbreviated Buick.

The lawn of the house next to his father's was unmown, brown and fading. His father's lawn was green and freshly cut. The house still looked tidy, the way it always had. It was a good old three-story house with leaded windows, big trees in the yard, and wide porches that ran all the way around. The iron fence in front was freshly painted. It was like the old man had decided that even if the rest of the world went to hell his part was not going the same road. Then McDowell thought of all the junk his father had sold in his life and he was momentarily confused.

Then he remembered his earlier realization—it was all junk, most of it. Some junk just cost more than other junk. That was the only difference.

As he went up the walk to the front doorway McDowell felt nearly morbid. The curtains and drapes were drawn, which, of course, was all right on a hot day. Still, when he rang the doorbell he figured no one would answer. He could not say why, but the house already felt deserted. He rang the bell again, heard it tinkling inside, and there was still no answer. He stepped to one side of the door and tried to peer through the window. The drapes were pulled. He walked along the encircling porch, looking into windows, but still could see nothing through drawn curtains. When he got halfway around, he knocked on the back door and waited. The kitchen curtains were slightly drawn. Through them he could see packing boxes from a storage warehouse. There were only three, and they were packed and sealed. He told himself that whatever the old man was doing he was not totally selling out.

Further around the house he could see a narrow strip of the living room through curtains that were not pulled tight. Furniture still sat around the room. There were more packing boxes, also sealed. The old man was obviously not in the house, and neither was Shag. When Dan McDowell returned to the front door he tried the knob. The door was locked.

The weather was getting downright muggy. The air conditioning unit that was hidden in shrubbery beside the front porch was silent. That, more than anything else, told him that the old man was not home and not planning to be home, at least not today.

McDowell sat in a porch swing and looked out on the street that had once been familiar. He had been raised in this house. He had walked that street hundreds of times, going to school or loitering along on hot noons like this. He sat in the swing, believing he was due for one more realization, waiting. What happened was not a realization, although he was not surprised.

The presence was sitting beside him, and it was easy in its mind. It was not particularly strong. It was like a man sitting in the cool and licking away on a julep, like a man who had worked all morning and was taking his ease.

McDowell, having been with Peg, and listened to Peg, was terrified. After what Peg said, McDowell wanted nothing to do with the presence, or with Enoch. He began to stand, then told himself to forget it—the presence could go anywhere he could go. Maybe Peg could drive it away, but he, Dan McDowell, could not.

"You want something," McDowell said, and he could hear the failed bravado in his voice. "What the fuck is it?" He gave the floor a little kick, to get the swing moving. The springs were rusty. They creaked, but the creaks were normal. There was nothing ghostly about them. In the street the sunlight was now strong. It glared from the new Buick and his Cad. The dirty windows of the van and the tin pots gave off dull glows.

The presence remained content, like a man who had just finished a good piece of work. McDowell looked around, looking for Enoch. Nothing. The sunlight was as hot and intense in the street as the sun in Spain. A beat-up, old Chev cruised past, the driver longhaired and looking tired. He wore old work clothes and looked like he was going to a job he did not like. Either that, or home to a wife who did not like him.

"I don't pay you no mind," McDowell said. "You plagued me enough." He stood and walked to his Cad. He got in, started the engine and the air conditioning. The presence slipped onto the seat beside him.

McDowell pulled the mouthpiece from his shirt pocket and blew into it as softly as he could. That was not very soft. The presence seemed content, as happy, McDowell told himself, as a pig in shit.

"You done a job on him, didn't you," McDowell whispered. "Now you're sitting at his house, bragging." He continued to fool with the mouthpiece, blowing into it. He felt like he was playing poker. "Is Pop dead?" he whispered.

The presence seemed to be chuckling. It was giving nothing away.

"I wish," McDowell said, "I could get my hands around your moley neck." He leaned over, feeling beneath the seat. His hand hit the paper sack containing the pistol. The presence seemed to stir happily. McDowell fumbled in the map case and pulled out Margaret's picture. The presence stirred, but not as happy this time. McDowell blew into the mouthpiece and looked at the picture, at the hair that was light and cloudlike, at Margaret's nearly patrician nose.

It almost seemed like he could hear her voice, like she was trying to help him. It was not a jazz beat, but more like a revival beat and he did not recognize the music. Listening, he could almost hear a stump preacher panting back there someplace, waiting to get in his licks.

Then Margaret's voice was joined by Peg's voice. Then their voices were joined by Becky's voice, Becky singing.

The presence vanished like blown smoke. McDowell sat waiting, playing the mouthpiece. When nothing more happened, he pulled away. There were a couple of things he wanted to check out.

Chapter 28

WHEN HE RETURNED TO THE MOTEL, IT WAS COMING ON TOWARD evening and time to meet Peg. McDowell had spent the afternoon checking out the Lincoln dealer. He figured that if the old man was leaving he would have his car serviced. He had drawn a blank. Mc-Dowell, remembering the name of the storage warehouse that had been printed on the cartons in the Citizen's warehouse living room, called the warehouse. The outfit had no order to pick up anything. Next he checked with a couple of the Citizen's oldest customers. The men claimed to have heard nothing from him. McDowell called his father's attorney, who said he no longer represented the Citizen. Dan McDowell did not check with the old man's bank. It would do no good, and it might foul his pop up if he was trying to pull something smart. Banks were awfully dumb. All you had to do was establish credit, and they could be conned immemorially.

Somewhere during those errands he had stopped at a music store. The horn was now in good shape, and a beat-up old Gibson six-string lay on the back seat along with a pair of sticks. McDowell left the whole lot of instruments in the car when he returned to his motel room. He wished he had called for laundry service.

He had time for a shower before meeting Peg, but he sat for a moment on the edge of the bed in which he had not slept.

He tried to feel guilty about sleeping with Peg, or at least he tried to feel apologetic toward Margaret. He could do neither. In fact, he thought, without understanding it, that he would have been disloyal to Margaret if he had not stayed with Peg. Then he mournfully told himself that if he did not understand it, how in the world was Margaret supposed to? He fumbled for the mouthpiece in his shirt pocket, undid the neck of the tobacco sack. His lip was sore, but he could feel it beginning to come around. He told himself that he had better get working with the guitar and the sticks, and soon.

He stood up slowly and headed toward the shower to rinse off the sweat from the day. He felt tired, old. So much had happened, so fast. Now he was worried about the Citizen. He told himself that he did not even like the old sonovabitch and knew that he was lying as he said it. The man was his father, and he was in trouble. Dan McDowell told himself that he mostly felt sickly because of his pop.

The phone rang. McDowell hesitated. Likely it was crazy Samantha, but there was just an outside chance that it might be the Citizen. He decided that if it was Samantha, crazy or not, he was going to once and for all tell her to get out of his life.

He answered the phone.

"I'm just starving," Peg said. "Like a bobcat trapped in a cabbage patch. Get on down here."

"I smell pretty bad," McDowell admitted. "Was headed for the shower."

"If your nose can stand it, mine can." Peg hung up brisk, not giving him a chance to alibi.

If her nose could stand it, his could. McDowell grinned thinking that no matter how poorly a man felt, Peg could make the feelings seem a little silly just with her presence. He bailed out of the room and headed for hers. The sky was luminous and the heat was not letting up. It felt to McDowell like the weather was arming itself to make one final blowout before fall. He looked for gathering storm clouds but saw none.

When Peg answered his knock, she looked puny in spite of her directness. Peg was dressed in a frilly, white and blue western shirt and pale gray jeans. The outfit should have helped draw attention to her blue eyes. Instead, it seemed to be taking color from her complexion. Peg was pale, and for all of her bodaciousness she seemed frail. She took his hand, pulled him gently into the room.

"I wish the hell you were my man," she said. "It don't happen often but there's times when I get nervous. Dan, you got to tell me everything you remember about this business between your pop and your sister. You got to tell me what you remember about that raggedy old fella."

"That is one whale of a long story."

Peg looked at her watch. "You got to be nowhere until nine. Let's go eat and you tell it."

He looked at his own watch. It was nearly six o'clock. "We'll take my car." He watched her, seeing her frailty. "Hang on just a minute." He reached for her and held her close. She at first seemed passive, and then he realized that she was not. Peg huddled against him. She was afraid, not passive.

"Bad day?"

"I trust my feelings," Peg said, "and the feelings are bad." She drew away from him, took only a moment to grab her purse, then headed for the door. McDowell followed. When they were both in the car, he turned to her as he started the engine. "Anything special happen?"

"Nope. Some very unspecial shit happened, but none of it is exactly unusual. That don't mean that things ain't sour." Peg was looking backward, through the rear window, as McDowell backed from the parking slot. Peg looked like she was searching for someone. "Your pop called. Your pop is one fine man."

"Where'n the hell is he?" McDowell was so startled that he nearly forgot to brake. For a moment the Cad rolled backward and out of control. Then he got it stopped, turned, and pulled away.

"I asked him where he was," Peg said, "but he chose not to tell. We had a good talk. He soothed me." Peg looked toward him. "Dan, I'm not the nervous type. I ain't neurotic, or at least no more than anybody else."

"Never thought you were."

"Sure you did. First time you ever saw me I was drunk on my can."

"Not that drunk." He entered traffic that was still heavy, even this close to suppertime.

"Pretty drunk, though."

"What did Pop have to say?"

"You be there tonight at his business. I'm to stay home. He don't want me there."

"Say why?"

"Just said it wouldn't be fittin.'"

A couple of kids stood beside the road hitchhiking. The boy was long-haired, the girl kind of butch looking. Neither could have been more than eighteen, yet they had the bored appearance of a couple who had been together for years and were running on habit, not success. They were being careful with the hitching as they checked the approaching traffic for cops.

"How did Pop soothe you?"

"Same way I soothed him. We talked about old times . . ." Peg paused. "Of course, his times are older than mine."

McDowell knew better, but he did not want to get into all of that. The Citizen had come from a slightly more civilized place than Peg, but not much.

"Dan, your pop talked kind of bravelike, but sad. Like he was saying goodbye. Dan, I fear for him."

Dan McDowell feared for the Citizen as well. It was not like the Citizen to reveal any personal feelings.

"He said to tell you that Enoch was right. He said to tell you he's sorry, and he doesn't even know why."

McDowell was looking for a restaurant, any place that looked clean. He was thinking as he looked. He could not figure out what the old man meant about Enoch, but the sense of dread he had felt earlier returned.

A family-type restaurant sat a ways off the road. McDowell pulled into a lane, drove to it and parked, but made no move to get from the car.

"How was work?"

"That's the unspecial shit," Peg told him. "Bad rehearsal is bad rehearsal, but usually I don't cause it."

"What was wrong?"

"Nervous-like, just uncollected-like." Peg opened her door. "I'm starving."

When they entered, McDowell saw that the place was larger than it looked from outside. It had obviously been a roadhouse, back in the days before the city had grown outward and encircled it. McDowell could almost see how it would have been in the 1920s, the booze and the bands, the tables crowded close together, the banalities and dizzy-headed wit of booze.

The room was not narrow but seemed that way because it was

so long. Worn blue carpet gave a family-type effect which was good atmosphere but which meant high maintenance. McDowell figured that he had stumbled onto a pretty good restaurant. There was a small stage and mikes at the far end of the room. Once, he supposed there had been a large stage, or at least a thrust-type stage. Now the place was set up for three musicians, at most.

A stooped old man greeted them and led them to a table. He was dressed in a casual suit that he should not have been able to wear because of his age. Somehow, he pulled it off. McDowell figured the guy owned the place, and that he had been putting this act together for years.

"We've not seen you here before," the man said. Then he seated them halfway up the room and along the wall. "It's a pleasure to see new faces." The man's voice was gentlemanly. He reminded McDowell of the man who had saved him embarrassment back at the hotel.

"You have a nice place," McDowell said.

"A little shabby." The old man smiled. His voice was gentle but not apologetic. "We like to keep it that way." He made a small bow to Peg. "A waitress will be with you. The entertainment begins at seven."

McDowell checked his watch. Seven was still a half hour away. At least there was no electric organ on the stage, so there would be no cocktail bar jock pumping out mechanical versions of "Stormy Weather."

"We lucked out, didn't we?" Peg was speaking low, not whispering. She was regretting the jeans and western shirt, wishing instead that she wore a dress. McDowell was amused. In spite of her bodaciousness, Peg was pretty old-fashioned in a lot of ways.

"You feeling better?"

"Safer, anyway," Peg said. "Start telling me about all this."

"I've seen Enoch off and on for years. Sammy and my pop have been scrapping all the time for years. Only, their fights were never real before. Somehow, this scrap has gotten out of hand." McDowell began to tell his story. He went slow, trying to remember all of it so that Peg could get the feel of the matter, not just the facts. A waitress brought a menu. He was interrupted by that. Peg ordered quickly, and so did he. Peg sat quietly, waiting for McDowell to continue.

"They play act," McDowell said. "Sammy swears she loves Pop, and you know how the old man thinks. She's his daughter."

"Wait a minute. Don't say nothing more." Peg did not lean back, but she did close her eyes. She was studying something. McDowell waited, was about to say something, waited some more.

"Got it," Peg said. "My aunt was play-acting when she helped her man hang himself. I remember my aunt."

"You sure?"

"Yep," Peg said, "because they had no miseries. They had no kids, and nowhere to go, and they had the Lord, but that's all. They got to play-acting." Peg's voice changed. It sounded as positive as a preacher. "Your sister isn't crazy," Peg said. "The play-acting has gotten out of hand."

"That amounts to crazy. It comes to the same thing."

A middle-aged waiter who was doubling as a wine steward interrupted. McDowell okayed what the guy had brought.

"Feeling gloomy," McDowell told Peg after the man had left. "Maybe it's just this place."

"Naw, this is a good place. You worked as many places as I have, you know a good one."

"This is a good place to work?"

"Low pay," Peg said, "but long engagements. They don't jack you around in this kind of place." Then she changed back to the original subject. "It's not the same as crazy. When you're crazy, you don't cure." She grinned. "After the funeral, my aunt cured."

"What happened?"

"She kicked the Lord, moved to town. Last I knew of her she was emptying bedpans at a hospital."

The waitress brought their salads, which McDowell was not immediately interested in because of the bedpans. Peg was more practical. She was digging right into that salad. "Now tell me about Enoch."

McDowell looked up. The small stage was lighted, but with low light. A woman was setting up. It looked like a single act. He figured he could stand it if the amp was not too high. He sat thinking. "I've seen him several times, and once when Pop was there." He felt the amp come on, and it was not going to be too high. If anything, a little low. On the other hand, there were not very many people in the long room. It was still pretty early. A guitar started

walking mid-range, warming up, doing nothing special. The guitar was a good one, and in good control even if nothing much
was happening. Then it headed toward an intro, still doing nothing
special, and the song arrived.

McDowell sat stunned. Disbelieving. Speechless. He laid down
his fork as history rushed at him, overwhelmed him. He looked at
the tabletop, as if it were a page from a book in which the truth was
written, somewhere.

The south was song. Nowhere, at no other time in history
probably had a land been more a land of song than was the south.
Sad songs, blues songs, jazz songs, folk songs, and riff. The south
was the song of hounds beneath moonlight and mist, and it was
the cruel songs that rose from the beat of confused traffic and the
whip, whip, whip of the helpless police.

The south was sound. It was the cries of women without anesthetic, women in labor. It was the happy hollering of kids who did
not yet know what life was dealing them. It was the voice of mothers and grandmothers, calling kids home from play through hot,
steaming evenings. It was the rustle of down-falling creeks, the
rapid run of water. The south was the sound of storm, of the cracking, lightning-thrusting, bombarding storms that swept the rivers.

The south was pain-song, and nowhere, at no time in history,
had a place asked more of a man. In the sounds of the south were
the drunken groans of black men who could not find jobs and
could not then keep their women. There were the grunts of heartsick men following mules who cursed the hills, were entrapped
and encircled and who finally loved the trapping, encircling hills;
loving that which killed them. The sounds of the south were lung-
rot cough of men who lay flat on their backs in ground water,
reaching over their heads backwards with a shovel as they took
coal from a low seam.

The south was sound, echoes. The south was music that could
be found nowhere else, unless maybe Siberia. The south was the
frontier, unrelieved by modern tools. It had always been the frontier in this country, and it seemed it always would be.

McDowell knew that he had to look. He knew Peg was watching him, concerned for him, and that Peg was not understanding.
She could not. He raised his head.

The lights were low on that stage. The long room made the

small stage look subdued, unimportant, nearly apologetic. There was an old lady up there. Her long hair was cut with streaks of gray. Her shoulders were narrow, thin as they raised with the position of the guitar. Her breasts sagged against her shirt like sorrows of the unloved. She was popping the guitar the best she could, which was not bad, but not so good, either. And that lady was Becky.

"We got to go." McDowell tried to stand, but his legs were not helping him. He looked at Peg, at her face that was blurred as he felt his tears. Men did not cry, but with Peg, already, he had felt free to do it twice."

"Dan?"

"I used to live with her." He kept his face turned from the stage.

"That's no reason to go," Peg said softly. "She can't see you sitting out here."

He was having a hard time with his voice. "I told you that you and Margaret were two of the three best women I ever knew. That's the other one."

"The one who left?"

"Yep."

"Then," said Peg, "that's maybe a good reason to stay. It's surely no reason to go."

"But look at her. Just look."

Peg sat silent, fooling around with a fork, and she was clearly trying to control her temper. "I thought you had an ear. What is this bullshit about looking? Dan, whatever in the world is wrong with you?"

"Look at her."

"I'm looking," Peg said. "I see a singer working. Most singers aren't. She's making it. Did she ever ask to be rich?"

Becky had never asked for that. Becky had not left because he was drawing nonunion pay, or because they only had a cheap apartment. "No."

"Did she ever ask to be happy?"

"Yes." Then he thought about Becky, about the tall and beautiful and crazy lady who had tried to love him. "Nope. She always hoped for it."

"Then leave it be, Dan. She's working. Give it your respect. Give her what she's earnin'." Peg was past her temper, though it was still back there someplace. He could feel it, and he almost understood it.

"It does hurt, though. It hurts like hell."

"Sure," Peg said gently. "What do you think this is all about? You think this business is nothing but amusement?"

"You ought to know me better than that."

"Then you take your share of hurt." Peg reached toward him, touched his shirt pocket where the mouthpiece hung like a question. "You're not fooling me. Maybe you fool yourself." Then Peg's expression changed. "I recommend," she drawled, "that you quit being a horse's ass. Quit your sorrowing and bawling around. Listen to the lady's music." She picked up her fork and began chomping on the little salad that she had left. "Them steaks," she said lightly, "I wonder if they had to go out and catch the cow."

He found that he could do it. He could actually listen, once he got past those on-top emotions that were slugging him. Becky's voice had more control than it used to have. Through experience, or hints from other singers, or from lessons, she was breathing better. He listened through three songs, trying to credit her with what she had earned. Becky was still not the world's best singer, but she was lots, lots better than she used to be. She was not a flashy performer, but lots, lots better. Becky was up there doing a job. McDowell sat remembering how he loved her, had loved her and remembered her for a big part of his life. Then, without knowing he was there, Becky punched him hard.

It was not an old song. It had been written probably in the '60s, but it was in the tradition. Becky began to sing "When They Close the Minstrel Show." The guitar work changed, smoothing out, and the on-top sadness of the song was layered with underneath sadness. The underneath sadness was wrapped, thin layered but bound, with an old, old sadness; old like lost and remembered love. The guitar was working with the sadness, not bringing it forward but backgrounding with just a hint of weeping.

"I can't do that," Peg said. "Margaret does something different from that. Margaret can't do that." She had stopped eating and was listening. She looked at Dan McDowell like she might slap him. "And you," she said, "were bawlin' like a lost calf."

The sadness was even more than about lost love. It was lost music. Becky, who had loved folk music so well, was singing sor-

row over the diminishing past. For a moment it seemed to Mc-
Dowell that the songs were passing quicker than ever before, the
songs embalmed in music collections, in books. But books could
not inflect the songs, could not bring forward that voice that died a
little each time an old person headed for the grave. Becky sounded
like she was praying over the vanishing songs.

"I was surprised," he told Peg. "Of course I was bawling. Maybe I'll do it again."

"I might help you." She reached to touch his arm, no longer
indignant. "Margaret won't leave you," she said quietly, "not if you
don't hold too tight." Then she got practical again, checking her
watch. "We got to get going pretty quick. What about Enoch?"

McDowell explained quickly about seeing the Citizen laughing through fire, and about the times he had seen Enoch. "He killed
seven men," McDowell told her. "He was traditional, old-timey."

"Why'd he kill them?"

"They raped his woman. Women."

"I've never been," Peg said, "and I pray to the true God I never
will be." She shuddered. "Seven."

"He killed them in pretty awful ways."

Peg, who always seemed to McDowell to have the appetite of a
bear, seemed disinterested in what remained of her dinner. "There's
no answer to it," she said sadly. There was indignation mixed with
her sadness. "They're the ones who cause hurt but never get hurt."

"They sure as the world got hurt that time." He looked up.
Becky was offstage, the end of her first set.

"Dan, run me over to the motel. Do see your pop. Then come
back to me. Come back."

"We still have some time."

"I want to sit and figure why I have poor feelings. I figure best
when I have my guitar." She stood, looking down at him. "I do
truly wish you were my man, but even if it wasn't for Margaret,
there isn't a chance."

He knew that what she said was true, but he wished it was not.
He did not know how to answer her, and he found no answer as he
drove her to the motel.

Chapter 29

IT SEEMED LIKE SHE, BECKY, WAS RIDING WITH HIM AFTER HE dropped Peg at the motel and headed for his father's warehouse. Becky, who for so long had been part of his love and his memory, was now free of him. At least it seemed so to Dan McDowell. Now he could love her not as a memory, as a ghost of yesterday, as a wraith that on midnight roads had followed him. He could love her for her working, professional, and independent self. He felt that Becky was not saying goodbye riding beside him, but saying hello.

Then he heard her voice. The voice was not like memory. It was alive and singing, conceptual, the way the strong voice of song would live in the mind of a composer.

Then he heard all three voices: Margaret's and Peg's and Becky's. He heard them in the way that shapes and color would be alive and hot in the mind of a painter. In this tiresome, wearisome hour, when he drove toward a confrontation he did not want, their voices were giving him energy of mind.

Physically, he felt exhausted. His mind had received too many facts in a short time. In keeping his mind alert, he felt that his body was being drained.

Margaret singing. Peg singing. Becky singing.

Somewhere, behind the tall buildings, a storm was headed for the city. The air felt electric, the way it did before storms. In back of the tall buildings somewhere, the thunderheads were gathering and the wind was picking up to blow across the dying late summer fields. The storm had been threatening all day. Then he told himself, nope. Storms did not threaten. Storms did not need to threaten. Dan McDowell drove through streets that were not deserted, but traffic was lighter than usual. His instincts for storm were not well honed, not like the instincts of people who had lived for years in Centerville. There were folks out there, lots of them, who could predict within five minutes when a storm would arrive, and they could make that prediction hours in advance.

One more cop checked him out as he was stopped by a light. In the shadowed car the cop looked vague, undefined; the green lights on the dash lit only the high planes of his face. He was a balding guy who was sweating like rainwater in the hot night. The windows of the police car were rolled all the way down. It was not the brightest way to run a cop car. Any punk with a brick could catch him.

It was only Thursday night, but kids were out cruising. When McDowell pulled away from the light, the cop lagged behind. Then he suddenly goosed the patrol car. He was running only on blue lights, no siren. He was going to a break-in, a hold-up, or some other trouble where he had to get there fast with a minimum of noise. A carload of kids, driving a raggedy old Mercury, took off after the cop. They were fucked up, drunk or high, and chasing the cop just to see what he was up to. As they passed McDowell the driver flipped him the bird.

This cop-ridden, booze-ridden, helpless south.

The old codes said that a man protected the weak, and the weak were slaves and kids and women. The old codes had been conceived before engines, even before steam engines. They were older than that, as old as the eighteenth century. Cruising through the streets, in the face of the coming storm, McDowell had to wonder about weakness. The strongest man in the world was weak if he could be rendered helpless—if he could be tied down, as the Citizen was tied down, by old ideas of honor. McDowell sincerely dreaded the coming meeting with his father and his sister.

He checked the clock on the dash. He would be ten or twelve minutes early. In a way that was good. He could sit for a minute, absorb some peace of mind, or at least try to.

Peg singing. He again pulled up to a red light. A tired woman with short scraggledy hair was stopped beside him. Her man was on the rider's side, slumped into himself with fatigue and not anger. If they were having a fight, the woman would not look so tired. Her lips would not be lax. Hard-working folk, headed home after a day that must have seemed like forever. They owned a small business, probably, or they would not have worked so late. A physical-type business, probably, or the man would not be so wiped out. He would be driving. That woman, in her way, was protecting her man.

Margaret singing. Two teenagers cut him out in traffic. The boy was black and the girl white. They had to cut him out, he understood that. There was stuff you had to do when you were different. Margaret, being colored, could not afford to slur, any more than Billie Holiday could ever slur. Neither Billie nor Margaret had ever blown an 'r' in their lives.

Becky singing. McDowell passed a woman who stood at a bus stop, the woman frail and defenseless. She was trying to pretend that she was not at the mercy of chance. She was watching all around her, but not for a bus. The night was dark and she was alone. Becky had not known who the hell she was, only what she loved. For a moment it seemed to McDowell that he could hear a chorus, a hundred voices of singers who had made it and were strong; of others who were only strong.

The brick warehouse bulked three stories high, dark beneath the darkening night sky. He looked for lights as he approached. Even the nightlight at the corner of the parking lot was out.

Still, something was happening. The headlights of the Cad picked up a small group of people who were standing on the sidewalk at the entry to the parking lot. They were staring back into the lot, back toward the old poplar tree. Some of them were talking, gesticulating, and a couple of them seemed to be laughing. McDowell slowed, coasted, signaled to show them he was coming into the lot. He hung a left and rolled in easily.

A police car sat in the middle of the lot. Its searchlight was pointed toward the tree, about twenty feet up. McDowell pulled in behind the cop and shut off the Cad's engine. As he climbed from his car he heard music, strident and demanding. Behind him from the small crowd he heard a loud haw-haw and a couple of giggles.

The music was accompanied by high whines that were thin and harsh, electronic whines. McDowell slammed the door and walked forward. To his left the warehouse rose dark and silent. The Citizen's Lincoln was nowhere to be seen. Ahead of him, rising nearly a hundred feet into the night, the poplar stood like an enormous dark umbrella before the coming storm.

A cop stood by the police car. He was looking up, along the direction of the searchlight. He was a young cop, New Orleans high yellow, and McDowell had a flicker of thought which wondered what'n the hell this guy was doing here. The cop stared along the beam of light like he was in a trance.

No man in his right mind ever tried to surprise a cop. When McDowell was still twenty feet away, he spoke loudly and moved slow. "What's going on? What is it?" As the cop turned, McDowell walked steady but slow toward him.

"Mister," the cop said, "you get yourself back there with the rest."

Close up, the cop looked afraid. He was really only a kid, and his fear had to be coming from his puzzlement. What was happening was ordinary, but at the same time it was strange. In daylight it would not seem so strange.

"I belong here," McDowell said. "This is my pop's place, and mine." The lie was easy.

"In that case," the cop said with a mixture of gladness and relief, "you're cited. Get that thing shut off." The kid was speaking without the least trace of a drawl. He was cop-pissed, not man-pissed.

"I didn't do it." McDowell peered up the beam of light. "What the fuck is it?" He walked closer to the tree. March music, trombony, drum-popping, and strong, came loud and whining through the light breeze that was moving the summer-seared leaves of the poplar as the storm put out its first feelers of wind. McDowell saw what it was.

Someone, and it could only have been the Citizen, had tied a bullhorn to that tree. The Citizen had surer-than-hell wired down the trigger on the bullhorn and rigged in a tape deck. Surer-than-hell, that was John Philip Sousa who was blazing away up there in that tree, totally out of reach. The music seemed to rise with the early gusts of wind, like it was in tune with the wind. McDowell, who knew less than nothing about march music, supposed to himself that he was hearing "The Thunderer" or "The Conqueror" or some such fucking thing.

"That is the cheapest goddamn advertising stunt I ever saw." The cop had his hat pushed back. His forehead was broad, Indian looking, and not bulgy. "I guess," he said, "I'll call the station. Have them send a pickup with a ladder."

"It isn't advertising." McDowell suddenly felt urgent, alarmed, and the dread that he had felt over the past few days was back. The dread told him that something true and awful was about to happen.

"Because," the cop said, "I can't be frittering time away here. That street is beginning to heat . . ." The cop was interrupted, as was McDowell, because both of them were hitting the deck.

The whomp exploded in shattering glass, and the whomp was explosion-deep, like an enormous grunt as, at their backs, brilliant orange and ruby light flared hot into the parking lot. McDowell went forward on his face beside the cop, then turned toward the warehouse. A rapid-running line of fire rose from the concussion and traveled along the ground floor of the warehouse. Shatters of glass bounced and pinged between the burglar-proof steel screens that covered the windows. As he turned the flames were already sinking down into the steady, ambitious burning of a well-tended fire.

McDowell got to his knees, watching. The cop was already on his feet. His mouth was open and he was staring.

Black smoke began to pour from the area where McDowell knew that those hundreds and hundreds of cans of paint were stored. As black smoke rose through the open windows it was swirled by the popping gusts of wind.

"Gasoline," the cop said almost reverently. "Kee-rist." The cop seemed stalled, knowing that he had to do a dozen things and not sure which of them to do first.

McDowell got to his feet. "My pop's in that building," he whispered. "At least I think he is." For the first time he really felt the breeze, and in the distance was the voice of thunder. The march music swelled as a goddamned flotilla of tubas underlay the thunder like they were its foundation.

"You're under arrest," the cop said almost hysterically. He paused. Then he changed his mind. "Get that shitbox out of here. We got fire trucks coming."

"My pop's in there. I got to help." McDowell started toward the warehouse, but was grabbed by the cop. The cop, even if he was hysterical, was talking slow and reasonable as he stopped Mc-Dowell.

"If your pop's on the first floor," the cop said, "he's dead. If he ain't on the first floor, the best you can do to help him is get that car out of the way. I got to make room for a ladder truck." The cop released his grip on McDowell's arm, then ran toward, his car. As he ran he was hollering at the knot of people to move back. It was wasted effort. Most of them were already across the street, and the rest of them were running.

McDowell headed toward his Cad. The cop was leaning into the patrol car, reaching for his radio. McDowell was halted, struck nearly motionless, and then automatically hit the deck a second time. The march music was drowned beneath the deep voice of another whomp as a line of fire traced its way past the windows on the second floor. Glass pinged, shattered around him like a grenade, and the cop was all the way into the patrol car, lying with his face on the seat. As the fire settled into business the march music took over. The cop was yammering into his radio, leaning half in and half out of his car. He was holding the mike with his left hand, and waving people away with his right, even though there were no people.

A battalion of trumpets was trotting along in two-quarter time, swelling their chests like they were trying to pop their buttons. The march music accented the busy fire on the second floor, and it sang proudly into the wind and the distant but rapidly approaching thunder.

McDowell sprinted for his Cad, got it started, and cut rubber halfway across the lot. He got down to the tree, hung a left, and squalled tires as he passed the loading docks. He entered the street, searched for a place to spot the Cad, but the street was parked up. He was desperate, gunning the car, braking, looking for any spot where he could get over the curb and park on a lawn.

Farther down the next block was an alley. He hit the gas, fired the Cad forward, and braked to spin it hard, pointing into the alley. There was space in front of a garage. He goosed it and pulled in behind a short row of junkers. In front of him was a little van, and over the Cad's hood drooped the summer-burned leaves of a lilac. He bailed out of the Cad and ran back toward the fire, wondering how he had come such a distance.

After a block he was winded. Ahead of him, people ran around and yelled and were having a wonderful time. They were shadows in the hot summer night, dashing between the arcs of streetlights. A teenage kid dashed past him, hollering and happy. Far in the distance the sound of a fire siren rose squalling through the night. The street was crowded with running people, relieved of boredom and happy to be going to a fire.

McDowell slowed to a fast walk. There was not much he could do now anyway. As he walked he did not even realize that he was weeping. All he knew was that he could not get his breath, hardly, that he could hardly draw enough air to handle the choking in his throat. It was all happening so fast. He had not had time to think. Then it came to him with the rapid flash of lightning that was now blue and silver in the sky. *This* was the way that the Citizen was curing Sammy. This was the Citizen's way to make Sammy well. McDowell remembered it all as he half walked, half trotted. The old man had misunderstood Peg. Either that, or he had understood Peg too well. The old man figured that if the business was Sammy's one and only friend, then without the business she would have to find a new friend.

No one. No one but the Citizen would ever have the nerve to be that dumb. No one would have the bodaciousness to be that direct. No one, but a man filled with old notions of honor, could ever have been that self-sacrificing.

A fire siren, still distant, was covered over by a heavy burst of thunder. From half a block away the warehouse was an orange, luminous glow behind the business fronts and houses that blocked the view. It rose high enough that McDowell, approaching, could see third floor. Lights were dancing up there, but they were not the reflecting lights of fire trucks or police cars. Those lights were inside the building, reaching out through open windows. They were powerful. Maybe they were battery-powered searchlights, or maybe the old man had a 500-watt bulb rigged behind a light wheel. They came through the open windows that were drafting smoke, and the lights were diffused by the smoke and fire on the two lower floors. McDowell once more broke into a run.

People were in the way. It was not a crowd, it was a throng, and the people were watching openmouthed. Some were making jokes. A kid was bawling somewhere, lost and hollering for his mama. McDowell shoved people aside. As he did he explained in a loud, apologetic voice. He had to get there, had to, because his pop was in that building. Some people pushed him back, while others dropped away from him like he was crazy or diseased. He fought his way to the front of the throng, looking up. The young cop was in the street, trying to make room for a fire lane. Traffic was stalling, uncooperative.

It was a fucking light show up there on third floor. Even with the interweaving flames, the roar and heat of the fire, and the distant sound of march music; even with the approaching thunder, it was the lights that were stealing the show. They were silhouetting the figure of a man. He was first at one window, then at another. It was like the old man was running all around the top of the building, doing some last important chore. The crowd gasped, pointed, and a few people were hollering for somebody to save that man on the third floor. A lot of people were hollering, but no one was doing anything.

The lights were flicking back and forth, back and forth. Smoke was pouring dark, heavy, and thick from the third-floor windows. The lights and the silhouette seemed in combat with the smoke. The smoke poured sideways in the stream of wind from the approaching storm. Not far away a bolt of lightning smashed into a tree somewhere; the thunder cracked like an enormous rimshot from a gigantic drum.

Suddenly, unexpectedly, an orange light detached itself above the smoke. It seemed launched by the lights, and it reached upward into the wind. The skyrocket went high above the heads of the crowd, climbing over the street, and blown off trajectory by the wind. The rocket was slowed in its arc and was pointed straight up.

Next, a blue ball of fire from a roman candle shot into the street, followed by a green ball that headed right into the crowd. Another blue ball shot out, then a red, and then another green. The crowd pulsed, pushed backward, started to break and run. Now rockets rose from all of the windows.

McDowell, weeping, wondered where in the hell the old man had gotten hold of fireworks. In the wind, the popping of fire, and the hysterical flight of the crowd, the march music was thin, tinny, and faint. McDowell, weeping, told himself that it was a damned fine try. It was just, he told himself, that the old man had no business messing with civilization. Even when he used a bullhorn.

Now fire, carried by a heavier wind, was blown sideways with the smoke. The fire was blown toward the popular, scorching the already sun-scorched leaves, the tree standing just out of reach from total damage.

McDowell stood, awed and sniffling. While he had watched the fire one fire truck had finally gotten through. A fireman pushed him sideways. He staggered, caught his balance, and backed up. There was no way in the world they could save that warehouse. The most they could do was contain the fire. All that would be left of it would be a brick shell.

That was his pop in there. His Pop.

A hand touched his arm, gentle, almost tentative.

He turned, looking at her, at Samantha; at her drawn face, her plainness and thinness, and at her eyes that for the first time ever that he could remember held tears. Sammy stood beside him, supported by the Wimp, and Sammy was weeping from a stock of tears that she must have been accumulating for a lifetime. As she wept she looked at Dan McDowell, looking at him not as he had once looked at her—not back in the days when he thought she was a smart goddess—but looking at him finally like he was someone who could be loved. Sammy said nothing. She could not.

The Wimp spoke softly to her. He was not whispering, not talking under his breath, but McDowell still could not hear.

"What'd you say, Wimp?" McDowell could not smack his sister, but he was going to take no foolishness at tall from that Wimp. He watched the possibility of love in Sammy's face and wanted to slap her for it.

"I was not speaking to you," the Wimp said. He continued to hold Sammy, but he shrugged his ass like he was getting squared around to fight. "Why are you here?"

"Pop told me to be here." McDowell's voice choked. "I never dreamed of this."

"It appears," the Wimp said, "that Charles even cut off the sprinkler system." He paused, and there was genuine grief on his face. His free hand, the one not holding Sammy, hung at his side, unclenched, helpless. "Difficult to accept," he said, "that I spoke to him only a half hour ago."

"You saw him?"

"He telephoned to say that he had an urgent situation." The grief on the Wimp's face was deep and genuine, highlighted by the red and orange and ruby glows of fire. Twenty feet away a fire hose was unrolled, lying flat. Pressure came on the hose. It swelled quickly. The fire was not just popping and burning now, it was roaring.

"You wanted an estate," McDowell said bitterly to Samantha. "You sure got your wish." Even if he could not smack her, he could give her guilts a licking.

The Wimp suddenly stopped looking wimpy. His grief faded as his mouth tightened, and across his fire-illuminated face came the old southern look that told McDowell that the footing in this situation was getting treacherous. The Wimp's look was not pretending that he was going to fight. The Wimp was telling McDowell that one more wrong word would mean that only one of them walked away. Sammy, weeping, was not so far gone that she did not pick up on the situation. She tried to speak: wept, gulped, clung to the Wimp.

"You believe it is easy, Daniel. Easy to explain." The Wimp was speaking just loud enough to be heard above the roar of fire. "I know who you blame, but ask yourself this—exactly how much did you have to do with this?" The storm had nearly arrived. Wind was blowing against the Wimp's shirtfront, and it made him look even skinnier above his round and well-upholstered ass.

McDowell was stopped. What the Wimp said seemed to ring true somehow, if only he had time to figure it out. McDowell began to defend himself.

"Sammy," he said quietly, and with no trace of vengeance. "You were never crazy a day in your life. Sammy, you've been play-acting."

It seemed to do Sammy some good, what he said; but what he said made McDowell feel like just nothing. Sammy nearly stopped weeping. She tried for her practiced control, could not get a handle on it, and seemed surprised. She had found some different kind of control. "I wanted," she said, "a father. I used to have one. I even used to have a brother." Her words choked, and she returned to weeping. The Wimp held her close. Sammy looked so thin, so frail and vulnerable as she leaned against the Wimp that McDowell was heartsick.

Sammy had not needed to be respectable after all. Sammy,

who had no children, must surely have been trying to imagine, or make happen, a family.

"Exactly," the Wimp said. "We all were. Acting. You and Charles, myself and Samantha. Since we could not state our fears, we acted out our hopes and our memories." The Wimp was holding Sammy firm, but gentle. His sadness, his deep love for the Citizen and for Sammy, caused his face to seem painted with fire and regret and grief.

McDowell watched, incredulous. The Wimp was not a wimp after all. He was exactly the man who the Citizen had claimed he was. McDowell felt the heat of fire at his back, and that heat was nothing compared to the heat of embarrassment over his own waywardness and stupidity. He looked at Sammy, stepped toward her.

"Gerald," McDowell said, "you've taken such good care of my sister for so long. Gerald, please take care of my sister." He hugged Sammy, gentle-like, feeling the opening burst of rain approaching across the still hot pavement.

"I rather expect," Gerald said, "that you may trust me to do exactly that." He was removing his jacket, placing it around Sammy's shoulders as the rain arrived.

The rain came riding a bolt of lightning that cracked a tree somewhere, a big one, but the old poplar still stood. The rain came as it always did in thunderstorms, sweeping in hard and fast and drenching. There was no sprinkle or shower, only curtains of down-rushing water that turned red in the glow of flames. Thunder cracked overhead, ear splitting, violent, sucking hot air like a rush of electricity. The onlookers, those who had misgauged the storm, fled through the washed streets as the rain pounded, beat, and brought the gutters almost instantly to overflowing.

In the flood of rain bellowing downward, firemen in yellow slickers shot streams of water upward into the building where the third floor was now alive with fire. As McDowell watched, the high streams of water fell away as pressure came off the hoses. The rain was controlling the fire. The fire department had written the warehouse off.

McDowell, instantly drenched, turned and walked away. He was chilled by the wind, and he was walking and weeping and guilty. Somewhere in that blaze, and dead now . . . he could not think about it. Could not.

By the time he reached his Cad he had a bad chill. He climbed in, started the engine, and got the heater running. The car was stuffy. Technically, the night was still hot and humid. He sat in the car, thinking, feeling the last of his sobs as his throat stopped choking. He felt in his shirt pocket. The mouthpiece did not mean a thing. He listened for Margaret's voice, Peg's voice, Becky's voice. No one was singing.

Time to shove life back into gear. Time to get back to Peg. How he was going to tell Peg about this he could not begin to guess. McDowell turned on the headlights and prepared to pull away. He sat, instead, once more stunned.

There was something damned familiar looking about the back of that little van. He sat staring through rain at the rough-painted surfaces. The headlights did not reach high enough on the van, but as McDowell leaned forward and looked through the windshield as the wipers threw rain, he could see something—maybe just a spot of paint—right beneath the marker light. It looked like a decal, and not a spot of paint.

He told himself that he would be damned. He turned off the headlights, shut down the engine, and climbed from the car.

He walked along the side of the truck. It was a three-quart ton '67 Chev. There were a million of them. He could tell the make and year by the bend of the fender. He reached the cab and found that there was only one like this. A low snarl, deep throated and vicious, came from the cab of the truck. The windows were rolled halfway so that Shag could get air in the hot and humid night. Shag's teeth were bared in the snarl, and his muzzle was right at the edge of the window, ready to strike. Then Shag recognized Dan McDowell and immediately looked bored. Shag stretched, yawned, and his hind end was up, his yawn right in McDowell's face. Then Shag, as bored as any one dog ever got, lay back down on the seat.

McDowell's first reaction was hate. He would like to take that Shag and wring his neck. The Citizen was cooked like a chitterling, and there his dog was trying to get some sleep. The reaction passed as quickly as it came. It was as wrong-headed as any reaction could be.

You could not fool a good dog. Anyone who knew anything about dogs knew that. You could not fool them about important things.

The rain was easing, but not much. It was still a down drench. McDowell stood, getting his chill back, and told himself, doggonit and gracious God. He did not know how the old bastard had pulled it off. He did not know what combination of rigging and silhouettes and long fuses and electric gimmicks the old man had used. But, he told himself grumpily, if his pop were here right now, he, Dan McDowell, would personally kick the Citizen's ass right up between his shoulder blades.

McDowell walked back to his car and once more got the heater running. He was shot, beat-to-hell, exhausted, and had been nearly crazy with grief. Now he found himself pounding his fists on the dashboard, trying to catch his breath, and laughing like don't-give-a-damn Saturday night.

This play-acting, crazy-making, clown-show south.

And this was the final result of the clown show. This is how the clown show ended—joking about things that were important, strutting high and star bursting like skyrockets; joking when destruction was in the wind—the loud yuk yuk and haw haw that masked the pain which worked in hearts and minds.

This roman-candle south. This clown-show south.

It all fit in. Of course. Of course this is the way the Citizen would handle his troubles. With style. The Citizen had rigged a deadfall for everybody, while he was making Sammy well.

Right now *they* thought that the Citizen was an arsonist and a suicide. It would take a couple of days before they sifted that mess enough to know that the Citizen had not been burned in that fire. By then, the old man would be miles and miles away.

He, Dan McDowell, was going crazy. He could not stop laughing. He grabbed the steering wheel, rocking back and forth in the seat with his mind filled with anguish and his mouth filled with laughter. He could not believe he was this crazy.

He choked, laughing, imagining a bunch of insurance company jocks trying to get out of paying the claim. With the old man enjoined, he was automatically breaking the law when he entered that warehouse. And he was enjoined because he was allegedly crazy. The insurance company was going to be crawling the walls, because it either looked at arson—payable—or arson through madness—payable—at least it was payable when Gerald and his smart lawyers got through.

McDowell clung to the steering wheel so that he would not spasm and fall off the seat. He felt afire with pain, but he was choking with laughter because something else was even funnier.

Right now, he, Dan McDowell, was fucking the Citizen over. Somewhere, standing out there in that rain and cussing, the Citizen was waiting for McDowell to move his Cad. The Citizen was still trying to pull this deal off without anyone knowing.

McDowell gargled with laughter, kicked the brake like he was trying to kick away anguish, and bounced up and down on the seat as he tried to get his breath. He told himself to take his time. If the old man got wet enough, it might wash off some of the bullshit.

McDowell struggled for control and achieved enough to lean down and reach beneath the seat. He pulled out the pistol and took it from the paper sack. He checked the loads, then shoved the pistol back into the sack. Where the Citizen was headed, he just might need this pistol. McDowell leaned down and pulled out the antique Cad emblem, the hard and brilliant colors smooth beneath his fingers.

There was only one place the old man would go, because there was only one place he could go.

The old man was headed back to where he came from, and where McDowell's mother had come from. McDowell even knew the name of the post office. He could imagine how the post office looked. It would be a tiny shack sitting at a crossroads, deep in the Kentucky hills. The Citizen was going home.

Somewhere, and sold for cash at a loss, a Lincoln with a busted fender sat on a used car lot. Somewhere in the mail, from a dealer in used trucks, was the registration for an ordinary '67 Chev. The old man had bought something common and country. As he drove that thing into the hills the truck packed with necessary gear and a few sentimental things, the Citizen would blend right in. McDowell wondered what the old boy had used for an alias. The whole deal was so pretty that it would make you cry if you had any tears left.

Maybe now, the clown show was over. There was nothing McDowell could say to his pop. He could not say thank you. That might not even be true. He could not even hardly say good luck, because the old man made his own luck.

At the same time, he could not fault his pop.

He picked up the pistol, which the Citizen might need. He picked up the antique Cad emblem, which would have to stand as his only message and endorsement. McDowell climbed from his Cad, and as he walked toward the truck he was talking loudly to Shag. He did not want Shag to ruckus. McDowell stuffed the emblem through the window opening. It bounced on the seat. Shag yawned. McDowell dropped the pistol onto the seat. Shag curled up, bored. McDowell turned away, walking through rain to his car.

It was only after McDowell had pulled away, cruising slowly through the rain-swept streets, that his real trouble finally arrived.

He thought tiredly, almost idly, of the Citizen. He understood now why he had seen the Citizen laughing in the middle of fire. Then, mildly suspicious, McDowell thought of Enoch and of what the Citizen had called predictions. His foot moved on the accelerator, only a little. The Cad speeded up, but McDowell was still cruising.

Thinking of Enoch, he was unsure that he had even seen Enoch. His memory was like a dream, almost. He cruised and thought of all the things he had perhaps dreamed that Enoch did. Then he straightened in the seat, tense, as he finally understood.

The real ghost was the presence, the thing that Peg had called "Old Man." Enoch was only a picture, always had been. The presence showed Enoch, but it was the presence that was real and not Enoch.

Enoch was a picture, used to show predictions. McDowell thought it over, thought about the predictions. When Enoch had left his place and took his women away, Enoch had turned back and shot his own house. The Citizen had done the same thing, so to speak. He had shot his own business with fire.

If the predictions were real—and they must be real—then the predictions had to be read on the level of signs. Those predictions were a little bit symbolic, so they came out a little bit confused. Black turned to gray, and gray turned to white—McDowell paused. Enoch's women were both colored, but one was dark and the other was light. In the predictions a black woman might symbolically become light like Margaret, and a light-skinned colored woman might become white like Peg . . . and the clown show was not over.

In terror—absolute, concentrated terror that pressed him over the wheel and had the Cad's tires skidding and throwing clouds of water through the nearly deserted streets—McDowell drove for Peg's motel.

Chapter 30

HE DROVE IN TORMENTED FLIGHT, AND HE WAS A MAN ALONE. HE no longer had the Citizen for support, and he had never realized what kind of support the Citizen gave. He thought of his pop as he drove. There might be some further clue, something he had missed that was important.

He was alone. He no longer even had crazy Samantha. Sammy either was going to be sane, or she was not. No matter how it went, though, Sammy would be different. In a day, or next week, or in a month, she would need her brother. He would try to be there, he *would* be there; but for now he could not do a thing. The predictions were pressing him toward a desperate situation.

The Citizen had given Sammy his best try, and he had given a lot. The old man made himself into a criminal in order to help Sammy; not, of course, that being a criminal made much difference. Once the Citizen cleared Ashland he was long gone from any police. There was not a cop in his right mind who would chase the Citizen back into those hills. You could hide an army of ten thousand men in those hills. There were places in there where even federal booze agents were afraid to go.

McDowell drove in a frenzy. He shoved the Cad hard, running red lights when he had to, and when the way was clear. Even with fast driving and luck, it would still take fifteen minutes to get to Peg's motel.

The city flashed past his speeding car, the bars, the cowboy joints, the pawn shops, the motorcycle hangouts. Churches, hos-

pitals, high-rise apartments and tenements. Fast-food joints, restaurants, junk stores, and antique stores selling older types of junk.
The Cad's headlights swept the rainslick streets, streets dirty with
crud and crap and discards, with busted wine bottles and squashed
beer cans. Headlights occasionally appeared from ahead, or from
side streets. When that happened, McDowell slowed, twisting the
Cad down, catching the rear end as it broke loose. He had no time
to be arguing with cops, no time to con them. The clown show
might not be over, but the days of play-acting were over.

He passed occasional pedestrians, mostly drunks coming from bars. Water splashed high where the storm drains had
backed up, and the Cad hit the sheets of water like it was a power
boat. The wipers threw rain, and streetlights were dimmed by the
rain. Overhead, the storm had marched past, banging and crashing above the tall buildings. When he arrived at Peg's motel, the
rain was slacking but still heavy. It was no longer driven by wind.

He spun the Cad into the parking lot and nosed it in beside
Peg's Cadillac. He jumped from the car, ran, and banged on the
door. For a moment he heard nothing in the room. Nothing. Then
a small, timid voice, Peg's, asking who was knocking.

"I gotta get in. It's Dan." He pressed on the door, like he could
unlock it with the flat of his hand.

"Thank God." She opened the door, and he got into the room
fast.

"Are you okay?"

"I am now." Peg had not changed from the western shirt and
jeans. The light colors seemed bold because her face was so pale.

"Nothing's happened?"

"It's threatening." Peg's mouth was drawn tight with fear. She
looked more like a little girl than a woman. She walked to the bed,
sat down. Beside the bed a bed slat leaned. The bed itself was cocked
sideways, because she had torn it up to get at the slat. She touched
the thing, like it was her last and only friend. "I figured it out," Peg
said. "You claimed that Enoch killed because of a woman."

"Women. There were two. This could be coincidence."

"I believe in this stuff. If I had known sooner . . ." Peg sat, rocking back and forth, and her voice was filled with horror. "Margret."

"Do you know who he is?" McDowell was headed for the
phone. He paused before picking it up.

"I don't even know where he is. It could be anybody. Some studio guy, somebody maybe I've never seen. It's the prediction . . ." Thinking of Margaret, Peg's voice steadied. She leaned back on the bed, trembling, but anger was beginning to overcome fear.

"I've got to make a call, and then I've got to go. But I won't leave you." He knew that she would not understand the contradiction, but he had no time to explain. He picked up the phone, got the desk, and Jackson was not on the desk. He spoke, spoke harsher, and the desk connected him with Jackson's room.

"I got a real problem," McDowell said quickly when Jackson answered. "You're the only man I trust. The only man who'll understand."

Jackson came awake immediately. He had been yawning when he answered the phone. "Where are you?"

McDowell gave the room number. "I need you now. I need help and quick."

"You drinking?"

"No. Nor ever will again, I reckon."

"I'll be right there." Jackson hung up.

McDowell turned to Peg. He quickly sketched what had happened at the warehouse; the fire, the Citizen's trick, and his fear about predictions. "This guy who's coming down," McDowell told her, "is queer as a seven-dollar bill, but he's okay."

Peg seemed not to be listening. Color was coming into her face. She seemed tough, resilient, ready to fight.

"Do you know where Margaret's working?" McDowell asked.

"Yep. I know the name. One of those sophisticated dives."

"When I leave, get on that phone. Stay on it until you get her. If you got to, call the cops."

Peg bounced on the bed, stood, and seemed ready to scream. "Are you kidding? Cop sonsovbitches couldn't even find the address. If they did find it, they wouldn't hassle some guy, they'd just hassle her."

Peg was right. He knew it, because that's what cops did. He was in despair with the knowledge. "I think you can still get hold of her. Her last set must not be over."

"I'll try, Dan, and I'll keep trying."

There was a knock on the door. McDowell spun toward it opened it, ready and even hoping that the sonovabitch was tryin' something . . . but it was Jackson. Jackson yawned, as much impressed with McDowell as Shag had been when Shag yawned.

"Get on in here," McDowell said. "I got to go fast, and some sonovabitch is after this woman. Stay with her until she can get a rent-a-cop."

Jackson's tall frame was kind of hunched with sleepiness. Now he straightened up. "Which sonovabitch?"

"We don't know."

"Then, brother, how do you know he ain't a rent-a-cop?" Jackson grinned, totally in control of the situation. He turned to Peg. "Gets excitable, don't he?" He walked to the phone, dialed an extension, and ordered coffee. Somebody on the other end gave him an argument. He gave them an argument in return and won. He hung up, grinned. "If we got a long shift, we're going to need some coffee."

"She'll explain it," McDowell said. "I got to go. You got a gun?"

Jackson peered at McDowell. He seemed to be wondering if he was looking at a madman. "Shore," he drawled, "up in my room. All us down-home boys got swords." He glanced toward the bed. "An' I got a bed slat. There ain't a man born can come past me if I got a bed slat. You need a gun?"

"Nope."

"Goodbye."

"Dan," Peg walked toward him. "Drive. Go." She hugged him, hugged him hard, and then nearly shoved him into the door. He opened the door and ran to the Cad, moving out quick, skidding and splashing across the night-covered rainslick lot.

The Cad flew to Atlanta, a seven-hour drive that he made in five. He had never really understood why he had ever loved the Cad, but now, clear of the city, the heavy wheels beat on the striped, concrete pavement, thumping and in motion, running across bridged rivers and heading south. The headlights of the Cad cut wide swaths in the darkness, across the flat Bluegrass and through hilly terrain. The Cad was like an arrow on the road, a piece of the road, and for all of the many, many years that the Cad had existed, it seemed to him that it had been waiting to do this one job. The engine cried into the wind, and the wind tore around mirrors, over the canvas top; and the wind called like hot and humid voices, wailing. The Cad was good for one thing, and it was doing it—carrying him to Atlanta like heat blazing through darkness.

He called on his knowledge, his years on the road, and his instinct for smelling cops. He had no time to fuck with them, with their powerless cop problems and their silly cop laws. He watched the dark terrain, the trucks on the nighttime road, and he listened to his instincts. He had never installed a CB radio. A CB was a joke, a thing you learned to trust, and trusting it, you got busted. At times the Cad ran at ninety, at times it ran nearly legal. He kicked it through the night, and he thought and paid attention to the road, and thought some more.

The south was a retard. Always had been. Cars were loved and mistreated here. They were like bright, shiny axes traded to primitive cultures. They held the promise of power in a powerless place. The south was as helpless as he was.

Into the dark heart of the south, to Atlanta. The Cad drove roads that ran between fields, beside broken fences, walls, limestone and melted with age. It passed beneath limb-drooping trees and beside scrub pine.

For one hour of the long journey he played the mouthpiece, talking into the mouthpiece, crying into it with a tearless, buzzing wail. When his lip was raw, he continued to blow, listening to the failure, the indifference of jaw and gut, the failure of his body to supply the strength for his need. The mouthpiece cracked staccato, then wept, and then screamed.

To Atlanta, the dark heart of the south; and he rolled onto the broad, broad streets of Atlanta which ran between the high buildings. It was four AM. He gave a taxi driver a twenty to lead him quickly to Margaret's motel, where he found that he had saved Peg, a woman he loved. He had not saved Margaret, the woman he loved the most.

The dark, early morning that should have seemed cool at his back was hot as he stood before Margaret's door. He knocked, then waited, but there was no answer. He listened carefully, straining, attempting to hear movement in the room. From the road a solitary automobile passed, and in the distance was the buzz of a light plane. At his back the city seemed filled with low sound, a dark murmur of inarticulate dread. He knocked again, called softly to her. He believed he heard movement. He backed away from the door, ready to kick it down. Beside him, in the window, a drape moved.

The door opened and Margaret stood before him, wrapped in a bath towel. Her hair was wet, dripping. Her eyes were dull, dead looking, and the left one was badly bruised. She stood trembling. He could see suspicion on her face, although her eyes continued to look dead.

"Peg called," she whispered, "and I've been washing. It won't come off. Dan, I can't get clean."

He entered the room slowly, so he would not frighten her. It was a small room, and tidy, except for a wad of clothing that had been tossed into a wastebasket. A blouse hung over the edge of the basket. From the bathroom came the sound of water running.

"Been washing for an hour." Her voice was low, fearful. She stood before him, submissive and trembling. He thought that their pain might kill him, might cause muscles and tendons to tear apart, rip his heart loose from the rib cage.

"I got to get clean. Please."

"Can you talk?"

"I got to get clean."

He saw that she could not talk. She was fixed on a single idea. With her right hand she brushed at her left arm, rubbing, trying to brush away the feeling of dirt. He reached for her hand, and she took a step toward him, moaned, like a sigh. He thought she would fall. He stepped to her, put his arm around her, and that was a terrible mistake. She tried to lift his hand away and she began to weep.

"What?"

"Baby, I hurt so bad."

In a fury of helplessness, McDowell found himself behaving more gently than ever before in his life. He carefully led her to the bathroom, unwrapped the towel and helped her into the tub. She could not move well, strained or injured in the back or legs. Her rib cage on the left side looked inflamed.

"It's going to hurt, Margaret. I'm sorry, but I gotta." He felt the rib cage and satisfied himself that nothing was broken, only badly bruised. She sat weeping, enduring the touch. There were bruises on her arms and deep scratches on her back and chest. Her black eye was purplish, green, with the swelling of a bad bruise.

"I don't have anything," McDowell said. "I don't even have an aspirin."

She seemed to be listening carefully to him, but not understanding what he said. McDowell began to touch her tenderly, soaping her back. "Do you know anybody, anyone I could call? Even some codeine would do it."

"No junk. I never touch shit. Never. No."

He reminded himself that she was a singer who was nearly superstitious about booze. Any drug would naturally scare her off.

Well, he thought, and yes. Drugs had caught a lot of them, but he still wished he had just one pill. One pill would not hurt. He soaped her shoulders, rinsed them, soaped some more. The little bars of soap were not doing much good. He had regular soap in his suitcase, but his suitcase was still in a motel room in Centerville. Then he told himself that it was water she needed anyway. He rinsed her, then began pouring water across her back cupping the water up with his hands.

"How did you get here?" He did not see how she could have walked.

"I was here. My ride dropped me at the corner. I was outside in the parking lot." She was bent forward, whispering, and then she was quiet. She gave a little snore, woke, startled. Terrified. Then she remembered who he was.

McDowell, in a fury of helplessness, cupped water in his hands and washed her arms. She had to be exhausted. He had to get her to sleep. Then he told himself, no, he had to get her clean. Only if she felt clean would she be able to sleep.

Until dawn was light in the window she slumped and sometimes closed her eyes, sometimes came full awake. Her eyes remained dull and seemed sightless. McDowell changed the water, changed it again, changed it again. He murmured to her, consoling, loving, helpless words that he worried over. He did not know whether the words were helping or hurting. While all of it was going on, hatred was so deep in him, fury, that he made himself go even more slowly, more gently. His mind was silently talking to him about death, and his fingers were talking love.

By the time dawn was light in the window she was sleeping in longer stretches, slumped over.

"I have to move you," McDowell told her. "We've got it all off. It's all gone now." He figured that it might be years before it was really gone, but as exhausted as she was, she might believe him for a little while. He helped her from the tub and guided her to the bed.

She lay curled up, and he rubbed her back until she fell asleep. Her breathing was shallow, interrupted by deep gulps of breath and occasional snoring in a hard, raspy way.

He was exhausted himself. Last night, even before he had gone to catch the Citizen's act, he had felt exhausted. Dan McDowell took a pillow from the bed and stretched out on the floor in front of the doorway. He pulled out his knife, opened it, and put it beneath the pillow. The door opened inward. Anyone who came in had to push him aside first.

He slept in short spells, dreamed in short spells, and came awake, drowsy, looking at Margaret before he returned to sleep. He blinked his eyes open at sunlight, turned his face to the door, sank back into sleep. The dreams came at him like blades of violence, sharp, gleaming. For a while he dreamed only of knives. The knives were brilliant, clean, unblooded. The blades turned, circled, searched, and were impotent.

Another time while dreaming, he dreamed only of screams. Hoarse, deep-throated with terror. The screams were man screams, and the terror fled and the screams turned into his own screams of helplessness.

The sun was brighter and brighter each time he woke. The room heated up, as the old air conditioner throbbed and blew warm air. His clothes were soaked with sweat. The pillow was wet. He woke finally and checked his watch. It was one o'clock in the afternoon. From the bathroom came the sound of water running.

He got to his knees, then to his feet. He was dirty, rumpled, smelly, and wet. He felt like he was coming off of a bad, bad drunk. The sound of water stopped. Margaret's voice was making little hums: cold, mechanical, frozen hums like emotions encased in ice.

"It's me," he said so that she would not be frightened. "I'm awake. Up and about."

"Dan . . ." Her voice was hesitant. "Dan, come here."

He walked to the bathroom. Margaret was in the tub. "This is embarrassing, babe. I just can't seem to get it off." Her eyes were still dull, but at least they no longer looked dead. She glanced down at her arm where a bruise was nearly black. "Wish I was darker. Bruise don't show good when you're dark." There was no self-pity in her voice, no accusation. She was talking to herself, taking interest in some logical problem. "Going to have to work in sleeves. I hate that."

Of course she hated it. When they worked too much in long sleeves, the word got around among the punks and second-raters that the woman was a junkie.

"You can't work anyway," McDowell said. "Not for a little while."

"Don't say that to me. I can't hear that." She shrugged, trying to fight it off. Her dull eyes momentarily were sharp with pain.

"Margaret, quit fooling me around."

"I'm not fooling." She looked at him, and she was sad but determined. "We're out of soap," she said irrelevantly. She seemed nearly ready to cry because there was no more soap.

"How's the ribs?"

"Like a boil."

"Then you can't breathe deep, babe. If you can't breathe, you can't work."

"I don't hear a word of that. You take that, and you do with it what it deserves."

He was happy. Happy. He actually believed for the first time that she would eventually be all right. At least the submissiveness was past. Her bodacious self was trying for a little sassiness, a little smart mouth.

"We'll see," he said inconclusively.

"You bet we will." Then she looked repentant. "Dan, boy, pay no attention to my mouth. These are hard times."

"Get you to a doctor. Check you over."

"No," Margaret said, "I got to ride this one out. Go to a doctor, and he's going to want to yell cop."

He understood it. The last thing her career needed was any publicity about this. You did not command a stage when people thought of you as a victim.

"And," Margaret said, "no lousy pervert cop is going to go pawing me with his pervert eyes."

At least her hatreds were starting to turn outward. They were not going in against herself. He figured that Margaret was every bit as tough as he had believed. She was resilient. She was going to work her way through this, although it was going to be tough on them both.

"You got to eat. And besides, I got to get you some soap."

"Don't leave me."

"Not a chance," he told her. "Ever again. Ever."

She raised her head and looked straight at him. Her hair had dried, but it was not yet brushed. Her eye was darker, the bruise deeper, but the swelling had gone down a little. He could see doubt in her eyes, but he could also see hope.

"Is that true?"

"Count on it," he told her.

"I got to know," she said. She seemed nearly apologetic. "I got to figure things out." She stopped looking at him, and looked at her body instead. "Tell me true. Did you fuck Peg?" The apology was still in her voice, but fear was there as well.

"I made love to Peg," McDowell said truthfully. "She had poor feelings about herself." Then, determined to say nothing dishonest he admitted the rest. "I wanted to. It wasn't charity."

"How was it?" She looked dull-eyed again, like she was too lacking in feeling even to cry. She ran her hand along her bruised ribs, touched her small, badly scratched breasts. "I'm not used to being behind in any game I play."

"You never have been. At least not in this one."

"She's prettier. I can't help that. And I got this. Can't help that, either." She was moving her hands over herself and watching, almost wonderingly, as her hands touched bruises. Then she moved her hands, using them to cover her face.

Peg was not prettier, not more beautiful. Besides, that had nothing to do with anything, but how could he explain it? Of course Margaret was feeling ugly, of course.

"Quit fooling me around, Margaret. You're both beautiful, and you know me better than that."

"Still, I got this." She did not remove her hands from her face.

It was maybe taking a chance, maybe not, but there would never be a better time to say it. "Peg didn't tell me about you two," McDowell said, "about loving each other. I guessed. It was all right then, and it's all right now."

She hesitated, and then slowly lowered her hands. She looked nearly incredulous. "You know about that, and you're still here, saying what you're saying?" Her eyes were not as dull as before.

"It's actually even a pretty fine thing when you think about it."

"Yes," Margaret said softly, "it is a pretty fine thing. Are you telling me true? Are you going to stay with me?

"I got more to tell you than that," he said, thinking of the horn. He wanted to reach his hand toward her, touch her, but made himself stop. It might be that she could not bear that kind of touch. "I got this true thing to tell you." He stopped talking, wishing the room was really quiet, wishing that there was no buzz of traffic from the street, no rattle of the air conditioner. "If you want a man, then I want to be your man. If you want that, then I'll be here for always."

Her weeping was quiet, not choking or sobbing. He could not tell whether she was sad or happy or both. She pulled a towel from the rack and wiped at her eyes. Then she sat for a couple of minutes, regaining control. She pulled the plug from the tub and attempted to stand. He helped her up.

She stood, still weeping, but only a little. Margaret was looking at him, in love and not just lovingly. "I can't be your woman just now. I can't deal with no man just now." She began to dry herself. "But if you want a woman, and if you give me some time, I want to be your woman. I'm all the woman you'll ever want."

It was not sex, but intimacy. It was not sex, but love. There was no way in the world for him to explain that, at least not now.

"All the time you need," he said gently. "I'll be here." Hearing his own voice, he heard the honesty, open and strong in his voice. He knew what a singer must hear when that singer was doing her absolute best.

She began to move a little better. She was still moving stiff and painful, but with more directness. Margaret finished drying herself, then dropped the towel beside the tub. She did not seem at all shy now. She was as easy with her nakedness as Peg had been with hers.

McDowell understood it, and he felt better than anyone was supposed to feel in church. Margaret trusted him. He really was her man, she trusted him. Now she would not be shy, not ever again. He was her man.

This south, where the women were the strongest women in the world, and where the men were the most womanly men in the world. And the toughest.

She tried to smile, and the smile almost happened. "We got to get going. I have to get some shades and we have to eat. I got to walk some of this soreness off."

"I got to buy some clothes, get cleaned up. I smell like the pig business."

This time she actually did smile, a little. "You just go ahead, Dan. Smell any old way you want." She braced herself against the wall. "The dark blue slacks in the suitcase. And the darkest blouse. Let's get me dressed."

It took ten minutes to dress, and three more for her to make it to the car. Out there in the streets of Atlanta the traffic poured, pressed, rushed like a flash flood. The wide, wide streets were not handling the traffic. The tall buildings were like iridescent blocks against the hot sky. Margaret seemed almost comfortable in the seat beside him.

"You taken to selling out of the trunk?" She was talking about the instruments in the back seat.

"Those are mine. I'll tell you about it at lunch." He pulled away, entered traffic, and began looking for a drugstore. When he found one, he parked the car right in front, where he could be inside and still look out and see her. Margaret sat quietly, head down, hiding her face. He bought the widest, darkest sunglasses he could find. As he did, he felt the hatred return, threatening to overwhelm him. He got it under control and went back to the car.

"Never worked in these before." Once she was wearing the glasses she obviously felt better, or at least safer. McDowell began looking for a restaurant. He was pushed for time. He still had to change motels, get her somewhere else.

The restaurant was one of those mass production, Oldsmobile salesmen type of places where the seats were washable and the tables were plastic slabs. Well-dressed men and women sat around, but not too many of them in the middle afternoon. Three waitresses dawdled, taking it easy after the heavy lunch traffic. It was just another restaurant, and his attention was all with Margaret. He had no time for anyone else.

Lunch was going to be tough. Life would remain that way for quite a while.

A guy entered the restaurant, walked in McDowell's direction and took a nearby table. The guy was dressed in a business suit. He was preoccupied, worrying over a sheaf of papers in his hand. The guy was a good deal darker than Margaret. When a waitress arrived, he looked up, chanced to see Margaret, and then McDowell. His mouth hardened. His hands clenched. He looked at McDowell like he had just been served a piece of shit. He stood, spoke briefly to the waitress, then moved to a table at the far end of the room.

A white kid, sitting at the counter, stood up to leave. The kid had a kind of arrogant, smartass way of walking that probably meant he owned a motorcycle. His hair was blonde, but his eyes were deep, dark brown, nearly black. He passed McDowell, slowed down, and seemed to be trying to make up his mind whether or not to stop. Then he shrugged his shoulders contemptuously, and his mouth looked as repulsed as if he had been told to kiss a dead dog.

"I'm sorry," Margaret said.

"Can't be helped. I've done the same thing to guys, and maybe some of them didn't deserve it."

"Tell me about the other. You buy a music factory?"

He began, and the more he told, the more it seemed there was to tell. So he started over. He was talking with an intimacy and openness that he had never known before. He was not talking about problems, about the hard, uphill fight he would make over the next couple of years. He was trying to tell about meaning, about music and song and Margaret. Half the time he felt incoherent, and the other half he felt like he was singing, himself.

His talk lasted all through lunch, and he was still not done. Margaret was quiet during all of it. Once in awhile she poked in a question, like she was priming him.

He just kept talking, and as he talked it came to him that maybe the years were not wasted after all. Maybe the driving and the selling and the ass-kicking were all things he had to do, before he could do this one thing that always, all his life, was the thing he was supposed to do.

He kept telling it, breaking in on the story all afternoon as he bought clothes, changed motels, and walked with Margaret. She was stiff, sore, but by the end of the walk she was moving better. Once, during the walk, she actually reached down, took his hand, and held it for minutes. In a way, it was the most intimate thing she had ever done with him and she was not shy when she took his hand. When they returned to the motel, he managed to get her to bed for a short rest before dinner and work. He once more slept in front of the door.

Again his dreams were like knives. He woke in this different motel room, knowing that while life was different, and always would be, that other old life was not yet over. It might be a coincidence, it might be. He did not believe it was. If it was not a coincidence, then the predictions had not yet run their course.

He was going to say nothing to Margaret. As he woke he found himself in disciplined control. He felt for his knife, and it was little more than a toy. Unless, of course, you could get it into a throat, or up the back of a neck. The knife was a feeble thing. He did not dare stop at some store on an errand that would take him away from Margaret, not yet. Besides, Margaret was not dumb. If he went looking for a switchblade, she would know.

He remembered the predictions. The Citizen claimed to have seen Dan McDowell hurt. He shrugged. If these were predictions and not coincidences, then the predictions were only warnings.

If you figured them out ahead of time, you could beat them. After all, he had saved Peg.

He sat before the door and wondered how to wake Margaret. Then he thought of Peg and how she would worry. Since he had changed motels, Peg would not know where to reach them.

This room had an air conditioner that worked, and the room was larger. It had the chintz and cheap plush that you found so often in redneck cities. The paintings were antelopes from Africa, or some such-a place, on velvet. He wished they had a better place, but from now on it was best to live economically.

Dan McDowell touched the mouthpiece in his shirt pocket. His disciplined control was in charge. He put the mouthpiece in his pants pocket. When whatever was going to happen came down, he did not want to be dropping anything that looked like evidence. He opened a drawer of the dresser and emptied his pockets of change and cigarettes and a lighter. He counted his cash, left his traveler's checks. He left anything that might carry a fingerprint. McDowell listened. Out there in the street, traffic was running, and he expected to hear a siren. The sirens were temporarily silent. He debated about leaving the mouthpiece. Somehow that did not seem the right thing to do.

Margaret sighed, turned, and continued to sleep. McDowell took off his watch, checked the time, and put the watch in the drawer. He had to wake Margaret soon. Light was fading in the window. McDowell pulled the mouthpiece from his pocket and began to play, low and fairly soft. The control he needed was still a long way off, but the promise of control was there. The mouthpiece buzzed, which it was supposed to do, but McDowell could hear the difference. He was pulling up at least a short range of tones, and not just notes.

If he touched her she might be startled, afraid. As he played he watched her. In spite of the bruises and the bad eye she seemed better. If she was not relaxed in her sleep, at least she was no longer so tense. He thought lovingly of Becky. Of Peg. Margaret was the most beautiful woman he had ever seen. His woman. He found that he was playing the mouthpiece for her and to her. Even then it took her awhile to wake. When she opened her eyes, she lay quiet for a minute, then rolled toward the bed stand and picked up her watch.

"We have to get going."

"We have to call Peg," he said. "She'll worry."

Margaret sat up, took a deep breath, and grabbed her side. She took another deep breath. "Is that all right, what you're saying?"

"We got some talk ahead of us, but none of it bad." His voice was gentle, explaining. "It's the right thing to do. You know that."

"I know it. I'm just grateful you do." She sat up, winced, shook her head. "I got to get moving, walk this off." She stood, a little wobbly but without help. She walked slowly to the phone, got the desk, dialed. Holding the phone, she looked down at herself like she was surprised at being unclothed. When Peg answered, Margaret smiled.

"No," Margaret said into the phone. "Getting better, but still not good. It won't kill me. Are you okay?"

Peg took a long time answering. At least Margaret took a long time listening. Since the conversation might be private, McDowell went to the bathroom and splashed water on his face. He had bathed earlier and was in clean clothes. That was nearly as good as sleep. He tested his mind to see if the discipline was still there. It was.

"He's here," Margaret said to Peg as McDowell reentered the room. "Talk to him." She motioned to Dan McDowell.

Peg's voice was worried when he answered.

"Is she telling the truth?" Peg said seriously. "Is she okay?"

"Nope, but doing as well as can be expected. We'll get through this. Are you okay?"

"Well, now," Peg said, "yes." Her voice sounded happy, or at least optimistic.

"Because," McDowell whispered, "I don't think it's over yet. The whole thing hasn't run its course."

"I know it," Peg said, and she was grim. "But I'm okay, and going to be that way."

"Jackson's still there?"

"Like a tick on a pup's ear. Right now he's in the can, being discreet."

"You tell him I'm grateful. I owe him."

Peg actually giggled. "I dunno about that," she said. "It could be he owes you. I thought you said this guy was queer."

"He is. At least I'm sure he is."

"Quite a talker," Peg said happily.

"That's the God's truth."

"I expect he is queer," Peg said. "In spots." She once more giggled. "Dan, me and him have made no heavy moves on each other, but there ain't many good men. I know a good one when I see him."

McDowell told himself that he would be damned.

"And we won't be making any heavy moves, not for a good while. If this turns out to be what it could be, then it's going to take some time. I'm hopeful." Then Peg's voice got serious again. "Your pop called. Just after you left."

There was a shock. It made him sad, but it also made him glad.

"What did Pop have to say?"

"He said take care of yourself."

"Is that all?" McDowell was uncomfortable.

"Goodbye," Peg said. "He said goodbye."

"That's all?"

"All that's worth anything." Peg sounded apologetic.

"But not all?"

Peg took a deep breath. "He said to get a haircut."

This clown show. Would this clown show never end?

The old man had done his best. That was as close as he could come to saying thank you. That was as close as he could come to saying I love you. The old man could not have said those words to Sammy, either. Despite he had burned down a lifetime of work to save her.

McDowell looked at Margaret, who was getting dressed. He

felt in his pocket for his knife. This clown show. The clown show had its own style, its own pace, and it laughed and joked with a man up until a minute before it killed him.

"Dan," Peg said, and her voice was fearful. It was also loving, if not in love. "I trust this stuff. That means it's your turn next, at least I think so."

"I'm taking care. I'm watching."

"Does Margaret know?"

"Nope."

"And she'll be okay?"

"Nothing is broke, but you can imagine how she feels. She'll be okay, but not right away."

"Dan, I want to say so much. All I can say is be careful. Be real, real careful, Dan."

"I will. I am."

"How in the world am I going to say it? I love you, but not the way it sounds when I say it."

"And her."

"I already told her," Peg said, "and I'm going to hang up now, while I'm still ahead."

He hung up the phone and checked his pockets for the mouthpiece and the knife. He thought dismally that maybe the clown show never ended, not until you were dead.

Chapter 31

MARGARET TOTALLY BUTCHERED THE FIRST SET. HER VOICE WAS thin, airless and cold. It was hard, abrasive. He voice was worse than Samantha's, assuming Samantha could sing. Margaret was desperate. For a while she tried to play it little-girl but that sounded so awful that she came off of it fast.

McDowell circulated. The joint was a big one, and it rapidly filled with well-heeled people; ladies in simple and expensive evening dress, men in light suits, jackets, and some of them wore ties. Margaret might not have a national reputation, but in this south, which ran from Atlanta to Chicago and Detroit she drew the crowds. During the first set the crowd was talking. What was being said was not pretty. It was a credit to Margaret's reputation that most of the crowd did not leave.

McDowell circulated, eased around the long, wide room with the bar down the middle, and with the stage at one end. The bar ran nearly the length of the room. It was a fairly efficient setup. There were four waitress stations and eight waitresses. The four bartenders were moving fast.

As he circulated McDowell halfway listened and all the way grieved. He told himself that she should not have tried it. This was going to be one of those long, worst nights that you never forgot. Margaret had nothing going for her but professionalism. Her attacks were clean, her phrasing clean, and her voice made her sound like a witch.

Plus, she had professionalism behind her. It was a good band of local guys who had been together for a long time. Margaret had worked with them. That was clear. But it made no difference.

Halfway through the set, McDowell wanted to stop circulating and go clobber the guy on the lights. As the bad music did not improve, and seemed to get worse, and as the crowd began to chatter, the guy raised the brilliance of the lights. Margaret had makeup over the bruise. She was wearing dark glasses. Yet, as the light level rose she seemed to shrink. She was getting shy right there on that stage, and she had never been that way with an audience.

McDowell told himself to concentrate, to keep his discipline. He passed by tables and mostly ignored the well-dressed men who sat by well-dressed women. He checked tables where there were only men. There were only a few of those tables, and the guys were obviously fags. The fags were being catty, educated in their talk, and they would not know music if they heard it. McDowell moved slowly, seemingly indifferent, concentrating on the bar. With the lights turned so high it was impossible for Margaret to see the bar.

Once, he thought he had his man. A guy sat toward the end of the bar, staring right at Margaret. He seemed lost in the stare. He was mumbling, muttering, paying no attention to his drink. McDowell approached from behind, checking the guy out. He was a working-type guy, a machinist's apprentice or something. He was out of his element in this higher-class joint. He was wearing no jacket. McDowell looked at the guy's pockets, which were flat. The guy was wearing low-cut shoes. McDowell eased up behind him, listening.

"You don't wanta do that to me, Ruth Ann, not never, ever again." As McDowell listened, the guy mumbled his complaint to Ruth Ann. He was oblivious to the men sitting along the bar, and in less than a minute McDowell knew that he was oblivious to Margaret, although he stared at her. McDowell turned away and circulated. He told himself that there was no reason to believe that the guy he wanted would show up. On the other hand, there was no reason to believe he would not. Most guys like that were on power trips, not sex trips. They often showed up to look at a woman and gloat with their power.

Besides, there was the prediction. The Citizen had seen McDowell hurt.

McDowell stood at the end of the bar, looking across the crowd and toward the stage. He was nursing a soft drink that was masked by a whiskey glass. The guys up there were trying to cover for Margaret. They had been doing showmanship stuff, fine, strong jazz. They had raised their volume, but Margaret was still stiff. She moved stiff, holding the mike like it was a club. Those guys were working hard, but they were not drawing attention from the lousy singing.

On the last number of the set they played it different, trying to make the whole thing into a joke. The piano tinkled, schmaltzed, made phony runs. The trumpet barked, triple-tongued in the most corny manner. The trumpet made sharp notes, fluttered and trilled. The drummer tossed his sticks, laid onto a tickety-tick that would have been funny if he had not been trying so hard. You had to be relaxed to play it, and even these professionals were no longer relaxed. The noise level in the joint was high. People were bored or offended. They concentrated on the easy talk that came from booze. Even the hard-eyed bartenders seemed nastier and more efficient. The waitresses scurried.

McDowell was relieved when the first set ended. Margaret came down, sat at the band table off in a far corner of the room. The piano guy was with her. He was a balding white man. Even in the air-conditioned room the temperature was high. The guy had been working like a madman and even his head was sweaty. McDowell approached, slid into a chair beside her.

Her shame was all over her face, although he could not see her eyes. Her mouth was drawn with shame.

"You got an ear," she said. "Don't go telling me it's all right."

"There ain't a musician alive who hasn't blown a few."

"St. Louis," the piano guy said. "Once upon a time I shit all over myself in St. Louis." He leaned back, watching the crowd. "A'course, I was younger then." He looked at Margaret, then McDowell. "You need to be alone?"

"Nope," McDowell said. "Let's figure this out."

"I never been this cold," Margaret told them. "I mean really cold. How can you catch a chill under lights?"

"You're wired," the piano guy said. "You keep trying to get up there and it don't pay. Pays to go down. Couple of drinks."

"No." She looked frightened.

"Lower the lights," McDowell said. "Tell that guy to get them on down there."

"I'll freeze. Already I'm freezing."

"Yeah, and that's what's freezing you. You got no place to hide." He almost wished he had not said it, then he was glad he did. She looked at him gratefully, if not for help, at least for understanding.

"I'll get you something to drink. No booze."

"I couldn't keep it down." She looked at him and she was fighting back tears. "Can't afford to cry. Can't streak this stuff. Dan, this ain't me."

"Nope," he said with conviction, "It's us. It's you and me, and right now we got a problem."

That helped even more. She suddenly took off the glasses. "How does it look?"

"Not good from here. When you're up front, it can't be seen." He was almost not lying. You could not see it unless you were really looking.

She was staring across the long room, at the entry. She made a feeble, nearly pushing-away gesture with her hand. She put on the glasses, quick. McDowell sneaked a look. Three guys were over there, coming in, looking for seats along the bar. At first he thought they were together. Then he saw they were not. He kept his big mouth shut, pretending he had seen nothing.

Margaret was trembling now, and he pretended not to notice.

"Start off jumping," McDowell said, "because you just about gotta. Then sing me some blues." At least if she went to blues, the lights would get on down there. "Are you sick?"

"Sick and tired, Dan, tired and hurting."

"Bag it."

"Nope." She stood slowly. "Don't talk to me no more right now. But talk lots to me later. Keep an eye on me." She moved away stiffly, toward the can. She carried her purse like it was a heavy weight.

"I'll do what I can," the piano guy said.

"You've been doing it," McDowell told him. "Just stay with her."

"I wish I had my hands on that sonovabitch."

"I think I've got him spotted," McDowell said. "For God's sake don't tell her."

The guy looked pleased, then furiously happy. "Don't leave two of his bones hanging together. Take him apart." The piano guy stood, stretched. "Get a breath of fresh air, an' then we'll get back to it." He headed for an exit.

McDowell slipped away from the table. Here, in the dark corner, he believed and hoped that his man had not seen him with Margaret. He moved along a far wall, passing between tables. The noise level was even higher. If matters did not improve, and if the crowd kept slopping booze in this nervous way, McDowell figured there would be at least one ugly fight. Then he told himself, no, nope. Two ugly fights. He eased along, dawdling, checking the three guys. He could not tell which one he wanted. He stood at the bar and ordered another soft drink.

When the set started, he could tell tight away. He had his man, and having him, had to figure his next move.

The band jumped it without Margaret. She stayed back, stage side, waiting. The guys moved right out. If they were not relaxed, at least they no longer had the tension of the last set. Probably they were less tense because they did not have to carry her as they opened this one.

McDowell's man was looking straight at Margaret as she stood in the shadows. He was drumming his fingers on the bar, and his lips were moving. The guy was dressed in a phony, linen-looking suit. Tipped back on his head was one of those hundred-dollar straw cowboy hats. He wore low, flaring boots.

McDowell yawned, made himself look bored, left his drink on the bar, and started on a slow amble toward the john. He paused behind the guy, checking him out. The dumb sonovabitch was carrying his gun in his right-hand jacket pocket. A phony. A guy playing games. A guy without a holster. McDowell could not see the man's pants pockets, but he saw the bulge in the pants leg beside the top of the boot. He told himself, hot damn. The guy was an armament factory. It would save some trouble.

A cowboy guy. One of those total turds who would faint in the presence of a horse. As Margaret stepped onto the stage McDowell had already passed the guy and looked back. The guy's gaze was fixed on Margaret. McDowell hurried to the john, waited a minute, then returned. The intro was coming. Margaret was holding the mike, but this time not so stiff. Her voice started, tentative, and then began to come in strong. McDowell sat, watching the guy, and listening. The noise level of the crowd was still high.

The guy was actually wiping spit from his lips, like he was drooling. Margaret was singing blues. The blues began to pick up authority, take form in the air. Before anyone else knew it, Mc-Dowell knew it. Before the band knew it, before the few people in the crowd who could listen knew it, McDowell knew. Margaret was washing herself clean. She was fighting back.

That girl was singing white smoke and blue mist, like a heat-struck morning among the pines. He had never heard her sing this way, or anyone sing this way. The blues throbbed, wept, moved in the cigarette smoke-filled air, pulsing, hurting, throbbing, full of tears. These were not trick blues, not technique blues. These were the bluest blues there were. Dan McDowell sat wide-awake and choking. He reached for a cigarette, found none, fumbled. The blues should be rising, kicked on up by hope or maybe memory, or even just the love of music.

Instead, they dropped. Margaret pulled it right on down there, to the limit of what he thought was her range. The blues beat like surf. The blues washed over the audience like a sea, and even the drunks, the loudmouths, the guys preoccupied with trying to make a woman, stopped their talking. The blues walked like con-demnation, like hospitals, like jails. They cried more than lost love, cried like love was white smoke and blue mist.

The trumpet picked up, weaving slow, crystal, silver, talking back to Margaret. The guy played muted, soft, and as the blues ac-cented, the horn followed with a loving, decent accent. The horn was making love to her right there in front of the smoke-filled room, the women trying to make a man, or trying not to get made; the waitresses rubbing the pinch marks on their legs. The bartend-ers darting about, indifferent, and cruel. The horn kicked a little, asking a question, asking Margaret if she wanted to come off of it.

The blues walked, cried, were not about to leave, not just yet. Dan McDowell touched his pants pocket, felt the mouthpiece. The gray and white and silver that was walking across that stage made him feel like his heart would stop. He looked down the bar at the cowboy. The cowboy was rared back, a smirk and a drool on his lips. The powerless sonovabitch was doing it all over again, waiting, imagining, playing with the only power he owned. And, McDowell told himself, the only power the guy would ever own, because his time of power was past.

The blues went where Margaret could not go. A voice could not stand that. The throat, the hurt ribs, could not stand that. Yet, the blues cried, growled, stepped like heartbreak to an empty bed. The trumpet questioned, and then it began to insist. The guy was telling her it was time to leave, that she really had to come away from it. It was telling her more than that. It was loving her like no man could ever love a woman, or a woman a man. Love like this did not happen, except over years and years of music. It was not even Margaret, it was her voice. Margaret's voice and the voice of the horn were talking love.

Now the drummer started, laying away the brushes and sticking with his left hand, gentle. He was on the snare with the fingers of his right hand, the left stick moving on the snare rim like a walk down a dark and lonesome alley. He dropped the bass entirely, paid no attention to his deep drums. The snare spoke like snares were not supposed to speak, that soft, that respectful. The blues began to rise.

As they rose, a murmur rose from the crowd. Someone laughed tinnily, embarrassed. Then the laugh cut off, sharp. For a moment after the song was finished the crowd sat silent, waiting, tentative. Then it went crazy with applause, with the loud enthusiasm of people who did not know what they had heard, but enough to know that they had heard something so fine that they would not likely ever hear such a thing again.

The cowboy was leaning forward, his fingers nervous, drumming, and he was so pleased and proud of himself that McDowell tensed. The guy looked nearly ready to take action. He was a big, burly, black-hair sonovabitch who would take a lot of killing. His heavy hands drummed on the bar.

Hatred flowed through Dan McDowell as he sat loving it, loving how long it was going to take that man to die. He had to act but could not figure his best move. It would be best to wait until the guy left the joint. That was not going to work. As high as the guy was on his power, he would be there through the last set. McDowell yawned, pretended boredom. The guy's perversity was giving Dan McDowell time to plan, because sure-n-hell you could not just pick him off from along the bar. The guy was leaned forward, completely absorbed in overpowering Margaret again. McDowell was willing to bet that the guy did not even know that Margaret had a man with her.

McDowell slid away from the bar, walked to where the guy was sitting, and looked toward the band table. He saw that unless the guy moved his seat he would be barely able to see the table. McDowell figured the man would not move. His power depended on invisibility. If Margaret saw him, the guy had no reason to believe that she would not holler cop.

During the rest of the set McDowell dawdled, waited, worked his way back to the band table. Margaret was helping him. She was in charge of that stage. The noise level in the joint was low, and she was singing confidently. She was having some trouble breathing, but she was still in command. Later, when his mind was not in such tight control, he would be happy. The band was relaxing. It was swinging.

When the set ended, Margaret came from the stage fast. She was smiling. Then she saw McDowell and was obviously remembering that he had an ear. There was no possible way for Margaret to hide the fact that the cowboy was in this joint. As she walked to McDowell the trumpet player was staying with her. He followed her to the table.

"Dan, boy," she said rapidly, "it's okay now. Leave it be."

"You did good. You did so good." He leaned back, watching her, loving her, but hanging on tight to his discipline. The trumpet guy sat down. He was watching McDowell, to see what McDowell would do. The trumpet guy did not look like he was in any mood to go easy with anyone.

"Dan," Margaret said, "I know you. You aren't reaching for your balls. Give me your knife." She held out her hand for all the world like a tough deacon with a collection plate.

"What knife?" He tried to make it sound like a joke.

"Give me your knife, baby. So help me, I'll holler cop."

He dug it out, a lousy little three-inch knife that was not going to do much good anyway. "I'm not going to hurt him," he lied. "Just going to remonstrate with the sonovabitch. I got to, you know that."

"I know it," Margaret said, and she was sad. "But do it right." Along with the sadness, she seemed both happy and pissed at the same time. "Darnit, Dan, it's all a fantasy, you know that."

"I don't," he said honestly.

"Some of us pick one fantasy, some pick another."

"Just going to give him a talking to."

Margaret dropped the knife in her purse, handling it like it was a bayonet. The trumpet guy was still sitting there, and his face told McDowell that he was totally disgusted—disgusted with McDowell.

"I got to do something with this makeup. Keep an eye on me." Margaret stood and walked slowly toward the can.

McDowell turned to the trumpet guy. The guy was dark and thick lipped. His shoulders were heavy but his fingers were stream-lined. "Brother," McDowell said, "I need a favor."

"I got enough family trouble," the guy sneered. "Don't give me any of that brother shit. You liberals are all alike."

"I got a man I got to kill. You know what happened?"

The guy right away got over being disgusted. He leaned forward . "Either you got no ear, or I got no horn."

"I ought to be back by the end of last set. If I run into trouble can you see her to her room, and make sure she's safe inside?"

"I got a jealous wife. If I hurry, I can manage."

McDowell pulled the mouthpiece from his pocket. He set it on the table.

"What the hell's that," the guy said, "a dildo?"

"It's all I got. Way I figure, it's a pistol. I'll shove it between my fingers like those old Chicago guns. Put it in the guy's back. Fool him."

"It's by your foot," the man said. "I just now dropped it there."

McDowell looked around. No one seemed to be watching. He leaned over and picked up the knife, loving the knife, the feel of it. It was not much better than his own knife, but a little better.

"I owe you."

"Yep," the guy said. "I don't want to see that thing again until that boy's balls are hanging on it."

McDowell had a happy thought. "Let her open. Then let her rest three times."

"We're resting her."

"This guy's a pervert," McDowell explained. "As long as she's singing, he won't move. I've got to move him."

The trumpet guy grinned. "I will bore the living shit out of him."

The crowd was happy, as happy as any boozers ever got. There was no indignation left, only anticipation. The joint felt like it ought to feel during intermission. People were up and moving,

311

headed for the toilets, or checking out friends at other tables. The movement of the crowd was slow but steady. Margaret returned. She sat silent for a while, taking it in, and she was pleased.

"I've got your word."

"You've got my knife."

"How much good can you do me in jail?"

It was safe to kill him. No police department in the world would keep the books open on a punk like that for more than two weeks. That bastard had been born with the word "unsolved" written across his forehead.

"I'll just put the fear of God in him."

"Do that, but do it right." She stood, touched his arm warm and personal. She wanted to get back to work, like she still had something to prove.

McDowell caught his man on the third number. Margaret opened strong, and the guy went through his pant and slobber and finger-drumming number. McDowell stood at the end of the bar and watched. On the third number, when it was obviously instrumental, the guy pushed his hat to the back of his head, yawned, and stood up, heading for the can. McDowell waited for what he figured was exactly thirty seconds, then moved quick.

When he entered, the guy was standing before the long, mass production urinal. He had his cock in his hand and was reading the graffiti. Three toilet stalls were at the end of the room. One pair of feet showed. McDowell moved quick, like a man who had to piss, but he talked slow.

"A man with liver trouble ought not to drink," he said to the room in general. The knife was open in his hand. No one said anything.

"And your trouble," he said to the guy, "is that your liver is right in the way of this knife." He pressed the knife firmly against the guy's jacket. "Keep your hands where they are. Don't move an inch." He reached into the guy's jacket pocket and pulled out the gun. It was a lousy nickel-plated, two-shot, twenty-two caliber Derringer. The guy stood stiff, standing there with his hands hanging around his cock. McDowell prodded him with the knife, just to keep him stiff.

"What were you going to do with this cheap piece of shit," he said scornfully. "Shoot rabbits?" He prodded the guy again. "I ought to shoot you with your own gun."

"My money's on my hip, you robbing sonovabitch."

"You raped her," McDowell said. "You hurt her bad. She can't hardly walk."

The guy actually relaxed a little, and when he spoke he almost sounded proud. "Prove it."

"She saw you, you dumb shit. It's proved."

The guy glanced down, wiggled one foot, like he was checking the knife in his boot. "Women ask for it, they always do." He sounded like he was trying to start a discussion group. "Besides, she's a nigger. You ain't going to do nothing to a white man because of a nigger."

"Zip up," McDowell told him. "I'm a nigger. Black as the handle on this knife. Keep your hands where I can see them. I'll shoot you with your own gun, I swear."

"If you do shoot him," said a third voice that was husky and dark, "point him away from this stall." The voice got apologetic. "Because the bullet might go all the way through, you see."

McDowell could not tell whether the voice belonged to a black man or a white one. It occurred to McDowell that for quite some time now no one had been drawling. The feet shuffled. "I've got my pants up," the voice said, "but I'm not coming out. I don't want to see you boys, don't want to know you."

"I appreciate it."

"Call the police," the cowboy said.

"Get him out of here," the dark voice said. "I hope you cut his fucking heart out."

"Move. I hope you try something. All I need is an excuse." As McDowell herded the guy through the doorway two other men came in. The guy looked at them, desperate, and then said nothing. The men were executive types, but their mouths were southern.

As they walked through the long room the guy tried to dawdle. McDowell pressed him from behind. The little Derringer was concealed in the flat of his hand. "One word and you're dead." The lights in the joint were low. The guy stumbled, then walked on.

Past waitresses, past tables where men and women sat, past the hatcheck lady and the guy collecting the cover. McDowell watched his man and tried to estimate how drunk he was. If he was too drunk, he might get impulsive.

Onto the sidewalk. The hot, late night air was like an oppressive hand above the nearly deserted street. A Lincoln pulled to the curb. A well-dressed man got out, then opened the door for a well-dressed woman. The cowboy reacted. The man spoke to the woman in a soft, courteous drawl. The cowboy slumped, like he was in despair.

"That way." McDowell nudged the guy. "We're going to have our talk in that next alley."

A couple of white kids passed, coming toward them, holding hands. The girl looked no more than fourteen, the boy not much older. They should not be out so late. They were scared. The boy was walking tough, his jaw poked out like he was one mean man.

The cowboy started whining. "I'm a sick man. It's a sickness. A guy like me, he needs help."

"You fuck up and you'll get some help," McDowell promised. "I'll piss on your grave."

A cop cruised by, the car slowing as the cop checked out the white kids. Then the car moved away slow. The cop had decided that the hassle was not worth it. The cowboy again reacted.

"One shot in your back to stop you. One in your head to kill you." McDowell grabbed the guy's belt and pulled him backward into the gun.

"If they don't want it," the cowboy said, "then why do they stand up there in sexy clothes? Advertising."

The cop car cruised, the cop looking to bust a drunk or hassle a punk, a whore, a pimp, or a traffic violation. The cop did not seem at all interested in murder.

"You're digging your grave with your mouth," McDowell said. He had his man to the alley. He peered into the alley. A half block away a light hung from the side of a building. Over his head was a light. Between the lights the alley was all darkness and shadow. "Walk." He shoved the guy forward.

They passed beneath the light, entered into the darkness, and there was a glow in the darkness that McDowell did not at first recognize. The glow was dull, low, like the faded dusk before an evening storm along the rivers.

"You moley, old-timey bastard, you stay out of my road."

"What?" The cowboy was confused. Maybe he was sensing something.

314

"Get on down that alley."

The guy moved slow. He began to limp, only a little at first, then more pronounced. "Got to stop," he whined. "Can't hardly walk."

"You got a knife in your boot. You're just trying to get to your boot."

The light flowed, layering in blue, deep tones of blue, and the light seemed like a carpet of blue shading to purple across the filth and trash that lay in the alley. The light layered in the air and twisted deep blue and purple, with beginning tones of red.

"You stay out of this, you rag-tag old sonovabitch." McDowell gave his man a shove. "Spread against that wall. I'll take that knife."

The guy was a real punk. He thought he was smart and shifty and sly, but he was so obvious that McDowell wondered how he had managed to live this long. When he spread against the wall, he was backed away enough to get leverage. When McDowell went for the knife, the guy obviously figured to kick backward, turn, and fall on McDowell. McDowell backed up and momentarily paused, gauging his distance and loving it. The guy's legs were spread, but not really far enough. The guy was a dark shadow in the luminous dark.

McDowell kicked hard, as hard as he could kick. It was a good kick but not a great one. His boot glanced off the guy's leg, slid into his groin, and the toe of the boot missed but McDowell caught him with the instep. The kick was good enough.

The man did not scream as he fell. He grunted. He whooshed air, groaned, grunted, and doubled up as he grabbed at his crotch. His legs extended, then drew up, then extended, then pulled toward his chin. The pain was searing him, and he could not decide in which position the pain burned the least. The pain had him walking, nearly, as he lay on his side in the alley. The groans and grunts were cut with gasps. The guy was in an agony of disbelief. He could not believe that such a thing had happened to him.

McDowell stood above the man. He was watching the pain, enjoying it, and his mind was in a singing and celebrating fury. Light pulsed dim, low, blue and gray light. Light as silver as mist flowed into the blue light. McDowell waited. He watched the guy's hands, which pretty soon would be going for that knife, or for another gun. Then McDowell had a pleased and furious thought. He backed up, and as hard as he could, hard enough that he felt the heavy shock through his boot; he kicked the man in the back. His boot nearly rebounded, then was cushioned in a kind of rubbery softness as a rib or two broke and gave way.

Air jumped from the man's mouth in a huge gasp that faded to a huge sigh. He remained doubled, then stretched and doubled again, gasping. McDowell watched carefully. The guy would have figured by now that he had to stop McDowell or die. The light in the alley was accented. The blue and gray currents of furious light held the dull glow of dying fire, orange, red, ruby. McDowell leaned over the guy, watching.

Somewhere he had heard that you could kill a man if you kicked him in the balls hard enough and often enough. He stood back, measuring, judging the distance as he waited for the man to turn to the right position. The light glowed, moved like currents, pulsed and tried to take form. A vague shape, a face seemed trying to come into focus.

"You're dead," McDowell said to the light. "If you were not dead before, you're dead now. I don't pay the least attention to you." He watched the man, and the guy had his legs clamped together. He was gasping and still holding his balls. McDowell decided that he would have to shoot him after all.

If he had to shoot him, he had better get it over. It was best to shoot him in the head. McDowell pointed the cheap little pistol. The guy was moving his head around, getting his breath or trying to. He was sneaking his left hand down to his right boot as he lay on his side, and he was holding his balls with his right.

If the sonovabitch wanted more, then he could have some more. McDowell tensed, waited, watched the hand until the man's fingers were actually touching the knife. Then McDowell jumped high, stomping down on the man's hand and boot, crashing his weight on the man. It was a mistake. The guy was quicker than he should be, considering how badly he was hurt. McDowell felt the knife glance off his own boot before the sharp bite of it entered just below his calf. His foot hit wrong, his left foot, and he felt his ankle give. The sharp pain was so abrupt and fast that it was as vivid as sound. The pain from his ankle easily covered the pain from the stab wound.

Something had given way on the guy as well, a broken hand, probably. The knife click clicked against the alley as he dropped it.

McDowell was pulled sideways and stumbled against the wall, holding himself up. He was momentarily on defense. He leaned against the wall. His left foot was not good for much, and it felt slick inside the boot as blood ran down his leg. He figured he could still get a little more good out of the left foot. He braced on his right leg, kicked the man hard in the head with his left foot. The ruby light changed to red, rising through a range of color. McDowell felt something more give way in his left ankle. He lost his balance, falling beside the man, and lay helpless for a moment in the filth of the alley. The cowboy smelled, sweat smells and hurt. The smells were mixed with dog piss smells and the rotten smells of garbage. The filth of the alley was slick beneath McDowell's hands. He braced himself and struggled up to stand on only one foot.

The gasps, groans, and sighs had stopped. The man was out cold, his chest heaving, his breath drawn in sobs as his body gulped air.

McDowell braced against the wall. He could feel his ankle swelling in his boot. He had to kill the man, so he figured he had better go ahead and do it. McDowell was breathing hard, gasping. He pointed the gun. The light rose, violently red, and McDowell did not know whether the light was outside of him, surrounding him, or whether it came from his own mind.

Becky singing. For a moment, through his pain, he could hear her voice. The red light pulsed, urged, seemed to promise. Enoch had killed seven men, and he, Dan McDowell, only had to kill one. Becky had been crazy-as-hell sometimes, but Becky had never lied.

His finger tightened. He pointed the pistol at the man's temple.

Peg singing. The light whirled red, more red than the lights of ambulances. The light surrounded the pistol and actually felt like it pressed on his hand. Peg worked, had worked hard, and Peg believed in things that were maybe even bigger than music.

His hand was trembling. It was shaking so badly that he was afraid he would miss at a range of two feet.

Margaret singing. This man had raped Margaret. McDowell tried to steady himself. The pistol shook. Margaret had fought back, had gotten clean. Margaret had fought for the clear-eyed truth of music all of her life. Margaret had said leave it be.

The red light pressed, then dimmed. McDowell tried to point the pistol, but his shaking hand and arm drew the pistol away. He could not control his hand and arm.

He could not kill him, and he stood listening to the sounds of song. Margaret singing, Peg singing, Becky singing.

He could not do it. The woman self of his man self would not allow him to do it. Or maybe the musician self of his real self would not allow him to do it. The illusion self that had ridden loud and fakey and ass-kicking above all of his true selves for most of his life; that illusion self was as impotent as the presence, as impotent as Enoch. McDowell felt the true power of helplessness. He could not kill his man.

He could not, but he had to do something. Maybe this man would never rape Margaret again, but he would rape somebody. He was hurt, but he was not badly damaged.

McDowell staggered and half knelt, half fell beside the man who still lay on his back, gasping. McDowell could hardly see. He told himself that he could use some light, and he wiped his eyes with the back of his hand. He knelt above the man's legs. "You so-novabitch," he whispered, "if you loaded this thing with hollow points, it's going to hurt."

He felt with the muzzle of the pistol, feeling just under the kneecap, and the shot was muffled, like a weak firecracker. The knee and leg jumped, then sagged. The upper leg moved, the lower leg flopped. McDowell grabbed the other leg. He felt beneath the kneecap and fired. The bullet exploded, and a piece of it ricocheted from the knee and bounced with a leaden thud against the wall. McDowell felt the knee, and the knee was mush.

He shoved the gun in his pants pocket and struggled to his feet. He had a Cad parked around here somewhere. His foot was big inside his boot, pressing and sharp with pain, big and pulsing with pain. He half hobbled, half hopped his way deeper into the darkness of the alley.

Chapter 32

THE DARK STREETS OF THE SOUTH AND THE BROAD, BROAD STREETS of Atlanta. The dark heart of the south and the streets of Centerville. The streets of Nashville, Knoxville, Asheville. The dark streets of the dark heart of the south. The streets ran in his mind, a road map of the mind. The streets of Detroit, the dark heart of the south, and the streets of Pittsburgh and Chicago. The streets of Louisville, of Hamilton, of St. Louis; the streets of Roanoke, Lexington, Toledo, and Wheeling. The deep, dark streets of Richmond.

He made it to the Cad, and once in the Cad he felt safe. It was not the ninety-mile-an-hour strength of the Cad that caused the feeling. It was not the force, the engine-howling power that shoved him along night roads. The Cad felt like a cave, or womblike, soft and dark. McDowell sat, catching his breath, and slumped into the seat. He hoped the pain would not cause him to pass out. The parking lot was still full of expensive cars dark-gleaming beneath lights. Inside that nightclub Margaret sang.

His pants leg was soaked with blood, and the swelling in his boot was too huge to allow him to remove the boot, even with the slickness of blood. He pulled out the trumpet guy's knife, cut off his right pants leg, got out of the right boot and eased the fabric over his good foot. He used the cloth to bind the knife wound and stop the bleeding.

Time to get moving. *Time* to shove life back into gear.

He sat, feeling the pain, and understanding in a nearly detached way that he had some permanent damage in that ankle.

319

It was past time to shove life into gear. The pain did not throb, it swelled, and the pain was, of itself, an explanation. McDowell sat thinking. Life already was in gear. It always had been, only he had not noticed. The gears of life had been muffled by illusion. The movement of life had been covered by illusion and the movement was problematical, indecisive, vague. He had not noticed, because illusion was the most real thing in the world. He thought of the cowboy, and how the cowboy had come to the end of his illusion. He felt that he and the cowboy had both discovered just how real illusion was.

He got the Cad started, in gear, then pulled away into the broad streets of Atlanta. He drove slowly, but not so slow that a cop would think he was drunk. McDowell found himself smiling around the pain, but there was no Saturday night in the smile, only bitterness.

He patted his pants pockets. The mouthpiece was in one, the knife and the Derringer were in the other. Such small things, such little pieces of metal. He had to wipe the gun clean and get rid of it. There was a big river around here somewhere.

Then he told himself that he could not. The pain would roll him over before he drove that far. He pointed the Cad toward the motel, using his discipline to bring him soberly through the streets. He watched for police, but the police seemed to have disappeared.

He passed a woman and she beckoned to him. Working, she was working. He passed tired and drunk-looking guys who shuffled from bars, shuffled toward lonesome rooms. A wino sat on a curb, a bottle by his side. McDowell passed silent storefronts, dark, and storefronts lit with displays. He passed clubs, restaurants, hockshops. Two women walked together, and they were not holding hands, but their bands sometimes touched. The women were looking around them, looking backward, being careful, trying to take care of each other. At one stoplight, a kid in a ragged-out Oldsmobile convertible pulled alongside. At another light a lemon-colored Lincoln driven by a fur-collared pimp idled. The guy was deep, dark black, and he tapped long fingers on the wheel according to some rhythm on the tape deck. An old lady stood at a bus stop, shopping bag in one hand, her purse in the other. Tall buildings rose, and lights were on where night people cleaned away the grit of the daytime world. A filling station glowed where a kid attendant leaned tiredly against the side of a pickup as he filled the tank.

Through the broad streets of Atlanta until he reached the motel. He pulled into the parking space in front of the room. The room was dark. Margaret had not yet returned.

McDowell pulled out his shirttail and wiped the gun. He climbed from the Cad, staggered against it, bracing himself. He hobbled and hopped to the rear, wondering if the thing would fit. It did, just barely. He dropped the Derringer in the gas tank and replaced the cap.

Maybe the Cad would be bought by some car museum guy. The gun might rest in that gas tank for always. At any rate, it would be there long enough. McDowell turned and hobbled and hopped to the room. The pain seemed to be making him dizzy, or maybe he only imagined that he hopped sideways. He got the door open, and got inside.

Margaret came home to him ten minutes later. The trumpet guy was with her. Margaret entered the room fast, because she had seen his car. The trumpet guy followed.

McDowell sat on the edge of the tub, using the knife to cut away the boot while he attempted to sop up blood with a towel. He was painfully, dully, regretting that he had to ruin that boot. He was concentrating on that regret, because it was an easy regret and cheap. He concentrated on the boot. It was a simple thing to look at. McDowell wanted to think that everything was simple.

Margaret stood hesitant for a moment, watching. Then she moved toward him as quickly as she could. "You did, you did something. How bad is it? Where are you hurt?" She leaned over him. "Dave, come help."

The trumpet guy's name was Dave. McDowell thought dully that it was an interesting name.

"We got to lay him flat," Dave said. "I'll take care of all this." He helped McDowell to his feet and half carried him to the bed. McDowell tried to cooperate. He watched Dave, and Dave looked concerned, but more than that. He looked brotherly, or maybe like a friend. Dave was tying, wrapping, putting pressure on the cut with a towel.

"Dan, Dan," Margaret said. She had forgotten her own hurt and soreness. She was beside Dave, bending over McDowell. Tears came from beneath the wide sunglasses.

"It's just the ankle. I turned it is all." He heard his voice fumble and thought that he must be a little bit stupefied because of the pain. The trumpet guy was working on the boot, cutting, trying not to move the foot. Still, it moved. The pain was large enough and wide enough that the movement did not seem to make much difference. When the boot came off, the pain worked right on up to the surface, hot and swollen.

"We'll get you to a hospital, baby. We'll get you there." Margaret was holding him, kind of rocking his head back and forth. Her touch was gentle.

"We can't," he mumbled. "No. The timing's wrong." He hurt, but with the pressure of the boot removed, the hurt was less.

"I know someone," Dave said. "He has a good, closed mouth, but he's not exactly a doctor."

"You got anything," McDowell said. His tongue still felt thick, but he believed that he did not mumble.

"He will," Dave said, "this guy I'm getting. Actually he's a veterinary." Dave moved quickly to the phone. "I'm calling my wife. She'll get hold of the guy, and I'll pick them both up." He began to speak quietly into the phone.

"You're both crazy. There's nothing crazier than this." Margaret was still holding him, angry and loving both.

"It isn't," McDowell said carefully. "I'd better not show up at any doctor for twenty-four hours."

"You done it, Dan. You promised."

"I'll be right back. Twenty minutes." Dave headed for the door, turned back to Margaret. "Shoot the bolt on this door when I leave. They'll have to have a warrant." He opened the door. "Get him out of his clothes."

Margaret stood, like she was suddenly tired. She looked like she had lost everything she owned. She walked slow, and she was slumped with sadness. She shot the bolt, then turned back, helpless.

"You're my man. What in the world am I going to do?" She walked to the bed and began to undress him. "Don't want no hand on me that has killed no one. I don't think I can get used to that."

McDowell told himself that he was feeling better. Either that, or the hurt was making him clearheaded. Margaret had his other boot off, was peeling the sticky sock from his bad foot.

"He isn't dead," McDowell whispered. "He isn't exactly happy, but he ain't dead."

She looked at him, amazed.

"It's a rat's nest," McDowell whispered. "If I don't kill him, there's something wrong with me. If I do kill him, you can't stand it." He took a deep breath. "Before this goes any farther, I got to tell you this. I wanted to, I tried."

She had removed the sunglasses and was openly weeping as she worked to ease his pants off. "You're my man," she said, "and we have to say something here. Don't lie, ever again. I won't lie to you."

"He'll walk with canes if he ever walks at all. Women don't get raped by men driving wheelchairs."

"Oh, Dan." She shook her head back and forth, back and forth. Tears ran across the makeup, streaking it, and the dark purple of the bruise looked black in the low light. She got his pants off without wiggling the foot very much. "We got to live with this. We got to figure some way to live with it."

"He would have done it again," McDowell whispered. "Lots of women play this town. Peg plays this town. Margaret, if I didn't do it, we'd have to live with that."

She was unbuttoning his shirt. She stopped. She did not answer quick but sat thinking, maybe remembering other times. "I think," she said slowly, "that I needed for you to say the right thing. I think you just did that."

In the distance a siren was calling, a fire siren that was accompanied seconds later by the whip, whip, whip of the helpless police. McDowell wondered if the guy would talk and then knew he would not. He would not want to take one rape charge. If he had done it once, he had likely done it before.

When she raised him, trying to get him out of the shirt, he swung his legs over the edge of the bed. His ankle gave him a jolt. He laid back down, fearful that he would be sick. His stomach clenched. He fought it.

"We'll live with it," Margaret said. "Maybe someday we'll understand it." Her voice was different. He had heard these tones before, but never this intimate and loving. He had heard it strong, but not in the way that it was strong right now. Her voice had strength of people who were together, absolutely. People who nothing could drive apart. Margaret trusted him.

323

"I won't lie," he said. "Not ever again."

He loved it this way, with her lying fully clothed beside him, holding his hand. He loved the shape of her face in the low light, the hair that surrounded it like a cloud. He loved the long form of her beside him, her strength beside him.

And then for a moment it seemed that he had dreamed. Maybe for a moment he had actually slept. It seemed that a world of mist, a lifetime of mist had passed him by after encircling him in white smoke. He lay beside her, her fingers touching his, and Dan McDowell understood his ghost.

It was the ghost of all of them, and it was the ghost of his mind. It was the ghost of Peg's husband, even, dead with a knife in his throat. It was the mind of the Citizen, of Samantha, and the mind of the helpless police. It was the hockshop guy who let no one die in his doorway, and the minds of the kids who kicked their shitboxes through the hot streets. It was the mind of illusion, but it was more than that. It was the mind of song that rose above illusion. It was the mind of the past. Finally, and absolutely, because illusion was the most real thing in this world, it was the mind of the south.

And he, Dan McDowell, had been haunted by the ghost of a fool. The fool was well intended and the fool was honorable. It did not want to be a fool, but it was held and circled and deceived by illusion. It was a creature of emotion, of want. It was ignorant but hopeful, and it was the often smart mind of the south. It was a mind that laid down bullshit, but which would take none. It was mist and heat and smoke, ancient valleys and worn hills. It was of the past, reaching from the past, and it took shape and form whenever people gave it leave. It was a mind of honor, of antique dread, of fear, superstition, and independence. It was a mind that for as long as the south did not fade, would never, ever, apologize or be sorry.

He loved it this way, with Margaret lying clothed beside him, singing low.

The south was song, but particular songs. The wails of Jews and gypsies, the old, old songs of folks from the hills, the sad songs of whores and pimps, and the dark people who did not know whether they were black or nigger or colored. It was the song of queers and madmen and misfits. The south was beauty, no matter the crazy forms that beauty took. Song happened, and *they* paid no attention.

The south was direct, as direct as fire. It was as direct as Shag's voice, which in a couple of months would be calling through those hills. He could almost hear Shag running, could almost see his pop standing along the side of a high hill listening to the run of hounds. The moon low. The night cool. Mist rising against the moon.

He loved it this way, with Margaret bending over him, a little worriedly, trying to keep him awake as she rubbed his wrinkledy face.

And then he had a fantasy, but it was not one of those cheap ones like you had when you were alone. The fantasy would not come true this year, and it would not come true next year. But soon, it would come true.

He would tap some guy on the shoulder, and he would do some explaining. The guy would give it over to him while Margaret was singing. He would slip into the chair, nearly invisible, and begin to back her up. He would tell her how much he loved her, how much he loved Peg, and how much he loved her loving Peg. He knew Margaret's voice. He knew it better than any other horn who had ever lived. He knew she would understand him as she stood out there in the light and smoke of some future stage.

He was a lead horn now, and he would be a lead horn for always. Not this year quite, or maybe next, but soon. And, he told himself from that dreamlike, pain-filled state, that he was a lead horn, finally, because finally the clown show was finally over.

Jack Cady (1932-2004) won *The Atlantic Monthly* "First" award in 1965 for his story, "The Burning." He continued writing and authored nearly a dozen novels, one book of critical analysis of American literature, and more than fifty short stories. Over the course of his literary career, he won the Iowa Prize for Short Fiction, the National Literary Anthology Award, the Washington State Governor's Award, the Nebula Award, the Bram Stoker Award, and the World Fantasy Award.

Prior to a lengthy career in education, Jack worked as a tree high climber, a Coast Guard seaman, an auctioneer, and a long-distance truck driver. He held teaching positions at the University of Washington, Clarion College, Knox College, the University of Alaska at Sitka, and Pacific Lutheran University. He spent many years living in Port Townsend, Washington.